THE BOOK OF
FORBIDDEN WISDOM

THE BOOK OF
FORBIDDEN WISDOM

THE BOOK OF FORBIDDEN WISDOM

GILLIAN MURRAY KENDALL

HARPER
VOYAGER
IMPULSE

An Imprint of HarperCollinsPublishers

This is a work of fiction. Names, characters, places, and incidents are products of the author's imagination or are used fictitiously and are not to be construed as real. Any resemblance to actual events, locales, organizations, or persons, living or dead, is entirely coincidental.

EPub Edition MARCH 2016 ISBN: 9780062466105

Print Edition ISBN: 9780062466112

10 9 8 7 6 5 4 3 2 1

To Callie, my sister,
with love—as always.

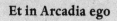

Et in Arcadia ego

THE BOOK OF
FORBIDDEN WISDOM

PART I

PART I

CHAPTER ONE

THE WEDDING

My name is Angel.

All of this is true.

They said the straight roads were old beyond the memory of memory. I dreamt of them from time to time and of the deep past and the cataclysm that had brought Arcadia into being. Everyone knew of the wars and the sickness that had preceded the creation of the Great Houses. But perhaps not everyone had dreams about the long ago.

On my wedding day, which was also my sixteenth birthday, I awoke from a dream in which I walked one of the Old Roads as my dead mother destroyed the world. She whispered in my ear—something about *The Book of Forbidden Wisdom*—as I continued my journey to a destination beyond my understanding. I could feel the earth close down like a paper box, and the casteless rise where the Great had been.

I sat up and blinked for a while in the darkness. My mother had died rather suddenly some years before, and perhaps it was natural that she should come to me before I wed Leth. I would, however, have expected something more celebratory from her than this odd and, even as it faded, vaguely upsetting dream.

I had no wedding jitters to keep me awake, so I lay down and went back to sleep. Details of the ceremony weren't the sort of thing that kept me up worrying—I was unimpressed by lavish marriage ceremonies, although mine was going to be more lavish than most. Yes, I was ready to marry Leth. But I wondered if we needed quite so many flowers and quite so much food—and bards and jugglers and body artists and a Ceremonial Bath constructed just for me, just for this one occasion.

My younger sister, Silky, felt quite differently about marriage. She had thought of her wedding constantly when we were children. She would drag me away from the edge of the swamp to play Wedding Day. I much preferred the swamp. If I were lucky I would catch a snapper turtle and add it, carefully, to my basin. Swamp turtle soup. But I always let the turtle go back to making bubbles in the waterweed. It would not have done to give it to Cook.

Cook was literal-minded about turtles and soup.

Silky held her nose when she got near the swamp, and she only would go near when she wanted to play with me. Although I was two years older, she was always Bride when we played Wedding Day, and I was content to play the bit parts: flower-maid, ring-bearer, bard, even Groom, stiff and silent (as they always were). Silky took the game seriously. If it were summer, she picked small bouquets of Queen Anne's lace, blue cornflowers, purple clover, red poppies. The bouquets varied with the seasons—in winter she had me carrying herbs and twigs. The game, however, was always the same. Silky would walk across meadow grass (if she could get me away from the swamp), while I would trail in her wake, holding flowers and the woven grass that served as a ring. On occasion she would chide me.

"Come *on*, Angel," she would say. "Play as if it were *real*."

If it were real, it would be unlikely that she would be the bride. From the time she was a child, Silky was a beauty with a heart-shaped face and a rain of golden hair, but, as eldest, I had inherited our mother's estates. Until I could create a dowry for her, she would be un-marriageable. But she never envied me. There was no avarice in Silky.

Sometimes, if our father were away, she would sneak into our dead mother's room and find a long dress to wear. Then my job was to hold up the edges like a train—all of our mother's clothes were too long for her. But she never put on Mother's wedding dress, although I knew she wanted more than anything to wear it to her own wedding. She couldn't, of course. As eldest, the dress was supposed to be mine on my wedding day. Frankly, I wished there were a way it could be hers.

But there wasn't. The rules forbade it.

When I opened my eyes for the second time, I saw Silky at the foot of the bed.

She was sitting on my feet.

"I'm not going to let you sleep away *the* most important day of your life," she said. I looked her over. She was wearing a wrapper over her Honor Gown, and her throat and arms were already intricately decorated with the lacy designs that were a sign of our House, our land status, our aristocratic roots.

"The day I was introduced to Leth was probably the important day," I said. "Or the day his parents asked Father if he could marry me."

"*Boring*. Plus, after this, you'll get to see Leth all the time, Angel," said Silky. "No chaperones anymore. This is the day that changes *everything*. You only get married once. Unless he dies, of course. But second ones are never so nice. There's always *gloom*."

"Silky—" I began to object. My sister was a romantic about weddings, but about the rest of life—less so.

"Come on, Angel," she said. "I've already spruced

up your bouquet with wild roses. I know you love wild roses. The flowers they sent were *not* adequate."

"I'm sure they were fine," I protested. The flowers were from the groom's family.

"Come on," said Silky. "I'll sneak you out so you can look. Some of them are wilted, and I *bet* they came from the pre-contract dinner."

"Flowers are expensive," I said. "And who cares?"

"*Angel*—"

"It's all right, Silky. I'll come and look at them."

I sat up in bed and threw back the covers. I had my favorite coverlet on the bed. I was supposed to start my married life with everything new, but there were more than a few items I planned on smuggling with me. I would take the coverlet, for example, and certainly the lucky quartz pebble that my best friend, Trey, had given me. It wouldn't be politic, of course, to tell Leth I was keeping something from Trey, but I could hardly help it that Trey was a boy. A man, really. He was on the cusp of his eighteenth birthday—and a thought occurred to me:

Time for him to find a bride.

He would have to marry someone with land, of course, because, as a younger brother, he had none, but he was handsome in a dark and interesting way, and a landed girl might well feel drawn to his green eyes. Trey's parents would probably seal such a match immediately. Trey didn't have the option of having sentiments. Sentiment was no substitute for land.

There were, however, worse fates than not loving your land-partner. I myself had chosen something better than love: I had chosen affection and respect and a most suitable of matches. Between the two of us, Leth and I would own much of Arcadia—not, of course, the Arcadia set apart by *The Book of Forbidden Wisdom*, but a considerable chunk of the rest of it. We would hold in common forests, meadows, mountains. Lumber, cattle, mines.

Of course with my land holdings, my father could have married me to anyone, but the merger with Leth of the House of Nesson made sense—the only single man with nearly as much land as Leth's family was ten years older than my father and wrinkled like a winter apple. My father never considered that match. I didn't know if it was from care of me or because the old man didn't have quite as much land as the Nessons.

But I knew Father's final choice had nothing to do with love.

Neither had mine.

Love was a great unknown that, as far as I had seen, generally led to trouble and then went away. I had seen girls in love. They made bad land deals; they lived with regret.

Silky broke into my reverie. "Are you *dozing?*" she asked suspiciously.

"No," I said. "I'm up."

Silky threw a wrap at me and then quietly, contemplatively, she went over to the closet and gently fingered the lace on our mother's wedding dress.

"So fine," she said. Her voice was low.

Once more I wished she could be the one to wear it, but the dress could never be hers, and we both knew it. It would pass to me and then to my female line. The least I could do to make up for the huge discrepancies between our fortunes was to let Silky shepherd me through the wedding. She cared so deeply about all of it—down to the last petal on the wild roses by the great door of our House.

"Shabby," she had proclaimed two days previously. The gardener had been hard-pressed to prepare the grounds to her satisfaction. First he left the wild roses too shaggy, and then he lopped them too closely. When I found him trying to tie some of the branches back on, I gave him a silver piece, told him to desist and did the best I could to rein in Silky.

"Where's Leth?" I asked when I was out of bed and in my wrapper.

"*His* Ceremonial Bath," snapped Silky. "Come *on*, Angel, you should have had yours an hour ago. And you shouldn't *mention* the groom when you aren't dressed."

"You're the one who had me picturing Leth in the bath," I said. "Besides, in not too many hours, Leth and I will be—doing the required." I couldn't resist teasing Silky, despite the proprieties.

Despite my own anxieties.

Silky put her hands over her ears. "La, la, la," she said. "I can't *hear* you."

"Well," I said reasonably, "something like that has to happen after the wedding. Or else it's not valid."

"Angel." Silky was shocked. "You *promised* not to talk about that. It isn't maidenly."

And I had indeed promised. I had told Silky I would behave and let her play Wedding, this time with me as Bride. She had always left out what happened after the wedding. Sometimes I wondered if she, in all her play weddings, had ever thought beyond the ceremony itself. Truthfully, I was a little nervous about that part. The matrons had been so vague about everything. Luckily, only yesterday, when the chaperone was looking away, Leth had taken my hand for a moment. That small intimacy had felt good. Everything would surely be all right.

I changed into my robe before the Ceremonial Bath and then walked outside, Silky right behind me, and into a crowd of people from the village and from villages beyond. One man stood by the door, bent under the burden of all the flowers he was carrying for me to inspect. But I focused instead on my friend Violet, who had crimped her red hair for the occasion and who waited to escort me to the Ceremonial Bath. I looked past the skin artists, with their tiny brushes and elaborate pots of color, and the baker, who wished me to see the sweets for after the feast. And I deliberately ignored the legal advisors—our father's, mine, Silky's, Leth's, that of Leth's parents—all making sure that not one iota of land changed hands that shouldn't. They all began talking at once.

"Later," I said. "I have to go put on something to

take off for the Ceremonial Bath." The Ceremonial Bath was done naked.

There was silence. No one so much as smiled. Not even Violet. Not even Silky.

"Angel," said Silky. "Can't you be more *discreet?*"

"I'll try," I said. "Lead away." Silky and Violet, my witness, escorted me to the Bath. Violet was sixteen, like me, and with her round figure and face, she reminded me of a lemon drop. Once I was married, she would be considered the best match for five hundred miles. Coal and opals.

Other women, most of whom I knew from the village, were waiting at the Bath to act as observers, witnesses and guardians of the ceremony. All of them would receive presents from my father.

Under Silky's critical eye, I played my role to the hilt, immersing myself completely and then bursting to the surface as if reborn—which was, after all, the point.

Then it was the turn of the skin artists. Luckily it was a fine day, and they chose to work outside. I knew that Leth admired the skill of the decorators, so I tried to be patient with them, although it meant keeping still for ages and ages and ages. I sat for four hours as they sent a fine filigree of paint up my arms, over my shoulders and, in terrifically fine detail, across my chest and onto my throat.

I only jerked away once.

"Angel's ticklish," Silky explained indulgently. I

sometimes had trouble remembering she was only fourteen.

And then my father was there, and it was time for our final father-daughter conversation. He had asked the question every month since Mother's death, although I think he had long given up believing there was an answer. When we were done today, the question would become Leth's.

"Come," he said, and gestured toward the house.

"Am I done?" I asked the skin artists.

"For now, Lady Angel," said one of them. "We'll do your hands right before the ceremony."

We went into my father's study, a dark room filled with shelves of old books. He favored treatises and books of law, but there had been times I had caught him reading improbable traveler's tales or a romance set down from a bardsong.

My father was always direct when he questioned me, but it had become more of a ceremony than anything else. The questions and answers were always the same.

"Did your mother tell you the secrets of *The Book of Forbidden Wisdom*?" he asked. Recently, he had grown more intense in his asking, but I was sure that if he really thought I had an answer, he would long ago have hit me to try and get it. *The Book,* after all—if any of the stories were true—would have made him the richest man in Arcadia. That hope would end once I passed into Leth's hands.

"No," I answered.

"And the Spiral City?" he asked. "Does it exist? Is *The Book* there?"

"The Spiral City is a fantasy or a ruin," I said. "You know what I know. I don't keep any secrets from you."

Almost true. He didn't know that Trey and I had continued in our friendship to the present moment. He didn't know everything.

"Angel," said my father. "It would be better to tell me than have Leth try and force it from you."

"Leth would never hurt me," I said. "I thought you liked Leth. What more could he want than the dowry I'm bringing him?"

"He could want *The Book of Forbidden Wisdom*," said my father. "He *would* want that. As do I. But I like Leth, Angel, or what little I know of him. I'm less fond of his parents. Happily, you aren't marrying them."

It was one of the longer speeches he had made to me since my mother's death.

I left his study confused and uneasy and crossed the courtyard to rejoin Silky. She had been waiting.

"Did he ask you the question?"

"Yes," I said.

"I bet there is no *Book of Forbidden Wisdom*," Silky said. "I bet it was lost a long time ago. If it had really been passed down for generations in our mother's House, Mother would have passed the knowledge to you."

"There wasn't much time."

There was a moment's silence. We didn't allude to Mother's death.

Then Silky collected herself.

"I still bet the wisdom's long gone," said Silky finally. "And if it's *wisdom*, why is it *forbidden*?"

"I don't know."

The sun was beating down now, and there was little shade, but I saw, sitting under our lemon tree, a man with bundles scattered around him. He looked up as if he had known I was watching. Thick, dark hair, deep blue eyes, maybe ten years older than I was. But his face took me aback—it was a face like that of one of the great Classical paintings. I should have looked away, or, better, put up my chin and glared at him, but I did neither. I simply looked back.

"Who is he?" I asked.

I had addressed Silky, but it was Violet, who had come up beside us, who answered.

"A bard," she said, in a voice that conveyed she didn't think much of him. "Can't you tell?"

"He was just passing through." Silky sounded worried. "Father told me. I'm *sorry*, Angel. I didn't want to *upset* you. But Cal sang himself hoarse at Bertin's funeral, so Father heard this one and approved him. He says the man's good at his job and has a sweet voice."

"I see," I said. I didn't. I was thinking of those strange eyes. Neither Violet nor Silky seemed to have noticed anything unusual about him—but I found it hard to take my eyes away.

"So you don't mind the change?" asked Violet.

"It doesn't matter," I said. "But Cal must be truly

hoarse to miss this occasion to show off." Cal, our village bard, had a fine voice, but he was, perhaps, a little too proud of it.

I looked over at the itinerant bard again. And now I saw what Silky and Violet saw: that the man looked travel-stained and, oddly, angry. He was sun-darkened—a testament to life spent on the road enduring the vagaries of sun and rain. Landowners, on the other hand, were usually fair-skinned. We did not, after all, work the land.

We just owned it.

The man turned to one of the bundles and pulled out a lyre. I wondered if Father had given him a low price for the wedding since he was, essentially, a vagabond and did not have to hold us to the usual rate. It was the kind of thing Father would do. The man surely looked discontented enough.

The normal wage for a wedding would have made a bard rich for half a year.

The bard raised his head and caught me looking at him. He looked right back at me, full in the face. And then he smiled—except it wasn't a friendly sort of smile. It was patronizing. As if he knew me. As if he knew all about me.

Me. A child of the House of Montrose. Me. Lady Angel.

I could have had him turned out, of course, but there was something fascinating about him. Perhaps he was a poor castoff from a landed family. It happened. Besides, it would dismay Silky if we had no bard, and it seemed pointless to get rid of him because of one glance.

At weddings, bards were expected to give the news (keeping early guests occupied), sing the wedding songs, perform an epic and provide music at the party following the ceremony. If Father really had heard and accepted this bard, the performance wouldn't be bad.

I went back to the skin decorators, who started the final work on my hands. Suddenly the marriage ceremony seemed very near. I could touch nothing until after the wedding now. Silky would dress me. It would be her last chance to hold the wedding gown.

The bard gathered his bundles and instruments and went toward the kitchen, where I knew he would be well fed. Cook had a weakness for bards—she liked the gossip they carried. Soon I would be part of that gossip, slipped into a recital somewhere down the road. Lady Angel Montrose married Lord Leth Nesson.

And that was that.

I had to confess to myself that I really didn't know just how happy I would be. I didn't think I'd be miserable—far from it—but as a married woman, I would probably never speak to Trey again, except formally. The time had finally come to cut the tie. We were adults now, sacrifices to the endless ceremonies and formulas that drowned friendships made in childhood.

"What's the matter, Angel?" asked Silky. She was good at reading my mood.

"I want this to be over," I said.

"How can you want your wedding to be *over*?" asked Silky. "It hasn't even *started* yet."

"I wish Trey could be here," I said. "Father didn't have to ban him from the wedding."

"Trey's a *boy*," said Silky. "The bride can't invite a *boy*."

"Then I wish Leth had," I said.

"Right," said Silky.

"He could have."

"*Right.*"

We went into the house and made our way through the halls and up the staircases until we were back in my room. Silky slipped Mother's gown over my head, did up the pearl buttons and began the lengthy process of pinning and sewing me into it.

"There," she said. "Almost done." Her eyes brimmed with tears.

"I'm sorry about the dress," I said. "I wish it could be yours."

"Mine will be beautiful, too," she said, but her eyes still glistened in the light. She finished with the pins in the back and turned me around.

"*Wow*," she said. Her sorrow was gone.

"'Wow' what?"

"You're *gorgeous*."

"We both know who the gorgeous one is," I said. Silky just laughed and shook her head, and her white-gold hair was a cloud around her face.

When we reached the wedding tent, where the ceremony would take place, where I would finally be able to see Leth without a chaperone at my side, I saw that Silky must have been up very early tending to all the wedding details. The path to the tent was sprinkled with rose petals, and there were flowers everywhere—a riot of color and scent. Nothing had been left undone.

It was as if Silky could read my mind.

"I added stuff," she said. "So there's nothing to complain about *now*."

"Silky," I said, "you know I wouldn't have complained."

"I wasn't thinking about *you*."

I laughed. "I thank you, but I'm sure what Leth's parents had was fine."

"You'd *think* it would be, considering the dowry," said Silky. "But they're stingy, and you know it. I'm *sure* Leth wouldn't have approved."

It was indeed a good dowry. This marriage was the biggest real estate transaction the village had ever seen. And despite Silky's romantic enthusiasm, I was perfectly able to see the wedding as Father and the Nessons saw it—as a good land deal. A sensible merger that would add to the power of both families.

And I got Leth in the transaction. He was a good choice. Other Ladies even accounted Leth the most handsome man they had seen, although I preferred Trey's dark looks to Leth's fair coloring. To be truthful.

Another thought came on unbidden: *Leth's not as handsome as the Bard, either.*

I laughed out loud at that. After all, the Bard was

nothing more than a landless vagrant with a goodish face.

Leth was a good man and extraordinarily generous: he had agreed that Silky would live with us until her marriage. As eldest girl, I had received my mother's inheritance—but now I could make sure Silky had a good dowry when her time came.

Silky and I went to the side tent, where I would wait until Leth and Father and the Nessons and the witnesses and guests and all the nobility father could muster were in place.

I began to fidget.

"Stop that," said Silky. "You'll ruin the pattern on your hands."

"Sorry."

"At least you're *acting* like a bride."

"I suppose I am a bride." Perhaps I was curt. Silky didn't reply. I held my bouquet firmly in my hand while Silky put flowers in my hair. I was dark, like Trey, and for effect she wove tiny white roses into the braids coiled around my head. The scent of the roses was strong, and as I watched Silky work, I saw that she had added some wild roses to enhance the scent. And because she knew I liked them.

Violet—who was looking more like a lemon drop than ever—popped her head in the door.

"It's the Bard," she said.

"Drunk?" asked Silky, concerned.

"He wants to check whether you want the traditional music," said Violet, "or something different."

"Traditional," said Silky. "What else?"

"Don't I get a say?" I said.

"*No*," said Silky. "You're just the *bride*, Angel. Traditional."

"I'll have the servant tell him," said Violet. She was too old, three months older than I was, for direct contact with a lower-caste man. That meant she had to communicate with the Bard through intermediaries.

Violet returned shortly and stood behind me, ready to lift the train of the dress. Silky and I would enter together, the two scions of the House of Montrose.

"Ready?" asked Silky after giving me one more critical examination. I must have passed. She looked radiant. I wished I could look that radiant. I prepared for the traditional music.

A minute later the preliminary music began, and it was something very *un*traditional, something haunting, in a minor key, but before Silky could run out and throttle the Bard, he launched into the wedding theme.

For the first time, my stomach fluttered. And at that moment, I really wanted Trey, to whom I could talk and who would make me calm. It would have been nice, I thought, to have had an un-chaperoned, informal parting with Trey. Because everyone knew friendships changed after marriage. For one thing, the married were much higher in status than those who were uncontracted.

But there was no precedent for a farewell to a male friend. We had been awkward in our snatched goodbyes. We had only had a moment before the chaperone descended upon me, and she had been livid, and while I hadn't cared, I knew that was the end of it.

I couldn't tell if Trey liked Leth. I rather thought not.

The music began to swell.

"Are you ready, Silky?" As if I had to ask.

"Of *course*," she said. Her body decorations were exquisite. Dark red flowers glowed in her golden hair.

The music had almost reached the moment when I would begin my walk, Silky behind me, toward Leth. And soon the legalities of the land transaction would be over, and Leth and I would be married.

It would be a nice life. And I was sure that, after a few initial questions, he would leave alone the issue of whether or not I had knowledge of *The Book of Forbidden Wisdom* or the Spiral City. He had never once mentioned *The Book*, but I knew he thought about it. All of Arcadia did. The St. Clares, my mother's line, had passed forward knowledge of *The Book* all the way to my mother, who had died young.

All Arcadia knew that, too.

Silky took my arm for a moment and then kissed me before taking her place again.

Then I set my foot on the narrow walk, and the servants pulled open the flaps of the tent. I smiled, but it felt forced, and the considerable weight of the dress seemed to hold me back. They were all there: Father, the Nessons, my aunts and uncles and cousins, Gurd—the head of the village—the minor nobility, each with distinct and colorful liveries. It seemed everyone except Father, who had dressed as always in his endless mourning, had chosen to wear something vivid. The tent was a riot of color, and a profusion of flowers lined the path. There was a shower of rose petals as I entered.

It might not have been the happiest day of my life, but I wasn't unhappy. I thought that perhaps one day I would be able to make amends to Trey.

The sky was blue. The bard was in voice. Silky was with me, and I was going to take her away from our father's dreary house of eternal mourning.

I saw Leth waiting. He looked real and solid and ready to take me as his bride. Behind Leth were his brother, Benn, and his sister-in-law, Lorna of the House of Tern. My father—a head shorter, stern, rigid in his mourning—stood next to Leth. This was a big day for my father, a triumph, really. For years he had feared that Trey had some hold on my heart. He didn't like Trey very much—or maybe he just didn't like Trey's landlessness. It came to the same thing.

Then had come Leth, with his vast holdings, and my father almost—*almost*—perked up. At least enough to be almost attentive when it came to my new suitor.

On our second arranged meeting, Leth had said, "Stifling, isn't it?" And he had not meant the weather.

I began to consider that Leth might make a suitable partner.

Shortly thereafter, the Nessons approached Father, and I let him know that the merger could take place. Why not? I was almost sixteen. It was time to marry.

And now I walked into the tent and took my place next to Leth. Silky went and stood with Father. I wasn't supposed to look at Leth until after the ceremony, but I leaned forward and peeked at him.

He looked a little pale, and I knew that he, too, was finding the tent, as he would put it, stifling.

Two books were open in front of us. The Marriage Book and the Land Book. The witnesses were in place. The music ceased. The Arbitrator called for the rings, and then made the motions over them. Then he opened the Land Book. And I couldn't help but think: land first. Always the land first. The marriage contract bound earth to earth as much as bride to groom. The marriage ceremony came second to the land merger: it was an excuse for a party and a license to produce children, but ultimately it was a formal contract signing.

I certainly thought about it that way, especially since I didn't even know what I thought about having children. I remembered what we tried never to speak of—the night our mother and the baby she bore died. In the chaos, the midwife left the door to the birthing room ajar, and I had seen the bloody sheet and one of my mother's arms dangling limply off the bed. My father had gone in, and the midwife tried to stop him, but he pushed her away and went down on his knees next to the bed. From that moment, our father wore only black, and he never sought another marriage.

These were not auspicious thoughts. I gave my head a little shake.

The Arbitrator handed the pen to Father. There

was a small intake of breath, and I looked up, surprised. I was suddenly aware that Silky's breathing had changed. Of course, her life, as well as mine, was about to be forever altered. And it occurred to me then that the two books open in front of me were the twin volumes in which my life would be forever sealed. The Montrose estates—my family's land—would merge with the Nessons'. And the Nesson name would become mine.

And then they would close the books. And my life would be written.

The Arbitrator held the pen out to me. I looked at it. Silky, even though Father could undoubtedly see her, poked me. Leth, against all decorum, turned his head to look at me. I took the pen.

Then a voice rang out.

"I stake a claim."

At first I didn't know where the voice was coming from.

But while the Arbitrator may have been as surprised as anyone there, he had been well trained. He had the pen he had given to me back in his hand before anyone else moved or spoke.

"I stake a claim to the Montrose land."

I tracked the voice this time. A man in silhouette stood in the entrance of the tent, the afternoon sun blazing around him so that I couldn't see his face.

My father moved toward the man, stumbling over the table the books were on and pushing the Bard out of the way.

"Who *dares*?" said my father. "Who *dares* interrupt this marriage?"

Land greed. I saw it all the time, and now it was in his eyes.

I wondered if Leth had any idea of what was happening.

And I thought that no, probably he didn't.

My father was scrambling for the entrance. When he'd pushed past the Bard, the man had dropped his instrument, a stringed thennet. It made a harsh, discordant sound now as he picked it up. The bodyguards of the minor nobility, unsure of what was happening, were pushing away the crowd and trying to gain control. I watched the scene as if it no longer had anything to do with me. And then it seemed that all at once everybody was talking, chattering, speculating. There were a couple of shrieks as people in the back of the crowd pressed forward to see the man who had staked a claim to the Montrose estates. In so doing, they threatened to trample those caught in the middle.

I had been to a lot of marriages, and I knew, at that moment, better than anyone in the tent, how carefully the Wedding Director choreographed everything in advance—right down to the color of polish on my toenails and the color of ink in the pen the Arbitrator had just snatched from me.

We were dangerously off script now.

Leth's mother called out something to him, and he turned his head away from me. But then he looked at me again.

Silky crept up on one side of me and put her arm around me, breaking what decorum was left.

The dress, the flowers, the music—I knew that Silky envied none of it now.

Again the voice rang out.

"I claim the Montrose estates. And I do not approve this marriage."

Silky held me close. "It's going to be all right," she whispered.

But we both knew it wasn't.

"What's going on?" asked Leth, but nobody answered him.

My father was clearly trying to figure that out himself as he pushed his way to get to the man in the doorway. But the Arbitrator's assistants, on a gesture from the Arbitrator, stopped him.

"Who *dares* do this?" My father was repeating himself now. "Who *dares*?"

I wondered, as if from a very great distance away, why he kept on asking the question. By this point, it was clear there was only one person I knew of who could possibly make such a claim.

There would be no marriage this day. I suddenly felt absurd with the wedding flowers in my hair, and I began pulling them out and throwing them onto the grass. Then, abruptly, everything in the world was stilled. The scent of wild roses, more heady than that of the blooms from Leth's parents, was overpowering. A bee lazily circled my bouquet. There was sweat on Leth's brow, but his pale blue eyes were fixed on me.

The moment passed. My father raged. The mundane smell of food from the dining tent overcame the scent of roses; the bee flew off; the only thing still connecting me to the earth was Silky's arm around my waist, because I couldn't see the blue of Leth's eyes anymore—he had dropped his gaze.

"This marriage is void." The words echoed in the tent.

I gripped my bouquet, and one of the rose thorns that had not been entirely removed pierced my finger. I bled onto a petal. Red on white.

I knew the voice. I had known it from the beginning.

Kalo.

My older brother, Kalo.

Of course.

CHAPTER TWO

THINGS FALL APART

Leth only had time to remove the garland of flowers around his neck and put it over my head before his parents were on either side of him and hustling him away.

"I'm sure we'll settle it," he said over his shoulder.

"Well *that's* comforting," snapped Silky.

Leth's father, a large bluff man with a red face, looked back at me apologetically, but he didn't let go of his son.

"Land dispute," he said to me. "Happens. Sometimes it works out, Lady Angel." He nodded at my sister. "Lady Silky." Then he and Leth's mother and

Leth were gone, part of the crowd headed for the open air. I saw Leth begin to turn toward me, but just then his mother must have said something, because he bent his head to her.

"Shrew-faced *witch*," said Silky.

"What are you talking about?"

"Leth's mother. She's only ever had her eye on the land. Are you *blind*? She doesn't care about *you*—or Leth—at all."

"Silky," I said, "you're making that up."

"Am I?"

I sighed. "All right—maybe it's true. But you shouldn't throw around the word 'witch.' It's danger- ous."

"She should be burned at the *stake*," said Silky. Her face was like stone in stark contrast to her airy blue dress and the dark red flowers in her hair. "She got Leth away from you fast enough."

"Not for long," I said. But that was as much hope as it was truth.

"It's a land dispute," Silky said. "*Anything* could happen."

Meanwhile the Wedding Director was smiling until all her sharpened teeth showed. Sharpened teeth were a sign of her guild; Wedding Directors, as well as Arbitrators, were a landless guild that, even so, gar- nered respect.

The Wedding Director was shepherding the guests to the feast, I suppose in the hope that food would dis- tract them from the main drama—at least for a while.

The canopy of flowers under which Leth and I were to sit at the feast, however, would now remain forever unused. Even if we later married, the thing would be done quickly and secretly; marriage after a land dispute was tainted.

I felt tainted.

Silky and I walked through the crowd over to Father and Kalo. As I went, I noticed that Trey had managed to come to the wedding after all. He leaned against one of the support beams of the hall, and although I didn't want to call attention to his forbidden presence by staring, I saw that his face was bloodless. He stared at me as if he'd never seen me before. Then, as the crowd pushed me toward him, he reached out and almost touched me. But not quite. His hand fell to his side. I didn't move toward him.

For the first time that day, I wanted to weep.

Kalo and Father were no longer screaming at each other. In fact, they were locked in what looked like a painful embrace—all, I knew, for the benefit of the crowd.

Father embraces long-absent son.

How he hated Kalo.

When Kalo had gone to Shibbeth, the great country to the north, we had expected to find his body returned to us, the limbs and head in a heap on the torso. The Alleusanuslidans of Shibbeth weren't subtle. But in the end he married well and acquired land, and then his wife died, and he married again, this time to a woman with even greater estates. By then the 'Lidans, as we called them, had realized he knew better than they how to use land for profit, and he gained money from being a Steward and bought more land.

His worth was close to mine, but, it appeared now, that wasn't enough for him. He had always resented the riches that came from my mother to me, and now he was taking pleasure in my ruin. The fact that he had no actual right over my inheritance was going to make no difference. Women might hold land, but men made the laws. And no matter what happened, he had already sullied the land merger with the Nessons.

Kalo was a bully. I hadn't missed him for a moment when he had gone to Shibbeth.

Now I loathed him.

As a child, I fought him when he tried to smash the eggs of the flash red meadow birds, and he made my life as difficult as possible in return.

To Silky, he was simply cruel. When she turned eleven, he told her he had arranged with Father to marry her to Wilcomb Surry, a boy rich in land but twisted in mind.

Silky couldn't turn to Father. He was locked up in his grief over our mother. She was left to her anxiety. She barely ate and grew ever more despondent despite anything I could say. Her relief had only come when, for whatever reason, Wilcomb Surry paid the penalty attached and backed out of the pre-contract. Later he died during the great sickness. Meanwhile, Kalo had turned his attention back to me. He tried to find out if I knew anything about *The Book of Forbidden Wisdom* or the Spiral City. He burned my upper arm, where father couldn't see it. But I said nothing. There was nothing I could say.

So he took pleasure in burning me some more.

Shortly after that, Kalo left for Shibbeth.

Now, by the time Silky and I reached Kalo and Father, I was too angry to retreat into formula.

"Kalo," I said. "You ruin things."

"You will follow the protocols of greeting," said my father, who had always found a refuge—from anger, from grief, from his family—in formula.

"You are welcome to me," said Silky obediently. Father diminished her as no one else could.

"I can't say the same," I said. But neither Silky nor I had a chance to say anything more to Kalo before the Arbitrator and his assistants were pushing us back to the house. The Arbitrator dealt with me directly, and he was gentle. After all, until it was proven otherwise, I was a lot of land on the hoof. When we were in the library, we all sat, except for the Arbitrator, who propped open the Land Book and the Marriage Book on my father's desk.

"My Lord," said the Arbitrator to my father. "Is this marriage now null?"

My father said nothing. He looked as if he were in another world.

"It is," said Kalo. "She doesn't have my permission."

"I have Father's," I said.

"She *does*," said Silky.

"And do you really think our father is still head of this house?" asked Kalo.

"Would you dispute it?" asked my father, and I could see his rage building.

"I just don't want you to be burdened," said Kalo. "And I have an even bigger merger in mind. One that will make us all rich."

"We *are* rich," my father said grimly.

"Richer. Besides, she can't marry without co-consent," said Kalo. And it was true. But he had been gone so long, it hadn't seemed to matter. And besides, what was there to object to about a union between Leth and me?

"You can't just come back and destroy my life," I said, although I knew in fact he could. He just had. "The match with Leth is a good land match."

"There will be a penalty if you renege," the Arbitrator warned Kalo and my father. "And the Nessons will not be happy if you do."

"I'll be able to pay that penalty tenfold," said Kalo.

That caught my father's attention.

"How?"

"My land extends far into Shibbeth," said Kalo. "More than that, I'm Steward and advisor to the greatest of the 'Lidan Lords. They plant as I tell them, and they reap more grain than they can imagine. They pay me well, and I buy more land and make more gold. It's a rather wonderful cycle."

"Be that as it may," he said, "what's wrong with Angel's match?"

"What's wrong," said Kalo, "is that I have a better one for her with a Lord of Shibbeth." I recognized the crooked smile on Kalo's face. He was about to inflict pain.

I fingered the flowers around my neck; they had already begun to wilt. I took my hand away and reached for Silky. She came willingly to my side. She was shaking. I felt sick, dreading what was coming.

"Through Angel's marriage," said Kalo, "the 'Lidans will bring untold land holdings and wealth to this family. And they won't be our rivals anymore."

"'Lidans," said Father, "have been known to break faith."

And I have none in you, I thought, looking at Kalo.

"I've dealt with them for years," said Kalo. "And I'm going to seal an alliance with them—through Angel's marriage. An ironclad alliance."

Of course.

Silky continued to tremble, but I didn't think she had cause—not for herself. Kalo wouldn't touch her, at least for now. He was after the one who had the most to lose.

"We can't make enemies of Leth's family," said my father. He seemed uncertain, and I thought that perhaps, finally, he was going to stand up to Kalo. I wanted to get down on my knees and kiss the ground in front of his boots in the ultimate gesture of deference.

The Arbitrator broke in. "Even if you pay the penalty," he said, "if the marriage and merger do not proceed, there will be bad feeling."

Now I wanted to kiss the ground in front of the Arbitrator's boots, too.

"All right," said Kalo. "Let Leth take her. But if she marries without my consent, she forfeits her dowry."

"No one will take a woman without a dowry," said Father.

"In that case, it will be Leth's refusal," said Kalo. "We won't even have to pay the penalty."

Leth's refusal. Suddenly the fear within me turned to hope.

Because it didn't matter what Kalo or Leth's father or his mother-the-witch thought. I had some money from my mother that I had hidden away. I knew that Leth himself had some land that belonged solely to him and not to his family—enough to yield a kitchen garden. Not much, but enough, if we were frugal, to live on. Leth was an honorable man, and we were pre-contracted. Minutes away from being contracted. We would find a way to get by.

More importantly, I would *not* marry an unknown 'Lidan. The rumors said that the 'Lidans branded their women—a small brand, an indelible mark of ownership—and enforced them to silence. I didn't want to be branded, and, besides, I wasn't good at silence.

Then I looked at my father. I knew he loathed to side with Kalo, but I could see the land greed in his eyes again. Once Mother had died, the love of land was all that was left him. I was a noisy, willful disappointment. Silky was even worse because she looked exactly like Mother. She was a constant reminder of his loss. He didn't dislike us, but he didn't have much affection for us, either.

Land was easy to love.

"If Leth and his family refuse the penalty," said my father, "and if they freely give her up, you have my leave to make this alliance." He wouldn't meet my eye.

"Thank you, Father," said Kalo. His tone was mocking.

I should have kept silent, but I couldn't.

"You're not going to have your way, Kalo," I said. "'Lidan alliance or no 'Lidan alliance."

"You think Leth will take you without a dower?" Kalo smiled. The smile turned into a frown, and he looked speculatively at Silky. "I'm going to work out something for you, too, Silky. Perhaps a 'Lidan Lordling."

"I don't want to marry a 'Lidan," said Silky. "I want to stay in Arcadia."

"You'd certainly have to learn to be silent," said Kalo, as if musing to himself.

"They'll hurt me."

"That part doesn't take long at all. It's a small mark. Many 'Lidan women consider it a sign of beauty."

"Then they're *idiots*."

The Arbitrator ushered Silky and me out of the room. As we left, I heard him say, "It's time to bring in the Nessons. Send a servant who knows how to hold his tongue." He was speaking to Kalo now—ceding to my brother what should have been my father's prerogative.

Silky and I went to my bedroom. We were to be no part of the planning and negotiations.

Silky slumped onto the cushioned long-chair and took off her chaplet of flowers. It had seen better days, although the small red sun-discs in her hair still glowed. I noted how beautiful she was. I was pretty enough but had missed beauty somehow—maybe it was the set of my nose. Silky said it was because I wouldn't stick in my chin and that green eyes were just unfashionable. Not unbeautiful. But Silky thought the world of me, and I didn't expect her to be the most objective judge.

Now she stared into space; she was miserable or in shock or both. I had to keep her out of a 'Lidan match. I would not let her be branded and owned and silenced. Their practices were not our practices—and my sister would *never* be on the receiving end of a brand.

Nor would I. Ever.

I had tasted despair the night my mother died; Silky, young then, had yet to know real despair. My job was to protect her.

Our mother would have wanted that.

Silky and I sat.

"You know they're deciding our fates," Silky said finally.

"I know."

"Is Leth going to rescue you?"

I hesitated. Then I spoke firmly.

"Yes."

"Are you sure?"

"Yes."

"Who's going to rescue me?"

"I am."

She didn't reply, because she knew it was true.

I would make sure that wherever Leth and I lived after he rescued me, there would always be room for Silky.

My thoughts turned back to what was going on in the other room—without us. Trust Kalo to insinuate himself with the 'Lidans. I supposed I was glad they hadn't simply killed him, but it was possible I was experiencing the kind of family feeling that they drilled into women from infancy on. Early training was hard to overcome.

I noticed that the beautiful decorations on my hands were smudged, and I imagined that I had sweat away those on my throat. Perhaps the tendrils from the nape of my neck and down my back and arms still remained.

The tarnished, wilted exhausted bride-that-almost-was. All the ceremony was rubbing away. What flowers remained fresh would soon fade. Like me.

We waited.

And then there was a knock on the door—a knock, meaning a stranger to the household. But before I could get to the door to lock out whoever it was (my father or Kalo would have simply walked in), the door opened.

The bard stepped inside.

"I'm sorry," he said. But he didn't look sorry, and he didn't drop his eyes. He pushed his thick hair back out of his face, and again I saw depth in his blue eyes.

I felt as if a chair had been pulled out from under me.

"I've been wandering the house," he said. "They wouldn't let me in at the feast. Although the cook gave me scraps in return for the news." I wondered why he was in the house at all.

"What do you want?" I asked.

"I need to get paid," said the Bard.

For some reason, I was disappointed, although I didn't know what I expected.

Silky was on her feet and halfway across the room before I could move.

"Go *away*," she said. "This is the *Lady Angel*. This is the *bride*, and you don't even *bow*."

"Oh," said the Bard. "Sorry. But."

"You still need to get paid," I said.

Silky blazed. "You come in here for *money*? You have no *right* to bother the Lady Angel. No *right*." And then she broke down in tears.

"Wrong room, I suppose," said the Bard. "But I've tried all the others." Yet I noticed he made no move to leave.

I felt strangely calm, but it may have been because of the Bard's behavior. He looked around the room with interest—at the books, at Silky, at me in my wilted state—but I could tell he meant us no harm; I had no sense that he was covetous. He probably needed the money badly.

He shrugged. "I just need to get paid for the wedding music," he said. "I never got to the epic or the comic ballads."

"And for how much of the wedding music do we owe you?" I asked. We stood there staring at each other.

And it wasn't about the money.

Silky had gone back to the long-chair, and, although she continued to weep quietly, I had no sense that she was going to fly at him again.

"I stopped when the yelling began," said the Bard. And I was almost sure I saw the flicker of a smile on his face. Then he grew serious. "If needs be," he said, "I can do without."

But I knew he couldn't. He was landless, and he needed to be paid, in spite of the fact that the tale of the Montrose-Nesson wedding-that-wasn't would get him hearers (and pennies) for weeks.

Pennies didn't last long. Even payment for part of a wedding would last much, much longer.

I went to the big chest in my room and took some gold coins from the hidden cache in the bottom of it, and then I put the coins in the Bard's hand.

I had given him three times the amount normally given to the Bard of a wedding, and that for less than a third of the music.

"Thank you, my Lady." He looked taken aback.

"Try and be kind to me in your songs," I said.

"I would do that without the gold," he said. "Is it supposed to be a bribe? Because I don't take them. Bribes."

Silky stopped weeping instantly.

"How can you be so *evil*?" she cried out. "My sister, the Lady Angel, is being *kind*, which is more than can be said of just about *anyone* right now."

"Of that," he said, "there's little question. I suspect you're both kind." And he gave me a smile that reached right down inside.

"You *annoy* me," said Silky.

"I'm sorry, my Lady," said the Bard. "I've been said to have that effect." And then he gave a laugh.

"What's so *funny*?" asked Silky.

"Oh," said the Bard, "I have a feeling that all those fools out there will pay in the end." He nodded his head. "Lady Angel. Lady Silky."

And then he was gone.

The light began to fade, and strange shadows began to fill the room. The skin under Silky's eyes looked bruised from tiredness.

"It's time for you to sleep, Silky," I said. "They're doing a lot in the arbitration room tonight, and we need to be fresh and ready to engage in some undoing."

"Why did you give that bard the gold?" asked Silky.

"I'm not sure."

But then I thought for a moment, and it was almost as if I could reach out and touch the dark shapes that were future things. And there, hard to make out in the deep gloom, I finally saw the Bard. His eyes were full of more than wisdom, and he was waiting for me.

CHAPTER THREE

CLOSED BOOKS

Silky slept in my bed that night. I knew she would feel safer there.

I sat on the long-chair, dazed, still dressed in my finery, and I held her hand as she soon fell asleep. I looked at her closely. She was curled like a puppy, her fair hair fanned out against the pillow. I knew she believed that I would let no harm come to her, and that thought was terrifying to me. I didn't know what I could do to keep Kalo from crushing her spirit. The last thing she said before sleep took her was "What are you going to do, Angel?"

And I said, "I don't know."

I thought about trying to eavesdrop outside the library, where the arbitration was taking place, but the huge oak doors and walls were thick—and I had a terrible fear of being caught. It might occur to my father—or more probably to Kalo—to lock me in my room. My father had done that in the past on one pretext or another. Mostly if he found out I was seeing a lot of Trey—but he always made sure I was fed. I wasn't so sure that Kalo wouldn't just forget about Silky and me completely for a couple of days while he solidified arrangements for the 'Lidan alliance. Or, if he remembered me, that it would be to torment me as he dismantled the world I had created in his long absence.

I had a network of servants on whom I could depend—and who could depend on me. He would never stand for that. And he would find intolerable the degree of independence I had achieved as my father had continued his retreat into mourning.

He would soon find out I even had a horse, Jasmine, and rode wherever I chose on our lands and in the village. Kalo would sell Jasmine. Or give her away. Or even kill her, if he felt he had to assert his authority. As if I needed any point to be made in order to know who was the new master of the house.

The hour was so late it was almost morning, but I was wide awake; I was in no way ready to join Silky in my bed.

It was true I couldn't hope to gain anything from trying to listen at the door of the library, but if I knew anything, it was that Kalo and Father would make sure the Arbitrator would have plenty of food and drink—and that meant servants. Servants coming and going. And, while they were in the room, servants hearing and seeing.

I took off the lace veil that had been pinned into my braids and left it on the long-chair. I tried not to wake Silky, but I needn't have worried; she slept soundly. The veil was a liability—likely to catch on things and make noise. My mother's beautiful dress—now dishonored, now never to be worn in a ceremonial wedding—was another liability. The ivory train of thick silk would only thump and drag behind me as I went up the stairs. But there was no time to change. For one thing, I was partially sewn into the dress, and getting out of it would take me well over an hour. It had taken far more than that for Silky, with my help, to get the dress on and adjusted in the first place.

So I hiked up the back of the dress and tied the train to the lowest button in the back.

Still, the delicate dress was not made for sneaking through the house. I would be an ivory ghost in a fitted low bodice of pearls and swan feathers with a cloud of silk and lace below. I was likely to frighten any of our older servants. In my mother's dress, even unveiled, I might easily be taken for her spirit.

I hurried to the stairs, and I saw no one. Most of the servants, all but the most trusted—who would be waiting on Kalo, Father and the Arbitrator—would be in the servants' hall and kitchen. There was, after all, a lot to gossip about, and the feast and flowers had to be cleared away and everything cleaned and washed. Most Great Houses used dishes several times before washing them, but Father would not eat off a dirty dish. People thought he was peculiar.

I crept up toward the library, but I heard nothing and saw nobody. The house, always kept dim and quiet because of Father's mourning, seemed to swallow me up in its darkness. The huge mahogany staircase and banister dwarfed me, and the enormous carved ancestor-lions at the top of the stairs looked stern, as if they knew what I was thinking.

If they did, I wonder if they would have tried to stop me.

Because I was thinking that I would do everything in my power to thwart Kalo. In anything he wished to do. Certainly I wasn't going to let him marry me off to a man I'd never met—a man I'd never even heard of. What if this nameless 'Lidan groom beat me? What if he kept me mewed up and friendless? What if he *smelled*? And there was no getting around the implications of marrying a 'Lidan. He would brand me, as if I belonged to him.

Surrounded by gloom, I could feel the ivory dress glow with a preternatural light.

Still no servants. Now I was next to the library.

Without warning, the solid grim door was flung open, but it was no servant sent on a hasty errand to bring food or fire or one of the land-law books from Father's study.

It was Leth.

He was moving so fast that he almost knocked me over in his haste. Then he stopped and stared, as if he'd never seen me before. As if—I could no longer remember how many hours earlier—we hadn't stood side by side. I stared back at him. He was pale, and his cool blue eyes were opened wide, but he didn't seem to see me, although I could see a tiny ivory bride reflected back in those eyes.

The vacant look left him, and he stared at me as if in horror.

"Angel," he said. "You shouldn't be here. Not now. Not in this place." His voice was hoarse and low, as if he'd been talking for hours. I lifted my hand to him and, since there was no chaperone present to tut-tut over the gesture, I expected him to take it. But he didn't touch me. He took a step backward, and I dropped my hand.

Perhaps he thought my breach of etiquette inappropriate for such a time. He said my name again.

"Angel."

He had left the door to the library open a crack, and I could hear voices rising inside.

"What is it, Leth?" I asked. "What's happening?"

"It's over," he muttered. "The only thing left is—they're talking about *The Book of Forbidden Wisdom*."

"I don't know anything about it," I whispered. "Nothing. The mother-daughter chain was broken."

He looked at me closely, and suddenly his voice was clear.

"Are you sure?"

And that's when I realized with a certainty that, for the Nessons, it had been about *The Book* all along. Oh, the Nessons loved my timber, my meadows, my mines, but more than that they loved the prospect of the power and land that was supposed to come with *The Book*. They thought I held the secret. And they had believed that, somehow, Leth would get it out of me.

I looked at my almost-groom and, for a second, I shivered.

Now, through the door, I recognized Kalo's voice as he laid down the law to somebody. From the measured response, I guessed it was Leth's father, who had an even temper—unlike his avaricious wife.

Leth continued to stare at me. I pulled my dress up and put the bulk of it over my arm. Then, without waiting for Leth to reach out to me, I took his arm and almost pushed him to the stairs. A chaperone would have been appalled—what passed for high spirits in a man was lewdness in a woman, and I had done much more than casually brush against him. I had practically been in his arms when we collided outside the library door, and there were never any excuses.

We were almost at the bottom and out the side door when a servant holding a tray of food saw us. She stopped and stared. She was new to our house, and I didn't know if I could trust her.

"Lady Angel," she said abruptly. "Do you need me to get the Lady Silky?"

This was as close as a servant could come to overtly

challenging me, but the situation—no chaperone—
must have seemed outlandish to her. She probably
thought she was helping to maintain my reputation by
offering to get Silky. Being so physically close to Leth
was odd for me, too. But I wasn't in the mood to ap-
pease the servant.

"There's no need to rouse my sister," I said.

The door gave out onto the orchard, and in a
moment we were out and under the trees. As I closed
the door behind us, I saw the servant still standing at
the foot of the stairs and staring after us. If her alle-
giance were to my father and not to me, then Leth and
I had time counted in minutes.

But the moment I felt the grass under my bare feet
and saw the vague shapes of the gnarled apple trees
looming in the darkness, I felt better. There were stars
and fireflies. I had forgotten how late in the summer it
was. The apples hadn't been harvested yet, but some
had fallen and been left to rot, and their sweet-sour
scent filled the night.

I found I didn't want to ask what kind of bargain, in
terms of penalties and forfeits, Kalo and the Nessons
were working out. I didn't care.

"It's going to be all right," I said. That's when Leth
stopped me and turned me so that we were facing each
other. I had always liked Leth's face; occasionally it was
bluff and blank, but an acute intelligence sometimes
filled his light eyes, particularly when he looked at me.
Now the intelligence was there, but I found I didn't like
the look he was giving me at all.

"No," he said. "It's not going to be all right. I thought it was. But it's not."

"The land merger was almost complete," I said. "In two minutes, we would have been married. Two minutes. Do we have to worry so much about two minutes? There are others who can complete the marriage portion of the ceremony, even if we lose the land."

"Your father has agreed with your brother to retract your dowry."

It was as I had feared. Unless the Nessons were generous, Leth and I faced hard times. Then I looked more closely at his face, and I knew I was in trouble.

"So," I said. "No dowry."

"I'll marry no one else," he said.

"But you won't marry me."

The door to the house opened, and light streamed out, gilding the trees. I saw Kalo on the threshold. He staggered for a moment, and I wondered if he were drunk.

"You're compromising my sister," said Kalo, and his words were slurred. So yes—drunk. "If word gets out you two were alone, I won't pay any of the penalty."

"If word gets out," countered Leth, "she won't be any good for a 'Lidan marriage."

I stared at him. I doubted what I had heard.

"Leth," I said, "you have a little land. Enough to live on. I have some money."

Kalo laughed at me from the doorway. "Without his parents' consent, he doesn't have enough to plant a rock garden on," he said. "We've established that. Cut your losses, Leth, unless her charms have made you change your mind. Unless you want to say she is herself a dower."

Now Leth seemed in some kind of stupor.

"I'm sorry, Angel," he said, staring at my feet. "We would have made a good match, but this way we have no means to live. My parents wouldn't pledge us anything. I *did* ask. They've taken the penalty and rejected the union. You wouldn't do badly to make a fine 'Lidan marriage, even if it did mean leaving Arcadia. This almost-wedding taints you, Angel. You know it does."

"You've given this some thought."

"Forgive me, Angel."

"No."

He didn't seem to hear that, though. He pressed on. "You've always been practical. You could save us if you had the key to *The Book of Forbidden Wisdom*. We could forget Kalo and your father."

"But I don't have it, Leth."

His eyes glittered. "The House of St. Clare had the key, and the House of St. Clare was your mother's House, before she married into the House of Montrose."

"I know all that, obviously. Just as you know my mother died before she could tell me anything."

"You would have told me," he said. "After we were married. I would have seen to that."

"Don't."

"Maybe we are a bad match, Angel." I had never seen this expression on his face before. This was not sorrow; it was anger.

"Is the forbidden wisdom all your family wants?" I said.

"I don't care about wisdom," said Leth, "but *The Book* carries the titles to all the lost lands. We would be rich beyond what either of us can imagine. I want you, Angel. And my family wants only what it would be easy for you to give. So very easy."

"I think you've been talking to your father."

"My father is wise."

"And you've been talking to your mother."

"Is that so bad?"

My Leth was gone. Subsumed into his ambitious House. I realized that I didn't know him at all. And I remembered some of the things Trey had said about Leth before the contract had been drawn up—words that had brought down silence on our old friendship. He had once called Leth weak, and I had stormed at him.

Perhaps Trey had been right, though. And perhaps— and this chilled me as I looked at the man before me— perhaps Leth had thought he could beat the secret of *The Book* from me after the marriage.

Kalo still stood in the doorway, watching us. Then he addressed Leth.

"Your parents are waiting," he said. "And we need the final signatures."

Leth turned from me and walked toward Kalo.

"Leth," I said.

"My Lady Angel?"

"Not yours. Not ever, now. Good-bye, Leth." Perhaps the finality in my voice goaded him.

"You would have told me, Angel," he said. "Maybe not on the first night. But you would have told me."

I flinched. The nights were absolutely not to be spoken of. Leth turned away from me and walked to the door. When he reached Kalo, Kalo put an arm around him.

"She's worth nothing," said Kalo.

The deep shadow shapes of the future played so close to me then that I could breathe the air of tomorrow. The scent of rotting apples was overpowering, and then it was replaced by the scent of moonflowers and roses.

I was in a quiet country, and my dead mother whispered in my ear.

CHAPTER FOUR

THE RESCUE

I don't know what woke me up. I barely knew how I'd made it back to my bed. The moon had risen; it was full, and the pale silver light streamed into my room. Silky was next to me, asleep, her fair hair glowing strangely in the moonlight. She looked soft and fragile.

For a moment, I thought it was my wedding day. Leth. The ceremony. But my wedding day had come and gone, and yet my life was still not sealed in the Marriage Book and the Land Book. It was like a children's riddle. What did that mean I was? Neither married nor lone. Not uncontracted maiden and yet, after what should have been the sealing tie, still in my original state. What was I?

I was nothing.

I was brought to myself by a small tap.

Now I was wide awake. Flowers filled the room, and I breathed in the heady scent of blush roses and wild roses, hyacinth and purple bells. And yet the odor was slightly off—a little sour, a little rancid. They were flowers that had, in one day, passed beyond their peak moment of bloom and were now overblown. Like me, I thought. Like me. And I saw my wedding bouquet on the floor by the bed, wilted now, and some of the petals crushed, because I had thrown it to the ground in petulance and anger and self-pity.

Tap.

I couldn't locate the sound. I saw the wedding dress, which I had torn in order to get it off, crumpled at the foot of the bed, the train stained with the grass of the orchard. In the bright moonlight, I could see Silky's bouquet in a glass of water by the window. Perhaps she had hoped the ceremony would go on tomorrow. Perhaps she couldn't bear watching the flowers wilt and fade.

Tap.

The noise was coming from the window. I didn't light a candle; I didn't need one in the moonlight. I opened the window and leaned out the casement, just in time for a pebble to fly out of the darkness and graze my cheek.

"Ow."

"Sorry. But we've got to go." The voice was low and

urgent. Luckily my room was at the back of the house and no one was likely to hear. I tried to imagine that I was hearing Leth's abashed words, but I knew that Leth was neither abashed nor the type to throw pebbles at windows.

"Trey?"

"Of course. Who were you expecting?"

It was beyond belief, and I felt some of my fear ebb away.

"I wasn't expecting anyone," I said.

"Did you really think," said Trey, "that just because we're not speaking I'd leave you to Kalo? Or, for that matter, to the 'Lidans? The word is out about the new match. Kalo. 'Lidans. Even Leth's better than those options."

"You know a lot."

"Everyone knows a lot. The servants know even more than everyone else, and they're spreading the word. And tomorrow Kalo will have you locked down so tight, your life really will be sealed."

"If Kalo catches you here, he'll kill you," I said. I said it first without thinking, but in that moment, I knew it to be true.

"I know," said Trey. "Now stand back from the window."

The ivy root against the house there was thicker than my arm. When Trey and I had been children, we had climbed it many times. We had played out the tale of the witch and the girl in the tower. And now I was the girl in the tower, and it was all too real.

In a minute he was in my room, and then, and then I was somehow in his arms.

If Kalo had walked in then, it would have meant death for both of us.

I couldn't have cared less—not about myself.

"And you an almost-married woman," he said, his voice muffled in my hair.

Silky moaned in her sleep and turned to her other side.

I stepped back and out of Trey's arms.

"This isn't right," I said. "You can't—I can't allow you to—because—" I was incoherent.

"It's all right, Angel," said Trey. "I have no designs on your virtue."

"We shouldn't have touched." I was scared. I was scared because it had felt far too natural.

"We used to touch all the time."

"We were five years old, Trey."

"Anyway," he said, "we have to go. I drugged the stable boy, and the horses are saddled."

I drew back even farther. "What are you talking about?"

"Do you really think I'd let Kalo contract you against your will?" Then he paused. "Unless you want the 'Lidan match. You'd be very rich."

"Trey—"

"I didn't think that would tempt you. I'm rescuing you, Angel. So try not to raise your voice."

And then fear was back. It swept over me. The nameless, incomprehensible fear of the unknown. He wanted me to leave, but I had nowhere to go, nobody to be once I wasn't in Arcadia. Everything I knew was close to home. I was no coward, but I was no fool, either. I would be giving up everything I had ever loved. Everything I was.

"You don't understand, Trey," I said. "I can't leave— all this. Everything I know. I can't give up me. The Lady Angel."

"I will call you 'Lady Angel' seventeen times a day, if you'll only hurry. Your options are limited. Now get some clothes; I have enough supplies for us for three days."

"You're coming?"

"Of course," said Trey. "You'd be hopeless on the road alone and prey for any vagabond who—for any vagabond."

"You don't have to come."

He laughed.

Trey's House was a small one, and he stood to inherit no more than a negligible piece of land. But even so, by leaving and taking me he was making it so that he could never return. And I, scion of a Great House, able to make a rich marriage, would never be able to return, either.

Perhaps, I thought wildly, what they said about the 'Lidans wasn't true.

Silky, who was a sound sleeper, murmured something and then turned over again. She must be having a dream.

And that's when I knew I really couldn't go with Trey.

"I can't leave Silky," I told him. "Kalo will blame her. He'll make her pay in every way he can. He'll punish her for my actions and for not having land and just for being someone to punish."

"Of course you can't leave Silky," said Trey. "Three horses are saddled. Your Jasmine. Silky's pony. My Bran. And while I was busy stealing horses, I took one of Kalo's pack animals as well."

"Trey," I said, aghast, "they hang people for horse stealing."

"What about bride stealing? Come on, Angel. We have to put some miles behind us tonight."

The scent of the flowers was stifling, and I couldn't think. But at Trey's vehemence, Silky rolled over and opened her eyes and lay there, staring at the two of us. She looked from me to Trey.

"Are we being *rescued*?" she asked.

And all I could say was "Yes."

CHAPTER FIVE

THE FLOATING ISLAND

I changed out of my nightclothes. Trey kept his back turned, but I was already shamed. He had seen me in night garb.

He had held me in night garb.

He had *held* me.

Despite the shame, however, I can't say that I felt particularly soiled. Not the way the chaperones had all pledged I would if anyone but my husband did so much as touch my hand. Trey had smelled good: of soap and leather and clean air. And he had felt good: strong and comforting.

I packed some clothes in a satchel. I was not going to risk trying to get to Silky's room, so she would have to make do with my things. She often wore them anyway.

Trey stood by the window, waiting.

We were ready, but before I committed myself to the night, I had one question for Trey.

"Is there any talk—" I hesitated. "Is there any talk that Leth might want to marry me after all?"

"Do you care?" asked Trey.

I thought for a moment. "I do," I said finally. "If he defies his parents, the Arbitrator will have to allow the marriage. If he defies his parents, I'll still marry him. He was only weak. He would never hurt me. I really believe that."

Trey smiled, but it was a bitter smile. "'He would never hurt me.' There's a basis for matrimony. Leth wanted your land, Angel, and more. The Nessons want the knowledge in *The Book of Forbidden Wisdom*. I imagine Leth's piqued he didn't get it for them."

"Is that what *you* want?" I asked, but Trey just laughed.

Then he said, "Leth's parents have already licensed the Arbitrator to search for another alliance for him."

"He said he'd never marry."

"I'm sure that's what he said," Trey answered. "I don't doubt you. But his parents are very strong-willed." He wasn't smiling now. Silky looked from one of us to the other.

"What about the *rescue*?" she asked.

We took almost nothing—some clothes, blankets. I handed my crossbow to Silky, who didn't dare go to her room for hers. We all knew she was the better shot.

Outside the stables, the horses were tethered to a post.

"All right," said Trey. "Let's ride for it."

I thought for a moment of what would happen if we were taken now. We would all be dead, but they would make Trey suffer before they killed him.

At first we stayed off the path and in the shadows; the grass absorbed the sound of horses' hooves. But once we had moved beyond the shadow of the house, Trey picked up a canter, and Silky and I followed suit, Silky's pony, Squab, taking two strides for every one of Trey's great horse, Bran.

"*Angel.*" Silky had to raise her voice to be heard. "*Angel*, look at the house. It's full of light. Like a *lantern.*"

I called ahead to Trey and pulled up Jasmine. We stared at the house. There was light everywhere. I could see my window, and I could see the silhouettes of men crisscrossing the room with flaming torches.

They were looking for me. I didn't want to think about why, in the middle of the night, Kalo would send men to seek me in my bedchamber. He must have feared I would bolt.

It was only a matter of time before they would realize that I wasn't in the house at all. With Silky gone, Kalo's suspicions would crystallize. The disappearance of Silky would make him believe what would otherwise be inconceivable: I had run.

And then, as we watched, a river of torches flowed out of the house.

"Let's go," said Trey urgently. "We have to keep moving."

I was suddenly afraid that he had no real plan, but then, beautiful and fully formed, an idea came to me.

"Our chance is the river," I said. "If we walk the horses through the shallows, they may lose our trail. As it is, we might as well have left 'we went this way' signs."

"We stayed on the grass," said Silky.

"We *squashed* the grass," I said. "They'll make out the prints in the dew easily enough. We go to the river."

"That's what I had in mind," said Trey shortly.

Trey urged Bran to a gallop. I stared up at the house one more time, mesmerized. Light was everywhere. Now I could see men holding torches and trying to mount their horses in the front courtyard. Fire and horses didn't mix, and the mounts were wheeling around in protest and skittering away from the flames. I hoped such stupidity would buy us enough time to reach the river.

And then a winding silver ribbon was in front of us, and Jasmine went crashing into the slow-moving water.

"Downstream," I said. "In case the horses have to swim for it. The current will carry us."

Silky's Squab had followed Jasmine and now stood fetlock deep in the river shallows. But Bran—Bran, a bold horse— had stopped at the edge.

Trey groaned. "He only likes water he can jump over—puddles, streams—and this does *not* qualify."

"Now might be a good time to show off your horsemanship," I said.

"My horsemanship is just fine."

Trey urged Bran forward—finally, reluctantly, using his switch on the sensitive horse. But Bran only backed up; he would not enter the water.

"Hurry, Trey," I said.

"I *am* hurrying," he said. I looked over my shoulder. Not so very far away, I could see lights bobbing through the trees.

I swallowed hard. "You'd better leave Bran and take the packhorse," I said.

"Bran's faster and fitter," said Trey.

"It won't make any difference if you can't get him into the river," I snapped.

The dark water swirled around the horses' legs. The moon shone down on us, and it occurred to me that, as in the old bardsong about the lovers and the coming storm, the moon didn't care.

And I thought ahead to the humiliations and death that probably awaited me. If word got out that I had fled with a man, there would no marriage, 'Lidan or otherwise. I would be stripped to my petticoat, and, if Kalo went for the full extent of the law, I would be tied to a stake to be either stoned or burned. Kalo's choice. And my father's, of course—technically—but I was under no illusions about who was making all the decisions now.

I wondered, too, if Leth would want to come after me. It was one thing for him to back out of our contract, it was another for *me* to run away from *him*.

Trey hit Bran on the flank as hard as he could with his fist. Bran half-reared but would go no further into the water.

Then I had an idea.

It's not hard to lead a horse. One can lead a horse places it would never take a rider.

In a moment I was off Jasmine's back and sloshing in the water toward Trey and Bran.

"This is cold, and this is wet," I said to no one in particular. Then I had Bran by the reins.

He followed me meekly into the water.

"Looks like you're doing some rescuing yourself," said Trey.

I remounted Jasmine, and we moved deeper into the river, but we were still in the shallows. In the moonlight, I could easily see the swath we had cut on land—it reached to the river's edge and then stopped.

"It's obvious what we've done," I said.

"There wasn't much choice," said Trey.

"What *are* we doing?" asked Silky.

"Further down there are reed beds and floating islands of wild hassow," I said. "I've been this way before. We'll be hard to find—they'll be searching the other side to see where we came out of the river."

"Where *are* we coming out of the river?" asked Silky. "The packhorse is shivering already. *I'm* shivering, too. So you know."

"It won't be for a while," I said. "First thing, we need to get around that bend in the river, or they'll see us the minute they break through the trees. The moon isn't helping. And couldn't you have picked a bay pony, Silky? Your Squab doesn't exactly blend in."

"Squab is *perfect*," said Silky.

"Not now, Silky," I said, and my voice was grim. "We have to go carefully. They're almost close enough to hear us."

We moved through the water.

"We could outrun them," said Silky.

"On Squab?" Trey said to her. "Your pony's a pet, Silky; he's not built for speed."

"He's built *exactly right*," said Silky.

"Quiet," I said.

We were very near the bend in the river now. All I could hear was the swish, swish of the horses moving through the shallows. My fear of leaving my home had been replaced by desperation to get away, to escape the land and marriage laws that would seal my life—or my shameful death.

The fireflies were gone, and the moon was cold—everything was bathed in chilly silver light. There was no solace in the night, and still, still the moon didn't care.

I was nobody now. No better than a vagabond. I had brought money, yes, but money was nothing when compared to land. I felt this was easier for Trey because he was land-poor. I had come from a Great House and thought my fall was greater.

I knew nothing.

Swish, swish. Rivulets and waves of silver. But no night birds or singing frogs or even the plop of fish rising for insects. The night, except for the sound of horses moving through water, was silent.

We were at the bend in the river.

I turned. The torches continued to bob among the trees, but then, just as we were beginning to round the bend, the band of riders broke out of the woods. They gathered together for a moment, as if to confer about their course of action. Luckily they hadn't seen us yet, but once one of them looked in our direction, our movement would give us away.

I pulled up Jasmine.

"Get ahead, Silky," I said. "Bran will shield that light-colored Squab of yours. It's not far now."

I could see a knot of riders go down to the river-bank, break up and cast about as if they had lost the trail. We had moments, if we were lucky.

The riders held their torches high above their heads, and, even at that distance, I could make out some familiar forms. I saw Kalo, tall, broad, grim, suddenly wheel his horse around and whip it to the place where we had entered the water. Close behind him was our land steward, Farnam.

And at Kalo's side, his face a mask of darkness, was Leth.

So.

It was possible he still harbored hopes I would trade knowledge of *The Book of Forbidden Wisdom* for a patched-up marriage with him. But, more likely, he saw my flight as a betrayal and wanted to ruin me. For disloyalty. For disobedience. And, if he found out about Trey's role in my escape, for harlotry.

Trey followed my line of sight.

"I'm sorry, Angel," he said.

"It would have been better not to know he was riding with them," I said.

"Maybe he's there to try and make sure they don't *hurt* us," said Silky.

"I assume you mean before the executions," I said drily.

"Angel," said Trey.

Trey's word was neither a reprimand nor an endorsement. It was just my name, that's all. But when he spoke it, everything fell away: my great lineage, my pride in my House, and my feelings for Leth. I wondered whether there was anything left of me. Then I looked up at Trey's clear face, and, for some reason, I felt better.

We rounded the bend at last, at the very moment I heard the sound of Kalo's party of horses crashing into the river.

"They're coming," I said.

"Now we ride," said Trey. "They won't hear us over their own noise."

"Do we even have a chance?" asked Silky.

"Of course we have a chance, Lady Silky," said Trey. I smiled grimly into the dark. Lady Silky. Trey was reassuring her with her title.

"But where are we going," she asked, "when we follow the river?"

"It doesn't really matter where we go right now," Trey said to Silky. "As long as we get out of sight."

The great moon was low in the sky now, and I could see, spread out in front of us, a long spit of sand on one side and an impenetrable bed of reeds on the other.

"Go straight down the center," I said. "The water's not deep. Don't leave a print on the sand; don't get tangled in the reeds. Single file. I used to do this for fun."

"Kalo's group won't care about leaving prints," Trey said. "They'll just gallop through—"

"They don't know this river," I said.

"You do?" Trey asked.

"I do. There's likely to be a floating island beyond the spit and the reeds."

"You never showed me that," said Trey. He looked at me in surprise.

"It was after I grew up," I explained.

"Oh," he said, and I couldn't make out his tone.

The horses scrambled through by the side of the reeds without leaving prints on the spit of land, and then we were galloping. The river opened in front of us; it was a sheet of silver with a large dark mound in the middle.

"We can get behind that island," said Trey. "While we're there, they'll start trying to pick up our exit trail on the other bank."

"Exactly," I said.

"That's what you had in mind all the time, isn't it?" said Trey.

"It is."

We hid and moved with the island—it was a floating hassow island, and no more substantial than the famed bottomless marsh of 'Lidan territory. Meanwhile, a few members of the pursuing party thundered across the spit but then pulled up at the silver lake opening in front of them. I could see through the hassow stems. There were three men in front, and Leth was leading them. I couldn't see Kalo, and I thought he might have gone upriver.

Their voices carried on the wind.

"They're probably gone," said one. "They could have left the river back there."

"They're far ahead of us," said the other.

"Those marks in the grass were fresh," said Leth. "They can't be far."

The third man, whom I didn't recognize, didn't speak.

"We should look for signs on the other bank," said Leth.

"You said there's a reward?" said the first.

"Oh, yes," said Leth. "Lord Kalo of Montrose is putting it up—and the reward is land. Enough to raise your caste. I have a purse of gold to go with it—if you bring them to me first."

"He's a *snake*," hissed Silky. I shushed her.

Then the third man, the one I didn't recognize at all, spoke.

"I'm going to speak freely, Master Leth," he said. "Because I'm a freeman, and it's my right. I saw the Lady Angel yesterday, on her wedding day. And I saw the Lady Silky. You showed them all the deferences and ceremonies then, and that was right, because I could see their virtue. Now you hunt them down."

"If Master Trey is with them," said Leth, "the Lady Angel's nothing better than a harlot."

There were no words for what I felt then. In a very low voice Trey said, "Sorry."

"You won't have second thoughts when we get the reward," said the second man.

"I think I might," said the third man, and his voice was cool. "I'm going home. I don't have the stomach for this."

"You think too highly of the Lady Angel," said Leth.

"What I think, I think," he said. "As I said, I'm a freeman. I'd wish you good hunting, but my heart wouldn't be in it."

Leth was silent. He and the second man rode to the far bank and, for a while, cast around for prints. Then they turned back. The man going home passed close by our island—at one moment I could see his outline clearly. We all stayed very still. Then, as he went by,

Jasmine shook her head, and her bridle jingled. The man turned. Our eyes met.

He bowed his head and put his hand over his heart.

And then he was gone.

We waited. The horses' legs must have been numb with cold, but they were obedient and still. Jasmine made no further move. Cries in the night floated across the water, and from time to time I could see torches on the far shore. The island drifted; we moved with it. No one spoke. I thought of Leth with the hunting party. I wondered what had happened between the moments in the orchard, when he swore he would marry no one as long as I lived, and now. Kalo must have persuaded him of something. Or, perhaps, he simply wanted to be true to his vow. With me dead, he could marry without breaking his word.

I told Trey my thoughts.

"You may be right," he said.

"I am right."

Silky looked cold and miserable, but before I could pull out an over garment for her from our satchel, Trey asked, "Do you know what's ahead?"

"There's a ford a mile downstream," I answered. "Then there's a stream that makes its way to the road. We'll have gone a long way without leaving prints."

"Angel," said Trey, "Kalo's spies are going to be everywhere tonight. The roads will be watched."

"We'll freeze if we stay in the water much longer. I can hear Silky's teeth chattering from here."

"They *are* clacking together," said Silky. "Sorry."

"All right," I said. "Let me think."

I noticed a streak of pink in the eastern sky. Dawn. Soon we wouldn't be able to trust to darkness.

I thought of my mother.

"All right," I said. "We go north. Toward 'Lidan country—toward Shibbeth—and away from here. They won't expect that." North. My mother had always talked about the north as if it were a magic country, but nobody really knew much about the northern territories, where Shibbeth bled back into Northern Arcadia—where, after the border-place of The Village of Broken Women, the ancient Spiral City was supposed to be.

"We need to move fast," said Trey, "if you really want to go to Shibbeth. They'll be watching all the ways out."

"We won't take the country roads," I said. "We'll go by the Old Roads."

"But the Old Roads are *haunted*," said Silky.

"Exactly," said Trey. "It's a good plan."

The Old Roads ran straight and true, and time did not eradicate them, although their builders were long gone. Except for the ghosts most thought they had left behind.

But in the end, the choice was simple. Kalo and death, or the Old Roads and ghosts.

We found the tributary with no problem, and the horses, after swimming the ford, heaved themselves up onto the bank and shook themselves like wet dogs. Silky laughed. Trey made us get off the horses and rub them down so they didn't cramp up. It was probably more work than Silky—or, I'll admit, I—had ever done. We were used to grooms brushing and blanketing and tending our mounts.

Once the horses had stopped shivering, we continued our journey. Trey took charge again, riding forward confidently, as if he'd been here before. We wove through the trees as dawn broke, and then we were in open country. After a long detour around a farm, we found ourselves pushing through undergrowth that came up to my stirrups. The morning sun cast long shadows, and everything was bathed in yellow light.

"I love this time of day," said Silky. "I could *eat* anything this light touches. It's like golden syrup. And I really like golden syrup."

"We have to be quiet," I said. I didn't mean to be sharp with Silky, but I needed her to concentrate.

We came out of the shrubbery, and the Old Road was in front of us, grassy and overgrown.

"This will lead us out of the country," said Trey. "But it's going to be three days of hard travel."

I set foot on the Old Road before Trey and Silky did. I was the one who had caused all the trouble; I was the one who had needed rescuing. I felt that I should be the one the ghosts got first.

I urged Jasmine forward.

No ghosts.

A moment later, we were all on the road. The future nudged at me, and I did not look back.

CHAPTER SIX

AN OLD ROAD

We rode in silence. The road was unnervingly straight—it didn't go around hills, it went through them, as if moving all those tons of earth had been nothing. I thought for a moment about those ghostly builders who couldn't be bothered with going over hills but who just charged straight through them. As a people, they must have been very powerful. And they must have been very impatient too.

There had been no sounds of pursuit since we had climbed onto the Old Road, but once, off to the west where the sky was still inky, we saw flickers of light on the hills—men on horseback with torches. Then they were gone.

Everywhere, as night gave way to day, the birds joined in the dawn song. Our long shadows stretched out to the left. I looked at Silky and Trey; I thought that they looked washed out and tired, and I was sure I looked no better. Any romance that might have attached to our wild night ride was gone, and we were just shabby fugitives now, going from somewhere to nowhere.

I thought about Kalo hunting us down. I thought about what he'd do. If he caught us on the road, he might kill Trey outright, without waiting for a tribunal. I realized that it looked bad—Trey had taken away a land-rich virgin on her wedding night and ruined her for a match. Kalo would be, in the eyes of others, merely protecting the family honor.

Leth, whom I had dishonored too, might be even worse. I thought about his shallow eyes, and I couldn't imagine that any pity lay behind them. It would be convenient for Kalo if I were dead, but for Leth, it was more personal. He would make sure Trey and I would pay before we died.

As for Silky—if Kalo let her live, he would make sure she was a broken thing. He would marry her to a 'Lidan, to be branded and silenced, and I had no doubt she would not last long. 'Lidan women whose husbands or fathers thought they talked too much were bridled. Unsatisfactory brides were sold or traded for cattle to whoever would have them. I knew that Silky was strong, but, in Shibbeth, her strength of character would only end in servitude.

We could never return—not to Kalo, not to Leth, not to my father. Not unless we came wielding the power behind *The Book of Forbidden Wisdom*.

For a moment a vision of *The Book* came to me, my mother stroking its pages, but I shook the image off.

I had promised.

There was no sound beyond that of the birds and the click-clack of our horses' hooves when they struck parts of the road that were still hard and black. No rustles in the underbrush. No shouts of discovery.

"We need to put in more miles before we rest," Trey said.

"But where are we going?" asked Silky.

"The Old Road meets up with the Great North Way," said Trey. "We'll follow it."

"Are we *doomed,* Trey?" asked Silky.

"No," he said shortly.

I understood her fear. The Great North Way was the finest feat of engineering left by the old ones, but it was also considered to be especially haunted. But there was something else very much on my mind.

"This rescue marks you, Trey. This may end terribly."

"Yes," he said. "There are, however, no circumstances under which I wouldn't rescue you, Angel. You should know that."

He picked up his reins and was about to urge Bran on when I reached out and took his hand in mine. Silky gasped at behavior a chaperone would have called wanton.

"You're my brother now, Trey," I said.

"I don't want to be your brother," he said shortly.

I was going to release Trey's hand, but he pulled his away first.

Silky, meanwhile, was watching us curiously. "Are you going to marry Trey, Angel?" she asked. "Because you *did* just touch him. That means a wedding, right?"

"I'm running from marriage, Silky," I said. "Remember?"

"I just *wondered*," said Silky. "I've always wondered why you and Trey didn't just—"

"Silky."

"Sorry."

Throughout this exchange, Trey rode with his head bowed, and I found I didn't want to know what he was thinking.

We began gently jogging the horses, but the road was slow going in places. The edges had crumbled away into a hard black scree that embedded itself into the horses' shoes.

"Maybe we're safe," said Silky. "Except for the *ghosts*, of course."

"You heard those men," said Trey. "There's a reward out—word will spread quickly. I doubt they'll give up pursuit that easily with land at stake. And with gold to go with it."

I thought of the kind of land reward Kalo could offer, and I knew Trey was right. Kalo could easily raise someone's caste or even set up a freeman for life.

We continued jogging. Ahead of us, I saw a puddle filled with yellow and red butterflies drinking. Jasmine, never breaking stride, waded through the puddle, and butterflies scattered like blown petals.

Bran jumped over the water.

"If you hadn't taught Bran to jump over puddles," I said to Trey, "he might not have refused at the river. You taught him to go over water, not through it."

"Jumping puddles is fun," said Silky, plunging into the conversation. "Squab and I do it all the time. And he's not afraid of *anything*."

"Too dumb," I muttered.

The sun was getting high. A deer made its strange coughing noise from the shade of a copse.

I don't know when the echo began.

But I knew, when I heard it, that we had been lazy and foolish and loud. We should have pushed the horses harder, and we should not have spoken at all, much less chattered idly. I should have shushed Silky, whose high, clear voice traveled.

Now I made a signal for silence.

"What's the *matter*?" asked Silky, without so much as waiting to take a breath.

I was right. She would have been doomed with a 'Lidan husband. A 'Lidan husband would have kept her universally bridled. At that moment, I wanted to put a hand over her mouth myself.

"Lady Silky," said Trey. "Be quiet."

Silky looked bewildered, but she held her peace.

A small miracle.

"Someone's following us," I whispered to Trey.

I looked around nervously. Yellow creepers and low green thorn bushes grew right up to the black scree. The horses could not breast their way through growth that thick—we were stuck on the road.

"I don't hear anything," Trey said finally, and Silky nodded her head in agreement.

But as we walked, I heard it again. A slow-moving horse whose hoofbeats were being masked by our own.

I moved away from Bran, reached down and grabbed Squab's reins, and jerked until he came to a halt. On my left, Trey pulled up Bran.

And then the sound was clear as the morning bell on the Montrose estate.

Clip.

Clop.

Clip.

Clop.

Then nothing.

We stood, our horses at a halt, and looked at one another. Squab chose that moment to stretch out his neck, delicately pull off the leaves of a wick plant and eat them one by one. I had told Silky a thousand times not to let Squab eat when his bridle was on, but this didn't seem the moment to bring it up.

It was Trey who broke the silence.

"We keep moving until we can get off the road," he murmured. "Then I'll wait for the follower."

"No, Trey," hissed Silky. "It could be *ghosts*."

"Silky."

"It *could* be."

"That's not the sound of a ghost," he said. "That's a solid sound."

"It's all right, Silky," I said. "We'll let Trey set an ambush."

"Angel?" Silky was taken aback.

"What choice do we have?" I said. "Trey can handle it. And if we stay, we'll just be in his way."

Silky looked skeptical. I was skeptical myself.

It wasn't clear to me what Trey could possibly know about ambushes.

We began walking the horses again, looking for an opening in the undergrowth. And then, as I looked carefully at Trey, I was suddenly less unsure about the plan. I saw someone who probably could overcome a single horseman. Maybe even two. He had grown into himself, and he was tall and broad shouldered.

Trey wasn't a child anymore.

The thought worried at me. For a moment I saw through Kalo's eyes—and Leth's. I really was the virgin stolen away on her wedding night. This man had asked me to go with him on the night of my wedding day, and I had chosen to go. He was almost eighteen, and we had gone away together—no chaperone in sight. Suddenly I wondered if I would ever see Violet again, my lemon drop friend, and, if I did, whether or not she would turn away.

But I had liked the rescue.

No—it was more than that:

I had liked being rescued from marriage.

The Echo-horse must have come closer, because now we could all hear it clearly.

Clip.

Clop.

Clip.

Clop.

Inexorable.

I felt sick.

Minutes passed, and the undergrowth on either side was as thick as ever. The Old Road took us through a copse of trees, and the branches met over our heads.

The air was close.

And then the way became broad, and the vegetation receded, and all at once I could see half a dozen places where we might be able to get down from the road and plenty of places where we would be hidden from view.

"Now," said Trey, and the horses scrambled down the bank.

We didn't have to go far; a wall of variegated vegetation soon camouflaged us. Squab immediately started munching on a string of vines.

"Silky," I whispered, annoyed.

"What?"

"Squab's eating again."

"He's *hungry*," she said. "As am I."

"Stay here," said Trey. "I'm moving closer. And please, I beg of you, Silky, be quiet."

She opened her mouth, thought better of it and closed it.

Trey turned his head toward us for a moment before moving forward.

"If this goes badly," he said, "get out of here."

"Don't let it go badly," I said. "Keep yourself safe, Trey."

We focused on the road. I saw nothing. I heard nothing. The only noise was the light breeze tossing the ends of the branches and the sound of Squab chewing.

The time passed. No one came for Trey to ambush.

Our mistake, of course, was to look so fixedly at the Old Road.

They came from behind.

I turned in time to see a fair man on foot, his face partially concealed by a hood, burst through the bushes. He pulled me off Jasmine before I could react. Jasmine reared and plunged as I wrestled with the man, almost overwhelmed by the smell of charcoal and unwashed clothes. I saw Silky reaching for the crossbow, but then another man was in the clearing, and before Silky could fit a bolt to the bow, he had dragged her off Squab by her hair. I saw her raking her nails over his face as they went down together.

Then Trey was there; he had galloped from the road, and he almost threw himself from Bran. The man holding me pushed me down, wheeled around, his leg high, and kicked Trey in the temple.

Trey fell.

The fair man then came for me again. I pushed at him hard, and when he fell to one knee, I kicked him and caught him in the chest. A moment later he dragged me to him and held my arms down. His breath was foul. He started screaming in my face, spitting out words.

"You be Lady Angel Montrose. Ain't you? You be the harlot. Ain't you? Ain't you?" Each word was accompanied by that foul breath and spittle.

And then he punched me.

I wanted to crawl away. Out of the corner of my eye I could see that Silky was trying to get to me, but the man who had her continued to hold her by her thick gold hair. Then she flung an elbow back and caught her assailant in the ribs; he released her for a moment, and the crossbow, which had fallen to the ground, was instantly in her hand.

"It's all right now," she said to me softly, even as her attacker was reaching out for her. "I've got it."

She breathed out evenly and took the shot. The bolt

hit the fair man holding me; it entered the back of his neck and burst through his throat. The tip of it grazed my cheek, and his blood spattered my face.

Silky turned to the other man, who, seeing his comrade go down, had hesitated. She was strong with a crossbow, and in a moment she had fit another bolt into the slot, but, with a great cry, the man ran away through the thickest part of the vegetation.

My assailant lay dead on top of me. Silky came and helped me push him away. She was distressed.

"There's blood *all over you*," she said.

I wiped my face with the hem of my shirt. "Not mine," I said shortly, out of breath.

"I never thought I'd kill a person, Angel." She looked woeful for a moment, and then she looked at my cheek.

"My bolt *scratched* you," she said. "I meant it to stop inside him."

"A scratch is just a scratch," I said. "You saved me."

"Of *course* I saved you," she said, and she burst into tears. I knew she must be feeling the beginnings of bloodguilt, and I wished I could figure out a way to help her. But one dealt with bloodguilt alone.

Trey was groggy, although what he said mostly made sense. We decided that the second man probably wasn't going to come back.

Squab hadn't gone far, and Silky walked over to him and took his reins. He nuzzled her with his big old shaggy head, and I thought of how I loved my little sister.

I walked over to Silky and hugged her, and she looked up at me in surprise.

Then Trey came over to Silky and me, and despite my thoughts and fears—against all the rules I'd been taught, against the decorum, the rituals, the modesty that had been instilled in me—I put an arm around Trey and drew him into our embrace.

Trey let go first, and we stood apart, awkward, embarrassed. Then Trey turned away.

Eyeing him, Silky leaned up and whispered in my ear. "Are you going to marry him *now*?"

"Like a brother, Silky," I murmured. "He's like a brother to me."

She seemed to consider that.

"Are you *sure*?" she asked.

While Trey adjusted Bran's saddle, I walked over to the dead man, knelt down and started going through his pockets.

I looked up for a moment and saw both Silky and Trey staring at me.

"Angel," said Silky. "You shouldn't *touch* him. You'll be unclean until sunset, and even then, we don't know if we'll find enough water for full immersion."

She was right.

I didn't stop.

"We let the landless prepare bodies for burial," I said finally, doing my best not to feel the flesh beneath the clothes. "And they sometimes aren't purified for days."

"But they have no caste," Silky said.

"We have enough water for me to wash my hands," I said. "That's the best I can do."

Silky looked doubtful.

"She's doing it for us," said Trey softly to Silky.

The dead man was clearly landless and of low caste—perhaps a vagrant. His clothes were dirty and torn. In his food wallet he carried only a small heel of bread, but in his breeches pocket, I found a sheet of cheap paper, dirty from handling. In large, easy-to-read letters was spelled out *REWARD*. Below was written *LADY ANGEL MONTROSE*. And below that (if any vagrant could read so far): *HARLOT*.

I doubted the dead man could spell it all out, but he must have known someone was wanted. Perhaps someone else read the words to him. Because he had known my name.

And he had called me a harlot. I would have expected a cruder term; someone educated had spoken to him. Trey seemed to read my mind.

"Kalo and Leth are moving quickly," said Trey. "They must have started distributing these before dawn. There's no shortage of landless who would want a land reward—plus Leth's gold."

There was no sign of the horse that had been echoing us, and so we hurried, assuming it belonged to one of the men, and knowing that when it got back to its stall, someone might sound the alarm. Before leaving, we cleaned the site and buried my attacker in a shallow grave.

"It's too bad he didn't have money," said Trey. "I brought what I had, but we'll need more eventually."

"I have some," I said.

"We're landowners," said Silky. "We don't *need* money."

"All that was yesterday," I said, and I wondered how long it would be before she understood that the Lady Silky of the House of Montrose was gone forever.

I saw The Book again. My mother looked into my eyes, put her hand over my heart, bowed her head and was gone. I had been given permission.

I was careful what I said next.

"If we were to return to Arcadia with *The Book of Forbidden Wisdom*," I said, "they'd take us back."

"Yes," said Trey. "*The Book* would open all doors. So what?"

"So north to Shibbeth."

Trey stopped Bran, and I stopped too.

"Your mother told you something before she died," said Trey.

I had kept the secret a long time. It was hard to speak, even to Trey.

"Yes," I said.

"You've been lying since you were a child."

"Yes."

"You could have told me," said Trey.

"You could have told *me*," said Silky.

"No—I couldn't have. It wasn't my secret to tell."

"So you've known where it is the whole time?" Trey asked.

"No. And I still don't know, exactly."

"What does that mean?" he said.

"It means Mother will guide the three of us. A stage at a time."

"Mother's *dead*," said Silky.

"It doesn't matter," I said.

"All right," said Trey after a long moment. "One thing at a time. I can do that."

"Well *I* can't," said Silky.

"You'll have to, Lady Silky," said Trey. "We're going to have to trust Angel." He turned to me. "I suppose this means the Spiral City is real?"

"It's real."

I couldn't read his expression precisely, but I knew there was no land greed in his face, no desire to wield *The Book*. He was no Kalo. No Leth. But I had always known that. He just wanted me safe—and Silky too, of course. That made me ride a bit lighter in my saddle.

We continued. After a while, Trey looked thoughtful. "I doubt Leth will follow us all the way into Shibbeth. He has no land papers."

"Yes," I said. "But he's very annoyed."

"I don't understand," said Silky. "*He* might be logical enough to stop—given he has no papers—but *we're* going to ride right in. With no papers at all."

"You're right," I said. "We are."

We set up camp at dusk, and we all felt awkward about it. There was no purple perfumed Women's Tent. No feather camp divans, soft as beds. No tent for a chaperone to stay between the Women's Tent and the place where the men slept. There were, in fact, no tents at all. I felt we were totally unprepared for a night spent together, much less a night spent together in the wild. Trey had brought bedding and a rain sheet, but the ground was hard, and even in late summer the deep night air carried a bite.

Trey built a fire. Before I foraged through the bags on the packhorse for something to eat, I stood in front of the flames and stretched my whole body, glad to be out of the saddle.

Then I saw Trey watching me. He turned away before I could speak.

Later, as Silky stoked the fire, he took me aside.

"I'll just speak frankly," he said. "I'll be sleeping outside the perimeter of the camp. Your modesty is safe." He thought for a moment. "So is Silky's," he added.

"I know," I said. "Like a brother. Remember?"

"All right, Angel," he said. "But no need to do all that stretching around me, all right? I'm not *actually* your brother."

And with that, he went to set up his sleeping area.

Silky and I put our blankets by the fire, but then she looked at me, hesitant.

"Remember the perfumed traveling tents?" Silky asked wistfully as we set out our bedding by the fire.

"I do," I said. "They were always too hot. And they made one smell of cheap incense." I was making the best of it. I missed those perfumed traveling tents terribly.

"*Expensive* incense," said Silky.

"All right," I said. "Now get ready for bed."

"I can't undress," she said.

"Trey's not going to look," I said. "Anyway, he saw you in your nightgown last night."

"That was *different*," said Silky. "It was a rescue. I didn't even *notice*—"

"Notice what?"

She leaned toward me conspiratorially. "He's turned into a *man*."

I tried to ignore her comment. Then I glanced at the perimeter where Trey was standing and looking into the darkness.

"I hope he won't be cold," I said.

"He's awfully far from the fire."

On a normal journey that required an overnight stop, we would have been able to pretend that Trey was sleeping somewhere else entirely, nowhere as indelicate as within thirty yards. But we didn't have the tents. Or the chaperones. Or the servants. Or the messengers to go between. All those ceremonies and chaperones hadn't given us much practice at being around men. We just didn't know how to do it—we barely knew how to converse outside of the regulation conversations. They might as well have bound our feet, as I heard they used to do in Shibbeth.

"Let me do your hair," I said to Silky. It was a ritual that soothed us both, and she eagerly sat with her back to me. She had put her hair up after the attack, and when I undid the pins, it cascaded down her back. I brushed it out as carefully as I could and then helped her with her nightgown. She got into her bedding quiet as a pet lamb.

"Thank you, Angel," she said.

"Go to sleep." I was soon in my bed, and the warmth of the fire made me sleepy.

"Angel?"

"Hmmm?"

"I was thinking," said Silky. "Wouldn't it be *safer* if Trey were closer to us? If we're going to break rules, that is."

"Maybe," I said.

"Will you ask him?"

"We'd be breaking rules that are quite serious, Silky."

"I'm sure he won't try to come too close."

I hesitated, because how close was too close? Still, I was sure my morals weren't eroding—much less the careful walls around my heart. And who would know?

I climbed out of bed and put my cloak over my nightclothes. I made ready to approach Trey.

He had been arranging his bedding as I approached, and he looked at me, surprised.

"Is everything all right?" he asked quickly.

"Yes," I said. "Silky thinks you should sleep closer to the fire."

"That's—that's kind."

"It was Silky's idea. She says you're harmless."

It would be hard to describe the expression on his face.

"I'll appreciate the warmth. But Angel?"

"Yes?"

"Just to be clear. I'm not sure I like being called harmless."

"But you are," I said. "You would never hurt me or Silky."

Trey, like the freeman who saw me behind the island, said nothing, but bowed his head and put his hand over his heart. I walked back to the fire.

The breeze was brisk, and as I made my way back to Silky, I felt cold. Visiting Trey at night, undressed, with only a coat as cover, had suddenly felt like visiting the rim of the moon.

Finally Trey, now closer to the fire, slept. Silky slept too. The fire burned low. A few late-summer Light Creatures blinked in the air; a night bird began her song. Soon the moon set, and I realized I had never seen so many stars. They were like jewels against the soft darkness.

I nudged Silky awake to share the night.

But I let Trey sleep.

Perhaps I was a little bit afraid of him—because of marriage, because of all it entailed.

Because I knew, of course, that if we ever made our

way back, I was going to have to marry Trey. No matter what happened—or rather, *didn't* happen—between us, Trey and I were now bound forever. I was tainted by my failed marriage to Leth, and now I was stained by my closeness to Trey. I would have to marry, and I would have to marry him. Or be an outcast.

That's where all the convoluted, twisted paths led. Out of some labyrinths, there was no safe passage.

CHAPTER SEVEN

THE RIVER WYS IN FLOOD

Breakfast was an awkward affair. I couldn't, of course, eat off any utensil Trey had put in his mouth, and we weren't supposed to share dishes, either, although since all we had was a spoon and a porridge pot, that delicate bit of behavior had to fall by the wayside. I could hardly fault Trey for not bringing enough spoons and forks.

"Needs be," I said, serving myself with the spoon Trey had been using.

"But, Angel," said Silky. "What about the protocols? It seems we're forgetting about *all* of them."

I handed the spoon back to Trey. Before Silky spoke

I had been wondering if, perhaps, I had natural immoral tendencies. Now I was simply annoyed.

"Do you really think," I said, "that we're compro-
mised by eating from the same spoon as Trey?"

"It's *unusual*."

"Do I have a say?" asked Trey.

"All right," I said.

"It's a pleasure to share with you."

I gasped and then laughed. Silky just gasped.

"This is so strange," she said. "And it's *so* wrong, in
so many ways."

"Come on, Silky," I said, bolder now. "Needs be."

"Even *married* people don't share the same spoon,"
she said.

I'd almost been a married person, and I had been
told by my chaperone the night before the wedding
that marriage, although no dishes were ever to be
used in common, consisted of another kind of sharing.
She hadn't been very specific, but some of the whis-
pers among the girls over the years had been pretty
raw. And everyone knew that after marriage, on the
very first night, the rules that we had been raised on
changed.

If the wedding to Leth had been completed, after
the Arbitrator had sealed us in the Book of Marriage
and the Book of Land, after the feast and the cake and
the dancing, after all excuses to avoid it were over,
would come the shaking of the sheets, the final ceremony. The chaperones would give me to the young

maids, who would dress me in my nightclothes. Then, after rose petals and lavender sprigs had been sprinkled on the bed, they would all withdraw. There I would wait for Leth. He would get into bed with me. He would touch me. Presumably he would know more of the rules governing this than I did.

Sharing a spoon with Trey bore no comparison.

Leth would have touched me, and I would have diminished into the House of Nesson.

We finished breakfast hurriedly. By the time we were actually packed up and ready to ride, we had broken so many rules that I had stopped counting.

Silky, on the other hand, was keeping a running tally.

"That's *twenty-four*," she said as Trey gave me a leg up on Jasmine.

"Someone always helps us get on our horses, Silky," I said.

"Not an eligible man from a Great House—who, by the way, accidentally touched your leg, which is *twenty-five*."

"I'm flattered by how dangerous I seem to be," said Trey. "Kalo has nothing on me."

"I think you're enjoying this," I said.

"*I* certainly am," said Silky. "Now help me up, please, Trey. And that'll be *twenty-six*."

"Happy to oblige," said Trey, who, instead of delicately holding his hands so Silky could step up onto Squab's back, picked Silky up and tossed her onto Squab as if she'd been a sack of feathers.

"Hey!"

"You're welcome, Lady Silky," said Trey. He looked over at me with a smile. "I held back with you, Angel," he said. "A few too many rules would have gone by the way. Given your advanced age."

"I'm getting used to fewer rules," I said.

"Angel," said Trey. "You love rules. They keep you safe from life."

I didn't say anything. I didn't understand what he meant.

We rode at a jog until the sun was beating down. There was no sign of pursuit, and as we rode, farms were becoming farther apart—Leth and Kalo could hand out all the Reward sheets they wanted, but word would be unlikely to reach this far.

It couldn't be long to the Great North Way now. It seemed as if we were being channeled toward the north by chance and by circumstance. All the better.

Perhaps, I thought, *we will find* The Book *quickly and go home in triumph.*

I was suddenly happy.

After all, I was with Silky and Trey, my two most favorite people in the world. I pulled some food from the saddlebag, and I started eating a dried biscuit, thereby breaking two more rules by Silky's count (don't eat with your fingers; only eat when seated at a table). We

THE BOOK OF FORBIDDEN WISDOM 99

passed close by a small tree, and I broke off a twig and started tickling Jasmine's ears. Just because.

Jasmine was very tolerant.

My happiness made me warm.

I was away from the Great House of Montrose, where my father moped and dreamt up land-merger marriages. Kalo was absent. And as for Leth's betrayal, well, it allowed me to see how lucky I had been that the wedding hadn't been completed.

Maybe everything would be all right.

That's when I heard the Echo again. As if it had never been gone.

Clip.

Clop.

Clip.

Clop.

Trey didn't need to say anything. I could see by his face that he had heard it too.

Silky looked at both of us. She was upset.

It seemed our Echo had not been made by the men who had attacked us, and whoever it was had been out there while we, vulnerable, had slept.

But then the Echo was drowned out by something louder—the sound of running, rushing water.

"The River Wys," said Trey. "It flows near the Great North Way."

"Maybe the Echo will lose our trail in the water,"

said Silky. "The way we lost Kalo and Father at the river."

"We're too visible," I said. "It was night then."

There was a bend in the road. We were in a forested area, and there was no way to see ahead to the Wys, even as I heard it bubble and sing.

Silky and Trey and I came around the curve at the same time, and the road simply ended. Water lapped at the horse's hooves. A long, dirty expanse of water spread before us, and in its center ran the wild river Wys.

The river had overflowed its banks; the Great North Way was nowhere to be seen.

"Is the Great North Way just *gone*?" asked Silky.

"It's there," said Trey. "But we have to cross the flood and the river Wys in the center. That's going to be the tricky part."

"Everything's the tricky part." My buoyant mood quickly evaporated. All that water.

There were some things I could do quite well: I had a prodigious memory—I mean really prodigious. If I read something once, I knew it. There were some things I could do fairly well: I was hard to beat at Nancalo. And there were some things I had never bothered to learn how to do at all.

Like swimming.

We were silent, contemplating the power of water. And then we could hear hoofbeats at our backs, above the sound of the wild rush of the river. Our Echo was no longer an echo, and the hoofbeats were coming closer.

"We hide in the trees, or we cross," said Trey, but he was already half dismounted, ready to lead Bran into the swirling waters. Silky was urging Squab forward. Only I hesitated.

"Where will it end?" I asked. "If we manage to swim to the Great North Way, where will it end?"

Silky looked at me in surprise.

Trey set his lips and then spoke. "It's not going to end here," he said firmly. "Not here." He pulled Bran ahead until the water was up to the horse's knees. Trey remounted and turned and looked at me.

"All right," I said.

"Angel can't *swim*, Trey," said Silky.

"I know, Silky." Then he spoke firmly to me. "Hang on to Jasmine's mane."

"Not the saddle?" I was near panic.

"Saddles come off," said Trey shortly. "Manes don't."

The three of us moved into the water. The smooth brown pond was easy to traverse, but the current that ran through its center—the old river Wys—was another story. We waded until we were at the edge of the current.

I could no longer hear the hoofbeats of our Echo over the surge of the water, but when I took a quick look back, I saw a horse round the same sharp curve we had. The rider pulled up suddenly, probably, I thought, as surprised as we had been by the flood.

But there was no time to think about the sighting of our Echo. I had other problems.

"I'll be the shield," said Trey. "Bran's the biggest."

I didn't know what he meant until he and Bran staggered into the current and tried to brace against it.

"You'll be swept away," I said, raising my voice in an attempt to be heard over the water.

"Hurry," he said. Silky moved Squab forward. She was almost at Bran's flank, and Bran was standing solid as a rock; the water split around him into two streams.

For a moment I really thought it was going to work. The current of the Wys wasn't so very wide. I briefly looked at the Echo-horse on the bank. The rider was beginning to move his horse into the flood.

Then Squab plunged forward. I let Silky go ahead, farther into Bran's shadow, where the force of the swirling waters was broken up.

After that, it was my turn.

Jasmine stepped into the river Wys, and almost immediately I felt her begin to lose her footing. That's when I saw something huge and knobby and black coming toward us from upstream. A moment later the shape took form.

It was an enormous tree trunk, and it was going to crush me.

There was no time to prepare myself for the impact, not that it would have made any difference.

The log reached me and knocked me off Jasmine. I saw Trey's appalled face.

After that, the water closed over my head.

When I came up, the tree limb was gone. I was holding nothing. I was nowhere near Jasmine or Squab or Bran or Silky or Trey. I flailed in the water knowing I would soon reach the end of my strength, of my luck. No more Lady Angel Montrose. No more Angel. Then I got water in my mouth and went down.

When I reached the surface this time, I was sputtering and swallowing water, and I could feel my legs fatally tangled in my wet clothing. If I went under now, there was no way I would be able to make it back to the surface.

I heard a great cry, and I realized that Trey was calling me, although I couldn't hear what he was saying over Silky's screams.

And I started to go down again.

I clawed at the water.

There was movement closer to shore. Time suddenly seemed to slow down, as if the river were going to take its time in finishing me off. As I struggled, the current swirled me so that I could see the bank. I saw the Echo-horse, and I saw someone dive from the Echo-horse into the Wys, which, I found myself thinking, was a stupid thing to do.

I tried to turn to get back toward Trey, and I saw he was trying to hold Silky, to keep her from the voracious current. To keep her from coming after me. To keep her from dying.

Thank you, I thought.

I went under, and the water closed over my head.

I knew I didn't have the strength to struggle back to the surface.

Sometimes, one just knows when it's time to give up. I didn't want to leave Silky alone, and, somehow, I didn't like leaving Trey. But trying to breathe meant swallowing more and more water. I went ahead and closed my eyes.

And then, as far as I knew, I drowned.

CHAPTER EIGHT

THE GREAT NORTH WAY

The thing is this. If an arrow pierces your heart, or a horse stomps on your head, you're dead.

Sometimes, though, with drowning, a person has a second chance.

When I became conscious again, the only thing I could think about was being sick. Then I turned to my side and *was* sick. Copiously. A figure that had been hovering over me sat back. It was Trey; he had been holding my hand. Silky was holding my other hand. I didn't feel well at all.

"I let him touch you," said Trey in a voice of anguish. "He said he might be able to make you breathe again. I wanted you to breathe again."

"Well," I croaked. "I'm breathing."

I felt as if I were waking into a dream. We were on the far shore of the flooded river Wys, and, as I sat up and looked around, I saw that the bank we were on was, in fact, part of the Great North Way. It stretched on and on before me. This road was meant for us to take. Or, rather, I meant for us to take this road.

Bran and Squab and Jasmine were cropping the grass, and the sun was quickly drying them. Nearby was the horse I had seen as I was being swept away. It was a scraggy beast with a notched ear—color: undistinguished. The question of where the rider had acquired the horse probably didn't bear much scrutiny.

I knew the rider at once, of course.

"He pulled you out of the water," said Trey. "I couldn't get to you. Silky tried too, but I had to keep her from being swept away."

"Then that man," said Silky, "took you to the bank and squished the water *right out* of you. Trey was going to punch him for touching you, but *I* wouldn't *let* him."

"My chest hurts," I said.

My rescuer spoke.

"Your heart didn't start right away. I had to pound on your breastbone."

Silky wiped away her tears with the dripping hem of her riding skirt. "He hit you really hard," she said. "Until he got you *alive* again."

"I'm grateful," I said. He seemed surprised at my words.

He knew me, too, of course.

Silky lowered her voice as she spoke to me. "I'm *certain* he's landless," she said. "Look at his clothes. Maybe he's even a *vagabond*."

I looked at her, my head tilted to one side.

"Don't be silly, Silky," I said. "He's the Bard who sang at my wedding."

There was a pause.

"The one who barged in and needed to get *paid*?" she asked.

"Yes," I said. For a moment I searched my memory. "The bard who was passing through and sang when Bard Cal couldn't. The Bard."

It was as if, at that moment, I had Named him. We all referred to him as the Bard from then on. I eventually learned that his name was Renn, but it made no difference. To us, he was the Bard.

"You sound as though you're feeling better," said Trey.

"Actually," I said, "I feel horrible."

"You sound a *lot* better," said Silky. "For a while you were *dead*."

I laughed weakly and tried to get to my feet. Silky started to lean down to help me. Trey just looked at me, distressed. All his training was keeping him from doing what I knew he wanted to do—put his arm under my shoulders and help me to my feet and support me as I stood. But there were too many taboos—my hair was as unkempt as if I'd come from bed, and I realized, with deep embarrassment, that my dress was clinging to me in a way that left little to the imagination.

I wished I could tell Trey to go ahead and help me, but I knew better. It changed nothing that I was cold and that I wanted his warmth.

I stayed silent—

—and the Bard left his crop-eared horse, came over to us and pulled me to my feet.

His grip was firm, and his arm was warm, and the act was done before I could protest.

Trey was immediately angry with the Bard, and I didn't blame him.

"The Lady Angel didn't say you could touch her," he said. "And you can move on now instead of following us."

The Bard released me. I was wobbly on my feet, but Silky was there to help me stay upright.

"I wasn't following," said the Bard. "I was going the same way. That's all. I found the shallow grave a day back. Who's in it?"

"A man who asked too many questions," said Trey.

"I assume the Lady's running away," said the Bard. "Most exciting wedding I've ever been at. But now I'll go if that's what you want—I'm certainly no company for those from Great Houses."

I looked at him more closely. There was mockery in his tone and defiance in his blue eyes and a whole world of experience in his classically beautiful face.

I remembered trying to calculate his age at the wedding. He was older than I. Older than Trey. Maybe he was twenty-five. And—bad timing is all—I was suddenly, strangely and irrevocably drawn to him.

I didn't like any of it. I didn't like the way I had felt when he had helped me up. His arm had been comforting and strong, but I didn't want his comfort or strength. I didn't want those feelings.

But what I liked or what I didn't like no longer mattered. The Bard had saved my life. Our ways, I knew, were forever intertwined.

Two chance meetings are not chance.

"What are you doing on the Great North Way?" asked Trey. "Surely you're not going to Shibbeth."

"When the pickings are lean here," said the Bard, "yes, I sometimes go to Shibbeth. I know the country. But I wouldn't worry about me if I were you. You have a lot more to think about. These woods are full of people, and I presume they're hunting you."

"It's not your business," said Trey.

"Then it's none of my business that I'm not the only one who saw that grave."

"What do you mean?" Trey demanded.

The Bard shrugged. "Horsemen came and dug the fellow up. I felt sorry for the landless who handled the body—they're all tainted now. That's the only reason they're so far behind you. The purification rituals. The long ones, that use no water."

"I didn't think they'd go on the Great North Way," I said. "Ghosts."

"Oh, they seem superstitious enough," said the Bard. "But they're trailing you along both sides of the road. There's only one place you'll be safe."

"Where would that be?" asked Trey.

"You need to pass the Cairns of Shibbeth. They won't dare follow you into Shibbeth. Unless they have land there—and permits to come and go."

"My brother knows Shibbeth," I said. "And he has land there."

Trey looked thoughtful. "I don't think Kalo's with Leth," he said. "And Leth won't pass into Shibbeth if there's the chance that a border patrol will pick up him and his riders. The 'Lidans don't like strangers. And they show it."

"What if a border patrol picks *us* up?" asked Silky.

"You're probably safe way out here," said the Bard. "But I doubt your almost-groom knows that."

Suddenly I knew we would end up roading together. We needed someone who knew Shibbeth. Besides, I wasn't ready to leave this Bard behind, prickly though he was, with his deep mocking eyes and the bold way he had reached down and helped me.

It may have been true that bards were like vagabonds, one step above outlaws, really, a caste so low it almost didn't count as a caste, a caste forbidden from marriage to the landed, from carrying weapons, from fraternizing with nobility. These things were so.

But it occurred to me, too, that these things were true not because bards were below us but because they were beyond us. We wouldn't know how to include them even if they had wished to be included.

"I suppose you want to come with us," said Trey to the Bard. "I suppose you want the job of guide."

I thought Trey was being rude.

"I wouldn't call you very safe company," said the Bard. "Not given your pursuers. But what does the Lady Angel say?"

I reddened. But I spoke clearly. "You know Shibbeth," I said. "If you keep us safe, we can pay you on our return to Arcadia. We can pay you well then."

The Bard laughed. "So you don't have the money now," he said. "And I can't help but wonder under what circumstances you would ever be able to return to Arcadia. But I suspect we'll end up roading together nonetheless."

Trey looked angry.

"The Lady Angel is offering you her company," he said at his stiffest. "And that's something more valuable than anything you own."

But that wasn't true. The Bard had held my life in his hands, and he had given it back to me. His action was above the value of things.

And I realized then that I would never be able to thank this Bard by paying him off with jewels or giving him the freedom of my lands. I would never be able to thank him enough: the debt ran deep, more deep than any I had ever known. And then, as it sometimes was, the future was there, and I reached out for it, and it was as if I could touch it, and somewhere there, in the darkness of time, were my thanks.

The great wheel turns.

PART II

CHAPTER NINE

THE CAIRNS OF SHIBBETH

The Bard joined us, but not before further infuriating Trey.

"I'll get you through Shibbeth," the Bard said. "The roads are easy enough to traverse, but you might need some help with the customs."

"That's kind," I said.

"We're paying him, Angel," said Silky.

Trey gave a snort.

"I notice there's nothing to put in my purse just yet," said the Bard. "But having saved the Lady Angel, I feel I have some sort of obligation to keep her alive."

I almost smiled, until I saw Trey's face. For his sake, I spoke.

"You go beyond the bounds," I said, and I saw Trey relax.

"I do that sometimes," said the Bard. "But nobody complained when you came back to life."

"Bard," said Silky, "you're being *fresh*."

"Enough," I said, but I couldn't help one tiny smile, just to myself. And then I saw that the Bard was looking at me, and he was smiling back.

We mounted. The Bard made a move to help me, but Trey forestalled him; nor would he let the Bard so much as touch Silky's foot to help her up.

Then we were on the Great North Way, and Shibbeth lay ahead.

Leth may have been trailing us, but there was no sign of him. We moved at a good pace—the Bard's crop-eared horse had stamina—and soon we had left the river Wys far behind us. It grew hot. I hoped that Leth's horses were as tired as ours—and that it would take his troops some time to ford the river Wys.

We kept going.

My breastbone hurt as we rode, and I had to keep wiping my nose as the water of the river Wys leaked out of it in a small, continuous stream. In the heat Silky drooped like a flower plucked too long ago. Trey and the Bard were silent; I could see the marks of fatigue on both of them.

Then, as we went over a rise, I saw something

shimmering in the heat waves on the horizon. At first I thought I was seeing small hills.

After an hour, we seemed no closer to the forms. Whether it was through some trick of the eye or because of the midday glare, it was only when we were considerably closer to them that I realized that these were no hills. These were the work of 'Lidan land slaves.

We had reached the great Cairns that marked the borders of Shibbeth.

The 'Lidan Cairns were frightening in their size. They loomed over the desolate landscape, and they cast inky shadows onto the flat brown ground. I knew from legend that one couldn't climb them; they were solid things of mortar and stone smoothed to a flat surface by those who had built them. No one could take or add a pebble, as one could with the small welcoming Arcadian Cairns that were at most crossroads, and no one would mistake them for guides to the lost or signs of hospitality.

In both directions, they just went on and on and on.

"Shibbeth," said the Bard.

"Can we go back?" asked Silky. Trey sighed, and I shook my head. There was no going back. There could be no patched wedding to Leth to save my reputation, my standing, my wealth. The sole ceremony Leth and Kalo were interested in was that of execution.

Our only hope of return lay in finding *The Book of Forbidden Wisdom*. Kalo had probably thought for a long time of the land deeds it contained—deeds to thousands and thousands of hectares of unclaimed Arcadian land. The contents of *The Book* might just be enough to satiate even Kalo's voracious land greed. And once rich beyond his dreams, Kalo would, in the end, call off Leth. Leth might feel betrayed, dishonored and even jealous, but people tended to listen to Kalo.

I would let Kalo have his happy avaricious ending, and I would marry Trey and so give Silky a home and have a patched up sort of honor again.

Perhaps the Bard could sing at our wedding.

I liked thinking about the Bard.

I couldn't seem to help it. I thought about his bringing me back to life—my chest continued to hurt where he had pounded on it. I turned in the saddle to look at him, and his deep-colored eyes immediately met mine. His mouth turned up into an almost smile, and the thought came into my mind: *This is a man who might prove dangerous to me.*

"Angel." Trey's voice was sharp, and I realized I had been about to guide Jasmine into a gorse bush.

"Sorry," I said.

"What are you thinking?" he asked.

"Clearly I'm not," I said.

"Why are you *blushing*?" asked Silky.

"It's hot, Silky," I said. "My face is red. It means nothing. I'm tired and hot and exhausted." I looked at the Bard. "And I just drowned," I added.

"Do you want to stop and rest?" Trey was obviously concerned. I wanted to hit him.

"No," I said. "I don't need to rest."

We were in a scrubby, lightly wooded area, but ahead of us, about a mile between us and the Cairns, the land had been cleared—and obviously kept clear—of all brush. The purpose was obvious to me: it would be easy to spot anyone trying to go from Arcadia to Shibbeth.

We were going to have to cross that flat open land. There would be no way to hide from Leth if he were behind us.

"Is this *safe*?" asked Silky, also seeing what I saw. "It seems so wide open."

"It's safe enough," said Trey.

"No," said the Bard. "It's not."

"We don't have a lot of alternatives," said Trey.

He and the Bard glared at each other. Silky looked puzzled.

"Well," she said, "it can't be safe *and* unsafe."

The Bard began to speak, but I gestured for silence.

I could hear something. And I saw something, too. The birds were rising, rank by rank, from the trees far behind us. Closer now, they wheeled into the sky, stirred up by something below.

"They're coming," I said.

The wide, clear area between the looming Cairns and us now looked terribly exposed. There wasn't even grass covering the dirt; it had been burned back; I could see charring on the earth. We hesitated at the edge. Jasmine could feel the conflict within me, and she began shaking her head, pulling at the bit, backing up and then moving forward.

"You and Silky," said Trey. He was trying to get Bran to turn away from the scorched earth, away from Shibbeth. "Go. Now. I'll keep them busy."

"We all go," I said to Trey. "We're not losing anyone to them. Not here. Not now. We ride together, or I'm not going to go."

Trey paused, but then nodded his head. Yes. He knew me.

"But," he said, "the packhorse won't make it." He dismounted and hauled saddlebags from the animal's back. A moment later, he put one of the bags across Jasmine's withers. The Bard's Crop Ear got two saddlebags, as did Bran. Trey left the rest on the ground—Squab would be hampered by an extra burden—and, after stripping the packhorse of saddle and bridle, he released it.

The animal stood there, ears pricked forward. Waiting.

"When they find the horse," I said, "they'll know we're here."

"They already know we're here," said Trey. He remounted. "Let's go."

"Come *on*," said Silky, but still I hesitated.

"This is your chance to leave," I said to the Bard. He turned his strange eyes on me.

"Time and chance have thrown our lots together," he said.

"That's poetic," I said, "but you'd better get out of here now."

"No," he said. "I haven't engaged in a last-chance gallop in a while. In fact, not ever."

"Come on, Angel," said Trey.

"Yes," said Silky. "I can *hear* something." She was hearing the wild clamor of the birds taking flight. And possibly my heart beating against my ribs.

"You can hide," I said to the Bard. "They'll only be looking for us."

"They'd find me, Lady Angel," the Bard said. "And they'd make me talk."

He was right. Our futures apparently lay together, and I knew then that we were tangled in some intricate design that I didn't understand.

Birds continued to rise from the trees in flocks—we must have been near some venerable nesting place. The sky grew black with them, and their cries were raucous. They were terrified by something below.

I gathered Jasmine.

"All right," I said. "Let's go." I gave Jasmine her head. Trey, Silky and the Bard were only moments behind me. Together we rode for it.

By the time we had all crossed onto the barren ground, we were at a hard gallop. The birds wheeled overhead.

We pounded across the open land. Silky was keeping up with me on Squab. Trey and the Bard were slightly behind us. Chivalry. I wanted to be chivalrous and heroic, too, but I had to get Silky across the border. I had to keep her safe.

And then the rising birds flew out of the last bit of cover.

I turned my head as men on horseback burst out of

the trees on either side of the ancient road. I saw Leth, who, in a kind of fury, seemed to have given up on superstition and was in a flat-out gallop down the *middle* of the Great North Way. He whipped his horse cruelly. I realized that all along his fair face had concealed a deeply embedded brutality. I should have watched the way he treated animals. I should have found out if he gave charity to vagabonds. I should have taken notice of how he spoke to his servants.

Those shallow eyes had kept me focused on his shallow courtesy.

I could not bear the sight of him. And, indeed, I didn't have time to stare at him; I could only hope we could stay ahead and that we were all moving too fast for crossbows to be effective.

We were going flat out. I fixed my eyes on the Cairns in front of us, and I despaired. They seemed to come no closer. They shimmered in the heat; they were no longer something forbidden and foreboding; they beckoned, offering safety.

I focused on Jasmine's stride. Out of the corner of my eye, however, I could see Squab beginning to lag. I was swept with fear. I wouldn't let Silky be taken alone.

"Stop them," screamed Leth. I could hear the pounding of hooves, the jingle of bridles, even the squeaking of leather as they gained on us. Above, the birds called and cried as if to mock us.

The Cairns looked closer now.

But maybe not close enough.

We were really going all out now. For a moment

Silky fell no further behind, and we rode as one. And then Squab lost more momentum. I turned my head and screamed at her.

"Hit him," I yelled. Silky shook her head. I was frantic. "Hit him! Now."

And Silky, her face as pale as milk, pulled her crop from her boot and smacked Squab on the rump. In a second, he was up with us again. As I had turned to Silky, I had seen arrows in the air, but they all seemed to be falling short.

And then the Cairns were no longer a shimmer in the distance; they were in front of us. We galloped without looking behind; my breathing was labored, and Jasmine was slathered with foam.

At last we surged forward between two of the great standing Cairns of Shibbeth.

Into the land of the 'Lidans.

Leth and his men had to pull up hard not to cross the boundary—so hard that two of the horses went down. I felt elated, but I knew that this was not the end. Leth—and Kalo—would find another way to get at me. But for now Leth didn't dare enter. He didn't have enough at stake to risk being taken by the 'Lidans.

We did.

"Harlot!" Leth screamed at me. "Harlot! Whore!"

We kept riding hard until we could no longer make out what he was saying, and the Cairns were well to our backs.

And I thought, *So this is Shibbeth. This is the forbidden country.*

"**W**e can give the horses a breather now," said Trey.

I dismounted, but Trey remained in the saddle, and I realized he had the reins in the wrong hand.

"Let me see your arm," I said, and he turned so that I could.

"Oh, *Trey*," said Silky.

A bolt from a crossbow had pierced the flesh of his upper arm; it had opened the muscle in a wide gash. Trey swayed in the saddle. In a moment, the Bard was at his side, helping him down, and I felt a great relief.

To help Trey dismount, I would have had to take his whole weight on me.

I tried to turn my mind elsewhere. I focused on the injury.

"How bad is it?" I asked.

"It looks *bad*," said Silky.

"I'll be fine," said Trey. The Bard eased him to the ground. The two of them spoke in low voices. The Bard ripped Trey's sleeve open and examined the gash.

"We set up camp here," the Bard said to Silky and me, and he began taking the saddlebags off Bran and then Jasmine. "Do your skills stretch to making a fire, Lady Silky?" he asked.

"Not really," she said. "*Sorry.*"

"Then you get to handle the horses," said the Bard. "I'll get the fire."

"What about Trey?" I asked.

"I thought that would be your job," said the Bard. "Squeamish?"

"No."

I wasn't squeamish, but examining a wound, touching hurt flesh, would have been too intimate an act even if I'd had a sanctioned chaperone at hand. The Bard should have known that.

"Come," the Bard said to me. Silky had stopped unsaddling the horses and was watching us.

"Why don't you just leave her be," said Trey wearily. "I'm fine."

"He's not fine," said the Bard and reached out and took my hand. I snatched it back.

"If I wanted to hold hands with you," he said, "I would try charm." The Bard sounded annoyed. He looked closely at my hand again, although this time he didn't attempt to touch me.

"You have small fingers," he observed.

The horses were left standing as Silky trailed over to us.

"What do you want?" I asked him as mildly as I could.

"Yes," said Silky. "What do *you* want? I saw you touch the Lady Angel's hand." Her tone wasn't mild.

"Trey needs stitches," the Bard said. "Small stitches made by small fingers. Lady Angel's will do. I never met a Great Lady who couldn't do needlework."

"Oh."

It all made sense now.

I gave way. Silky was better with a needle, but my reputation was already in tatters. No need to involve her in any immoral close contact stitching.

Besides, Trey needed me.

The Bard built the fire and boiled the needle and thread he carried in his pack. In the same pack, he found some healing powder for the wound and a length of clean bandage. Trey lay down by the fire and put his arm on a length of cloth I had prepared. He didn't say much, but his forehead was creased with pain. After that, as the others watched closely—to ask for privacy would have been lewd indeed—I held the lips of the ragged wound together with one hand. With the other hand, I made small, delicate stitches. The work required total concentration.

Only once did Trey break my focus. He moved as my needle accidentally slipped off the skin and into the gash, and I looked at his face sharply for any signs of shock. My mother had taught me about shock.

"Angel," Trey said.

I knew then. It was all in his voice, all that I had really known for years but had kept carefully buried. Yet there was nothing I could say or do. I hadn't learned to swim, and I hadn't—I felt it sorely now—learned to love.

"Sorry," I said. "I'm almost done."

Those were all the words I could manage.

My cold hard heart.

When it was finished, I sat back and examined my handiwork. Silky looked closely but was very careful not to touch.

"That's astonishing, Angel," she said. "Your needlework's usually *awful*. I wish Madam Ogilvy could see."

"She'd drop dead on the spot," I said.

Trey quickly fell into a healing sleep. Once he called out "Angel," and I was embarrassed. Men do not dream about modest Ladies of Great Houses. The Bard, who was near, pretended he hadn't heard; he showed delicacy. He turned away.

Later, when Trey woke up, the Bard tended him. Silky, who wanted to speak, walked with me to the edge of the camp.

"Angel?" she asked, and I feared her question. I had just set her terrible examples of modesty, chastity and discretion. I noticed I still had some of Trey's blood on the back of my hands.

"Yes?"

"I have a question."

"What's your question?"

"What's a *whore*?"

This was not the question I had expected. I thought for a moment.

"A small breed of horse," I said.

There was silence as Silky took in the information.

"Angel?" she asked.

"Yes?"

"Why did Leth call you a small breed of horse?"

"He wasn't calling me that," I explained. "He was calling out because he wished he had that small breed of horse. They're very fast over short distances. If he'd had a whore, he might have caught us."

"Oh," said Silky. "It makes a lot more sense when you use it in a sentence."

Later I left the three of them and went up the road so that I could see sunset and moonrise. The sun seemed to pour liquid gold along the horizon as it went down, and, at the end, I saw a flash of green light. Seeing the flash was considered lucky. The moon rose, ghostly and huge. I saw the West Star hanging against the rising night like a bright coin in a jackdaw's nest.

"The moon's sailing full," I said when I went back to the others. "Come on, Silky. You can see better away from the fire."

"I'll go with you," said Trey.

I looked down at Trey and opened my mouth to speak, when the Bard broke in.

"It's not a good idea to leave the camp, Lady Angel," he said. "There're worse things out there than your brother and your almost-husband."

I met his eye.

"Doubt it," I said.

And yet the beauty of the enormous moon and the low West Star had an ominous quality; it was so very fragile and ethereal, the sort of beauty that tears one's heart out. The sort of beauty that doesn't last. I didn't stray after all.

CHAPTER TEN

WHEAT

Before I readied for sleep, I examined Trey's wound again—with Silky close by my side. The wound had grown red, and I packed wild garlic around the stitches. I tried doing it with a spoon, but it proved awkward. Surely there was a purpose to having small and nimble fingers.

My morals were slipping.

I turned away and narrowly missed colliding with the Bard.

"That's good work," he said.

We needed to speak.

He had dumped his pack and saddle by the fire, and he had given no hint as to where he intended to sleep. It was one thing to have Trey near the fire—especially now that he was wounded. It would be quite another to allow a bard, a landless man, so close to Silky and to me at the vulnerable time of sleep. The Bard's beautiful face might edge its way into my dreams, where chaperones, no matter how much they might be needed, were in short supply.

I looked up at him. He was quite a bit taller than I.

"I wanted to tell you," I said, "that you can sleep inside the perimeter. Over by the horses."

"Lady Angel?" he said. He looked at me quizzically.

"By the horses. You can sleep there." I was getting a kink in my neck looking at him.

"Yes, Lady Angel," he said. "I understand the words that are coming out of your mouth."

"It's a position of great trust," I said, and it was true. "The horses will get restless if there's somebody out there."

Meanwhile, the Bard was scrutinizing me in a way I didn't like. As if he were summing me up.

"All right," he said finally. "By the horses."

"Inside the perimeter," I said. "That's a real—"

"Compliment," he finished. "I get it. I get the compliment part."

He turned his back to me and went over to the horses.

He was a touchy bard.

The next day, Trey's arm was stiff, but he said he was ready to ride. I packed the wound with more garlic. I wished the Bard would do it, but his fingers really weren't small enough to work the garlic in and around the stitches.

I started to mount.

"Veils," said the Bard.

"What do you mean?" asked Trey.

"Lady Angel and Lady Silky need to go veiled. Otherwise it's obvious that they aren't branded. Which would mean they aren't owned. Which would mean that any man we encounter might try and steal them."

"That's *horrible*," said Silky.

"Which part?" asked the Bard.

"All parts," Trey and I said in unison, and for the first time in a long while, we laughed.

But the Bard knew Shibbeth better than any of us, and I trusted him. Had I doubted him, we wouldn't be roading together at all. His sleeping near the horses was to keep up appearances; I knew he was sound.

We went through the saddlebags until we found material that would work as veiling, and after a little snipping and sewing, we tried on our handiwork.

"Stuffy," remarked Silky. She crinkled her nose and then pulled off the veil.

"If they notice you don't have a brand, you'll cause offense," said the Bard. "And they're more than signs of ownership; they're marks of beauty and status."

"Do you think I'd look beautiful with a brand?" Silky asked me. "It sounds *painful*."

"You're already beautiful, and yes, it is painful," I snapped at her. "A brand means you belong to someone."

According to the Bard, the 'Lidans were also great believers in the power of blood ties, and so we would be a band of brothers and sisters, as well as wives and husbands. The Bard, who was oldest, would pretend to be married to Silky, who, as a young girl, needed the most protection.

Silky was now in her element.

"It's like the wedding games we used to play," said Silky.

"This isn't real, Silky," I said. "Your supposed groom is a bard."

"I don't care," she said. "I'm a *bride*."

"Just play your role well," said the Bard. "If the 'Lidans aren't convinced, if they think we're Arcadian spies, they'll take us into their houses as slaves. Or worse."

"What's worse?" asked Silky, but the Bard wouldn't answer.

"I won't let anything happen to you," said Trey.

"No," said the Bard. "You'd be busy getting executed."

"The Bard's *gloomy*," Silky whispered to me.

"I don't know, Silky," I murmured. "I think he's just trying to protect us."

"Do you think he's handsome? In a landless kind of way?"

"Yes."

"Not as handsome as Trey, though."

"You're partial."

"Aren't *you*?"

So we rode veiled.

We were silent as we rode. I waited for Trey to speak. I thought maybe he would say something about the race to the Cairns, or his wound, or the stitches, but he didn't. I had no idea what he was thinking.

I drifted into reverie.

My mother. Smoothing the page of *The Book* with her cool hand. Showing me how to form strange letters. Telling me *The Book* was going away.

Trey spoke, and it was as if he were reading my mind.

"Even if you get us to *The Book of Forbidden Wisdom*," he said, "going back to Arcadia will be tricky. *The Book* isn't going to take care of all our problems."

"I know."

"*The Book* won't heal your reputation." He spoke carefully.

I was grateful to him for the opening.

"We might as well be frank," I said. "Only marriage will keep me from being shamed. And only marriage to you. They'll all have assumed the worst."

"The worst?" Trey looked at me oddly.

"You know what I mean," I said.

"I suppose I do."

"Our friendship will remain whole, Trey," I said. "I know it—and that's the main thing; it's the way I care about you. The other—the marriage—will be trivial by comparison."

"Do you think so?" I couldn't read his tone.

"I do. And the marriage *will* bring you land." Why did I sound so snotty? "And you're not pre-contracted, either. So that's all right. Under the circumstances, even my father will consent. All will be well."

"Of course," he said, and now he looked me in the eye. "Of course it will. Marriage to you will be an honor."

"You don't need to say it that way, Trey," I said. "It's just me. Angel."

"Of course, Angel."

"Our marriage will patch things up," I said.

There was a long silence. Trey tilted his head and looked at me until I dropped my eyes.

"Have you ever loved anyone, Angel?" he asked.

I thought about it.

"I love Silky," I said.

I saw his face, and I knew that everything I was saying was wrong-footed, but I couldn't help myself.

Of course, I had heard rumors and stories about love. I knew that some girls and boys fell in love, but they were silly and foolish to do so, because when they were finally contracted—almost never to each other— there were occasionally tears as they signed the Books of Marriage and Land. And those tears only marred everyone's enjoyment of the wedding feast. After one wedding, a boy hanged himself. There was nothing romantic about it. The boy was dead; the corpse was old when it was found.

Love was not just silly. It was stupid and reckless.

And the best bards knew it. The famous one, the blind one, sang that love was snow under a full cold moon. I knew what that meant.

Pain.

I could see the pain in Trey; I had heard it when he spoke my name in his sleep.

Perhaps there was a way I could make him learn to be heart-whole. And then perhaps Trey and I, if we ever made it back to Arcadia, could live together as brother and sister—and be married in name only.

Time passed, and we encountered no one. Then, late in the afternoon, we found ourselves riding by a vast field of golden wheat. The wind had picked up, and I could hear the heavy-headed stalks whisper against each other. In places the rows of grain were interrupted by a copse of trees or a lone bush, small oases in that golden desert.

It was beautiful, in a way I never thought land could be. And I felt for a moment as if our journey were little more than an excursion from the house rather than a ride for our lives—until Bran began limping. Trey dismounted and examined Bran's right fore.

"Swollen," he said. "We need to camp so he can get the weight off the tendon."

Trey walked beside Bran, at times stroking the huge horse's mane. The limp worsened.

Finally we came upon a path that led into the wheat field. We followed, Bran now drooping his head. The wheat reached up to my stirrup, and I brushed the top of it with my hand. It was like stroking a wild animal.

"It's as if the field could think," I said.

"Leave that thought alone," said the Bard. "Wheat is wheat. It doesn't think."

"Superstitious?" asked Trey, his hand on Bran's withers.

"I'm a bard," he said. "They pay me to be superstitious."

We neared a copse of apple trees: a green island rising out of the yellow sea. A spring bubbled up at the base of one tree, and I watched as it trickled down the slight rise and into the wheat. The apples looked as if they were almost ripe.

"We'll stop here," said Trey.

I was thinking about picking some of the apples when a group of figures—men and horses—came out from under the shadows of the trees. When we got closer, I saw that they had laden mules as well as horses. 'Lidan traders. Some of them were traditionalists—careful adherents to the customs and ceremonies of Shibbeth. I looked at the Bard, who had neither slowed his pace nor changed his expression.

My heart was beating hard.

"You talk," Trey said to the Bard.

"Why?"

"You're the Bard. People pay you to talk. Besides, you've been here before."

"All right."

There were six 'Lidans in all. The mules, heavily laden, pricked their large ears forward as we approached. The 'Lidan horses—fine and sleek—were nervy.

"Peace be with you," said the Bard, using one of the formal salutations.

"You're a long way from Arcadia," said one of the traditionalists, ignoring our greeting. "Where are you going?" His accent was strange, and I realized that we must sound odd to him, too.

"My contract-brother and I," said the Bard, "have business in the east."

The traditionalist took a crossbow from one of the mules and held it casually, bolt toward the ground.

"How do the women belong to you?" he asked.

"My wife," the Bard indicated Silky. "My contract-brother," he nodded at Trey. "My sister-in-name—sister to my wife," he nodded again, this time at me. "We're all bound."

The traditionalist addressed the Bard again.

"So your wife is twice a sister?" he asked.

"She is," said the Bard. I, meanwhile, was thinking to Silky over and over in my head, *Don't speak don't speak don't speak*. I wasn't sure she could keep her story straight.

She didn't speak.

"What about your papers?" asked the traditionalist. The Bard raised an eyebrow, and I wondered what on earth he was going to say, when one of the other 'Lidan traders, the best-dressed one, looked impatient at the words.

"We're two days late," the man said. "We don't have time for you to pick a fight over a piece of paper nobody bothers carrying."

"They're not nobody," said the traditionalist, nettled. "They're strangers. They should have papers."

The Bard moved Crop Ear forward slightly so that he was closer to the traditionalist.

"And exactly who are you," asked the Bard, "to inquire about our papers?" I was impressed by his calm.

Some of the other 'Lidan traders laughed.

"He has you there," said the well-dressed man, who seemed to be the leader. "Come on. The mules are rested."

"I want to see the papers."

The whole group looked exasperated, as if they had had disagreements with this traditionalist before. But finally the leader said to the Bard, "You better just show him your kin-papers."

"I don't think so," said the Bard.

There was a silence.

"You have me curious now, brother," said the leader. "Perhaps we should all see the papers."

"To show you the papers now is to accept imputations on the honor of our sisters," said the Bard. "And you don't have any authority to ask for them."

"Any man may ask," said the traditionalist.

"Arcan's right," said the leader. "Any man may. But I'm not going to allow this to come to a fight. We'll settle it by contest and save everybody's honor—but let's do it quickly. We're running behind. All right, Arcan?"

Arcan didn't look happy, but I could see that he wasn't ready to challenge the leader.

"All right," he said.

"What do you have in mind?" said the Bard.

The leader of the 'Lidan traders looked exasperated. "What do you think I have in mind? If you win, we apologize and you move on," he said. "If Arcan wins, we see your papers. So what'll it be? Arm wrestling? Shooting? Horsemanship? You pick the contest, we pick the terms."

"Shooting," said Trey quickly. The Bard gave him a look, and I could tell he wasn't pleased. Trey, as archer, was out of commission because of his wound. And bards weren't renowned for their handling of weapons.

"All right," said the 'Lidan leader. "Now Arcan picks the target. Unless you just want to show us the papers and forget any hasty words. We don't mean to dishonor your women."

"You have no reason to challenge us at all," said the Bard. He drew himself up and looked as indignant as any Arcadian Lord from a Great House.

"Let's just get it done," said the leader. "Unless you win the shooting match, Arcan's unlikely to be satisfied until he sees those documents. Go ahead, Arcan."

Arcan smiled as he picked the target. "One of the apples," he said. "The high one that's red on one side."

It looked as small as a grape to me.

I moved up to the Bard and lowered my head as if in submission to him, but under my breath I said, "Let Lady Silky shoot."

The Bard looked at me, startled. "She's a child," he said.

"Have you made up your minds?" asked the leader.

"Not yet," said the Bard. He murmured to me, "Our lives depend on this."

"Just let her shoot."

Trey settled the matter. "My sister, the Lady Silky, will shoot."

"Women don't carry arms," said Arcan.

"Let's get on with this," said the head 'Lidan. He seemed to have grown bored of the challenge.

The Bard gave Silky the crossbow reluctantly, and she put on quite a show, awkwardly putting the bolt on the bow and fumbling it in the process. Trey was clearly enjoying the little drama, and so, I could see, was Silky. The Bard looked grim. Trey seemed to take great enjoyment in saying to the Bard, "I just hope she doesn't shoot one of our horses by mistake."

Everything was riding on Silky.

Arcan took aim. Silky made some slight adjustment to her crossbow.

There wasn't a breath of wind. Arcan stood squarely. I saw Silky still Squab with her calves and knees. Even though she had dropped the reins to hold the crossbow steady, I knew Squab wouldn't move. Even if he had, I doubt it would make any difference to the outcome.

Arcan carefully lifted his crossbow.

Then he fired. The bolt went straight through the heart of the apple.

Almost simultaneously, Silky fired.

Her bolt hit the apple on its way down, pinning it, with the 'Lidan arrow already through it, to the far apple tree.

The Bard gaped.

"Well done." The leader of the 'Lidans spoke as though stunned. He was no longer bored, and some of the 'Lidan men gasped and then gave murmurs of approval. Arcan scowled, but as I examined the apple pinned to the tree, the leader pressed goat meat and dried figs on us.

"Magnificent," he said. "Your wife is a prize."

No one was more surprised than the Bard. Trey and I, naturally, already knew of Silky's freakish ability.

"Thank you," said the Bard faintly.

"Keep your papers close," the 'Lidan leader said. "If you have them. I've never seen such shooting. Ever. Give this to the Lady." He gave a small melon to the Bard. "You are fortunate in your wife."

"Indeed." The Bard was serious, but when I looked closely at his face, I saw a trace of humor in his eyes. He knew we had, in some sense, set him up, and he was enjoying the joke.

I liked him. Up to that moment, he had impressed me and intrigued me and attracted me and scared me.

Now he seemed human.

The traders made to move on.

"Why are you traveling so late?" asked the Bard. The sun was low in the sky. "Isn't it time to make camp?"

"We don't like too many questions, either," said the leader.

"I apologize for the intrusion," said the Bard quickly.

The face of the 'Lidan leader was serious, and I wondered what was in those mule-packs. I knew that there was a thriving illicit trade in gemstones in Shibbeth. It was a trade for the very rich, and I glanced at the leader's fine clothes again.

The leader gave the Bard a piercing look. "How long have you been married?" he asked.

"A year," said the Bard. He could hardly claim more, given Silky's age.

"I would keep her close if I were you," said the leader with a smile. "If you get into trouble, though, I'm Partin Coss. I live in Parlay, and I'm well known there. You and your wife may call on me if your way is toward Parlay. I would gladly meet again. You and your Lady wife."

The Bard was quick to speak.

"You honor our whole House," he said, retreating into formula.

And then the traders were gone.

"**N**ice work," said Trey to Silky.

"I take it that wasn't a fluke shot," the Bard said when the 'Lidan traders were out of sight.

Silky pulled her veil off. "'Fluke'? Of course not. I *always* win at crossbow contests," she said. "But I didn't get to have any fun being a bride at all."

"Marriage is just a contract," said the Bard.

"Be careful," I said. "You make your living from weddings."

"And funerals. I'm unlikely to run out of custom."

Trey's arm was sore, and I insisted that he rest and let me take care of Bran. When the horses were settled and I had poulticed Bran's hock, Silky, the Bard and I went under the trees to gather wood for the evening fire. I found a large dead tree and began pulling branches from it; Silky, singing to herself, moved from place to place picking up kindling.

Soon enough, I realized I was alone with the Bard. There was no sign of my sister—I had been too much in my thoughts.

"Where's Silky?"

"Your chaperone?"

"No." My tone was abrupt, but I was worried about Silky. "This isn't a time or place to be alone."

"She's right through those trees," said the Bard. He pointed, and, sure enough, I could glimpse Silky with a small pile of branches at her feet. And then I heard her soft singing again. She was singing a song she had heard from the Bard.

"All right," I said.

"She's a good girl," said the Bard, and he smiled, just a little bit, just enough that I knew Silky had charmed her way into his heart. Which was no surprise to me, because who could resist Silky?

And I could tell he had no designs on her. Otherwise, I'd have had his heart for breakfast.

I turned away from the tree and started to pick up some pieces of wood from the ground, but the Bard stopped me.

"Leave it," he said. "I'll get more wood from the tree. It's an Etchling Tree; it burns very brightly."

Silky's voice was clearer now; she was moving toward us under the trees.

"I like what Silky's singing," I said.

"My sister wrote that song. She wrote it before she came to Shibbeth. There's nothing but silence for women here."

"Why would a woman move to Shibbeth?"

The Bard pulled a dead limb from the tree and cast it on the small pile I had made; he leaned back against the trunk of the Etchling.

"Years ago," he said, "when I was still a child, she fell in love with a 'Lidan trader."

"Love." I narrowed my eyes. I hoped he wasn't going to start going on about love.

"It happens." His tone was sardonic. "They married secretly in Arcadia and then ran away to Shibbeth. But the 'Lidans have laws, and if one lives here, one lives by 'Lidan law."

It took a moment for that to sink in.

"Oh."

"Yes, 'oh.' She carried his brand."

"Are you looking for her here?"

"She died of the shuddering sickness two years ago," the Bard said. "Word came to me this spring. I miss her. I'll always miss her—she was like a second mother to me. They say her husband is still alive. I don't know where."

"Maybe you can find out."

"Maybe I can." He turned away from me and pulled more boughs from the tree. "And maybe when I do, I'll kill him. Love. He brought her here to be branded."

"Be careful," I said.

He just laughed.

"You're the one who should be careful, Angel," said the Bard. "This place is snakebite for someone like you."

Once we had all returned to camp and kindled the fire, I pulled a brush from my pack and began to smooth Silky's hair. I let my thoughts wander. I realized that, as we had gathered wood, the Bard had spoken to me without using my title.

Silky sighed.

"All right?" I asked.

"It feels wonderful," she said. "I haven't brushed my hair in *forever*."

"Wee pig." I started on the tangles, and then I brushed out Silky's hair until it was a bright gush down her back, a golden waterfall. It shone in the firelight.

And I suddenly looked closely at the fire. The flames were like pale candles; the wood was burning white. The Etchling Tree.

"The fire," I said. But Trey was already staring at it. Silky moved to get a better look.

"The wood from the Etchling Tree always burns white," said the Bard.

He sat across from us, cross-legged, and then he pulled his lyre from a bundle.

The Bard sang a few fragments from ballads. His scowl disappeared when he sang, and I examined that beautiful face closely. He was as fair as Trey was dark. His eyes were deep blue again in the firelight. He had full lips and a scar on his chin that pulled on the lower lip.

The Bard stopped singing and looked up at me. I blushed. I had no business taking inventory of his face.

He played for a while. I asked if he could sing the story of the Lady in the Castle, a favorite of mine, but he didn't know it well. And then I was very still, because, after a moment's hesitation, perhaps to make up for what he didn't know, he began the great old tale of The Taken. No hearer of that lay has ever confused the wild opening notes for anything else. Silky lay down and put her head in my lap, and I stroked her long hair. Silky was my weak point. Through Silky, I could be hurt. Otherwise, I was safe.

We listened to The Taken, and the fire burned white. As long as my life lasts, I will never forget the white fire, the Bard's voice, the old tale.

CHAPTER ELEVEN

THE TAKEN

When I awoke in the morning, Silky was gone.

I had awakened because I was cold, and I was cold because Silky wasn't sleeping with her back pressed against mine the way she had been doing the last few nights. I turned over and sleepily touched her bedding.

No Silky.

I felt the bedding more carefully.

It was cold.

I got up hurriedly and walked the perimeter. Still no Silky. She wasn't in the camp, and she wasn't at the place where we had dug the holes for the night earth. I was becoming increasingly uneasy, and I wanted to wake up Trey. I threw a shirt on over the top of my nightgown. The bottom half would have to pass as a skirt.

But when it came right down to it, when I was standing by the sleeping Trey, I was paralyzed. I didn't know how to wake him up—I didn't think there was any Arcadian etiquette on the matter. My desperation increased, but I couldn't overcome my upbringing: Trey and I weren't related. Trey was in what passed for a bed, and he was male, and who knew what he was wearing under the blankets. I needed servants or a go-between. Even a chaperone would refuse this job.

Finally, almost weeping with frustration, I poked his arm. It was the wrong arm: the one with stitches. Immediately, he rolled over and looked up at me.

"Angel?" Even from Trey, I had expected, initially, embarrassment, maybe even anger, but he just seemed puzzled.

"I can't find Silky," I said.

He looked at me drowsily. "She probably needed privacy," he said. "You know."

He shouldn't have referred to it. Bodily functions were off limits in any kind of conversation at all.

"I checked there," I said. I poked him again when he showed signs of going back to sleep. He didn't seem to understand the depth of my fear, or the rules I was breaking in order to get his help or how wrong every-thing had suddenly become.

Abruptly, Trey pulled himself into the waking world.

"Go to the spring we found last night," he said. "She might be down there. I'll wake the Bard."

I walked up and down the rivulet, trying not to rush, trying to be systematic in my search.

It took me precious minutes, but I found something.

In the marsh moss, where the footing was muddy, I saw a tangle of hoof marks. Grass and earth churned up. A single small blurred footprint and some trampled summer flowers.

Suddenly, without warning, I could see what had happened as clearly as if I were reading it in a book, as clearly as if it were happening in front of me: Silky, sometime in the early morning, came to the spring car-rying a small bouquet of summer flowers she picked from among the wheat stalks. A man on horseback rode up and pulled her onto his mount, and the flow-ers scattered to the ground. Silky struggled instead of screaming—that would be like Silky. And perhaps it was for the best; perhaps the man would have hurt her badly if she had called out.

The hoof marks, large as dinner plates, indicated a horse that could bear a large rider.

Silky didn't have her crossbow. I had seen it by the side of her blankets, and without it, she wouldn't stand a chance.

I picked up the broken flowers: cornflowers, water daisies, the sky bluebell, Princess Columbines.

Trey, who had been looking on the other side of the camp, found me standing there holding the flowers. The Bard was with him.

"Look at the marks," I said to him. "She tried to run, but the horseman plucked her up. She's so small. He plucked her as if she were nothing."

"Angel," said Trey. "We'll get her back. I promise. It may be some kind of mistake—these marks could be old. She might be back at camp already."

"Do those marks really look old to you?" I asked. "Do they?"

"The marks are new," said the Bard.

"If someone's taken her," said Trey, "we'll get her back. I promise."

He promised. But we were Arcadians. If she were with a 'Lidan for more than twenty-four hours would Trey really want her back with us?

Perhaps I should have known the answer. But I didn't.

The Bard was looking at me speculatively. The Bard, whose sister had left Arcadia with a 'Lidan. The Bard, whose only mission was one of revenge. But destructive as his sister's love might have been, I knew Silky was in danger of something different, something hideous. I was not naïve.

"We should have been together," I said. I did not cry. I was not weak.

"One of you would have been killed, and one of you

would still have been taken," the Bard said harshly. "Trey's right. We'll get the Lady Silky back."

"What if we're too late?" I said in a low voice.

"There is no 'too late.' While she's alive, we'll seek her," said the Bard. "We're roading together. That means something to my guild."

"Two don't travel fast on one horse," said Trey. "We'll catch them. Before—before much time has passed."

Trey had been trained as well as I—if too much time passed, he would, he must, shun her. No matter what, he wouldn't be able to help shrinking from her.

I didn't know about the ways of bards.

"Partin Coss," I said suddenly. "He liked Silky. Maybe too much."

"We need to ride now," said Trey.

I stood and looked at Trey. At the Bard. And I thought that Bran was lame, and Crop Ear was slow and Squab was also slow and crashed loudly through underbrush.

"Let me take Jasmine," said Trey. He seemed to read my mind.

"No," I said. "I'll go."

"You won't," he said. I thought for a moment, and then I nodded. There was no time to argue.

Without a word, I led Jasmine to him.

But Jasmine wouldn't take him. She was used to me, a ninety-five-pound burden who knew all her quirks and habits. She simply would not let Trey mount.

He hit her.

She bit him.

"Wait here," I said. "I'm going to get a different bridle."

Of course I didn't really have an extra bridle, and if they'd had any time to think about it, they'd have known that. Back at the camp, I checked once more for Silky, and then I put on Arcadian hunting clothes. I quickly plaited my hair into a long braid that coiled down my back in the style of traditionalist male 'Lidans. I grabbed the crossbow that I had lent to Silky and returned to the spring, where I saw that the Bard and Trey were arguing over what to do. I could see that they were at odds.

The Bard was the first to see me. He understood all of it at once, while Trey stood, surprised, confused.

"Don't do it, Lady Angel," said the Bard.

"I'll do as I please," I said. "And I'll do what needs to be done." I put a foot in the stirrup and mounted with the crossbow still in my hands. Then I hooked it to the saddle and picked up the reins.

But Trey wouldn't let go.

"I'm sorry," I said, and I kicked Jasmine, who half-reared and pulled herself free of Trey. "If I'm not back today, I'll meet you outside the walls of Parlay," I said. "In three days' time. I'll have Silky."

"What do you think you're doing?" asked Trey in a voice of despair.

"I'm rescuing Silky," I said. "What do you think?"

I was afraid to let either Trey or the Bard near me

in case they tried to pull me from the saddle. I paused and looked at them. I spoke very clearly so that they would understand.

"I'm an Arcadian Lady from a Great House," I said. "I can do this." I gave Jasmine the signal, and in a moment we were across the rivulet, and then we were on a narrow path to the east of the Great North Way. I signaled Jasmine to gallop. I did not turn back to the others. And then we were gone.

After a while, I slowed to a trot. The wheat on either side of the path had given way to woodland; we were leaving the open land behind. I took Jasmine under the low-hanging branches of sweeping trees, and I had to lean forward until my head was below Jasmine's neck so that we could pass. As I did, I saw where the hooves of the 'Lidan horse had churned up the earth.

It wasn't difficult to follow the tracks of the heavily laden horse, and I pictured Silky struggling, and Partin Coss trying to control her. I was sure it was Partin; I remembered the melon he had given the Bard for Silky.

They only had a lead of hours, if that, and I had the advantage of speed. Still, I couldn't ride Jasmine flat out. If she tired, I would never get to them. They would be moving slowly and steadily once he got Silky under control.

I didn't like to think about that.

So I focused on catching them. I *would* catch them. It was only a matter of when.

I came to a stream and let Jasmine drink. Patience was not part of my nature, but the sound of Jasmine drinking eased my mind.

They couldn't be far. But I had to find them before they got to Parlay, and I didn't know how distant that was. I had to find them before Partin's servants and friends and family and land slaves surrounded him. His protectors.

Silky would have no protectors.

I mounted Jasmine again.

We jogged and rested and jogged and rested. I wondered just exactly how much of a head start Silky's abductor had. The ride was deeply frustrating—I would lose the trail and have to circle until I could pick it up again. I wasn't much on broken twigs, although I could tell when a horse had pushed through undergrowth. Mostly I was following those enormous hoofprints.

By the late afternoon, I was seeing signs where there were none, and I feared I had lost them forever.

The birds stopped singing. The air was oppressive.

And I saw the hoofprints again.

This time I dismounted and examined them in the grass. They were no longer the sliding marks that indicated speed but clear, individual prints. The horse was proceeding at a walk. Within yards, I saw horse dung that was still steaming. I led Jasmine to the left, off their trail, and flipped her reins over a low-lying branch. On foot, I made a wide circle around Partin's trail.

In minutes, his horse was in sight.

It was hobbled at the base of a tree at the edge of a beautiful clearing—rays of sun scattered through the boughs, and the yellow light dappled the green moss beneath the tree.

I saw Partin Coss and Silky.

His pants were down, and he was trying to pull up her skirts. At first I was shocked into inaction by his partial nudity. Nothing looked the way I had imagined it might. Then I was lost to anger—Silky was gagged, and although I could see her trying to push him away, she was lethargic, as if she were ill, or very, very tired.

Silky saw me, and her eyes widened. Partin Coss looked around sharply and in a moment was looking directly at me. He immediately pushed Silky to the ground and lifted his crossbow—I had been so busy staring that I hadn't seen it lying in the grass. I was slow to lift my own crossbow; I was distracted and appalled by the sight of his naked flesh.

I wished he would pull up his pants.

He smiled at me. He had only seen me veiled, and there was no recognition on his face.

"Out wife-stealing, traditionalist?"

"Yes," I said. "I'll take her off your hands."

He frowned. He yanked at his pants awkwardly,

with one hand. With the other he balanced his cross-bow so that it remained pointed toward me.

"You have a strange accent for a traditionalist," he said.

"Just give her to me," I said.

He frowned again. "This woman's my property," he said. At that my eyes shifted to Silky. I started to speak—

He shot me.

Partin and I were so close that the bolt spun me around, but not before it passed straight through my shoulder. I knew I would be in shock soon—and use-less. Partin, smiling, carefully fit another bolt into his crossbow. He had all the time in the world. Because he knew I needed time to aim. And he knew I could only use one arm.

We both knew it.

Silky, still looking dazed, sat up. Partin ignored her, continuing to set his crossbow. She leaned over to him, cocked her head slightly to one side and bit him in the leg.

He yelled in pain, dropped the crossbow, and kicked Silky away, but she had given me the time I needed.

I shot him in the chest.

Then I fell slowly to my knees. When I touched my shoulder, my hand came away all blood. Silky got to her feet unsteadily and came over to me. She walked in a strange weaving pattern.

When she reached me, I pulled off her gag with my

good arm and then pressed the gag to my shoulder. I hoped for some brief strong bleeding both here and where the bolt had come out on the other side. Blood was a great cleanser. On this side, however, I saw that the gag was already red through. A lot more than enough blood to wash the wound.

"You're bleeding," Silky observed.

"I know," I said. Still I didn't feel the pain. I looked at her closely. "Did he drug you?"

"Yes," said Silky. "He did. It felt good at first. Sort of like living in gauze. But now I'm going to throw up."

I thought of the little I knew about violation: vague rumors alternating with vivid description.

"Did he touch you?" I asked. It was no time for niceties.

She sighed again. "No," she said. She hesitated. "He tried to, but I pushed him away. He was very angry. He hit me." I saw the bruises on her face.

I fell forward some more so that my head was resting on my knees.

"You have to pull yourself together, Silky," I said. "You have to help me."

"Pull myself together," she agreed.

A few feet away from us, blood pumped out of the 'Lidan's chest. He twitched a few times, and I was afraid for a moment that he would rise and somehow take vengeance on us. My thoughts were cloudy. I could feel pain now.

The Bard, who was road-knowing, would never have done anything so stupid as to get shot. Not the Bard.

Although it was Trey who had rescued me.

The Bard. Trey. It was very confusing.

I began to shiver.

"Help me lie down, Silky," I said.

Cheerfully she obliged and eased me—remarkably gently, given her drugged state—down on my good side. With my right hand I tried to keep Silky's gag pressed into the hole the bolt had made, but pain washed over me.

"You're cold," said Silky. She lay down next to me and curled her body around mine, the way she had when we were children and still slept together.

"I can see where the bolt came out," she said. "It looks—"

"Don't want to talk," I said.

"All right."

Silky held me close to her. We stayed that way for a long time, as the 'Lidan next to us bled to death.

Without Silky's warmth, I would never have made it through the night. Several times she got to her feet and tottered a little way away to make good on her promise to throw up, but she always came back to me. By dawn the effects of the drug had worn off, but her natural ebullience was gone as well.

The pain in my shoulder was agonizing. It spread down my arm and across my chest. Silky tried to wipe away the blood to see the wound, and I'm sorry to say that I fainted. When I awoke, I found she had put some crushed wild garlic in the wound. She gave me water. She unbraided my hair.

"You make a terrible traditionalist," she said.

"I was rescuing you," I said.

"That was a *rescue*?" she asked.

She sounded more herself.

"I did all right," I said.

"Angel," said Silky seriously. "You got *shot*."

"Yes."

"Well," said Silky, "it's *complicated* now, though, right? With you shot." She gently touched the wound, and the world began spinning.

I fainted.

When I next opened my eyes, it was to find Silky sprinkling water on my forehead.

"We need to get back to the others," I said.

"Yes," said Silky. "But can you ride?"

"If I can bind up the arm and the shoulder," I said. "I have to try."

Silky began the process of binding while I was conscious and finished after I fainted again.

She was about to look for a log for me to mount from when the other 'Lidans arrived.

There were three of them, and they rode up and stood at the points of a triangle. None of them were traditionalists.

"Harlots," said one, and spat on the ground.

"Arcadians," said another. "No 'Lidan women would be out alone."

"They aren't branded," said the big man at the top of the triangle and closest to us. "And it looks like they weren't alone." He gestured at the dead 'Lidan. "Perhaps they're warriors."

The other two 'Lidans laughed uneasily.

"They come with us," the big man said.

What happened next was muddled, but I found myself on Jasmine. Silky was on Partin's horse.

"You needn't worry," the head 'Lidan said to me, and his tone was gentle.

"And yet I'm worried," I said. "If you're so harmless, let us go. At least let my sister go."

"You both need tending," said the 'Lidan. "Then, as you wish. I can overlook the fact that you seem to have killed one of my countrymen. He doesn't look as if he was of high rank. But I can hardly just leave you here."

I was thinking toward Silky as hard as I could. *Not a word about the others not a word about the others not a word about the others.*

She creased her brow, but whether she understood or not, she said no word about the others.

We began a trot, and all went dark, and I tumbled over Jasmine's shoulder and into a prickly bush.

After that, we let the horses walk.

We walked them all afternoon and early evening, until the light was beginning to go. As the 'Lidans spoke of halting for the night, the head 'Lidan's horse flushed a pheasant out of the underbrush, and it took off in a flurry of bright wings. In front of me the future opened out like a path, and it beckoned, and maybe I should have felt hope. But I didn't. Not then. The world was soaked in pain and darkness, and the twilight settled over me like a shroud. We rode on.

CHAPTER TWELVE

CAPTIVES

It was clear we were the 'Lidans' captives, but the head 'Lidan insisted on treating us as if we were guests. This included the kindness of keeping the horses to a walk, despite some of the men's impatience.

But as we walked, my shoulder minded the jolting more and more. It wouldn't stop bleeding, and we kept halting so that Silky and I could change the dressing. I wondered how much blood I had left in me. I watched for red fingers of infection that I feared would spread out from the wound and creep toward my heart, but they didn't materialize. Silky had cleaned the wound thoroughly during one of my fainting episodes, and she may have saved me from sepsis. Or else the future had other things in store for me.

Like slowly bleeding to death, drop by drop by drop.

The head 'Lidan, whom they addressed as Lord Garth, seemed almost as interested in the condition of the wound as Silky and I were. I let him look at it, hoping he would have some poultice or medicine that would stop the bleeding completely. There was always a lot of fuss when Lord Garth approached me. None of the other 'Lidans were allowed near, and Silky was expected to supervise. Lord Garth always waited for Silky to cover all the bare flesh around the wound before he looked at it. Showing wounded flesh, apparently, was even more of a moral dilemma in Shibbeth than it was in Arcadia. All of Lord Garth's preparations to protect my honor went far beyond Arcadian constraints. He treated my shoulder as if it were some kind of dangerous object of desire—like the Woman Chalices of bardsong—that might doom us all. Silky took the precautions very seriously, too. But once I finally came to believe Lord Garth and his companions were neither going to kill us nor violate us, I found the extra rules irritating. After treating Trey, I had come to see some of the Arcadian modesty rules impractical when it came to tending the wounded, and I wondered how many men and women had died as the result of such customs.

As we rode, I thought a good deal about escape, but

I confess that I kept coming back to the conclusion that I was just too tired and too hurt to try to get away—and when I attempted to talk to Silky about escaping on her own, she became angry.

The most subversive thing we did was to call Lord Garth quite simply "Garth" behind his back. A few times we forgot to add the "Lord" when speaking to his face, but he just found it amusing.

Apparently, he did not take us seriously.

On the third day of travel, Jasmine tripped on a rock, and I found myself once again sliding to the ground. I was a good horsewoman, but the pain was making me weak and feeble. Blood loss had made me dizzy. I hit the ground and fainted. Again. I was only out for a few seconds, but when I came to, Garth and Silky were already off their horses. Silky ran to me; Garth strode after her; the wound began to bleed in earnest.

There were no finicky modesty preparations this time. Garth brushed Silky aside as if she were a summer moth, and he picked me up and put me down on the deep green moss that grew beneath the shade trees. I looked up at the pattern of leaves against the sky and wondered if it was possible to hurt more than this.

It was.

Garth removed the bandage, and I could see that, once again, the wound had bled through the dressing.

"Build a fire," Garth said to the others.

I just lay there, under the tree, hoping the pain

would subside. Jasmine, whom nobody had bothered catching, walked over to me and put her muzzle near my neck in a gesture I couldn't help but see as apologetic for my fall.

"Not your fault, girl," I said. "I'm just not doing very well." I stared up at her. She looked strange at that angle.

Silky held my hand.

"We have to close the wound," said Garth.

"Right," I said.

The other 'Lidans were busying themselves by the fire. Silky was watching them, and I was watching Silky. It was interesting to see the bloom on her cheeks fade away to paper white. I wondered offhandedly what had caused the change. Then I was dizzy again, and for a little while I went away.

When I came back, Garth was speaking to me.

"Drink this," said Garth. He had pulled a small bottle from among his saddlebags. "It'll help."

"I don't want it," I said.

"Yes," he said, "you do."

I lay on my back and looked at the wind playing with the leaves.

"I'm not going to drink some 'Lidan brew," I said. "Right, Silky?"

Silky was looking nervously toward the fire. "Drink it, Angel," she said. "I think they're going to seal the wound."

"We have no choice," said Garth. "If you want to live."

I glanced at the fire, too, and I saw that an iron rod was heating in the coals. I didn't like the thought that came into my mind as to what Garth planned to do. But I did want to live.

"I won't let go of you," said Silky.

I drank the 'Lidan potion. It was bitter and awful, and at first it made me numb all over.

But the deep searing pain broke through whatever Garth had given me. I opened my eyes and first saw Silky, and then, as if they were actually there, Trey and the Bard. It was Trey who reached out as if to touch my face. But surely that was all wrong. I wanted the Bard.

And then, for a moment, I was alone with my pain, and the ache of loneliness went into the very marrow of my bones.

"Am I dead?" I asked. And I was back in the present. Silky was crying. Garth, who, I realized, had been holding me down, sat back.

"You're not dead," he said. There was a new respect in his voice, and I wondered where it came from.

From that day on, the other 'Lidans, too, were different around me. Sometimes, after the cauterization, they forgot the formal deference owed to me as a woman, but it was as if they forgot because I was one of them. "You carry the brand of a warrior," Garth told me after that. "It makes you different."

The wound stopped bleeding.

Garth told us we were near his country house, which he preferred to his palace in Parlay.

He was clearly Somebody. But he seemed to like

it that Silky and I developed the habit of calling him "Garth." The other 'Lidans called him "Master" when they weren't calling him "Lord."

We, of course, were Somebodies, too. But it seemed best not to dwell on that. I carefully embroidered what little I told him. After one of my particularly convoluted explanations of who we were and what we were doing there, Garth said, "You're telling a lot of lies, aren't you?" He didn't seem angry.

"I may be leaving some things out," I said. "So, yes, I am telling some lies."

"You say you're here for a wedding," Garth said. "But you have no attendants, no provision carts."

"We're traveling light."

"Where to?"

"Back to Arcadia. The wedding is over, and we're not looking for 'Lidan grooms."

"What if the grooms were great Lords of Shibbeth? Wouldn't they be good enough for you?"

"There's no good answer to that question."

"You're still telling lies, aren't you?"

"Yes."

"I don't suppose you know about the Montrose-Nesson wedding?"

"What are you talking about?" asked Silky, genuinely taken by surprise.

"They're looking for a Lady Angel Montrose," said Garth. "And her companion-sister. Word of a reward has spread."

"I suppose you want the reward," said Silky.

He laughed. "I doubt very much that the reward's enough to tempt me. I think, if I found her, that I'd keep this Lady Angel for myself—she sounds intriguing."

We were in trouble.

Garth's words rang true. If he found out who I was, he was going to keep me.

As if I were a thing.

The marriage and land laws—in Shibbeth, in Arcadia—were not designed for women.

I was so wrapped up in the turn my thoughts had taken that I was almost knocked out of my saddle by a low branch.

Garth steadied me with his hand. Then—

"I apologize," he said formally.

"What for?" I asked.

"*She* was the one about to ride into a tree," Silky added helpfully. "I don't see what there is to be sorry for."

"I mean I'm sorry I touched you," said Garth. "We don't do that in Shibbeth. As you must know by now."

"You already touched her," said Silky. "You *held her down* to cauterize the wound with that hot iron."

"So I did," said Garth.

"That was different," I said, and then I held my tongue. I realized I had just defended Garth.

Garth nodded, but he looked thoughtful.

The next day I noticed a change in the vegetation. The rough underbrush had been cut back to reveal short stubby grass. The trees looked as if they had been trimmed of low branches like the one that had almost swept me out of the saddle.

Someone had tidied up the wilderness.

When I pointed this out to Garth, he simply said, "We're on my lands now."

"Does that mean we're close to our destination?"

"Yes, Lady," he said.

"Too much riding," said Silky abruptly. "My backside hurts."

"Silky," I said, "that's common."

"One more night of camping," said Garth. "And I'll be welcoming you to my House. Lady Angel. Lady Silky."

So he did know who we were.

But he might not know about Trey—and he certainly didn't know about the Bard.

We denied nothing about ourselves, but neither of us said a word about the others.

They set up the tents earlier than usual that evening. Garth's idea of camping surpassed anything I knew in Arcadia, and according to him, he was traveling quite simply after making a trading run to Caddis—the great Shibbeth city to the south. When I asked him what he traded in—I had quietly searched for sacks of grain or some sort of goods—his answer was almost curt.

"Jewels," he said.

Jewels. Like Partin Coss, only probably on an unimaginably grander scale. This fit with what I already knew of Garth. He was not only Somebody, he was a rich Somebody. Leth and Kalo would have been impressed by Garth's style. Trey—and certainly the Bard—less so.

The blue silk tents billowed out in the wind as Garth's men erected them. Garth's had the flag of Shibbeth sewn into the side. Ours had two lions embroidered on the door.

"The lions will look after you," said Garth, and he smiled. But when he said that, I was reminded of the guards he posted outside our tent at night. Garth said that these so-called guardians would keep us safe. I was under no illusions. They were there as a subtle reminder that we weren't voluntary guests. We had no chance of getting to the horses and heading to Parlay.

It seemed that, after all, I had made a hash of rescuing Silky.

That night, as we lay on our cots, under our light down coverlets and sheets of soft, finely woven yellow silk, Silky was unusually silent.

"Tomorrow Garth's journey's over," I said. "He'll be home."

"Why do you say it that way?" she asked. "*Our* journey will be over, too."

"Our journey's barely begun," I said. "We're going to find Trey and the Bard."

"Are you *sure*?" Silky was subdued.

"We'll be all right."

Silky sat up and put her arms around her knees. "I don't *feel* as if we'll be all right."

"Cover your shoulders," I said. "It's chilly."

"Are they going to brand us?"

Her voice was soft and low so that the guards couldn't hear us, but I could detect the fear in it. This was what was on her mind; this was why she had been so silent.

"I won't let that happen to you," I said.

"Garth and his men might tie us up and give us *drugs,* and there would be no way to stop them."

"Garth and his men will do nothing," I said. "It's a woman thing. The branding is done by women. They put the mark on the left cheek, and the fact that it's women doing it is supposed to show willing submission. But when the time comes—if the time comes— I'll make sure you're all right."

"In Arcadia I heard some women talking. They said if you were branded, you were owned. Like a dog. Or a cow."

"Silky?"

"Yes?"

"People talk too much."

"A brand might make me *feel* owned."

There was silence. The light from the fire outside made strange shadows on the walls of the tent. Silky spoke again.

"The Bard told me that some women *died* rather than be branded, and I didn't understand. But now I think I do."

"Enough of those thoughts, Silky," I said, a little alarmed. "It's going to be all right. Garth doesn't seem the type to hurt women."

"You said it wasn't a man thing."

"I suppose I did." I sighed. "Just trust me, Silky."

"Oh, Angel," she said. "I always trust you. I always will."

Soon I heard her breathing regularly. She was asleep.

The wound in my shoulder ached; it throbbed in time with my heart, and I knew I wouldn't sleep for a long time.

I had to save Silky. And I also had to save myself. And I knew, deep down, that there was a chance I could do neither. I would do anything to keep Silky safe, but what if anything wasn't enough?

I lay awake and looked at the shadows until dawn.

The next day we turned off into a long lane lined with shrubs cut in mysterious shapes. In Arcadia, bushes shaped like swans and deer and squirrels lined the front of our house; here, although the bushes were carefully shaped, they looked like unfinished letters, or like a code I hadn't been taught to read.

Garth saw me looking at the shrubs.

"Tributes to the *Word*, our sacred book," he said. "A generation ago, we were traditionalists. Times change, but I like reminders of the past."

"Garth," I said. "Before we reach your house. Before anyone except your men even knows we're here, why don't you just let us go?"

Garth looked at me for a long time.

"Two women traveling alone in Shibbeth wouldn't last long," he said finally.

"You've been a good host," I said. "But the time comes for guests to leave. Silky and I are willing to take our chances."

"I have plans for you, Lady Angel," he said. "And I have plans for the Lady Silky, too. And they're plans to your advantage. You will come to see that. Through the right marriages, you see, the sons of my House can gain a foothold in Arcadia."

"You want Arcadian land," I said. "Of course you do." It was hard to keep the bitterness out of my voice.

But he seemed to feel he had said enough.

We rounded the bend to his house.

It was a palace. A palace with what looked like a hundred windows winking in the sun. A palace built out of many-shaded marble, so that it glowed rose and yellow and green and white.

I noted that all the windows were far from the ground. We were about to enter an exquisite cage.

CHAPTER THIRTEEN

BATHS OF ROSES AND MILK

"It's beautiful," said Silky.

"You're acting as though you'd spent your whole life in a shepherd's cottage," I said, but my mind was elsewhere. We had to get away from Garth, and we had to get away soon.

We were already overdue in Parlay. Trey would wait for us—I knew that. But I wanted the Bard to be there too. I remembered how, that day he had helped me to my feet, he had seemed so warm—and he had chosen to road with us when I had asked him. Surely he would wait for us. For me. I was beginning to think that he

and I were bound in ways I didn't fully understand—
that maybe I didn't want to understand.

For only a moment did I entertain the idea that it
might be better for all of us if he had moved on.

As we rode up to the great doors, servants rushed
from the house and stood in two rows. Some women
wore veils and a few did not. A number of the older
men were dressed like traditionalists.

"I'm scared," whispered Silky.

But I was looking around hopefully. "There must
be a hundred ways out of this place," I murmured.

Garth addressed the oldest woman there.

"Take the Lady Angel and the Lady Silky to the restricted women's quarters," said Garth. "They are our
reluctant guests. See to it that the Lady Angel's shoulder wound is tended to, and treat them with every deference."

"Except, of course, liberty," I said.

"Yes," said Garth, nodding pleasantly. "Except that."

The old woman took us through the palace. Cor-
ridors and doors flicked by and embedded themselves
in my mind. It was time to use my prodigious memory.
Just as I could read a line from a book and know it
forever, I could memorize the patterns of a building.
From a hallway we didn't take—one less ornate than
the others—wafted the smell of cooking. I would remember that. And then I smelled incense, and the old
woman opened a small door, and we passed through.

We found ourselves in an open courtyard surrounded by high walls. Everywhere there were pots

filled with curious flowers and exotic plants, and in the center, water from a fountain bubbled and splashed through bells, making chiming sounds. Several women in long loose robes were resting on divans, their hair down, no veils in sight. They glanced up at Silky and me with interest.

I stared around me. The women's quarters were lavish beyond belief. Everything seemed overdone, from the gush of perfumes that greeted us when the old woman opened the door, to the gilded ornate musical fountain. Later we were to see luxurious sleeping chambers that had walls covered with tapestries— tapestries with a weave and patterns so fine that the weavers must have risked blindness.

"Mistress Charmian will show you around," said the old woman, and she called over a girl no older than Silky. Charmian's lips were painted into a small bow, and her eyelids were streaked with blue; she had a fine, heart-shaped face, but there was something sly about her. She gave us a small smile, and her bow-lips thinned unpleasantly.

"Is this a *harem*?" blurted out Silky.

"Silky," I hissed. "There haven't been harems in Shibbeth for over a hundred years."

Charmian laughed. "This is where the women of the house can come for privacy. It's perfectly safe here."

"Can you leave when you want?" I asked.

"The guard at the door lets us in and out," said Charmian. "But you're Lord Garth's special guests."

Her first non-answer.

"We'd like to go *out*," said Silky.

"You just arrived," said Charmian. "In a few hours they'll bring in tea, for those who want it. There's everything you could want here. Lord Garth even indulges us with baths of roses and milk. And this evening Bard Fallon sings."

"Why would I want a bath of roses and *milk*?" asked Silky.

Charmian laughed. "It's good for the skin," she said.

Charmian was beginning to grate on me.

"Are you Garth's daughter?" I asked. If so, I thought, he should have a word with her. She was far too young to be painting her face.

"I'm Lord Garth's wife," she said. "He has grown sons by his first wife, true, but we'll have children soon enough. I'll see that it's my children that inherit. His second wife was barren."

I could tell this was somehow supposed to impress me.

"Are you *branded*?" blurted out Silky.

"Of course." Charmian pushed back her hair to reveal her left cheek. Where she had been branded, the skin was taut and unnaturally white; the scar extended from her cheek onto her neck. She saw the look on my face.

"Lord Garth's brand is bigger than most," she said. "He likes to mark his possessions."

"Didn't it hurt?" asked Silky.

Charmian smiled and the lips thinned. She looked sly again. Then she said, "The branding is a time of great celebration. You'll see." I thought not. And I realized that this Charmian was filled with guile, all guile.

Tea was brought in by the door we had used, and when it was, Charmian, now veiled, took her leave. She was away for over an hour, and when she returned, her mood was not good. No more smiles.

"Is something the matter?" asked Silky.

"On the contrary," said Charmian. "I have been informed you are particularly honored guests." She couldn't have made it any more clear that the news didn't sit well with her.

The evening drew on, some of the other women left, and Charmian explained that they were the wives and daughters of Garth's companions and guards. They had homes to go to.

"But you're special," said Charmian, clearly making an attempt to speak brightly. "Or Lord Garth wouldn't bother with you. How long were you together on the road?"

I explained that we had been forced to move slowly because of my wound.

"But how lovely for you," she said. "Except for the wound, of course. So rustic. I'd love to go beyond the walls, but Lord Garth says it's dangerous. You must be very brave."

"Not really," I muttered.

"Yes," said Silky. "She *is*."

I gave Silky a look that would have quenched a forest fire. Charmian shook a finger at me. "Not ladylike, though," she said. "All that outside travel."

I couldn't believe this girl-woman was only thirteen or fourteen. She behaved like a matron. I wished she would observe the 'Lidan virtue of silence, but perhaps that was only practiced before men.

It was one of the longest afternoons of my life. Charmian wouldn't leave us alone, and she didn't stop talking. She prattled. And we did nothing. We didn't play games, or do needlework, or do anything practical, like cleaning horse tack or practicing archery.

Not that they would have given us crossbows.

I was bored.

Later, Garth's herbalist came, and Charmian stood by as he examined the wound in my shoulder.

"I'm healing," I said.

"You are," he agreed. "But unless you move that arm as I show you, it will freeze into place." He gave me some of the 'Lidan brew for pain and then had me raise and lower my arm. I tried not to cry out, but when I gave an involuntary moan, I saw Charmian's lips thin. She was smiling.

When the herbalist left, Charmian took us to the baths. The room was cool, and the sound of trickling water was everywhere.

"Lord Garth said to prepare the best," said Charmian. "Baths of roses and milk for both of you. Lord Garth's orders." She laughed. "All the women are jealous."

I looked down at the watery-white liquid that filled a copper hipbath. A few limp-looking rose petals floated on the surface.

"That's really milk?" I asked.

"Yes," she said. "And you're the first to bathe in it today. So privileged."

"I'm not getting in there," said Silky. "I'm not taking a bath in milk; I don't even like to drink milk. I'm not sitting in it."

But I could see that the more reluctant we were, the happier Charmian would be, and that all we did would be reported to Garth. I took off my clothes with Silky's help—it was too painful to undress alone—and climbed in. Charmian didn't even show the respect of turning her back.

I got out, dripping tepid milk, and helped Silky in for her turn. I would have given a lot for a bath of cool water. As the milk dried, it became sticky. Several interested flies buzzed around me.

"Can I rinse?" I asked Charmian.

"As you like." She didn't look pleased, but she provided us with washing water, and we laved off the petals and clammy milk as best we could.

I wanted to gather information, to speak to Garth, to escape—to do *something*—but the very air was filled with a stupefying kind of languor. Nothing here was going to happen in a hurry. In fact, nothing much at all seemed to happen in the women's quarters, baths of roses and milk aside.

"It's time for the afternoon rest," said Charmian. "Later we'll hear Bard Fallon and then have supper." She took us to our beautiful, stuffy, over-perfumed room. Silky examined the tapestries on the wall while I wondered if we could force our way out, but the tiny window was high in the wall, and too small for even Silky to wiggle through.

I thought about going back through the door and remembered how all the women looked soft and spoiled and languorous. Even Silky, small as she was, would probably have had no trouble overpowering one or two of them, but outside the door was the world of men and weapons, and the men, if they were anything like Garth and his traveling companions, were not soft.

As Silky and I lay on divans in our sleeping room, I slipped into a living dream—the 'Lidan pain brew was strong.

I was looking into the Bard's face, and he was leaning forward, and I realized he was going to touch me with his lips. Then the moment seemed to tilt, and the face was no longer that of the Bard.

It was Trey's.

I awoke feeling sick, and when I came to my senses Charmian was standing over me, as if she had been there for some time, and I thought, suddenly, *She could have killed me*.

"Lord Garth would like to see the Lady Angel," she said abruptly. "I didn't know you were a Lady."

Charmian walked me to the door leading out of the women's quarters. From there I was escorted through the palace by a guard, who led me to a room filled with books. I had never seen so many books.

Master Garth rose from his seat when I entered. He wasted no words.

"You hate the women's quarters," he said.

"After our travels, you must know that they suit neither Silky nor me."

"That's the point," said Garth. "The women of my House have thin blood. You and your sister would bring strength to us. I thought of this on our journey, and I've spoken to my advisors—I want you and your sister to marry two of my sons. When it's done, we will reconcile with your House, and I'll see that you receive your dowry."

He clearly knew about my vast estates.

So much for thin blood and strengthening the House and all of that. Marriage in both Arcadia and Shibbeth always seemed to come down to land greed.

"I don't think you'd find a reconciliation with my family possible," I said, thinking of Kalo. "Even if Silky or I were in the mood to marry. Which we're not."

"It doesn't really matter what you think," said Garth. "We'll begin the preliminary ceremonies tomorrow. Charmian will see to it. In a month, when the brands have healed and you've learned our laws, you'll be married. And then, finally, you will be silent."

And I had thought he liked our conversations.

"No," I said.

"There's no refusal," said Garth. "Now go and listen to Bard Fallon. You won't have much else to do in the coming years. Except add to our lands, and, of course, provide my sons with strong heirs."

So that would be the end. There would be no more Angel and Silky, just soft breeding women. The Garth

I had begun to like on our journey was gone. Here, in his palace, Silky and I were no more than pawns.

Trey, I thought, might still try and rescue me after the 'Lidan marriage. But the woman he rescued would not be the same Angel he had known since childhood.

When I returned to the women's quarters, I saw that Charmian had donned a blue spangled silk gown that trailed on the ground in back. It clearly wasn't made to be worn more than once.

She had also informed Silky and the other women of the coming ceremony.

The women congratulated me. You would have thought I had done something particularly clever—there were looks of envy and reminiscences of the fuss made around each woman's branding ceremony. They focused on descriptions of the food and drink provided, the camaraderie of the women, the extra baths of rose petals and milk. But none of them said anything about the branding itself. It couldn't be as painful as the cauterization, but Silky and I were not—we were *not*—born to be branded. And, if they only knew it, neither were these women.

I found Silky in our bedroom, in tears, her head turned toward the wall.

"Do you really think the branding's going to be *horrible*?" she asked me.

"Horrible," I said. "But it's not going to happen."

"How can we stop it?"

"We may have to fight our way out."

I saw Silky's resolve build, and I thought to myself,

Garth wants strong blood in his House? Then blood is what he's going to get.

Silky wiped her tears. "All right," she said. "But if we fight, *I'll* go for Charmian. She's starting to annoy me."

I pulled Silky in for a fierce embrace. My shoulder ached as I held her, but, at that moment, I didn't care about the pain.

Charmian escorted us to the courtyard for the evening's entertainment, utterly oblivious to the dangerous look in Silky's eye. Soon after, Bard Fallon arrived: he was gaunt, with thinning white hair—utterly unlike our Bard. Everyone settled down and relaxed on soft chairs or divans that had been brought into a circle. Silky and I shared a divan. An older woman whom I had seen before came and sat very close to us. She was wearing a great deal of face paint—even more than Charmian—and dark markings made her eyes seem huge in her small, lined face. Her pupils were hugely dilated, and I wondered if she put belladonna in them. Her lips were a deep red, and no one's cheeks, not even Silky's when she was embarrassed, were that blush. Under it all, I could see traces of a woman who must have been more than double my age, and a woman whose leisure may have been spent in thinking dark thoughts—a woman who had been thinking dark thoughts for a long time.

"I'm Danae," she said. Her voice was soft and low.

In a moment, Charmian was with us.

"Leave them, Danae," she said. "They have no time for idle gossip."

It seemed an odd thing to say. All that the women in the restricted quarters seemed to do was engage in idle gossip.

"I want to wish them well at the marking ceremony," said Danae. "Leave us."

Charmian's eyes narrowed, but she left us without another word.

Maybe the older woman had some kind of special status that called for obedience.

"There's a supper after Bard Fallon sings," said Danae. "It's a good time to speak."

Sometimes life only offers one chance.

"Will you help us?" I asked her. There was no time for subtle games.

Luckily, there was no hesitation in her answer.

"Yes," she said. "I'll do what I can." She rose and went to the other side of the courtyard.

Bard Fallon began tuning his lyre. He looked around nervously, although he soon became calm as he fell into a recitation of the news.

He clearly knew his audience: the focus was on marriages and births, and there were many gasps and cries of excitement from the audience.

Fallon then sang the little-known lay of the Lady in the Castle.

And that's when I knew he knew. I didn't know how much he knew, but someone had told him we were abroad in Shibbeth. If that someone had been Trey or the Bard, Fallon's presence might offer hope. Only our Bard knew, after all, that the obscure lay of the Lady in the Castle was one of my favorites.

After Bard Fallon finished the lay of the Lady in the Castle—which left many of the women in tears, including Silky—a light supper was brought in. I saw Danae watching me. The other women crowded around the table, and Silky looked delighted by the food. While I wanted to speak with Danae, I saw I had only one brief instant to be alone with Fallon.

I didn't want to look as if I were doing anything secretive, so I walked up as if to congratulate him.

He stared at me before he spoke.

"I knew I would be the one to find you," he said. "Worse luck for me. Word's abroad among the Bards. Has the day come?"

"The day has come."

"Lady Angel and Lady Silky?"

I wished Silky to my side, but she was preoccupied with the food.

"Yes," I said.

"Meet me at the water courtyard when the moon clears the wall. Then we'll see."

"What will we see?"

"If I can get you out."

I was about to say something more, when I felt, rather than heard, Charmian come up next to me. Her perfume signaled her presence.

"You shouldn't be talking to him," she said sourly.

"I was just complimenting Bard Fallon on his song," I said.

"You were just talking to a man you don't even know," she said.

Then Danae was there.

"Come to supper," she said.

"What do you want?" snapped Charmian. Danae ignored her.

"The food is very good tonight," said Danae and put her arm around my waist. The bard had turned away. Charmian left us to go back for the desserts.

"How can you help us?" I whispered.

"I'll set my bedroom on fire. That will have the merit of getting their attention."

It had certainly gotten mine.

"Why are you doing this?" I asked.

"Look around," she said. "This courtyard, the fountain, the sleeping quarters with tapestries and embroidered sheets, the bejeweled clothes, the solicitude of your new friend Charmian—this place is Hell."

"That still doesn't answer why *you're* helping *me*."

"Just be here at moonrise; the fire will be large; my life will probably be in danger. They'll all be busy." She made to walk away, but I grabbed her elbow with a grip strong enough that she was forced to look at me again.

"I need to know *why*," I said. "I need to know you're not going to trap us."

Danae paused. "You see what that little girl Charmian has become: spoiled, pettish, dangerous, damaged. I never want to see that metamorphosis again."

"I don't understand."

Danae gave a little laugh.

"How could you? You and your sister have the marks of courage and honor, and you're—you're close to Charmian's age. She could have been like you, in another life, in another place."

"I still don't understand."

"I was Garth's wife," she said, "when he finished with his first one. After me, he married Charmian."

"I see."

"No. You don't. Charmian's my daughter. My beautiful, ruined daughter."

Danae turned away from me.

I never saw her again.

CHAPTER FOURTEEN

DIFFERENT DREAMS

As we walked to our room, we passed Charmian. She gave me a smile, and when I saw that smile, I realized how much she hated me. I recognized loathing.

"Danae's not usually social," she said.

"She's pleasant," I said.

"Yes. Well. I've been thinking about you and Lord Garth." She narrowed her eyes. "Did Lord Garth use you on your journey?" When I looked blank, she became more blunt.

"Were you his concubine?" She switched her attention to Silky. "Or was it you? He likes them young." For a moment she looked smug. "Like me."

"We journeyed together," I said. "That's all."

"I see," said Charmian. "Well, you won't do that again after the marking ceremony. Not after you become 'Lidan women. The branding will change you. You'll see."

"I bet it didn't change *you*," said Silky. "I bet you were *always* awful."

I almost wished Charmian would say something nasty in reply so that I could keep from feeling sorry for her, but she didn't.

"When I was a child," she said, "my mother let me dream of being free. She's a stupid woman."

"You're still a child," I said softly.

"Just go to your room," said Charmian, and her eyes glittered. "Soon enough you'll dream different dreams."

We retired to our chamber of tapestries and great drapes and swaths of multicolored silk. Silky and I sat quietly. I drew the curtains over the opening where a door would normally be. It was stuffy, but I wanted privacy, and there was very little privacy to be had in the women's restricted quarters.

"We take nothing," I said to Silky after I explained the plan to her. I didn't know where our riding garments were; we were going to have to try to make our escape in the spectacularly useless outfits that Charmian had provided.

Finally the quarters grew quiet; the women all went to bed, and Silky and I pretended to do the same. I predicted that the moon would be over the wall at close to midnight.

Time went by.

I was wondering if Danae was going to make good on her promise, when a cry of fire went up, and I could hear women running past our chamber.

"Hurry," a woman cried, "the whole room's gone up."

"Get the guards," called another.

And then I heard Charmian, her panicked voice lifted over the others. "She's trapped!" Charmian screamed. "She can't get out. Get her out!"

Silky and I slipped away, leaving the curtains drawn behind us. As we left the women's quarters behind, I saw flames flickering against the sky. There was shouting and screaming from the direction of the glow, and then, abruptly, everything was still.

We crept to the courtyard. It was midnight, and the moon looked as if it were sitting on top of the stone wall, huge, orange, portentous.

Fallon was waiting in the shadows.

"Come," he said.

"The guards?" I asked.

"I sang to the guards. We shared wine. Theirs was drugged." We passed the doorway, stepping over the men who had been keeping watch.

"Are they *dead*?" asked Silky.

"I don't know," said Fallon. "Take their weapons

and come on. Do you know how to use a crossbow?"
I didn't answer, but I took the crossbow off one of the
guards and handed it to Silky.

Fallon led us through the labyrinthine passages
of the palace, and I had a fleeting impression of over-
sized paintings, many of battle and slaughter, statues
of men and women out of bardsong, a hall of portraits.
He stopped in front of the painting of a woman with a
parrot on her finger.

"We need to find the kitchen."

I remembered the corridor that smelled of food.

"This way," I said. I took us left and right and left
again and down the corridor I remembered. Then
we were in a huge kitchen. Once there, Bard Fallon
opened a small door in the back of the pantry.

"It's the door for the dog," he said. "I saw it when
Cook gave me food. We'll fit."

"It's small," I said.

"So are you," he said.

We did fit—my shoulder protested the entire time—
but Silky and I had to pull at Fallon until he popped out
like a cork from a bottle.

The air swept over us, fresh and cold, sweeter than
any of Charmian's perfumes.

We were free.

Or at least free of the house. We were still a long way
from actual freedom. So we moved in the shadows. As
I followed Fallon, I thought that the last thing Garth
would expect was escape. Any idiotic notions I might
have had about his kind nature, his polite demeanor

or his pleasure in our conversations were gone, and I saw us as he had always seen us. Except for that brief moment of the cauterization of my wound, he had seen foolish, noisy, chattering, undisciplined women, just barely on the right side of being fit mates for his sons. He must have been disappointed that Charmian had so little success at getting us to conform to 'Lidan ways with her baths of roses and milk.

As if a bath could wash away our essence.

That's when, standing in the moonlight like a giant statue of a man, I saw Garth. He stared at us in disbelief.

And then he roared. It was not a sound I had ever heard coming from a human being.

It was the sound of pure rage.

His face was contorted into a mask of anger, and I could see that in a moment he was going to come for us.

We would never have another chance.

He drew his sword and took a few angry strides toward us.

Silky and I stood side by side in the moonlight. She grabbed my hand. Fallon was behind us, as if we could shield him from Garth's wrath.

Yet, instead of attacking, Garth spoke, and the measured calm of his words was almost worse than his roar of anger.

"You'll come with me," he said. "And we won't speak of this again. Charmian will worry if she finds you gone."

"Just let us go," I said. "Please." I hated the begging

tone in my voice. "We're useless to you. The Lord Kalo of Montrose hates us. You won't gain an acre from him by marrying us to your sons."

"Why not?" he said. "A 'Lidan match will bring Lord Montrose higher standing here," said Garth. "And, in return, he can make me great."

"Ambition is *not* a pretty trait," said Silky. She was foolish to speak so, but she was angry.

And I didn't disagree with her.

"It's strange talking about land and dowry matters with women," he said. "It's as if dogs could speak."

Garth raised his sword. I knew that by the time Silky had a chance to level and sight the crossbow, either she or I would be dead. But I was not ready to give up. I was angry. I let go of Silky's hand.

The giant Garth with his silver sword stood in the way of the outer gate. He was blocking Silky and me from freedom.

He was keeping me from Trey. From the Bard. From life.

I began clumsily to run, but not away. I was no longer trying to escape. The garments Charmian had given us were hopeless for running, and we were still in the walled outer area of the palace. There was no place to go that led to freedom.

No, I didn't run away—I ran *toward* Garth. And as I came on, he actually took a step backward. This was not what he had expected.

When I reached him, he raised his sword, but my anger had become a kind of frenzy.

I slammed into him as hard as I could. I batted his sword away, oblivious to the deep cut that opened in my hand. He stared for a moment at his sword, and I punched it out of his hand. It lodged in the paving stones behind him, hilt down, blade up.

I didn't know how to fight, and that's probably what saved me. Everything I did was unexpected. I pulled out a clump of his hair, and I began working my thumb into his eye socket. I could feel the slash in my hand now, but the pain seemed far away. Later my shoulder was going to be in agony. Now my focus was on getting his eye out.

All this time, he just kept pushing me away, as if he could think of nothing better to do, as if one good punch from him wouldn't have ended everything right there.

Silky was beside me in a moment.

"Get out of here," I yelled at her. "Run for the gate and get into the woods."

"I'm not going," she said, and she kneed him, hard, in the groin. He bent over in agony. He was off-balance. I slammed into him.

His fall was slow and monumental. I followed Silky's example, and, when he hit the ground, I kicked him in the groin, but there was no need—the silver length of his sword poked through his abdomen. The blood began to flow.

Now I could hear noises coming from the guard-house at the palace gate. There were lights and the crashing sound of armor on armor. The noise of

Garth's shouting and our fight had roused the guard, but they couldn't possibly have an idea of where the sound had come from.

We had time. Perhaps not enough. But we had a chance.

Suddenly I realized that Bard Fallon was gone. Sometime during the scuffle with Garth, he had found a way to disappear.

We were alone. We would have to do this by ourselves.

I looked at Silky; she looked back, trustingly, hopefully.

Despair coursed through me like poison.

When I heard the sound of hooves on cobblestones, I thought Garth's troops were here. But a moment later, in a moment of disbelief, I could make out the shadows of three horses—one with a man already mounted on it, the other two saddled up.

Even in the dark I recognized Jasmine's silhouette. Bard Fallon had been true to us all along.

"Get on," he whispered. "We may actually come out of this alive."

Silky and I were mounted in a second. She had the crossbow we had taken from the drugged guards, and she held it in her right hand and the reins in her left.

We could see the great gate was not yet closed, and we rode for it, hooves sparking on stone. As we passed the gatehouse, the first guards tumbled out, still fastening their armor.

"Master Garth is down," I yelled. "And there's a fire in the women's quarters."

They stood and stared. I had hoped to gain time by sending the guards back to the chaos behind us, but it was soon obvious that I couldn't conquer the suspicions aroused by two women in gauzy nightclothes riding hard out of the palace in the middle of the night.

The gate began to close. I didn't even know if they were trying to keep us in or if they feared a threat from the outside. Silky and I just barely slipped through, but I didn't think the Bard was going to make it. Yet he did, grazing his legs against the monumental gate.

We galloped until we were under the trees, then we stopped and looked back at the palace. No pursuit, and plenty of fire and smoke. A moment later, we heard a high-pitched wailing—the women must have found Garth, and the keening for him had begun. I didn't think the cries would be for Danae.

I wondered, fleetingly, what would happen to Charmian now that the palace would have a new master. I suspected she would be seeing a lot more of the restricted women's quarters.

As we stood there, catching our breath, we saw the gate begin to open again. The first men were out, some of them buckling on breast plates, others leading horses and carrying saddles.

"We ride for it," said Fallon. "There's a trail to the left of the main road. Maybe they won't take it."

I could now hear the clash of swords and light

armor. The nervous movements of the troops' horses.

"Will you take us to Parlay?" I asked Fallon. My voice was high-pitched with tension. "We need to get to Parlay."

"Be quiet," he said. "I'm taking you to Niamh."

I knew of no city called Niamh. Silky, meanwhile, was indignant on my behalf. "But the *Lady Angel* wants—" she began. Fallon cut her off.

"What you *want* is your business," he said. "Niamh will decide what you need."

At least now I knew Niamh was a person.

"And how will he know what we need?" I asked.

"Niamh is a woman," he said. And it was clear the subject was closed.

We came out from under the trees, and there was a swath of open space before us. We galloped, hoping to reach the trees on the far side before we were discovered.

In bardsong the moon was indifferent, but tonight it seemed malevolent; the clearing was so filled with moonlight that Garth's troops would be able to see every spangle on our ridiculous garments. The stars were insignificant in the light of that awful moon.

Then we were on the far side of the clearing, galloping on the trail among the trees, but I knew that the trail would lead Garth's men directly to us.

I pulled up Jasmine. Silky came alongside.

"We have to get off the path," I said to Silky. It took Fallon a moment to realize we were no longer with him, and when he came back to us, he looked angry.

"We have to keep going," he hissed.

"They will find us on the trail," I said. "They will. Silky and I may be forced back to the palace, but you'll die here like a thing of no consequence. We have to get off the road. We have to let them go by."

Bard Fallon paused, his face in a deep frown. "They'll see our tracks."

"They'll be making too many tracks of their own," I said. "And it's dark. They won't even look." I hoped. Garth had underestimated us because we were women, and I assumed his men would, too. Silky was watching us. In her mind I knew there was no decision to be made; she was only waiting to see if Fallon would come with us.

Her trust was a beautiful and terrifying thing.

"All right," said Fallon. 'Lidans were famous for torturing captives before slaying them. Perhaps he was thinking of that.

There was a slim opening in the bushes lining the trail, and Jasmine, now in the lead, breasted them at my command. Silky followed. Fallon, his animal skittish, rode up on Silky's horse, and her mount kicked out.

"Sorry," he muttered.

Then I heard the guards. The moon was casting deep shadows, and I motioned to the others until we were all huddled in the black penumbra of a large oak. Perhaps the moon was not malevolent after all.

We waited, afraid to move, nervous that the horses would give us away by a shake of the head, the clink of a bridle.

The guards came close to us. Very close.

Silky lifted her crossbow. I made an abrupt motion, and she lowered it.

Silky could have easily picked off one of them, maybe two, but we would still have to contend with the rest of the mounted guards, not to mention the foot soldiers. And Silky would be incurring more bloodguilt.

The mounted troops passed us by. And still we waited, for fear more guards would follow them.

None came.

Finally I turned Jasmine off the trail in a direction that would lead us away from the soldiers. Silky and Fallon followed.

We rode under the trees at first and then under the night sky and that ominous moon.

"This is *spooky*," said Silky.

Fallon told her to be quiet. No "Lady Silky" this time.

The going was easy now; we were on old pathways that skirted fields of hay. Bard Fallon took the lead. In the east, streaks of pink heralded the dawn.

He stopped in front of a small farmhouse.

"Niamh lives here with her son," said Fallon. "Trust her."

"You're leaving us," I said. It wasn't a question.

"Our journey forks here," he said. "I'll make sure to

leave some visible tracks once I'm away from Niamh's. Perhaps the soldiers will follow them for a while—but I'm not going to stay to find out if they do."

He had put his life up for us, and all I could say was "Thank you."

"I saw you run at Garth," he said to me. "Even if I put that act in bardsong, no one would believe it."

"If I'd been thinking," I said, "I probably wouldn't have done it."

He looked at me speculatively. Then he mentioned our Bard by name.

"If you do see the Bard Renn again," he said, "tell him the debt is paid. Although"—he seemed to hesitate—"although I would rescue you again, even if there were no debt. I don't believe in pedigrees—those that know anything of *The Book of Forbidden Wisdom* don't—but I believe in courage. Lady Angel. Lady Silky." And his horse broke into a canter; he turned in the saddle once, and, like the freeman in the river, he put his hand over his heart; he bowed his head. He turned back to face the road, and was gone.

CHAPTER FIFTEEN

NIAMH

A moment later, a woman came out of the farmhouse.

"Get off the horses," she said without preamble.

We dismounted. She took the horses and began walking them to the back of the house. A young man, maybe a year older than I was, came out the front door after her with a broom.

"Better get inside," he said. And he began brushing away our tracks.

Minutes later we were sitting in the garden of Niamh's house, sipping icy water from the well and eating ripe summer figs. Niamh and the young man with the broom—her son—sat and listened to our story.

Niamh had deep black hair and wide dark eyes. Although I saw no signs of a husband—and she didn't wear the Shibbeth gold marriage bracelets—she *was* branded. I tried hard not to stare, but when I looked at her face, my eyes were drawn to the cat-shaped scar. She was, perhaps, thirty-five. Certainly no older, in spite of having an almost-grown son.

The son, Jesse, scrutinized us both carefully as we spoke, but I noticed, to my annoyance, that his eyes kept returning to Silky. I admit that she was looking particularly beautiful. She had unbraided her gold hair, and it tumbled, tousled, down her back and framed her delicate face. The excitement of the escape and the wind, which had been in our faces as we rode, had put extra color in her cheeks. There was a glow to her. No wonder he was staring. I saw, too, that she was looking at Jesse as much as he was looking at her.

As Silky took a turn with our story, I reached for another fig, narrowed my eyes, and considered Jesse.

Although he might be no more than seventeen, he was like a young giant; outside, he had towered over all of us. His hair was blond, but not golden, like Silky's, and his eyes were the same peculiar deep shade of blue as his mother's. His face still had the appealing softness of youth, and, despite his size, there was nothing at all about him that seemed dangerous.

Except the way he looked at Silky.

Silky reached the present moment in our narrative. She had been circumspect and had left out a great many details, including Garth's death.

"You don't need to worry anymore," Niamh said. "We've never refused to help a woman, and we're not going to begin now. I'll get you out."

"I don't understand," I said.

"This is a way-station," said Niamh. "The last way-station for 'Lidan women escaping Shibbeth for Arcadia."

"We're going to Parlay," I said.

Niamh continued as if I hadn't spoken.

"We can have you out of Shibbeth in three days," she said. "Jesse and I will guide you. The backroads to Arcadia are narrow and steep, and we'll have to go on foot. I'll sell your horses on the black market—with the money, you'll be helping the next woman in need."

I was near panic. We had to get to Parlay. As for Jasmine, on the black market horses became horsemeat—no dealer would leave a horse alive and risk having his merchandise recognized. Meat was anonymous.

"We're not going back to Arcadia," I blurted. "We're going to Parlay."

Niamh stood suddenly, but not at my words. There was a sound on the walk outside and then a loud knock on the door.

Silky's eyes widened. I picked up the crossbow. Silky reached over and took it from me.

"Wait," whispered Niamh. Jesse crossed the room

and looked out the side of the window, where the curtain met the frame.

"Two horses by the trees," he said. "Troops, by the look of the tack. I can't see who's at the door."

The knock came again.

"A moment," Jesse called out. "I'm coming. My mother's not fitly dressed."

"Come on," said Niamh. She pulled us into the bedroom.

"One soldier with the horses," murmured Jesse to us over his shoulder. "There may only be one at the door."

Niamh didn't appear to be listening. She closed the bedroom door behind us. A moment later she was tugging at the floorboards; Silky and I began to help her.

There was a crawl space big enough for two. Just.

Silky and I curled around each other so that we fit. Niamh threw our saddlebags on top of us and began to put the boards back.

We could hear Jesse speaking, but we couldn't hear what he was saying. Then there was a single angry raised voice. "I will search your house," came the voice. "And I will do it now."

Jesse mumbled something.

As Niamh prepared to put down the last floorboard over us, I saw the crossbow on the floor, grabbed it and pulled it in, hitting Silky on the head in the process.

"That *hurt*," she said.

"Silky," I said as firmly as I could. "You have to be quiet."

Niamh, her lips now pressed firmly together, shut us in.

At first there was light from a thin crack in the floor. I had a brief glimpse of Niamh lifting a rug, and then Silky and I were in absolute darkness.

I could hear Niamh rustling on the other side of the room, where the bed was.

The guard was very loud.

"There's been a murder," he said. "A great Lord. You've been thought to harbor fugitives before. It's said you deal in women."

"Does this look like a brothel?" asked Jesse. "We abide by the law. You'll find no murderers here."

The bedroom door creaked open.

"Who's the woman in the bed?" asked the soldier.

"My mother," said Jesse. "She's ill."

The rustling must have been Niamh getting under the covers.

"What's wrong with her?"

"The shuddering sickness."

"There's no quarantine mark on this house."

"We've let no one in," said Jesse. "I was going to seal the door within the hour."

Next to me, Silky moved suddenly and then was still.

"*Itch*," she said in my ear. "*Nose*."

Her arms were pinned to her sides, but my arm was around her shoulder. I scratched her nose.

"I'm sick, sir," said Niamh.

The soldier didn't answer.

I could hear him move around the bedroom. His footsteps came closer. I thought he was going to walk right over us, but he stopped.

There was silence.

He lifted the rug.

A beam of light fell across my eye. Silky gave a small gasp.

For an instant, the soldier and I were looking directly into each other's eyes.

He lowered the rug back into place.

"My comrade and I," he said, "could tear this place apart if we wanted to. Just for the fun of it."

"I understand," said Jesse.

I didn't.

I heard the soldier walk out of the bedroom.

An hour later, Silky and I were still brushing off dust and stretching.

"That was scary," said Silky.

"A murdered Lord," said Niamh. "We could do without that. They'll be watching the trails for weeks—our whole operation will have to be suspended until they catch the killers."

Silky looked anxious.

"We didn't mean to kill him," she said. "I thought *he* was going to kill *us*."

"Silky," I said.

There was silence.

"You?" asked Niamh. Jesse stared.

"Well," said Silky. "I helped. But it was *mostly* Angel."

In the end, I told her a more complete version of our story: how we had become separated from our friends and were supposed to meet them in Parlay.

"I don't like this," said Niamh. "They're very close on your trail."

"The roads to Arcadia will be closed now," Jesse said to Niamh, glancing at Silky. "We might as well get them to Parlay."

"How long will your companions wait for you?" asked Niamh.

"Some days more," I said. "A week. Maybe."

"Oh, more than *that*," said Silky. "Trey would *never* leave Angel."

"*Silky.*"

"Just saying."

And Jesse smiled. At Silky.

It took only a day to prepare for the journey. Jesse disappeared for a little while and came back with bread, dried meat, fruit and skins of water.

"There were soldiers in the village," he said. "We need to leave now."

I assumed we would take turns riding Jasmine and Silky's horse, but in the afternoon a man rode up leading two sturdy ponies and a small goat. He tethered them to Niamh's gatepost and then cantered away.

"Many people are in debt to my mother," Jesse explained to me. "For the lives of their friends, their sisters, their mothers. They would give her anything. I borrowed the horses, but the goat is a gift. We'll slaughter it, and what we don't eat tonight, we'll take tomorrow."

The goat was small and white and stood out against the green grass. When Jesse cut its throat, red streamed down the white of its chest. It didn't struggle.

With Jesse's guidance, I helped him cut it up, until both of us were soon in gore up to our elbows. Unlike most Great Ladies, I had seen animals butchered on my father's estates, but I had never dreamed I would ever help in the dressing of a carcass.

I had a handful of kidney, and Jesse was skinning the haunch, when he finally spoke of Silky.

"Is your sister running from a contract?" he asked.

"No," I said. "No contract. No pre-contract. No attachments. She's only fourteen." I put emphasis on "fourteen."

"She's old for her age," he said.

"You don't even know her," I said. "You'll find that, if anything, she's young for her age."

"I see."

"What do you see?"

"You wouldn't approve of my knowing her better."

"Not even remotely; not even hypothetically."

"I see."

"She'll never be ready for a pre-contract with a 'Lidan."

In one deft movement, Jesse removed the entire intestines of the goat without contaminating any of the surrounding meat.

"Niamh raised me well," he said. He began wash-

ing out the inside of the goat with water from a pail.
"Lady Angel, I help her rescue women from the branding and the silence."

"Good for you," I said.

Really. Silky. Marriage.

Not a chance.

I thought the subject was closed. Jesse cut out some
goat chops. "I'm saving her the prime ones," he said.

"You won't get Silky's heart with a goat chop," I
said. "And you certainly don't have my permission to
court her."

"I worry a little about your heart, Lady Angel," he
said.

I didn't say anything. There was nothing wrong
with my heart. Nothing. It was healthy and strong and
whole. It was safe. It was a fortress.

CHAPTER SIXTEEN

THE WALLS OF PARLAY

The roast goat was delicious.

Jesse, I saw at once, had saved the prime chops not for Silky but for me. He knew where he needed to gain favor; he was more astute than I had given him credit for. And while a nice piece of goat wasn't going to get him my permission to court Silky, I admired the effort—and the juiciness of the chop too.

We set out a few hours before dawn. I, in my veil, rode Jasmine, and Jesse rode Silky's mount, the one we had stolen from Garth. Niamh and Silky wore veils and sat sedately on the stocky ponies that the man had left the day before.

"Jesse will do the talking," said Niamh. "He's big and, more importantly, male."

Silky frowned.

Niamh and Jesse were in the lead, but Niamh soon dropped back to be with me, and Silky, on her coarse little pony, left the two of us in conversation and rode up to Jesse. I watched as Jesse edged his horse closer to Silky's. It was neatly done.

"My son likes your sister," said Niamh.

"I'm going to have to chaperone if he rides any closer to her," I said.

Niamh sighed. "You know, Angel," she said, "you can relax with me. My whole life is given over to making sure bad matches aren't forced on anyone, especially the young."

"The young are quite capable of making bad choices on their own," I said.

Niamh laughed briefly. We rode in silence for a while. From time to time Niamh turned in her saddle and looked back.

"Are you expecting someone?" I asked.

"I'm expecting pursuit."

"If soldiers were after us on this road," I said, "we'd have been taken by now."

"That's what worries me," she said. "That soldier said the house was under suspicion. Yet I saw no soldiers there this morning—we rode out of there as easily as if we were innocents taking the country air."

"Maybe we were just lucky," I said.

"Oh, Angel," said Niamh. "There is no such thing as luck."

We traveled two nights, sleeping roughly. When I made it clear that I expected Jesse to sleep at the perimeter, Niamh raised an eyebrow.

"Jesse knows how to behave," she said. "We've traveled with women a lot more afraid of men than you are."

"I'm not afraid," I said. "He can eat with us if he chooses." Silky's eyes went wide, and I knew she was remembering Trey's sleeping next to the fire and the Bard's sharing of food with us.

But she would never undermine anything I said.

Five hours into the third day, I saw a shimmer on the horizon. Soon a city seemed to rise out of the plain.

"The walls of Parlay," said Niamh. "We'll get as close as we can and then wait for dusk to approach the gates. There's a big bustle to get in at night. We shouldn't be noticed."

We stopped a good distance from the city walls and grazed the horses in the shadows cast by a small copse of trees. While Jesse groomed first his horse and then Niamh and Silky's ponies, I brushed the sweat off Jasmine. In the process, I transferred a lot of horsehair to myself. As I was trying to pick it off, I caught Jesse staring.

"I was going to groom your horse, Lady Angel," he said.

"No need," I said. I wanted nothing from Jesse, not goat chops, not horse grooming. The truth was that he couldn't possibly have groomed Jasmine even if I had asked him to. She wouldn't have tolerated him.

Jasmine hated men. She wouldn't have let him near her. Trey was the only occasional exception.

It seemed that evening would never come. I couldn't help but wonder if Trey and the Bard might be waiting at the entrance to the city, and that thought filled me with anxiety even as it filled me with hope. Finally the afternoon waned and evening set in. We mounted our horses and rode up to the great gates of Parlay.

They were enormous, taller than the gates of our House, and carved with intricate scenes of hunting, and gardens, and nobility with hawks on their hands, and scenes of battle and, at the bottom left of the door, a merry group of skeletons engaged in a dance of death.

The guards on either side were watching. They ignored most of the people, although some of them they greeted by name; others were pulled aside and questioned. But no one was denied entrance, and the guards barely glanced at those departing. I took note of that. Eventually, after all, we were going to have to get out.

It didn't help, though, that one of the guards was a traditionalist.

"Step it up, Lordling," he called to Jesse. "You slow the crowd."

"My sisters aren't used to riding," Jesse said.

"That's a nice horse," said the traditionalist guard as he looked over Jasmine with an experienced eye.

"My sister rides one of my best," said Jesse. "I'm taking her to her groom."

"I wish her happiness," said the guard politely.

"It will be a joyous day," said Jesse steadily.

Apparently I shouldn't have worried about the traditionalist guard. It was a good cover story and well delivered.

Jesse annoyed me.

I focused on the city of Parlay as it opened up in front of us. The streets were full of people, of colors and scents and movement, and the horses, even the staid, coarse little ponies, became nervous. Luckily, the crowd split in front of us as we negotiated the main street. Horses clearly had right of way.

Jesse eventually found an inn near the gate. It was set back from the main thoroughfare and built up against the wall surrounding the city. The innkeeper welcomed us and gave us two rooms—one for Jesse, and a women's room for the rest of us. Niamh and Silky and I went to our room in silence—it would have looked strange if we had done anything else.

"We'll wait two days," said Niamh as we began settling in. "If we haven't found your traveling companions by then, I'll take you to Arcadia. You'll find a life in a corner of your country somewhere. It's not safe to linger here."

"There's nothing for me in Arcadia anymore," I said.

Niamh looked at me sadly.

"You don't know how much that 'nothing' is, Angel," she said. "You have no idea."

Niamh had given us good used clothing when we were at her house, and now we pulled the excess out of the saddlebags and draped it on the bed to air. Then, careful to use the women's staircase, we went down to the public room, where Jesse was waiting.

"We're family," he told the innkeeper, and we were allowed to sit together in the small, airless room. At one of the other tables, a man and a branded woman wearing marriage bracelets sipped at tall glasses of water. We spoke of the weather until they left.

When they did, we confronted a problem I hadn't foreseen: neither Silky nor Niamh nor I had freedom of movement. Jesse, of course, could move around as he wished, but he had no idea what Trey or the Bard looked like.

"Your companions may be hiding in places women can't go," said Jesse. "Let me ask around. Perhaps your Bard friend has been plying his trade."

"The Bard's not my friend," I said sharply. "He's a bard."

"Go, Jesse," said Niamh. "But be mindful."

Jesse went out into the streets. We had no choice but

to return to the women's bedroom, where Silky and I couldn't stop fidgeting. Even Niamh couldn't sit still.

"We should rest," she said. But none of us were resting.

"Can't we at least go downstairs?" asked Silky.

"We could go and eat in the women's public room," said Niamh. "I'll tell the innkeeper's wife to let us know when Jesse returns."

It was, I suddenly thought, an excellent idea.

I waited until we were all veiled up and impenetrable to the male view. As Niamh opened the door to leave, I sat down abruptly on the bed, pushed away the clothing we had set out and lay down.

"I don't feel well," I said.

"What is it?" asked Silky.

"My shoulder."

"Your wound?" Silky asked. Her voice was subdued, and I was sorry to give her worry. Niamh knelt by the bed and looked closely at me.

"It hurts," I said. "And I feel so hot."

"That was *sudden*," said Silky.

Niamh's face showed only concern, but Silky was giving me The Look. As children we had not infrequently faked fevers to get out of unwanted tasks.

"Perhaps it's my childhood sickness," I said, and I saw understanding blossom on Silky's face.

"Are you *sure*?" she asked, but she wasn't asking me how I felt. She was asking me if I needed assistance with my lie.

"I'm sure, Silky," I said.

"Your wound could be *infected*," she said helpfully.

"Show me," said Niamh. I bared my shoulder, and she probed it with skilled fingers. I flinched. The pain never really went away.

"No oozing," she said. "No infection or swelling. I've never seen a wound this large so smoothly and thoroughly healed. A hole this big should have killed you for a dozen reasons. Infection. Blood loss."

"Garth cauterized it," said Silky.

"Impossible," said Niamh.

"Angel was *really* brave," said Silky. "When she passed out, she did it *very* quietly."

Niamh looked at me as if her perception of me had changed in some way.

"I'm going to sleep," I said. "I just need some rest."

"We'll bring you food," said Niamh. "You can't go out of this room alone—one wrong turn, and you might end up in the men's section. It's not safe."

"All right."

I lay there until they left. Silky turned back for a moment before they went out the door and looked at me with concern. She knew I was up to something.

As soon as they were gone, I went to the door and opened it a crack.

I saw Niamh and Silky at the end of the corridor about to take the stairs. Quickly I changed into riding clothes and braided my hair like a traditionalist. It was so unlikely that a Shibbeth woman would dress like a man that I was sure I could get away with it. I crept down the stairs and slipped outside.

The bustle in the streets almost knocked me over. Earlier, as a woman on a horse, people had given me more room. Now I was hemmed in, and the bright sun, the number of people, the greens and blues and reds and purples of 'Lidan garb confused me. It took me a moment to figure out the direction of the great gate.

As I moved through the crowds toward the gate, a plump woman wearing a veil and carrying a basket of purple turnips knocked me off balance. I stepped in a horse pile and almost went down just as three or four horsemen rode by—perilously close to me. A big man with a gruff voice pulled me out of the street by my arm.

"Watch yourself," he said, and was gone.

So when I saw a lone horseman coming, my first thought was to back up to the wall—but my way was blocked by an orange-seller. The horseman came so close that the man's stirrup was inches away from my head. I tried to step back, and, as I did, I looked up into his face.

Our eyes met.

And it didn't matter that I was in man's garb with my hair done in the 'Lidan traditionalist way, or that I was darkened by the sun and by the dust and dirt and grime of our journey. It didn't matter that the last place the horseman might have expected to see me in was Shibbeth. None of it mattered.

He would have known me anywhere.

"Angel," he said. Then he reached down his arm, and I grabbed his wrist, and a moment later he had pulled me up and into the saddle.

It was my father.

My father urged the horse to a trot, and the pedestrians in front of us scattered like geese, swearing, a few of them letting out screams, some shaking fists at us. Then my father took a narrow street that branched off to the left, and, when we were alone, he pulled up his horse.

"I'm not going to have you executed," he said. "Although given that you've come with me, I assume you've guessed that."

I had. With Kalo by his side, he was capable of almost anything, but alone with me, he was a different person.

"Will you help me?" I asked.

He sighed. "I don't know," he said. "You're certainly not safe here in Shibbeth, and especially not in Parlay. Kalo's estates aren't far from here, and he's in the city now. Leth told him you took the Great North Way. And everyone seems to be looking for you regardless—they say you killed a Lord of Shibbeth."

"It was mostly an accident," I said.

"Angel," he said, "if anyone could find trouble, it would be you. I make you a perfectly nice marriage, and you run off with Trey, a man not even related to you by blood. If you'd only waited, I might have sorted out your contract to Leth."

"Sorted it out?" I found it hard to believe what I was

hearing. "Father, you were allowing Kalo to dispose of me as he saw fit."

He avoided my challenge as if I hadn't spoken.

"Your will should have been subjugated for the family's good."

I felt angry, and I felt confused, too. Nothing he wished was supposed to anger me, but the old protocol of a daughter's absolute obedience to her father seemed like part of another life. I realized that I had begun, in very small ways, to live by other rules.

"You never subjugated Mother's wishes," I said, touching on forbidden territory. "The village still speaks of it."

Pain twisted his face. But only for a moment.

"We won't speak of your mother."

"We never do," I said. "Maybe we should. You mourn her endlessly, but you're indifferent to her living daughters."

"You've changed, Angel," he said. "You're not speaking as an obedient child—but I will answer you in this: I am not indifferent to you or to Silky." He looked thoughtful. "Perhaps this can be mended, even now."

"After traveling with Trey?"

"Someone might take you."

The words stung. And yet I felt exhilaration, too, because the conversation had veered completely away from formula. Normally fathers and daughters never—never—spoke truths to each other. There was only obedience and submission. Now I couldn't back away from truth.

"I'm not interested in 'someone,'" I said. "And I might as well tell you that I never loved Leth."

"Of course you didn't love Leth," said my father. "You don't love anybody—I know enough to see that. And you were perfectly happy with the marriage before you ran off with Trey. The Nesson contract was a good one." He sounded nostalgic. "All that land."

"Father," I said. "We'll never understand each other."

"Daughters aren't meant to understand fathers."

With that, my father let me slip off the horse and then dismounted. We walked down the empty street together. He was leading the horse; it was almost, after his harsh words, as if we were walking companionably, and I felt sorry for this man who lived in eternal mourning. I took his arm.

"Why are you in Parlay?" I asked.

"I'm here with Kalo," said my father. "I don't have the troops to go against him. You picked a bad place to be."

"I'm going north."

"I suppose you're going after *The Book of Forbidden Wisdom*. After all those years of denials and silence—of lying to me. Of saying you didn't know anything about it. Really, Angel. And I suppose you're mixed up with that bard too," said my father. "Kalo suspected it, but he couldn't prove anything. And, of course, it's bad luck to execute a bard."

"You know about the Bard?"

"You *are* mixed up with him," said my father. He frowned at me.

I simply asked, "Where is he?"

My father sighed.

"He was taken up by Kalo's men this morning, but he denied knowing anything about Trey or Silky. Or you."

"But where is he?"

"Do you even have a real plan, Angel?"

"If I find *The Book*, I'll return to Arcadia."

"I see. But you'll still be considered a harlot."

"I'll marry Trey if I have to."

"If you have to?"

"I'll marry Trey. I want to." I didn't sound convincing even to myself.

"You've gone too far down your own path, Angel," said Father. "I'm going to leave you now. I have to meet Kalo—he's become demanding and peremptory. But I'll say nothing about you to him. It's the best I can do. If you're caught, there's nothing I can do."

"Father—"

"I'm sorry, Angel," he said. "I hope you find *The Book* and come home in triumph. But I wouldn't count on it."

"Mother told me a time like this would come." I looked at my father's eternal mourning clothes. "She would want me to do this."

"She would want you safe," he said. "But now we need to speak of Kalo. Kalo likes public punishments. He probably put your bard in the stocks."

"I wish you wouldn't call him 'my bard,' Father."

"You're not denying it, though." He paused. "But, Angel, a bard?"

"He's a very good bard."

Suddenly Father laughed. "Of course you're mocking me," he said. "And perhaps I deserve it. Kalo's thoughts about your association with a bard are ridiculous—I realize that now that I see you. A Great Lady traveling with a bard! Really. You almost had me believing it, Angel."

And there we parted, I thought probably forever. My father rode away as I stood there. He looked back once. He was weak and fickle and strange. But he looked back once.

The stocks.

I didn't know where the stocks were, so I went in the direction the great crowd was moving in—men on foot, horses, litters with the insignias of Great Houses on them, scantily dressed peasants, freemen with their coarsely spun brown clothes. I listened.

It was two freemen who, out of a hundred conversations, spoke words that meant something to me. I was yards from them, but they might as well have been speaking directly into my ears.

"I prefer whipping," said the one with a cap.

"Over too soon," said the other, who had a ginger beard. "And there's only watching—no perticerpating. Give me the stocks for throwing garbage and doing a little poking and teasing with water promises. Perti-cerpation is best."

"I like to see blood," said Cap.

"Then throw something hard," said Beard. "Anyway, they have a bard in there now. I'll bet we can make him sing."

"What's he in for?"

"Vagrancy. Stealing. Corrupting women who should be at home instead of listening to bards. Singing out of tune. Who knows with a bard? He's been in since yesterday, and he should be pretty prime about now."

"If he's alive," said Cap.

"If that," agreed Beard. "But they usually is. Even if they can only crawl for a while when they're set free. It's not like whipping. Whipping does them in, often as not, and I don't much like the killing."

Beard went up in my esteem.

I followed them, and they went in the direction of the general crowd, which seemed to be converging on some sort of marketplace.

The stocks were in the center of the market square. There were two of them, and one was empty. The other held a man whose head was bowed with weariness.

It was, of course, the Bard.

I came to a dead stop; I was unable to move, and people streamed around me. A woman with a chicken in a cage bumped into me and almost knocked me over. I could see fragments of rotten vegetables and small stones around the base of the stocks. Then the Bard raised his head and looked out at the crowd with empty eyes. There was no intelligence in them; I could see that the life in him was ebbing away. As I watched him, all of the titles that caste demanded Arcadians use with one another—titles that kept the castes distant from one another—faded from my mind.

"Oh, Renn," I said.

I had never before called him by his name.

CHAPTER SEVENTEEN

THE STOCKS

I moved with the crowd until I could see Renn's parched lips and his red-rimmed, vacant eyes.

The stocks were evil devices that did not allow for sleep or movement—they pressed knees against the cobblestones for hours and hours and stiffened the legs and neck—sometimes forever. Many of those who were put in the stocks were left crippled, most in body, some in mind. And a particularly raucous crowd could abruptly end the occupant's life by throwing rocks instead of garbage.

The two freemen, Cap and Beard, inspected Renn closely.

"He don't look good," said Beard.

"He gets out tonight," said Cap.

"If he lives."

"Don't matter," said Cap. "Dead or alive, they'll leave him in till sunset. Want to throw something?"

Beard considered. Finally he spoke. "No," he said. "When I were a lad, I loved them bards, in tune or not. I could almost give him water myself."

"Don't be soft," said Cap.

They moved away. I wanted to reward Beard. I wanted Cap to be struck down by lightning.

Renn's hair was matted with vegetable matter and blood. His face was ashen—and there were hours to go until sunset.

He raised his head.

The crowd began to heckle him, and I realized that they perceived his raised head as a kind of rebellion. Maybe it was.

A potato flew toward Renn's head but missed and hit the stocks. Laughter and jeers from the crowd.

Put your head down, I thought. *Put your head down.*

He put his head down, and the crowd soon lost interest once more. The market was next to the stocks, and there were vegetables and chickens and ducks to buy and cloth to look at and more interesting things to do than harass an obviously broken man.

I went to the village water pump. I soaked my outer shirt so I could clean his face. I had no jug or jar to put water in, but I found I could cup water tightly in my hands.

Then I crossed what seemed to be a forbidden zone—although there were no guards—and knelt down next to Renn. He jerked as if to move from a threat. I couldn't say anything; I lifted my cupped hands to his mouth. His eyes were now on mine, and I saw to my relief that there was no madness in them, although there was no recognition either.

He licked the water out of my hands as best he could with his swollen tongue. I had never been that intimate with a man. I squeezed the water from my shirt onto his lips and wiped the blood and refuse from his face. He was trying to say something, but it was hard to make out what. I pushed his hair back out of his eyes, and I put my ear next to his mouth.

"Go away," he said.

The members of the crowd had moved in closer now. They were disgruntled.

"That man gave him water," a boy called out.

"Better leave it," said the woman with him. "He's a traditionalist."

I made my face expressionless as I walked into the thick of the crowd. Most of them looked afraid of me, and I wondered at a place like Shibbeth, where people feared mercy more than torment.

I saw him in the shadow of the column that marked the center of the market square.

Trey.

I made my way to him. Trey looked down at my small form with alarm.

"Trey," I said. "It's Angel."

His response surprised me. He touched my chin, tilted up my face and looked into my eyes. His touch was really no more improper than any of the dozens of rules he and I had already broken, but a shock ran through my body. I felt it all: sorrow and anxiety and suddenly both exhilaration and joy. I felt, too, Trey's longing. I had been afraid of that longing for so long; I had tried to deny it even after the rescue. Finally, now, I began to understand what he felt for me.

But there was no time to think. No time to feel.

"Angel?" said Trey.

"I found Silky," I said. "We're safe. We need to free Renn."

He raised his eyebrows at my use of the Bard's name, but all he said was, "They won't release him until sunset."

"We'll need a horse to get him away from the square when the time comes, then," I said.

"Squab and Bran are in the wide gully outside the gate," said Trey. "We can use Squab to carry Renn. Angel, I—"

"We have a sturdy animal," I said. "Easier to use him. Even Squab has a little too much breeding for this job. He'll call attention."

"I didn't know if you and Silky were alive," said Trey. "I thought they might have taken you—branded you."

"But you waited for us," I said.

"I'll always wait for you, Angel." He was upset. "No one hurt you?"

I thought of my shoulder.

"No."

I told Trey more before I went back to the inn to face the fury of Niamh and Jesse and, what I dreaded most, the wrath of Silky.

"I was *sick* with worry," Silky said.

"I'm sorry."

"I really mean I was *sick*. I threw up on Niamh. Next time, take me. Where you go, *I* go."

The sun was low in the sky when I returned to the square with Jesse. Trey looked Jesse over carefully; apparently he passed inspection.

Renn's face was once more bloody, and, as the time came close for his release, the crowd seemed to become interested again. They threw rotting vegetables from the market's refuse pit and yelled obscenities.

But they didn't kill him.

At sunset, the soldiers unlocked the stocks. When they released Renn, he crawled forward into the garbage people had thrown at him all day and then fell on his side.

Before I could move, a man from across the square went toward Renn. I tensed, but Trey put a warning hand on my arm. The man carried a water skin, which he held to Renn's lips. Renn tried to gulp down the water, and I could see that the stranger was trying to slow him down.

I couldn't wait any longer. I left Jesse and Trey holding the pony, and I hurried over to Renn.

"Thanks, friend," I said to the man and gently disentangled his arm. "We'll take him now."

"He be a bard," said the man. "Renn of Arcadia. I seen and heard him before."

"I'll take care of him," I said.

"I thought traditionalists be not liking bards."

"We just don't like it when they sing out of tune," I said. "Why are you helping?"

The man looked almost ashamed. "I heard this one right here sing the Tree ballads once. He made me weep." He leaned forward confidentially. "Shame to hurt a bard."

"You're a good man," I said.

It was impossible for Renn to sit a horse, so we ended up hoisting him onto the animal's back like a bag of flour. The stranger helped. Renn made no sound.

"Good luck to you then," the stranger said. "I hope someday I hear him sing again. Maybe The Taken. I never heard a real good bard sing The Taken." And with that, the man blended back into the crowd.

Renn's head, since he was slung across the pony, was even with my neck. I looked at him now and saw that he was watching me.

"Angel," he said.

"You're going to be all right," I said. Trey was looking at us, and I felt myself flush.

"You should," Renn said to me, "have gone away." His voice was hoarse.

"I did. Now I'm back." And my heart opened a little.

"Angel," he said. "Lovely name. Mustn't say so. The Lady Angel."

"Renn," I said. "It's Angel. Just Angel. I've been stupid."

"Angel."

The light was dimming fast. A woman from the market came close and pressed some bread into Jesse's hand. An herbalist from the market left his stall to pass Lorsum leaves and Calla powder to me. Lorsum dulled pain so that stiff muscles and tendons could be stretched out. Calla was a stimulant.

I had been ready to dismiss all 'Lidans, but I had been wrong.

"Angel?" Renn's voice surprised me.

"Yes," I said. "I'm here."

"All right," he said.

Together we moved down the street.

CHAPTER EIGHTEEN

REUNION

When we reached the inn on our way to the gate, Jesse went in to get Niamh and Silky. They were heavily veiled. Meanwhile Jesse, Trey and I managed to get Renn upright in the saddle. No guard would have let us go unquestioned through the gate with a man slung across the pony like a sack of grain.

"Move on," said the bigger of the guards as we approached the gate. He pointed at Renn. "We don't want that one dying here. It'd block the traffic for hours."

And so we left Parlay unchallenged.

It seemed to me almost a little too easy.

Once out of sight of the gate, Renn slumped forward, his cheek against the horse's neck, his arms hanging down.

"He doesn't look good," said Jesse.

"He'll be fine," I said. I gave Jasmine to Silky and added the herbs the man at the market had given me to a skin of water. I knew the strong stimulant would tax Renn's system, but he had to drink it if he was going to be able to ride. Trey and I pushed Renn up into the saddle again so that he could drink.

We moved on.

"We're camped in a deep niche of the oasis," said Trey. "We need to run the gauntlet to get back to the horses."

"What do you mean 'run the gauntlet'?" I asked.

"You'll see," said Trey.

We moved beyond the edge of the oasis that Parlay was built on, and I soon understood what Trey had meant. The gully near the oasis was a kind of haven for the disenfranchised—those who had been denied entry to Parlay and had nowhere else to go. The diseased and the criminal, the mad and the starving subsisted on what they could by the side of a fetid brackish rivulet.

A man made a move toward us, and I saw with horror that his face had been partially eaten away, but Jesse—strong, young and healthy—glared at him until he returned to his tiny camp. A woman there, her face marked as his was, pushed at him and began to weep.

We passed a dancing madman who whirled and swooped and spooked the horses, all but the staid pony conveying Renn.

A little farther on, close to the path, three women who were cooking something over a small fire stared as we passed. One of them stood and started to walk toward us. She wore no veil, and neither did those back at her small camp. One of the other women caught hold of her arm, seemingly to stop her, but she came right up to us.

"I be no beggar," she said, using some of the old-style speech. "We need food. We be desperate." She suddenly caught at Jesse's arm. "It be too late for us. You understand? We have no money for food. We trade."

Jesse shook her off, but not unkindly. To my surprise, he reached into one of the saddlebags and gave her some dried fruit.

"If you sell yourself," he said, "you just start the long spiral down into darkness."

"The choices are gone, Lord," said the woman.

"There are always choices," said Jesse to the woman.

"You're young," she said. She paused, as if afraid of going too far. "And you be a man."

She tucked away the food and looked sad—and a little bitter.

"Go to The Village of Broken Women," said Jesse.

The Village of Broken Women. Our passage back into Arcadia, to the Spiral City—a place of the northern territories.

"They have Arcadian ways there," said the woman. "We be 'Lidan women."

Jesse leaned very close to her, and she drew in her breath, as if afraid. But he did not touch her.

"You've lived like 'Lidan women," he said. "But you don't have to die like them. If you won't go to The Village of Broken Women, wait some weeks' time and go to Niamh at Negreb. She'll take you somewhere safe." He didn't look directly at Niamh, but she nodded.

"I thank you," said the woman.

She turned and went back to her little camp. I could see the other two women exclaiming over the food. They made gestures of reverence toward Jesse.

"What just happened?" I asked. "I don't think I understand."

"I *know* I don't," said Silky.

Jesse, Trey and Renn were silent. It was Niamh who spoke.

"They've been violated," she said. "Probably by the guards at the gate, who will no longer let them in because now they're harlots. No veils anymore. She offered Jesse sex for food. He tried to send her to safety. That's it."

"But why—"

"There are no whys," said Niamh. "Women can't travel alone in Shibbeth in safety—not in small numbers, and certainly not women of low caste."

"There were three of them."

"And no men."

Soon we passed a group of four roasting a giant ox heart over a fire. Their eyes were intent on it as juice dripped into the fire, and I wondered how they had gotten it—until the smell reached me. The meat was bad. They had probably scavenged the heart from a pile of butcher's offal, and now they were going to risk poisoning themselves in order to live a little longer.

Renn became more and more alert as the herbs coursed through his blood. Trey was on the other side of the pony, leading it, and the others followed, so only I noticed that Renn was also becoming freer in speech—a side effect of the stimulant.

"Lady Angel?"

"Renn, are you really going to call me Lady Angel again?"

"No. *And* I like that you're calling me Renn." Alert as he seemed, he almost fell off the pony.

"Is he all right?" asked Trey from the other side.

"Yes," I said. I helped Renn sit up.

"I like your hair in a braid," he said softly.

"Thank you, Renn."

We had left the path as we made our way to the niche Trey and Renn had found in the gully, and I saw no more people. We had left behind those pitiful cast-offs of Parlay.

Except that we were castoffs, too.

Abruptly, a figure like a scarecrow stepped out of the darkness; he held Crop Ear by a frayed rope loosely hung around the horse's neck. The scarecrow figure glanced at Renn and then addressed himself to Trey.

"I done what you asked, Lord," he said.

"Squab and Bran?" asked Trey.

"All's well, Lord."

"Take this for your trouble." Trey reached into a pocket, and I saw the glint of silver. "As well as our food gift."

"No point, Lord," said the man. "There be nothing here to buy. Nothing but food's worth anything."

"You've kept our bargain; you'll feast tonight."

"Yes, Lord." And the man vanished into the shadows, taking Crop Ear with him.

"Crop Ear?" groaned Renn.

"I'm sorry," said Trey.

"That horse—carried me far."

"That horse will keep at least one family alive. For a while."

"Trey," said Silky, "you *didn't*."

He gave her a little smile. "Dinner on the hoof."

"Trey," I said, "that's too much information for Silky."

Moments later we found ourselves reunited with Squab and Bran, and Silky spent a long time stroking Squab.

Silky was sentimental about horses, but less so about small edible game. We were all hungry, but we were low on food until Silky went to the nearest out-cropping to see what she could find. Guarded by Jesse, she killed an enormous rock hyrax.

We built a fire, and we ate stewed rock hyrax, and I have to say—it was pretty good.

Jesse made his bed at the perimeter and then came and sat by Silky's side. I saw surprise on his face when he realized how close to the fire Trey's bedding was, but Jesse made no requests to move far-ther into camp. Perhaps he thought I would refuse him. Perhaps I would have. Renn lay on a blanket near Niamh, who was making a poultice for him. Trey and I were side by side. He smiled at me, and his hand hovered over mine for a moment, but he didn't touch me.

"We can't stay here much longer," said Trey after a little while. "Those people out there are drawing closer and closer to the camp. It's only a matter of time before enough of them gather and attempt to overrun us."

"Should we go *now*?" Silky was alarmed, but I knew that travel would badly overtax Renn.

"The earliest we can leave is tomorrow," said Trey. "We'd never get out of this gully at night—but if we keep the fire up and keep good watch, we have a chance to make it until morning."

"A *chance*?" said Silky.

"A good chance, Lady Silky," said Jesse.

I closed my eyes the way I sometimes did when my mother's face would come to me, or when, sometimes, the future seemed near, so very near, and I thought that, yes, we would survive the night. I'm not sure it was foresight, but it was a feeling that had never failed me. I opened my eyes.

"We'll be all right," I said to Silky.

"But where do we go then?" Trey was looking at me.

"North. To the Spiral City. To *The Book of Forbidden Wisdom*."

Trey laughed. "Either there, or eventually we'll just fall off the top of the world."

"What's *The Book of Forbidden Wisdom*?" asked Jesse. We all stared at him.

"It's a key," I said.

"The key to more Arcadian land than you can possibly imagine," said Trey.

"I don't know," said Jesse. "I can imagine a lot."

"Me too," said Silky, and they smiled at each other like idiots.

So we prepared to stay the night. My words. My plan. My choice. If we had left at that moment, it's possible that everything would have turned out differently. It might have. But I saw the six of us live through the night, and I chose to stay. I didn't yet know much about near misses and last chances or actions that could never be mended. But even if I had known, it might not have made any difference.

CHAPTER NINETEEN

RAID

We were attacked just before dawn.

A ragged crew of ten or so men swarmed into our camp, overrunning the perimeter before we could react. One of them grabbed the rock hyrax stewpot from over the fire. He howled in triumph until another man tried to wrest it from his arms, and the entire contents flowed onto the ground.

Both men raised their heads, seemingly in unison, and the setting moon revealed them to us.

They had no faces. Slits for eyes and a hole for a mouth and everything else a red broth of disease.

For an instant, none of us could move, then Silky ran for the horses. I cried out "No," but I was too late. One of the men grabbed her by the hair and started to drag her behind the rock that marked the outer limit of our camp. I don't remember raising my crossbow or fitting a bolt to it, but I do remember my hands shaking as I took aim. Niamh was at my elbow.

"You can do it," she said.

I aimed for the man's chest, but the shot was far wide. I knew I was going to be too late, but in desperation I loaded another bolt and swung up the crossbow. Before I could take the shot, the man staggered and fell; a bolt protruded from what had been a face.

Jesse had saved my sister.

Silky ran to me through the crowd of men. She didn't weep or cower. She just took my crossbow and fit a bolt to it.

"Get back, Niamh, Angel," she said. The no-faces were among the horses now, and Silky had no easy target. I could tell that these men had no experience with the animals, though, and that was to our advantage. Jasmine snorted and whinnied, and then all of the horses were blowing and snorting and stamping their hooves. The moonlight was tricky, and the attacking men were weaving among the animals, but then I saw, all too vividly, one of them reach up with a curved knife and slice into the neck of Niamh's little coarse pony. Next to me, Silky aimed carefully. A moment later, the man with the knife fell backward. The wounded pony reared and shook his head, and blood scattered everywhere, further pushing the horses into frenzy. Another man grabbed Jasmine by her lead rope; Silky didn't hurry. As the man tried to control Jasmine, she carefully fit a new bolt to the crossbow and then dropped him.

Renn was on his feet fighting side by side with Trey. I had lost sight of Jesse. A man outside the circle of fire-light raised a crossbow and took careful aim at Trey.

I nudged Silky and pointed. A second later, her bolt hit his crossbow and drove it into his body.

"Give me a bolt," Silky cried. "Give me a bolt!" She fumbled in her bag and had one in her hand, when I pushed the crossbow down.

"Wait," I said. "They're leaving."

The faceless ones screamed with frustration as they backed away. The one who was nearest Trey spat in his face. Then they were gone.

The horses were still restless; the little coarse pony was on the ground, and its eye was cloudy. Blood pooled around its neck and head. Silky went among the horses and calmed them.

She turned her back as we began to butcher the pony. We were in such a hurry that I almost made a mess of it by puncturing the ropy intestine. Luckily Jesse pulled back my hand before the meat was pol-luted and useless. We wrapped huge chunks of flesh in oilskin and put them in the saddlebags. We had to leave a lot behind. The faceless ones would have their feast anyway.

I looked at Silky. She had killed three men in the

attack; I had seen the battle frenzy on her at the end. My little sister, who was charming and loyal and intelligent and beautiful, was also marred by bloodguilt— which she had incurred in order to save all of us. My precious, feckless sister was friends with death.

We made camp that next night miles from the gully and Parlay. There was nothing left of the rock hyrax, so we ate some dried fruit and as much of the dead pony as we could. The meat wouldn't keep for long. Even Silky ate her share.

It was there that Niamh told us she was going back to her work in Shibbeth.

"You *can't* go," said Silky. "Alone? *Bad things* will happen."

"I've traveled here before. There's a village an hour this side of Parlay," she said. "Jesse can get me there. Then I'll reach home with a convoy of women."

"Jesse will go with you?" asked Silky.

"In fact, " she said, "I'm hoping you'll give us half a day—so he can return. I'm hoping you'll take Jesse with you. Shibbeth shouldn't be his home forever. And eventually I'll make my way to Arcadia too."

"Of course, Niamh," I said. "We owe you a great debt."

"We'll miss you," said Silky, but she was looking at Jesse. I thought, perhaps gracelessly, that our debt to Niamh only went so far. I didn't owe her my sister.

"We'll meet again," said Niamh, and she gave me a small smile as if, perhaps, she could read my mind and found what was there amusing.

I slept fitfully the night before Niamh's departure. I woke up, wide awake, in the late night or early morning. The fire was only coals. I could hear the breathing of the sleepers. Trey was lying by the fire, and he seemed to be rubbing at his face. For one shocked moment I thought he might be crying, but then he gave a low sigh and began breathing deeply.

Renn, ever since we had left Parlay, had been sleeping by the fire as well. Only Jesse steadfastly remained modestly at the perimeter. Now I saw that Renn was sitting outside the circle of light. He was holding his lyre and silently testing the tautness of the strings.

"Renn?" I spoke softly.

"Angel." He didn't look up.

"Are you still in pain?"

"Mostly wakeful."

"Me too."

"I know. I heard you stirring. Come over, Lady Angel."

I considered. I thought that perhaps I should wake Silky to chaperone, but she needed her sleep.

It was important she get her sleep.

"All right," I said. "I'll join you."

I pulled on my overcoat, walked to the other side of the fire and sat next to Renn. Even as I sat, I realized that I had misjudged the distance between us. I was close, very close. But I didn't want to hurt his feelings by moving away—now, though, I wished I had woken Silky.

"You know," he said, "you're far different from that almost-bride I saw in Arcadia. I misjudged you."

"I misjudged you too."

"Maybe." He put down his lute. "You look cold."

"I am cold."

He moved his arm and put a blanket around me, and, in so doing, his arm brushed my shoulders. It couldn't have been for more than a part of a second, but I was very aware of his touch.

"Renn," I said. "I wish you were my brother." But I was saying something that wasn't true.

"You have enough men who are brothers to you," he said.

In the bright dawn, Niamh left us with Jesse by her side.

When he returned, he looked tired and sad, and I wondered what it must be like to say good-bye to a mother.

"He needs someone to talk to," said Silky. "I'm going to *comfort* him."

"No," I said. "You're not."

We packed up camp and mounted. Silky and I rode bareback together on Jasmine. The wind was brisk, and I tied back my hair with some string.

"I still don't understand," said Jesse, "what we're going to do with this *Book of Forbidden Wisdom*."

"Anything we want," I said. "Anything at all."

As we rode, Trey kept rubbing at his cheeks and

forehead, the way he had when I awoke in the night. At one moment, as we were in an extended trot, he dropped the reins and pulled at his face. Bran halted immediately, as a well-bred horse would, and Trey almost went over his horse's shoulder.

"What is it?" I asked. "Did something sting you?"

"I don't know," he said.

"Is there a swelling?"

"No."

I looked at him sharply. We were all halted, and Silky, who had been lagging behind and chattering with Jesse, came up on us abruptly.

"*Trey*," she exclaimed. "Your face is so *red*."

It looked as if he had a touch of sunburn. Or was overheated.

"Have some water," I said. "Sprinkle it on your face."

At midday we came to an enormous well-known Shibbeth market, where we had planned to buy more supplies. There was a livery at the entrance of the market where, for a few coins, we could keep our horses while we looked around and made our purchases. A small, wiry man with a cast eye and long, dirty hair came to take them. I remembered the stories I had heard about those who carried the cast eye—it could see beyond; it could mean evil; it could be luck. But this man just looked the horses over appraisingly and raised his eyebrows as he examined Jasmine. When he saw Bran, he exhaled slowly, in deep appreciation.

"How much for the bay?" he asked.

"He's not for sale," said Trey.

"Everything here is for sale," said the man.

"Not my horse," said Trey. "But we might be in the market for one."

"What kind?" asked the man, "well-bred or grade?"

"Grade," said Trey.

"Riding horse or pack?"

"Ready for either and able on long distances."

"I have what you need," said the man. He led the horses away.

"Can we trust him?" asked Silky. "Look at his *hair*."

"We'll pay him after," I said. "And give him a good price for the new horse. Besides," I added, "*your* hair could do with a wash too."

We walked into the market, and I was suddenly in an ocean of smells and sounds. I was assailed by the stink of rotting cabbage, which was replaced by the pale fragrance of violets as a cart went by. We walked by huge overflowing bags of a rainbow of spices—yellow, red, orange, green. We saw mounds of vegetables and, where the butchers worked, carcasses of cows and goats. No sheep. The 'Lidans kept their sheep for their famous blue wool. In the fish stall, live eels slithered over tilapia and bass; there were, too, small fried fingerlings to be eaten by the handful.

"We need cured meat," said Renn. "Dried fruit as well. And some fresh vegetables for the next few days. We can get part of a goat for tonight."

We were in a hurry, so we split up. Trey and Jesse

went to the fruit and vegetable stalls, Renn, Silky and I to the butchers.

We were dickering over the haunch of a goat when I sensed restlessness in the market. A big woman in a red apron with a trout under her arm careened right into me and then was gone. The butcher stopped negotiations. He put the goat haunch in a hamper and began taking down carcasses and dragging them to the back.

"Come back later," he said. "After."

"After *what*?" Silky asked. Renn grabbed the butcher by the wrist.

"What's going on?"

The butcher pulled his hand away. "Raid, of course," he said. "Where are you from? It'll pass, if this is just a tithing. Come back." He lifted his eyes, looked startled and turned, disappearing into the darkness of his shop.

Silky and Renn and I looked behind us to see what had spooked the butcher.

I had feared I would see troops pulling down stalls or burning and killing, but instead I saw just three soldiers, one leading a packhorse, striding down the main path of the market. The men stopped now and again to take goods on display. They took their time at the spice stall, wrapping up handfuls of yellow saffron and red turmeric. One tucked a live chicken under his arm. Another grabbed a brace of ducks. Eventually they came to the end of the stalls, and although they upturned some of them, they did no lasting damage.

The market now looked deserted, and I wondered where so many people could go so quickly.

The soldiers scanned the area and then started toward the butcher's stall. The one in front who was leading the packhorse narrowed his eyes when he looked at Renn. He came closer. Then his eyes flicked from Renn to me and then to Silky.

That mass of golden hair. Distinctive, even though streaked and dirty.

"Get Silky out of here," I said softly to Renn, and he turned so that she was shielded from view.

"Hey!" I yelled. I overturned the butcher's stall, sending a stream of calves' heads, tongues and livers—the delicacies—onto the ground. Renn was alarmed, but I didn't have time to say anything—he had Silky; I had to distract the soldier. I jumped behind the fallen stall and ran back into the store, hoping there was an exit.

There was. The butcher had backed into a corner, a knife dangling halfheartedly from his hand. In Shibbeth, after all, using a weapon could mean death.

I relieved him of the knife.

Behind me the soldier came crashing through the shop, the other two trailing him.

"Stop her," he shouted. "She's an assassin."

"What?" The butcher sounded bewildered. I realized they were Garth's soldiers searching for their Lord's killer, not Kalo's men.

I was already out of the shop and into one of the smaller ways through the market, running for any kind of shelter. I turned my head just enough to see the lead guard pull bags from the packhorse and then mount.

He was going to hunt me down on horseback. The animal didn't look fast, but I was on foot.

I ran. Suddenly I was among the vegetable carts. I overturned a barrel of sand potatoes into the street, hoping to slow the horse. I looked for help, or a place to hide. I knew what was waiting for me in Shibbeth for killing Garth.

The horseman had made his way through the sand potatoes and was bearing down on me.

I couldn't outrun the horse. As horse and soldier came even with me, the man leapt from the animal and pushed me to the ground, where we became a confused tangle of limbs and bodies—and a knife.

Immediately blood was everywhere. The soldier released me, and for a moment we both looked down at the blood spurting out of his arm. It did so rhythmically, grotesquely, in time to the beating of his heart. Blood sprayed my face.

His face was greying, and his breath came in short pants. I pressed on the wound with one hand, and with the other I tore off the string that was tying back my hair. He saw what I was doing, and with one hand, my teeth and his good arm, we tied a tourniquet.

He held my arm for a moment, and I flinched at the touch.

"We've been following you, Lady Angel," he said. He released my arm.

There was something odd about his words. Who was following us? Garth's heir? Kalo? Leth?

This was no time for questions.

The packhorse had run on for a few more paces and then stopped. I did a running mount and was on the horse in a moment. For one second I looked back at the man who was down.

His face was paper white and his eyes dark. But he would probably live.

I looked up and scanned the market. The other two soldiers, seeing that their comrade hadn't taken me, were running in my direction. But the packhorse didn't seem to pick up on my anxiety. He was a patient mount. I turned him in a tight circle to see where the various lanes led—I had to get back to the others.

I thought of Dirty-Hair-Cast-Eye at the livery in the front of the market.

If the others thought about it at all, they would realize it was the one place where we might meet up—where we *had* to meet up to get the horses.

"Come on, horse," I said, and I gave a few low clucks. I noticed that more people had emerged from wherever they had been hiding.

I glanced back at the soldiers. They were bent over their fallen comrade.

I hoped they would loosen and then tighten the tourniquet. Otherwise, it was a good way to lose an arm.

We cantered. A woman appeared next to me, materializing out of nowhere. She must have been hiding among the boxes that held up her eggplant stall. In a moment the horse and I had passed her, but not before I heard her speak.

"Go, girl," she said.

I went.

The two soldiers were after me now, and they did not look as if they were going to let me escape. I galloped down a narrow lane, always aware that I needed to circle around the market in order to reach the livery and Dirty-Hair.

My chance came. I saw a place where a large wheelbarrow of carrots was overturned. It blocked the narrow lane.

I took my chance.

I knew nothing about this big old shambling packhorse I was riding, except that he was accepting of my presence on his back, and all his reactions had shown him to be a good-natured sort of a horse. So I asked him for a favor.

Never command a horse if you really want to get what you want.

Ask.

We turned and trotted back toward the soldiers. I could see the surprise on their faces. Then we turned again.

To say we flew down the lane would be exaggerating the horse's ability, but we were moving fast, and the wheelbarrow loomed large. I felt the big animal's hesitation; his ears flicked back and forth as he looked ahead and listened to my reassurances at the same time. As far as I knew, this big, clumsy horse had never jumped over anything in his life.

We were three strides away from the wheelbarrow, and now we were committed. There were only two ways to go.

Over.

Through.

If the horse didn't make it, if we went crashing into the obstacle, we would both go down.

There are all kinds of bardsongs about the hearts of champions. About the deep reserves that a truly well-bred horse can call on. I didn't know of any bardsongs about a workhorse having the heart of a champion.

One stride. I felt the horse gather himself. I urged him once more with my legs, and then we were in the air over the spilled carrots and the overturned wheelbarrow.

He cleared the wreckage with a foot of air beneath him.

It would be nice if I could say he landed as lightly as a feather, but it was more like riding a potential disaster in the making. I don't know how that horse got a foot down clear of the wheelbarrow, but he did, and when he did, we were in a flat-out gallop, and nobody was going to catch us.

Renn was going to have to write a new horse bard-song.

The lane I was on led to a shed. We galloped behind it, and three roads opened in front of me. I almost hesitated, but I was suddenly deep in the world where the future opened like a flower, and we didn't slow as we hurtled down the third.

Seconds later I was trying to pull up the horse, who had a mouth about as sensitive as an anvil. Then Dirty-Hair was there. He stood in front of the oncoming horse—where he mustered the courage, I don't know—and the animal stopped at his feet. He raised a hand and stroked the horse's mane up and down. No pat pat on the face or good-hearted slap on the neck. He stroked the horse the way mares lick newborn foals.

I'll never forget Dirty-Hair.

"Your friends are in the barn," he said. "Looks like you got that extra horse you was wanting."

"Yes—I—they're in the barn?"

"Waiting. The little girl's not happy."

"She's my sister."

"She's not happy. Be glad to see you is what I think. What I don't think is you want that horse I got you. Seems you found one yourself."

"Yes. I need to get to the others." And I rushed past him to the barn, leaving him to lead in the horse.

Renn met me in the doorway. The odor of alfalfa wafted out of the barn and seemed to settle on him.

"Angel." He put his hands on my shoulders, and I was so surprised by the touch that I forgot to pull away. "I thought they would capture you," he said. Still he didn't release me. He looked into my eyes, and I didn't think to look away or remove his hands or to step back.

Yet I was very aware that he shouldn't be touching me; he shouldn't be looking at me that intensely.

He leaned down. My heart was beating fast, and I was afraid. I was afraid of what I was feeling.

He put his lips to mine. This was called a kiss, and I didn't want it to end.

I was a fool. I vaguely hoped that Silky wasn't watching.

After, as I gazed over his shoulder, wound up with desire and exhilaration and fear and the exultation of having escaped, I saw a crack in the barn wall that let in a pencil of light. I thought nothing of it—until I followed the beam to the back of the barn, where it lighted Trey's green eyes.

Where he stood watching us, stunned.

CHAPTER TWENTY

DISEASE OF THE FLESH

I disentangled myself from Renn. Silky had been sitting with Jesse away from the door, and they had not witnessed my return. When Silky saw me, she ran into my arms.

"I'm glad you're all right, Angel," Trey said, coming forward, and for just a second I hated him for his generous words. Then he turned his back on me.

Feelings. I hated feelings. Trey had been right all along when he had said I loved the rules of Arcadia, and even some of those of Shibbeth. They kept me safe.

Dirty-Hair came in leading my newly stolen horse,

which looked more unprepossessing than ever. I walked away from the others and took the lead rope. It looked as if nobody had taken a brush to the animal in months, and his hair was matted down with sweat. I took a handful of the dirty, wet mass and pulled it right out.

"That's a *very* ugly horse, Angel," said Silky, coming up beside me. Jesse was with her.

Considering what I had asked of him, the horse looked pretty good. And I realized that this was an animal that worked every day of his life, which meant he had muscle and stamina. I noticed that he was slightly knock-kneed, but he couldn't help his looks. Dirty-Hair-Cast-Eye joined us.

"So you want the one you stole?" asked Dirty-Hair. "Or you want to buy one from me?"

"We'll take the one I stole," I said. Then I caught myself. "We'll take this one."

"You want a jumper, I got a good one," he said—with not much hope, I thought, of actually making a sale.

"This fellow jumped well enough at the right moment," I said. "It wouldn't be luck to leave him." With the word *luck,* I could see the discussion had ended. One did not take chances with luck in either Arcadia or Shibbeth.

There was a piercing whistle from the direction of the market.

"That be the signal," said Dirty-Hair. "There're more troops coming. But there's a trail under the trees, close to a mile from the back of the barn and to the north. The troops be not knowing it. If you have a care to avoid them."

He turned to me, and for a moment his cast eye moved in his head until he was looking at me directly. The effect was uncanny, and I thought again of the stories of those with a cast eye and the special vision it was supposed to lend them. Then I came down to earth. This man was a practical, fair (and unwashed) keeper of a livery, and he was probably going to say something about getting away, or our horses, or my choice of the big ugly chestnut.

What he said was "You don't know what you want, Great Lady. And you won't take what you need."

I immediately forgave him his forward speech because I could tell he was Seeing. I felt no evil in his words but a kind of gentle sympathy that was at odds with his earlier manner.

"What do I want?" I asked. "What do I need?"

He leaned forward. "What be in front of you, Lady."

He smiled, showing his bad teeth, and I saw that the words were over; he was himself again.

"I thank you for your speaking," I said formally, although I wished he had said more. Seeing beyond was well and good, but it wasn't, I knew from experience, always very *specific*.

"I fed your horses well," he said in his normal tone, and the cast eye was no longer fixed on me, and he seemed not to know anything about what he'd said.

We spoke a little longer, and then he walked away

and became one more person who passed through my life only to be gone forever.

Silky named our new horse Shamble on the spot.

"The perfect name," said Jesse. Of course he did.

We didn't gallop away in a whirlwind of dust. We picked up our customary jog and, taking a narrow path that passed the barn, soon found ourselves under trees. When we didn't hear any sounds of pursuit, we slowed to a walk. Single file, we wove in and out of the trees. A few soldiers might have been able to keep up with us, but not numbers.

I cast a glance at Trey, who was behind me. His face was a patchy grey and red, and he looked unwell.

We hadn't spoken since I had kissed Renn. There was no privacy while we were riding. Of course, according to Arcadian customs, there wasn't supposed to be any privacy to speak to a man. And there were no scripted public words for the kind of conversation I needed to have with Trey. In fact, I could think of no words at all to explain to him what had happened.

My heart must, I realized, be coming alive. Because it ached for Trey.

After all our time together, I had let Trey stand by while I kissed a man I barely knew—kissed him, on thought, quite thoroughly, and on *purpose*.

Dirty-Hair had said that what I wanted and needed was in front of me.

I wished he had narrowed things down a bit more.

At that moment, the trail petered out.

"What do we do, Angel?" asked Silky. She and Jesse were riding too closely together again. We would have to talk. I was glad she hadn't seen the kiss.

"We keep going," I said.

Renn gave way, and I took the lead. The underbrush grew thicker. And then, without warning, we stepped out of the tangle of vegetation and onto a road: an Old Road.

This Old Road wasn't as wide as the Great North Way, but it, too, went north, as if some force had been pushing us inexorably in that direction. As if *The Book of Forbidden Wisdom* had, at last, been ready to be found.

We rode hard, and there were no sounds of pursuit. Late afternoon we stopped to give the horses a breather. I took the time to groom Shamble. Really it was Renn's job—he was riding the horse, and the job was far beneath me—but I had a great affection for that creature. He made horsey groans of pleasure that were almost embarrassing. He purred. His hair came out in handfuls, revealing a short, dull coat and a protruding set of ribs.

As I brushed, I remembered the day that Silky had counted all the rules we were breaking. We had started going down a slippery slope, and it had ended with my kissing a bard.

Trey came over to me and took the brush. He didn't look at me.

"Do you love him?" he asked.

I was unprepared for this.

"I don't know. I don't think so."

"Am I still first in line for matrimony? If we get back to Arcadia."

"I'll have no choice—"

"That's encouraging."

"That's not what I mean. That's not what I mean at all."

"No? Has Renn asked you?"

"No."

"So that's the problem."

"No. I don't know. Help me, Trey."

"I can't, Angel. But I will marry you if that's still what you need for your honor to survive."

"We could lead separate lives, Trey," I said finally. "And we could also still be friends. We would be happy enough. I ask nothing of you."

He gave me a strange half smile.

"Well," he said. "You're right. That is nothing."

Silky woke me in the middle of the night.

We had been keeping a watch, and my first thought was that the soldiers had come.

"It's Trey," she said. "Hurry."

Her voice was low and urgent. I pulled a dress on over my nightclothes.

"What is it?" I asked.

"He was making sounds in his sleep, so I went over to look—to make sure he was all right. Then the fire flared up, and I saw his *face*."

Trey was feverish. By the time I got close to him, he was shivering with the chills. Before he could say anything, I pulled a green Alla leaf out of the herb bag and put it on his tongue. It turned black immediately. High fever.

I reached out again to take the leaf back, but Trey recoiled sharply, as if my touch were snakebite.

"Get away," he said. "I know what this is."

The moon came out from behind a cloud. Trey's face was misshapen, and there were open sores on his left cheek and forehead.

"Steep the willow leaves," I said to Silky. "I'm going to get him a cold compress."

"Don't touch me," he said. "You have to stand back."

I looked at his face again, and in that moment, I knew what was wrong with him. During the attack on our camp in the gully outside Parlay, the man without a face had spat on Trey.

He had passed to Trey the disease of the flesh.

Trey's flesh would fall away; his face would be a scar—if he lived.

Trey tried to turn his head away from me, but once I knew what to look for, I could already see where the skin was pulling back from his eyes and mouth. His flesh looked ragged and raw.

"I'm not going to let this happen to you," I said.

"The world doesn't always do your bidding, Angel," he said, not without bitterness.

"It's going to be all right," I said. And I thought, *It has to be.*

By then Renn and Jesse were up, and I heard them whispering with Silky as she brewed the willow. The three of them came to us together.

"It's the flesh disease," said Renn after taking one look at Trey.

"Oh *no*," said Silky.

"You're too close," Jesse said to her. "Get back, Silky." She didn't move.

"Get back right now," I said to her, and she stepped back.

"I'll be delirious soon," said Trey. "You can't touch me. I'll be too weak to protest then, but you have to stay away."

"I'm going to keep you alive," I said. Silky brought over the willow brew; Jesse took it from her before she could get close, and he handed it to me. Sister expendable. Trey let me spoon some of the broth into his mouth.

"Put the spoon in the fire," I said to Silky afterwards.

"I'll help you, Angel," said Renn.

"No," I said. "You won't."

"I'll get another compress," said Jesse.

"My face is on fire," Trey said. "It's all I can do to keep from tearing off the flesh."

"Oh, *Trey*," cried Silky. I didn't change my expression. Trey needed me, and he didn't need to see shock, or dismay or revulsion.

"Jesse," I said. "Take Silky to the other side of the camp. I'm going to grind some herbs for a poultice."

"I can help," said Jesse.

"Just me," I said.

I finished the poultice and leaned down to apply it.

"I'm obviously contagious," Trey said. "You can't possibly use your hand to spread that."

"Easy does it," I said, as if I were talking to some sort of skittish animal. "I'll use something else."

In the end, I used Renn's knife to smooth the poultice onto Trey's face. Very carefully. Renn put the knife in the fire afterwards.

Finally Trey slept.

"You care about him very much," said Renn.

"Of course," I said.

I sat by Trey as the night deepened. Renn did not leave my side. In his sleep, Trey began to scratch his face. I tried to bind up his hands with lengths of cloth so that he couldn't mar his face further.

"Don't do that," said Renn. "You can't do that without touching him."

"I *will* do it," I said.

Renn got up and walked away as if I had somehow hurt him.

"There now, Trey," I said. And then I broke another rule. After Trey stopped trying to touch his face, I moved my bedding from Silky's side. She and Jesse were standing together whispering.

"What are you *doing?*" she asked me.

"What I please," I answered. "What I owe Trey. Both." When I was very near Trey, I lay out my bedding. In case he needed me.

I looked up to see Renn watching me closely, but when I met his eye, he turned away.

I was up every hour to change the poultice on Trey's face.

I was tired in the morning. Renn was curt as he prepared food. Jesse helped him. Silky didn't know enough about cooking to warm bread, and I, who had at least watched Cook work, had been too near to the contagion to touch food.

When I approached Trey to examine his face by the light of day, he tried to move away from me.

"That's near enough, Angel," he said. I had to hide my shock when I saw the soupy redness that had grown under and around the poultice. The herbs had done no good. He saw the bad news in my face.

"Well, Angel," he said. "I have no more than a sliver of land, and I'm going to have no face. The marriage is off, wouldn't you say?"

I ignored his words. "I'm going to try something else," I said. "An infusion of Aman fungus."

"That's poisonous," said Trey.

"It won't be strong enough to kill," I said. "Just strong enough to kill the disease."

I hoped.

I tried the infusion in the afternoon after searching for the fungus at the base of trees. It burned Trey terribly as I put the plaster on his face. The flesh had been eaten away on the left side and under his right eye.

Meanwhile, Silky went hunting and came back with two plump grommets. The birds were as large as turkeys and as fatty as ducks.

I changed the infusion. Trey seemed no worse, but substantial damage had been done. Even if the Aman fungus held the disease at bay, even if he didn't quite become a faceless one, he would be marred for life. I smeared the ointment liberally. If his nose and lips were eaten away, he would become the kind of horror that the Bards loved singing about.

I went to search for more Aman fungus. The day passed slowly—no one spoke of moving on. The disease moved over his cheeks, but it seemed to me that it was progressing more slowly.

That night I still slept near him.

In the morning he had improved. His fever was down. The lesions had ceased oozing.

He wasn't going to die.

But most of his face was gone.

PART III

CHAPTER TWENTY-ONE

PETRO

Trey pulled the hood of his coat up over his head after he mounted Bran, so that his face was in shadow. I had wanted to examine his face before we left, but he'd turned away from me. I caught Renn looking with pity at Trey—which made me angry. I knew I was being land proud, but Renn's good looks and dark attraction couldn't keep out the thought: who was Renn to pity Trey?

In a way, Silky was the worst. She couldn't hide her fear, and she avoided Trey; she could not seem to bring herself to look at him. I knew she couldn't help it, because I knew what was in her mind. There had been nights in the past when she had dreamt of beings like Trey—when she would come to my room, fresh from nightmare. She would pad to my bed and, after crawling in, whisper to me her dreams of faceless men.

Perhaps in those dreams she had been Seeing what would happen to Trey.

Only Jesse behaved naturally. Only Jesse behaved well. He kept between Silky and Trey. He was solicitous, but he never peered into Trey's face. He spoke naturally and easily. At one moment, something he said even made Trey give a short laugh.

That was when I finally realized he was good enough to be allowed near Silky. To be, in fact—and at a discreet distance—her friend.

In this crisis, he was the best of us.

After we had all mounted, Jesse fell in with Trey as if it were the most natural thing in the world. Only I was close enough to hear Trey's response.

"I don't need pity," Trey said. I cringed. But Jesse replied simply.

"I won't give it to you then," he said.

"Why are you here?" asked Trey. "Do you want to see the monster?"

Jesse looked around quickly. I pretended to be particularly interested in something Silky was saying, but in fact I could hear their every word.

"To be truthful," said Jesse, "I need advice."

"What kind of advice do you need?"

"You've been friends with the Lady Angel since childhood."

"Yes."

Jesse paused.

"How do I get her to like me?" he asked finally. "I need her to like me."

"You want the Lady Angel's good opinion?" Trey sounded taken back.

"Naturally," Jesse said. "But especially because"—he paused—"because she won't let me near the Lady Silky. Only to talk. That's all."

And just like that Trey gave a real laugh.

"From your words, I thought at first you were interested in Lady Angel," he said.

"Of course I hold her in high esteem," said Jesse carefully.

"Of course," said Trey. "But I have to tell you—it's tricky dealing with Angel on the subject of Silky."

"I noticed."

Trey laughed again.

"Listen—" he said. But at that moment Silky demanded an answer of me to a question I hadn't even heard her ask. Jesse and Trey rode ahead, talking, thick as thieves.

They were friends after that.

We rode for a while until I felt I could no longer bear the weight of the heavy dresses and veils required for Shibbeth women. We stopped, and I put on traditionalist garb and once again braided my hair.

"What about me?" asked Silky.

"You keep playing the bride," I said. "It raises our status."

Not long after this we came upon a shepherd. He wasn't on the road proper, but stumbling along the rocky shoulder. He led two blue Shibbeth sheep with ropes around their necks, and three dogs followed him obediently.

Strange.

Three dogs could, under normal circumstances, control a flock of well over a hundred. I hadn't spent my childhood exploring my father's great lands for nothing. I knew about sheep and orchards and vineyards, the fields of crops, smallholdings that kept flocks and flocks of heavy-wooled or fat-tailed sheep. Unless this shepherd had just sold off his flock, there was some small mystery about three sheepdogs and two blue-wooled sheep.

"Put your veil up," I whispered to Silky, and she obeyed. I sat taller in the saddle and prepared to play the role of a haughty traditionalist.

The shepherd stared at us. When he saw Trey, he began to back away from the road. The dogs, barking furiously, followed suit.

"Master Shepherd, you're a stranger to us," I said, using the Shibbeth formula to greet someone unknown.

"No longer," said the shepherd, warily giving the ritual reply. Then he added, "You be on the ghost road."

"But we're not ghosts," I said.

The shepherd looked hard at Trey. Trey gave no

sign, but I knew he was suppressing some sort of strong emotion, because Bran began fidgeting and pawing the ground, and Bran was a carefully mannered horse.

Jesse moved closer to Trey.

"Quiet down," snapped the shepherd, and at first I thought he was talking to me—until the dogs stopped barking and settled. The two blue sheep lowered their heads and began cropping the few blades of grass growing up among the rocks.

"We want to go north," I said.

The shepherd looked at us suspiciously. "The road goes north," he said. He paused. "Maybe you have food?"

"Food?" I said. "Where's your flock? Surely you're wool-rich."

"I was." He turned his head and spat. "Two hours ago I had more than fifty sheep. But there be troops on the move—some eighty strong—and not the standard 'Lidan troops. These be some Great Lord's troops. They took all but two of my sheep and called it charity. Fifty blue sheep. For slaughter! They would have taken the dogs and eaten them, too, but Kep and Nemo and Tigh wouldn't go."

"Who eats *dog*?" asked Silky.

"The woman is forward," said the shepherd.

"She's young," said Jesse.

"I'm surprised she doesn't be knowing that dog is a delicacy," said the shepherd. "But then you be having an accent. You're not from Shibbeth. Arcadia?"

"Yes," I said.

"Why are you dressed like a traditionalist then?"

"It suits me." That seemed to satisfy him.

"The troops be looking for two Arcadian women," he said. "And one other from Shibbeth. When I first heard you coming, I thought you was them."

"Tell me about these women," said Renn. He reached into his saddlebag and pulled out the uneaten grommet and some sand potatoes.

"The Arcadian women be murderers." The shepherd eyed the food. "A Lord of Shibbeth's dead, and his heir wants vengeance. That's what the captain of the troops says. The Shibbeth woman—I don't know. Be those sand potatoes?"

"Yes," said Renn. "Don't you believe the captain?"

"I believe. But I'd say he wants a piece of Arcadia as well as those murdering women. Those troops be following them women to the weakest point of the Arcadia border."

"The weakest point," I said. "The Village of Broken Women." And our road north would take us there. It was the last place to resupply before the largely ruined Spiral City.

The shepherd looked at Renn. "Mayhaps I could relieve you of some of them potatoes," he said. Renn leaned down and gave him what I knew was the last of our food.

"Keep talking," said Renn.

"The more I think about that juicy northern part of Arcadia," said the shepherd, "the less I believe in them two women what somehow killed a Great Lord."

"It strains credibility," I said.

The shepherd stared hard at me. "Have a care and keep to the ghost road," he said, "or those troops will take everything you have. The lady who travels with you won't be safe." He indicated Silky.

"Our way is north," I said. "The road is the most direct way."

"That be your business," said the shepherd, "but if there really be Arcadian Lady murderers, and you run into them, you might give them a warning." He pulled on the ropes attached to his sheep, whistled up his dogs, and turned to continue his way south. Then he seemed to hesitate. Finally he turned back to us one last time.

"The ones the troops seek," he said, addressing himself to me.

"Yes?"

"If you see them, tell them that veils are the best disguise. Passing for a man works in bardsong, but not so much in life." And with that he finally and resolutely turned his back to us.

"Well," I said when he was out of earshot. "Well."

"He *knew*," said Silky.

"Yes," I said. "He did."

"Of course he did," said Renn.

"What's that mean?" I asked.

"It means no matter how you tie your hair or keep your face dirty, it's hard not to see you're a woman," Trey said quietly.

"My face is dirty?"

Trey changed the subject.

"Eighty troops." He seemed to muse.

"So we're following eighty armed men," said Jesse. "Eighty armed men who would love to capture the Lady Silky. And the Lady Angel too," he added hastily.

"I wonder who the Shibbeth woman is," said Silky.

The others ignored her.

"Behind us are Leth and Kalo," said Renn.

"I don't like this," said Jesse.

"It can't be helped," I said. "*The Book* is north. We go north. If the soldiers are going to The Village of Broken Women, we need to get there first."

"Everybody in Arcadia acts like *The Book of Forbidden Wisdom* is the most valuable object in the world," said Silky. "What if it doesn't contain the deeds to the lost lands? What if it's a bunch of old herbal remedies? For frostbite. Or maybe *lovesickness*. Useful, but not—"

"North, Silky," I said.

It wasn't long before we began to encounter evidence of the 'Lidan troops in front of us. They were crisscrossing the north road and raiding farms along the way. We went off the road to try and find a farm where we could get cheese and maybe sausage or dried beef—perhaps some milk—but when we found a small holding, it was deserted. No people, no livestock, no sign of life.

Silky, as we explored one of the huts, found an overturned chair.

And a woman's body hanging from a beam.

"Who would do such a thing?" she cried.

But there were no signs of struggle. I saw Jesse and Trey exchange glances.

"Go outside," Jesse said to Silky. "I'll take care of it." When she left, he righted the chair and cut the woman down.

We were out of food, and the landscape seemed stripped of wildlife—no grommets, no sand potatoes, no deer, not even songbirds. We were too hungry to be particular, and Silky looked for raccoons as well as pheasants, and fat, slow brush snakes as well as rabbits.

Nothing.

As we cast a wider net looking for food, we began to pass burned barns and the occasional farm with pens and stables devoid of livestock. Sometimes the holdings were still occupied, and whole farm families would come out and watch us pass, and sometimes the women of the families were set apart, their veils rent, their sobs unheeded.

Jesse rode up to me. "Can't we do anything for them?"

"We don't have any food to give them," I said.

"That's not what I meant."

"There's nothing we can do."

"It's as well Niamh went back home," said Jesse. "This would break her heart."

We came to a hamlet that was still smoking; the huts and barns had been burned to the ground. Nothing remained but a few stone walls. This time the troops hadn't taken all the livestock with them—some pigs, two horses and a strange thing Renn called a llama had been corralled and set on fire.

The 'Lidans were having fun.

In front of the remains of a small house, the body of a man lay across the doorway, and I crouched down next to him. He hadn't been long dead.

A carrion crow gave a harsh call and hopped close to us, its head to one side. Silky threw a pebble at the malign thing; her aim was true, and she knocked it sideways.

"Up you get, Angel," said Renn. "Time to move on." He took my hand.

I looked up into Renn's face, and I saw that Trey was watching.

As I took Renn's hand and he helped me up, Trey started walking away, walking away into the shadows cast by the blackened trees.

He didn't come back until we had almost finished surveying the area.

We found only one structure left whole in the entire village, and that was a chicken coop. As I looked at it in surprise, a hen came out, strutting, cocking her head sideways now and then as if to see if there was anything edible in the ashes.

"That chicken's *food*," said Silky, getting right to the point.

"Don't point at it, then," I said. "Shoot it!" The hen was ignoring us and seemed in no hurry to go anywhere.

"Are you kidding?" said Silky. "With the bolts I'm

using, we'll end up with feathers and a head. *Do* something, Angel."

Before I could, Jesse took matters into his own hands. He walked up to the hen and threw his outer garment over it.

"There," he said. "Now it thinks it's asleep."

"They must be *very* dumb," said Silky.

"You have no idea," said Jesse.

"Let's check the henhouse," I said. But there was no need. Before I could move, a man poked his head out of the coop's door. His shoulders followed. He crept forward on his elbows, and I saw why. In each of his hands he carried a plump hen by the feet. His clothes were smeared with chicken droppings, and he had feathers in his hair.

"Don't kill me," he said. "I'm a bard."

Renn gave a long sigh.

"Petro," he said. "What are you doing with those chickens?"

Petro looked relieved.

"Hello, Renn," he said. "I stole them."

"How did you escape the soldiers?"

"As you can see, I hid, and, luckily, they overlooked me," said Petro. "There're more hens. And eggs. I'll trade for clean water."

"You know each other?" I asked.

Both of them turned to me and stared.

"We're bards," said Petro. "Of course we do."

"Those chickens aren't yours to trade," said Renn.

"Booty," said Petro. "The spoils of war."

"You're not going to tell me you fought with the 'Lidans," said Renn.

"True, I'm not a fighter," said Petro. "But I can also trade some very new ballads, as well as recent news from both Arcadia and Shibbeth. And I'm pleased to meet you." He bowed. Then he tucked one of the chickens under his arm and offered his hand to Jesse. He couldn't, of course, touch the hand of a Great Lady.

"Oh, Angel," said Silky. "Can we listen to the new ballads? Because they'll cheer us up. Even Trey. *Please?*"

"What about Trey?" asked Trey, coming out of the shadows of the trees.

Petro took one look at Trey's face and began backing toward the henhouse.

I went up to Petro and hissed in his face.

"He's not contagious anymore. And you will not stare, or shy away, or even think about putting this in bardsong," I said. "Or I will kill you."

Just so we understood each other.

The point having been made, we set up camp by the road, boiled water, scalded the chickens and began plucking.

Petro hummed as he plucked. "Have you heard the ballad of the Montrose-Nesson almost-marriage?" he asked. "It's beyond funny."

There was a silence.

"We'll hear the news," said Renn drily. "But leave out your wedding ballad."

Petro complied and began tuning Renn's lute as Jesse prepared the hens for roasting. Jesse knew wild herbs by sight, and, it seemed, he had often cooked for Niamh.

("He's *amazing*," said Silky.

"He's completely ordinary," I said.)

Petro's news was mostly of land mergers and births—one of which was unnatural. A child with stumpy wings, like those of a flightless bird, had been born to Lorna Nesson. I remembered now that at the almost-marriage she had been pregnant.

Prodigious births were a staple of the news. Of course, Lorna's child—which Petro said was stillborn—had probably been smothered at birth. Great Families could easily hush up such things. I pitied Lorna and her baby.

As Petro continued the tellings, the air grew rich with the scent of roasting chicken. The fat from the hens fell into the fire and hissed and hinted at the flavor of crisp perfection. The juicy chickens were almost ready.

Then Petro suddenly had my full attention.

"The Lord Leth of the House of Nesson has wed into the great forest lands and river valleys of Lady Rose, House of Cantreux. The telling is new—it is possible you have first hearing, for I was one of the Bards there."

I felt a flush creeping up my throat and onto my face. At the same time, I seemed to be having trouble breathing. Renn made a move in my direction, but Trey pulled him back roughly.

What a knot to untie.

Petro stopped the telling, uncertain.

"Are you sure about this news concerning Lord Leth?" Trey asked.

"It is part of the news," said Petro. "The telling is what it is."

"Don't speak in riddles," said Silky. "I hate riddles. I'm *terrible* at them."

Jesse looked at Silky as if this were the most admirable quality he had ever encountered.

Petro looked uncomfortable and fell back into the common speech.

"I was there," he said. "The wedding was lavish—five bards. And four witnesses were used instead of the usual two. Lady Rose wanted the merger inviolate—because of the broken ceremony of the Lord Leth and the Lady Angel."

"Leth is a *snake*," Silky muttered. "But he gets what he deserves. The Lady Rose *never* bathes."

"You're making that last part up," I said.

"I'm not," said Silky. "We did Comportment together, and I smelled her *firsthand*. Still, I feel almost sorry for Rose. She's only thirteen."

"The rumors are delicious," tempted Petro.

"All right," I finally said.

"Prepare yourself," said Petro. "They say that the pure and beautiful and intelligent Lady Angel of the raven hair is a *harlot*. Some say the Lady Rose took the Lord Leth out of pity. The Lady Angel ran away in the night with a man. In the night. With a man."

He couldn't seem to believe it himself, which might

have been why he was repeating things. And for a moment I thought I saw it through Petro's eyes—a sordid escape into the forbidden, the unspeakable. No wonder they called me a harlot. But Silky interrupted my thoughts.

"The Lady Angel is the *opposite* of a harlot," said Silky hotly. "And you are a *terrible* bard."

Petro cleared his throat. I saw him look at me again, and this time his glance took in Silky as well. All that golden hair. She had, before now, been described in bardsong.

He knew who we were.

"You will not speak of this encounter," said Renn.

"No," said Petro. "I see that now. I've made rather a fool of myself."

"Do you know where the Lord Leth is?" asked Trey.

"I—are you? Are you the Lord Trey? I'm sorry. Very sorry. About your face."

Trey said nothing more. His darkened face was like a mask.

"Tell us about Leth," Silky said. "Tell us about the *viper.*" Jesse went and stood beside her.

"All right," said Petro. "Lord Leth left the Lady Rose alone right after the marriage. They say he's obsessed with hunting down the Lady Angel—that the marriage is partly to spite her. I mean you. Sorry. He keeps talking about the Lord Trey. I mean you. Sorry. And what he'll do when he finds him. You. Sorry."

"Stop with your apologies," said Trey, "and tell us where Leth is."

"He's with Lord Kalo," said Petro. "They're behind you. I saw them. The soldiers in front of you seek you as well. I heard them—they seek you and another woman who's escaped from Lord Garth's heir."

I wondered what other woman would have left the restricted women's quarters. Whoever she was, I wished her well.

"You're caught between enemies." He fell silent.

"I don't understand," said Jesse. "I don't understand why they'd pursue Silky and the Lady Angel and the Lord Trey so far and for so long."

"Oh, they don't want to capture you," said Petro. "Not yet. At least Lord Kalo doesn't—and Lord Leth is letting him take the lead. You're being followed to *The Book of Forbidden Wisdom*. Do you really think a soldier is so incompetent he would not check under floorboards for fugitives?"

"You know a lot," I said.

"He's a bard," said Renn. "Knowing a lot is his job."

"Thank you, Renn," said Petro. "I listen. And people talk. Incessantly. You'd be surprised at how interested in themselves people are. Now let's enjoy these ill-gotten chickens, and I'll be on my way."

The chickens were almost buttery in texture, and with the herbs Jesse had picked, oozing flavor inside them. Coupled with the salt from our precious reserve sprinkled on their crispy outsides, they were indescribably delicious.

When I had eaten my fill, the world seemed a better

place. I felt slightly sorry for the Lady Rose. All those witnesses. She'd be stuck with Leth forever.

As for being caught between two lethal powers, well, we would just have to move on and hope for the best. Not, perhaps, my most clearly thought-out plan.

In the morning, Petro prepared to leave; he said his good-byes quickly, as if chagrined by the whole encounter. We sent him on his way with one of the remaining live chickens and a clutch of boiled eggs.

"It's a long walk to Southern Arcadia," said Renn.

"I don't plan on encountering those soldiers again," Petro said. "And besides, somewhere along the way I can probably steal a donkey."

"You're a *scoundrel*," said Silky.

"Yes, Lady," said Petro. And he set off, the chicken hanging from his belt, the eggs in a bag.

CHAPTER TWENTY-TWO

WHAT HAPPENED NEXT

Petro went south; we broke camp. Renn spent some time improvising a sling for the live chickens, and we wrapped the boiled eggs in soft cloth and put them in the saddlebags. Finally, Trey, Jesse and I spent some time trying to disguise the fact that we had been there—while Silky critiqued our efforts—but it proved difficult to hide the fact of the fire. We smothered it with earth and then covered it over with brush, but anyone looking closely would see the marks of our passage.

"Maybe Leth and Kalo will confuse our tracks with those of the 'Lidans," said Silky.

"That's possible," said Jesse. I just gave him a look.

We mounted and took the Great North Way. Ahead of us were eighty 'Lidan troops, and ahead of them lay The Village of Broken Women.

All the gold that I had worn at my wedding had initially come from that village. Once it had been a prize, the jewel of Arcadia. Back then, it had been called Gold River, but the gold was long played out. One of my lady maids had come from The Village of Broken Women and had told Silky and me about it.

Bards, too, sometimes sang the story. Renn, I thought, probably knew the tale. For years the river had yielded up soft lumps of gold—some the size of a baby's fist. But as time passed, and the gold in the river was depleted, the men had gone farther and farther into the hills in search of more. As years went by, they brought back less and less gold. Many of them left Gold River, while the widowed and unmarried women stayed. My lady maid had told us that now the village was almost entirely without men—some had moved on, some had died of Gold Lung, some had disappeared into the hills. A few stayed as shopkeepers or gardeners, she said, but gardens didn't flourish there, and no one had money to buy from the shops, and the shopkeepers had very little stock to buy. It sounded an empty, desolate kind of place.

But it was a weak spot. Largely inhabited by low-caste women, who, according to Arcadian law, were forbidden to carry weapons, the place would have been tempting as a point of invasion—had it not been for its rugged canyon and cliff topography. No large army could pass into Northern Arcadia there, but eighty troops? Eighty troops might be able to make it over the rough terrain before the villagers could sound the alarm. Garth's heir might be seeking Silky and me, but I was now more than willing to believe he was also seeking a way into the northern territories of Arcadia.

Late afternoon on the day that Petro left, after a hard day's journey, we saw a glow on the horizon. Eighty men move more slowly than a group of five; we were catching up to the soldiers in front of us.

"I have an idea," said Silky.

We turned to her politely.

"I say we get *ahead* of the troops," she said. "We do it *now*. This night. Then we warn The Village of Broken Women and send some of the villagers to warn the rest of Arcadia. Just in case these troops want to use Angel and me as an excuse for an invasion. By the time the 'Lidans arrive, there'll be an empty village and Arcadian troops massing on the other side of the canyon."

There was a silence.

"It makes sense," said Trey.

"It's a good idea," said Renn.

"It's absolute brilliance," said Jesse.

I was proud of Silky. I was deeply annoyed by Jesse.

"All right," I said. "We'll muffle the horses' hooves and check that none of the tack jingles or squeaks or otherwise gives us away. We move in absolute silence, no matter what. Silky?"

"*What?*"

"You know what."

We reached the place that had produced the glow. Once it had been a thriving farm, or so it seemed by the number of outbuildings and corrals. Now it was a smoldering ruin. Bodies were lying in a long row across the farmyard. So silent. So still. So damaged. I tried my best to shield Silky from it.

Not long after we left the ruined farmstead, we entered a wood. We were off the road now but running parallel to it. Daylight was fast disappearing. From under a thousand trees grew a thousand shadows.

We moved to the left until we were in untouched forest, and the devastation of the 'Lidans was to our right.

We went single file. Trey, Jesse, Silky, me, Renn.

We suddenly realized we were too near. Steaming horse piles and razed vegetation that still oozed sap showed that we were in their wake. We moved more to the left.

And we were upon them.

They had stopped to set up camp, and we passed so close to the troops that I could see the light of their fires and hear their voices carried on the wind. As we neared the back of their camp, I could smell hot horse and hear the sound of grazing. I thought perhaps they had corralled their horses, but I had no intention of getting close enough to see.

We were careful. We kept checking that none of us was silhouetted against the sky—a person-shaped darkness blotting out the stars would give us away.

And then, finally, I could no longer hear the voices of the troops, and their campfires were behind us.

I turned to look back at Renn, but it was too dark to make out his face.

When I looked forward again, something was wrong.

I couldn't hear Squab.

Squab was a stocky pony, and he had a heavy gait. The hoofbeats I could hear were coming from too far ahead, and they weren't Squab's. They belonged to Trey's horse, Bran.

Right in front of me, where Silky should be, was only empty night.

I stared ahead as if Silky might materialize if I looked hard enough, but she had simply disappeared.

It took only moments for me to gather everyone together. We could no longer hear the troops, but we knew we had to be very quiet.

Trey rode up to me. His face was a shadow, and he looked like a thing of darkness.

I wanted to cling to him.

"We'll find her," he said to me.

"It's all right," said Renn. "When you turned to me, Angel, she slipped into the bushes. I think she had to—I thought—"

"You thought she had to pee," I said.

There was an uncomfortable silence. The subject was taboo. Renn wouldn't have questioned her.

"Silky would never have to—you know," said Jesse.

"Everyone has to pee," I said.

"Stop saying that word," Trey said.

We stood in silence for a minute.

"But how do we find her?" asked Jesse, at last.

"She'll come back," said Renn. "It shouldn't take her long. You know."

But in fact, I knew that Silky was at the time of women. The shame she would have felt at leaving a mark on the saddle would have been greater than her fear of the woods. But the mention of such a thing was beyond. Just—beyond.

Women's business. To speak of such a thing in the hearing of men would have beggared belief.

But I had already broken a lot of rules, and now was no time for niceties. Especially so close to the troops.

"It's the moon-time with her," I said. "She wouldn't have talked about it. That's why she slipped away—she probably went farther than she should have so none of us would stumble on her."

They stared at me blankly.

I became exasperated.

"The time of women," I said. "The cloths that must be used. She would have needed privacy."

Immediately Renn and Trey looked as if they would have liked to disappear beneath the earth. Women's bodies were supposed to be whole things, objects of integrity. I had gone far beyond the boundaries and found myself in uncharted territory.

Jesse just looked bewildered. "I don't understand the words you're saying," he said.

I sighed. I was *not* going to explain women's business to Jesse.

"Renn," I said. "You tell him. I'm going to go in the direction she took. Take Jasmine, Trey—I'll go faster on foot."

"I'll go," said Jesse, but I was already among the trees.

There was no way I'd let Jesse embarrass her. If I let Jesse come across her doing what she was doing, she might never forgive me, and she'd be absolutely justified.

Immediately it was as if a curtain had been drawn between the others and me. Darkness. Silence.

I pressed forward.

Only minutes later, I could hear men speaking in normal tones of voice. I pushed myself against a tree, my face against its bark so that the whiteness of my complexion wouldn't give me away.

I had to get closer.

I crept forward until I could see the light of a small fire and the shapes of two small tents. Then I moved toward the fire some more until I was crouched in the bushes right next to it. I was perfectly visible to anyone in the camp if one knew where to look.

There were five men. Two of them were playing Nancalo, and I could hear the counting stones clicking against one another. The other three were huddled by the fire, eating something that looked like spoosh from a pot.

"I don't care what you say," said the spoosh-eater closest to the pot. He spoke as he chewed. "The captain won't stop till he be getting those women."

"Or till he be getting a piece of Arcadia," said the second man.

"Not our business."

The third man looked thoughtful. "I don't know why the new Lord be wanting these harlots so much— even if they killed Lord Garth. After all, the new Lord hated his father."

"Enough of that."

The third spoosh-eater wasn't satisfied. "The other woman—why does he want her?"

"Maybe because she don't want him." The man closest to the spoosh pot laughed.

Meanwhile, I began to wonder even more about this other woman. Perhaps our paths would cross; perhaps we could help her.

"Point is," said the first one, "the new Lord can't have people murdering his father and getting away with it. Looks bad."

"Master Garth were the better master," said the other.

"Best be quiet about that."

And they continued to eat their spoosh in silence. Not a word about Silky.

Then there was a disruption: one of the men

playing Nancalo suddenly stood and tipped over the board.

"You cheat," he said.

"Say it again," said the other.

I used the diversion to creep away. If Silky wandered too close to their camp; if she were just a little careless and they a little more vigilant, she wouldn't stand a chance.

But perhaps she was already back with the others.

I was among the trees again when I found her. She looked at me and started; then her arms were around me.

"I was just going back, Angel," she said. "I'm sorry I took so long—the belts got all tangled, and I couldn't see what I was doing *at all*. And then I got lost."

There was one moment of complete silence.

Just as I was starting to release Silky and lead her back, the 'Lidans came crashing through the trees.

I didn't hesitate; I pushed Silky in the direction of Trey, Renn and Jesse, and I took off running, making sure to make plenty of noise as I went crashing through the underbrush. If I lived, I was going to have to have a word or two with Silky later. I loved her for not being a squashed cabbage leaf of a woman, but sometimes her willfulness in wandering off maddened me.

At any moment, I thought the soldiers would catch me. But then I heard Silky call out, *"No."* There was a muffled sound and the low growl of men's voices.

My attempt to draw them away from her had proved useless. Not one of them had followed me.

They had her.

Still—if I could get back quickly, I had a chance. The 'Lidans thought of their prey as two silly, frightened, fragile women—like those in Garth's restricted women's quarters. Like Charmian.

We could use that to our advantage.

The others were where I had left them. I burst through the underbrush and panted out, "They have Silky."

And then I realized that Renn and Jesse and Trey were holding raised crossbows, and those crossbows were aimed at my heart.

"It's me," I hissed. I couldn't seem to catch my breath. "'Lidans. Silky. Hurry."

"Let's go," cried Jesse.

"We go quietly," said Trey. "If they hear us coming, they'll use Silky as a shield."

"You're—you're right," I said.

Trey reached down. He knew, as I did, that the time of contagion had ended when the open sores closed, and now he freely took my hand.

"We'll get her back, Angel," he said. "I promise you."

"Stop promising and start rescuing," said Renn. "And you might give the Lady Angel back her hand."

"And you might remember who and what you are," said Trey. I had never heard him speak so arrogantly.

"We're a little beyond the Arcadian niceties of caste," said Renn. "I would never touch the Lady Angel without her consent. And I had it. Her consent."

"You didn't even think about—"

"For Heaven's sake," I snapped at both of them. "Enough of this—I'm standing right here, and you're bickering over me as if I were a haunch of goat. The only thing that matters now is Silky. The only thing."

They both looked abashed.

We moved through the trees on horseback. The height would give us an enormous advantage over the 'Lidans.

As long as they didn't think to shoot the horses out from under us first thing.

When we got closer to the 'Lidan camp, we could hear men's voices, and, for a moment, muffled cries. I was terrified for Silky.

Silence.

Deep dead silence.

My heart was pounding so hard I thought the sound would give us away.

"Come on," Jesse whispered.

We were on the outskirts of the 'Lidan camp, but there was no noise at all. Nothing.

We slowly became aware of the bodies. Five of them. Four in the open area near the glowing fire. One half in and half out of a war tent.

I dismounted and ran to them. No pulses, no signs of life, but they were still warm.

In a minute I could see that Silky was nowhere in the camp. But even had she escaped, even if she had somehow gotten a weapon, she would not have been able to kill them all. They would have quickly taken her down.

"I don't understand," I said.

That's when I knew that we weren't alone. In a semicircle around the camp, silent and still and blending into the night, stood—women. They were women of all ages—from a girl younger than Silky to an elder—but all were dressed in muted colors and all were shadowed by the shifting patterns of foliage and shadow. They carried crossbows and longbows, and their raised weapons were pointed at my heart.

CHAPTER TWENTY-THREE

THE VILLAGE OF BROKEN WOMEN

One of the women, who was perhaps in her thirties, stepped forward into the firelight. They did not lower their weapons.

"Lady," she said to me. "Are these your men?"

For a moment I had no idea what she was talking about. Then I heard Renn murmur, "This isn't a time to be silent."

The woman looked toward him.

"You're right, but it definitely isn't *your* turn to speak," she said. She looked at me.

"Wait—yes." I was stumbling over my words. "We're traveling together. We're Arcadians."

"Zinda," said a woman from the shadows. "Let the young one see them. See if she confirms their story."

"All right, Caro," said Zinda. "Let her come forward."

And there was Silky. She ran straight into my arms. "Those 'Lidans took me back to the camp," she said, "but right away, the sisters came."

On my right, Jesse exhaled, as if he had been holding his breath for a long time, and I saw his immense relief.

At that moment, I liked him.

The women emerged from the trees. There were twelve of them, and I was struck again by the broad range of ages among them. It was unlikely that they were literal sisters.

"You're lucky to get the golden-haired one back," said Zinda.

"I'm the Lady Silky," said Silky.

"And where are you all going when you aren't being captured by 'Lidans?"

"We're going to the north," said Silky. "We're on an errand, and I don't think that Lady Angel, that's my sister, wants me to say anything about it. But when we're *done,* we can go back to Southern Arcadia. You see, it started when Lady Angel was getting married, and—"

"Silky."

She stopped.

"Your business is your own," said the woman called Caro.

"But given the proximity of the 'Lidans," said Zinda, "it's best if we all went back to the village."

"All right," said Trey. Zinda gave him a surprised look, as if a dog had spoken. Then she looked at him more closely:

"The disease of the flesh is hard to bear," she said. "And easy to spread."

Trey didn't answer.

"There's no more fear of contagion," I said. "The sores have all closed. Your village will be safe from the disease—and yes, we'll go with you."

She saw I was looking as the other women lashed the corpses of the 'Lidans to their horses.

"We'll bury the bodies elsewhere," said Zinda, "and we'll keep their horses. To the other troops, it'll be as if they'd disappeared off the face of the earth."

"Are you from The Village of Broken Women?" asked Silky.

I sensed amusement among them.

"We are," said Zinda. "But we're not as broken as you might have been led to believe."

We kept walking until Zinda paused near an old oak with carvings on it.

"You just passed from Shibbeth into the spur of Arcadia that reaches into Shibbeth," she said. "We're coming to the canyon that leads into the northern lands."

Home. I wanted to bend down and kiss the land.

Soon we were going steeply uphill. I was out of breath, and Jasmine, even without my weight on her back, began to labor as she made the ascent. Somewhere I could hear water. We left the trail, and cliff walls rose on either side of us—we had entered a canyon, and I could see the source of the sound of water. A shallow river ran through the center. At some time in a far distant past, it must have been a mighty force that had shaped the canyon walls. Now I would have been able to cross it without getting my knees wet. We stopped, and the horses sucked down their fill; I got down on my knees and scooped up the sweet water—not realizing until later that the brimming cup in Trey's hands must have been meant for me.

Without his changing expression, I saw him give it to Silky.

In another hour of hard going over rocks and scree we came to small huts, clearly long deserted and in disrepair.

"When there were more of us," said Zinda, "the village stretched all the way here."

"Was that during the days of gold?" asked Silky. "Angel has gold from The Village of Broken Women."

"I can imagine she does," said Caro. "The bed of this river was once strewn with gold nuggets."

"Bardsong," said Renn, "would have it that one nugget was as big as a cabbage."

"Ah, well," said Caro. "In bardsong, sometimes things grow."

We picked our way through the ruins until, finally, we were in the center of The Village of Broken Women.

I'm not sure what I had expected. Perhaps more half ruins. But these houses looked strong, compact and solid. They were all made of stone.

"That's hard work," said Jesse. "Building with rock."

"We're strong," said Zinda. She looked at Jesse, our young giant, appraisingly. As if she were judging a horse.

"Are you—are you married?" I asked. I couldn't exactly ask her if she was a Lady, but I couldn't place her caste at all. Marriage would have raised her status.

"I'm married," she said. "Unless my husband's dead. He left with the others." Her tone was even.

These women had clearly not disappeared into their husbands. I wondered who ran the village. Who sent out female patrols. Who called them sisters.

By the time we got to the village square, sixty or seventy people had gathered, almost all women. The men stood at the edge of the crowd. They were certainly not the leaders.

"Lark," said Zinda to a young woman by her side. "Pick out ten for corpse duty. We need these 'Lidan bodies underground. And hurry with the purification rituals—there's an invasion on the way."

"Easily done," said Lark. Zinda turned to Caro.

"The 'Lidan troops will be here soon," Zinda said. She put a hand on Caro's shoulder. "We need to be strong and ready. Get Farno to slaughter one of the 'Lidan horses."

"I can do it," said Caro.

"I need you here," said Zinda. "Get Farno."

"You're going to kill a horse?" asked Silky. "I thought you were *good*."

"There aren't many alternatives," said Caro. "We can't cook the dead 'Lidans."

Zinda tugged at a lock of Silky's gold hair. "Someday you'll understand, little girl," she said, but Silky pulled away, clearly not wanting to understand.

I looked over as one of the horses was being led away, and I couldn't blame her.

Then Zinda stood on an overturned crate and addressed all those in the marketplace. As she spoke of invasion, a wave of excitement spread through the crowd, but I didn't sense fear.

"Bring weapons and food to the square," she said. "The 'Lidans think they're going to overrun us. Their surprise is going to be considerable—if they have time for surprise before they die."

The excitement in the square turned to murmurs and shouts and then, at her final words, a roar of approval, and I realized that these women, faced with the possibility of death and oblivion, were responding with the blood-lust of warriors.

We went with Zinda and Caro and helped them

stable the 'Lidan horses—all but the one marked for slaughter—and the two women finally began speaking to Trey, Renn and Jesse more directly.

"Renn's a bard," I said.

"A good occupation for a man," said Zinda.

"I don't think," whispered Silky, "that's a compliment."

"Let's hear you sing," said Caro.

Renn's song was complicated, like an intricate dance to which I did not know the steps, and it was also very beautiful and sad. Some women came into the stables to hear. I looked up at Renn's face, and I saw that, as he sang, he was watching me.

When he came to the end of the song, we all walked back to the square, where I caught the aroma of roasting meat. The 'Lidan horse had, apparently, been dispatched.

Then I saw the weapons. Mostly I saw rocks and some kind of rope, carving knives and brooms. There were some longbows, and even a couple of crossbows, but it wasn't going to be enough.

"You should leave the village," I said abruptly. "Go further into Arcadia. Bring troops."

"This is our fight," said Zinda.

"But brooms," I said. "What on earth can you do with brooms? Sweep them away?"

"Brooms are useful," said Caro.

"There're eighty of them," I said. "Armed. Most on horses. You don't have a chance."

"We're going to be all right," said Caro softly.

"We'll take them at the canyon," Zinda said carefully, as if explaining to children. "They can only pass in threes—at most, fours. The rocks and the brooms and the arrows will spook the horses. And once a 'Lidan's down, he won't get up. Ever." She made a slashing motion with her hand across her throat. I glanced quickly at Silky, worried she was too young to see such a brutal gesture.

But Silky was staring at Zinda with openmouthed admiration.

"What do *we* do?" she asked. "I'm good with a crossbow, and I'm very enthusiastic about throwing rocks. And Angel, my sister, once killed a man after punching his sword. She just *punched* it."

I moved uneasily.

"Don't get so enthusiastic about death, Silky," I said. "It worries me."

"Would you worry less if she were afraid?" asked Zinda, but Zinda was not waiting for a response. She was looking at Trey.

"What about this one, Angel?" she asked. "Bards entertain. The man Jesse has strength. But the faceless one?"

Trey stood there silently.

"You won't speak of him like that again," I said. Zinda narrowed her eyes, but then she nodded.

"Trey *rescued* us," said Silky. "Angel and me."

Caro looked at Silky appraisingly.

"You should learn to rescue yourselves," said Zinda.

CHAPTER TWENTY-FOUR

BATTLE

That night the whole village ate outside in the square. In the end they had slaughtered two of the 'Lidan horses, and there was enough meat for everyone several times over. Garden vegetables went into a huge iron cauldron that hung over a fire, and woman after woman came up and added her produce. There would be enough for the next day and the day after that.

If these women lived that long.

Renn, Trey, Jesse, Silky and I ate apart from the other women by my choice; I didn't want anyone to stare at Trey's face. Silky was in a strangely ebullient mood that seemed at odds with the preparations for battle going on all around us.

"Land isn't so bad," she said suddenly.

"Land greed's what got us here," I reminded her.

"Affection is more important than land," said Jesse seriously. He may have had a point, but I wasn't ready, at that moment, to grant it.

"I *want* affection," said Silky, "but I want lots of land too. Timber. Meadow. Farm. *All* of it. Right now I don't have a thing."

Jesse suddenly looked forlorn.

"You'll have what you want, Silky," I said. "If Kalo doesn't manage to get my dowry, I'll give you half. I promise. And even half is a great deal."

Silky frowned. "I don't want *yours*," she said. "I want to get mine because of who I am. By marrying someone *rich*."

Jesse looked even more forlorn.

"That's not quite the same thing as getting land-rich because of who you are," said Trey.

"He has you there, Silky," I said.

Silky gave a great sigh. "I *hate* it when you're *right*, Trey. "When I was a child you always were. It's an annoying trait. I don't know why Angel feels so—"

She looked up to find the four of us staring at her. All of us, I suspect, wondered how she was going to end that sentence.

"Never mind," she said quietly.

We finished our horse soup.

Later, while Renn tuned his lute, and Trey and Jesse sat talking, and Silky was chattering with a group of girls her age, I went to find Zinda and Caro. They were going through the cache of weapons with some of the other women, and I took them aside.

"I must be direct," I said. "You need to take your people to the hills; you can't withstand this invasion—you have few horses and no soldiers."

"We don't need help," said Zinda. "We never have."

"We'll kill them all, you know," Caro said.

"They're going to come through," I said. "They're going to swarm over your village, and then they're going to try and take Arcadia."

"It's going to be all right," said Caro.

"They have the land greed, Caro," I said. "If Garth's heir has promised these soldiers land in Arcadia, and he would be a fool not to, they'll fight with all their hearts. They won't give in. They won't die easily."

"Who does die easily?" asked Caro softly.

"We're going to fight for our village," said Zinda. "And our hearts are greater than theirs."

"It's going to be all right," said Caro again. "Really."

The cliff walls loomed over the shallow river below, but as the canyon approached the village, they declined until the rock walls were only waist high. If the 'Lidans got that far, there would be no more women in The Village of Broken Women. There would be no more village.

I helped take carts of rocks up high on the canyon wall. Jesse pulled the heavier loads for me. Zinda and Caro had shown us all the vantage points from which we would be low enough to do substantial damage to the 'Lidans but still too high for them to reach us on their horses.

At the entrance of the village, a group of women pounded sharpened pikes hardened in fire into the sand, a last stand against any horsemen who got through. As Jesse and I unloaded the rocks, I noted that the pikes, from above, looked puny and insignificant.

In the square, Trey helped re-string longbows and crossbows. Many of the strings had long since perished from lack of use. Renn sang and did odd jobs. When Trey finished with the bows and began hauling stone, I saw how strong he had grown on our journey. Jesse looked tired, but he kept working—now with Trey.

Silky showed the women who would be stationed on the canyon walls how better to use their bows. They imitated Silky's peculiar but effective stance, and, if they were using longbows, learned to raise their elbows ever so slightly when they released their arrows.

It was the longbows that might give the women an advantage. Crossbows were for close contact, and if the 'Lidans got that close, we were in trouble. Perhaps the women I saw brandishing brooms could keep the horses at a distance.

But many of those whom I saw making preparations were no more than girls, girls who should have been sent to the mountains to hide.

"They're too young, Zinda," I said between loads of rocks.

"They won't leave," said Zinda. "And I don't see you leaving either."

"We've brought the 'Lidans down on you. And you saved Silky. But they should hide. They should—"

But then I stopped, because I realized she was right. I had seen the determination on their young faces; they weren't going to leave. It hurt to think of any one of them wounded or killed—and another thought struck me.

"Who's your healer? Do you have medicines prepared? Bandages?"

Zinda smiled. "According to you, we'll all be dead. No need of a healer."

"Just in case."

"Our healer died in the shuddering sickness last winter. If you know herb lore, you're all we have."

"I know some," I said, and I thought of my mother sorting through herbs in our giant kitchen.

"We're grateful for all you're doing," said Zinda. "Even your men are helping. Jesse is strong. The bard brightens the women's spirits. And the Faceless One has been tireless."

"His name is Trey," I said. "Trey. You can at least learn his name."

Zinda cocked her head at me.

"Your Trey has worked hard."

"He's not *mine*."

"He's not?"

I thought of Father calling Renn *my* bard, and I almost laughed at the absurdity of it all. But then I had a flashback. The summer I was twelve; Trey's peach trees laden with heavy, ripe fruit. We had been alone for a moment, and he had fed me portions of his peach until the juice ran down my chin. At that moment, perhaps, we had been each other's. Now it seemed as if my childhood had never been.

Caro, on Zinda's instructions, called a break, and an hour later the girls who had been practicing with the brooms started distributing food. I took my share of horsemeat and started off to find Silky. I found her still showing the villagers how to work with bows. Jesse had used the rest as an opportunity to find his way to her. When I took Silky aside, he looked at me woefully, but I wasn't there to speak of him.

"I don't want you so much as two inches from me when the 'Lidans come."

"You'll be with the bows?" she asked.

"I'm not much good with a bow," I said. "I'm going to be in the square, preparing for the wounded."

Silky looked troubled.

"But *I'll* be up on the canyon wall."

"You need to stay with me."

"They need me, Angel. Some of them are pretty good, but they will *not* keep their elbows up, and they've all learned that idiotic Arcadian stance, which almost guarantees a miss."

"This is dangerous, Silky," I said.

She looked at me in surprise. "Of *course* it's dangerous," she said. "And I'll see you back in the square."

She smiled. And then, for the first time in her entire life, she turned and walked away from me.

"Just—just remember to aim at the horses," I said, trying to be helpful. "They're the big targets."

She turned back. She looked surprised. "The horses are innocent, Angel. It's the 'Lidans who want to kill us. It's not as if I might miss."

Jesse looked as if he was about to follow Silky, but I held up my hand.

"There's more to be done," I said, and for some reason I said it gently. He left the archers and started to walk back to the square with me. Partway there he joined Trey, who was helping to bury ropes in the sand.

"We'll pull them taut when the 'Lidans ride by," one of the women said to me.

Trey turned his ruined face to mine.

Those peaches. Long ago.

As he gazed at me, I saw it all in his green eyes. All our lives together. I could not help but break one more rule. I went to him, took his hand in mine, and then I raised and kissed it. I didn't wait to see his reaction but left to steep willow bark.

Just in case any of us lived.

The signal came much earlier than any of us had expected. I was in the tent pounding herbs, and the girl assisting me called me to the entrance of the tent. Zinda and Caro had sent sentries south on the canyon wall. As I stood gazing out, the last woman visible to us on the canyon lip lifted a flag. The girl helping me said, "They must've just entered the canyon." She was fidgety and nervous and knocked over a bowl of hot water.

"If you want to go to the hills, go," I said.

She laughed. "It's not that," she said. "I want to go to the front of the pikes." Her face was shining. "When a horse goes down there, so will the man riding it."

"And what're you going to do once this 'Lidan's down?" I asked.

"I'm going to cut his throat," she said. Then she smiled, took off her apron, grabbed a kitchen knife and ran for the final barricade.

The 'Lidans would be here at any moment. Sure enough, as I looked out over the landscape, the 'Lidans rounded the corner of the canyon and came into view; they looked like a long wave coming in to the shore.

Another of my assistants came to me and looked out to the surge of 'Lidans and then to the women at the top of the cliff, who were signaling.

"The signals say," she said, "that half the 'Lidan force has come so far."

"But look at them," I said. "They're so many."

"You're the color of cheese," said my assistant, peering into my face. "You need to brace."

"I need my sister."

"Golden Hair? She's taking care of herself and the women around her. You don't need to worry about Golden Hair—about the Lady Silky."

I was surprised out of my worry. They normally didn't use titles. Silky must have impressed this woman, who couldn't possibly know Silky was only fourteen, who didn't know she needed protection. That Silky was a child.

Then I remembered how she had walked away from me to get back to the women working on the bows.

How she had killed men to save me.

How she had been brave time and time again, even when it seemed we would be subsumed utterly by the protocols around us.

And I realized that while she wasn't yet fully grown up, she could no longer be called a child.

All this time, the 'Lidans kept coming.

I thought the archers would never fire, and I thought of Silky up there with them, and I wondered if she would wait until it was too late. I wondered how much skill she had managed to inculcate into these women.

The horsemen came on.

I saw three figures near the pikes, and I realized I was seeing Renn and Jesse and Trey trying to hammer the pikes more deeply into the ground.

The horsemen were already halfway to the pikes.

It began.

I didn't see a hail of arrows—at first I didn't see any arrows at all—but here and there a 'Lidan was suddenly struck down from his horse.

Silky's work.

The arrows came more thickly—I could see them in the air—and now some of the horses were going down (not Silky's work). But then the 'Lidans were lifting their shields as covers, and not many more of them fell. Soon the women would be throwing rocks and using the few crossbows they had.

Which meant that the women would have to be dangerously close to their targets.

Then the 'Lidans who had been rushing forward changed their tactics. Instead of coming straight on, the horses on the outside were peeling off and making for the weakest point of all—the place where the pikes did not yet begin but where the canyon wall was less than a waist-high slope of scree. Their plan was obvious:

They were going to scramble up that scree, get onto the lip of the canyon and ride up and take out the archers.

Jasmine was a light-boned mare. She would be no help for me this day. I ran to the barn for Trey's great Bran instead. By the time I was mounted and on my way to the low canyon wall, at least four 'Lidan horsemen had managed to get up the scree on the left side, and three had clambered up the right wall.

Silky was on the left flank.

'Lidan horses were massing at the pikes, and it was only moments before they would find a weak spot and overrun the village. But even as I watched, women wielding brooms were upon them—and I suddenly understood their tactics. The woman in front ran close to one of the mounted 'Lidans, lifted her broom, and, with a carefully timed swing, swept him off his horse. Others followed, although not all of them brandished brooms. I recognized my young assistant, and I watched as she bent over a fallen 'Lidan who was still moving. She made a slashing motion. He did not move again.

I turned Bran around and took the first path that led to the left, and, sure enough, I was able to find my way around to the back of the canyon wall, where the way was steep but not impossible, and the terrain was grass, not scree.

I didn't fool myself. If they found me, I would be dead. But if I didn't get to Silky, she would be dead, too.

Bran struggled on the slope. He heaved with the effort, but he didn't slow. And I had gauged it right. We came out ahead of the 'Lidan riders, only yards away from Silky and the other women with bows.

One of the women gave a great cry, but not one of fear. She ran, and the others followed her, down in the direction of the roiling mass of 'Lidan troops and horses.

All but Silky. She stood her ground with her crossbow, and she waited. She didn't spare me a glance; all her focus was on the 'Lidan horsemen coming toward her.

She was giving the other women a chance to get to the main part of the fighting. A crossbow is not a longbow, and Silky was going to have to wait until the soldiers were on her to fire. I could only hope that the 'Lidans wouldn't cut me down on their way to her crossbow. I had no bow at all. I had only the knife I had been cutting the willow with.

Bran and I were on the crest of the canyon when Silky suddenly seemed to notice who I was.

She yelled something, but I didn't hear. Then she yelled again.

"Angel—you're in the *way."*

I was between her crossbow and her targets, and I didn't know which way to turn. She couldn't fire without killing me. She might as well have been unarmed.

I should have known Silky's skill better. She lifted her crossbow, and the bolt went so close to me that a little puff of air lifted my hair. The arrow lodged itself in the 'Lidan rider who was right behind me.

But there were more behind him.

"Best not to move *at all*," said Silky to me calmly. She lay in another bolt. And another 'Lidan went down, one whose armor should have been better fastened under the arm.

I did as she said; I pulled up Bran, and the 'Lidans, going full out, passed us.

Silky fit in another bolt. There were two 'Lidans left, and they were in battle rage, and they were facing down a slip of a girl who was unarmored and completely ignorant of battle.

The closest to Silky went into a full gallop, trying to end the distance between him and my sister. He carried a battle-axe, and he raised it as his horse bore down on her.

When he was half a stride away, she took him down. The horse had to scramble to avoid stepping on her. She stood her ground.

The fourth 'Lidan had been canny and had used the others to shield himself. He was close to Silky as she laid in her last bolt. The sun was behind her, and I saw her squint as it reflected off the 'Lidan's helmet. She wasn't going to be able to see well enough to take good aim. And I knew that she was too stubborn and too sentimental to aim for the horse.

Silky loved horses, and it was going to kill her.

Unless I did something.

I crashed Bran sideways into the 'Lidan's horse. For a second I thought I was going to fall, but Bran, because he was half-rearing, heaved me back into the saddle. It was the 'Lidan who fell, his armor clanging on the jagged rocks to my side. I was triumphant, and looked to Silky—

who suddenly cried out *"Angel!"*

I hadn't seen that there was yet another 'Lidan behind the one I'd unhorsed.

All I knew was that I felt as if an ox had stepped on me, and then, for a while, I didn't feel anything at all.

CHAPTER TWENTY-FIVE

THE HORSE

As I lay on the ground, I had no vision of my mother. Arcadian myth had it that when one was near death, one's mother came to help with the long journey. But really I didn't feel dead so much as muffled. Sound came to me faintly—I thought I could hear Silky calling my name, and then she was crying, "Get her out; get her out; get her *out*." The only sense of mine that was sharp was that of smell: blood and garlic. I wished that it would go away.

And then I was gone again.

When I regained consciousness once more, I became aware that a large, armored dead 'Lidan warrior, one who liked his garlic, was lying partially on top of me. We lay together like that, the dead warrior and I, for a while in a macabre embrace. Finally the weight lifted. The smell of sweat and battle (and garlic) receded, and a scent I recognized from my childhood took its place. But it wasn't Silky's scent.

It was Trey's. Without opening my eyes, I put my arms around him. Perhaps there would be nothing wrong with my sudden surge of need—and something else, some kind of want—if I just kept my eyes closed. But he let go as soon as he realized I was conscious, and a moment later, Silky had taken his place.

"I ran out of bolts," she said. "Trey was running toward us. He threw a knife—a really good throw."

"It had to be," said Trey.

"Bran?"

"He's okay," said Trey. "Next time take your own horse." And I could hear past the gruff voice, and I could see past the mask that was his face to the fear.

The fear that was not for his horse.

"Where's Renn?"

"He's probably singing the 'Lidans to death," said Trey. "Come on. The day is far from ours."

I looked down at the melee near the pikes. The women, with their brooms and their few horses and some crossbows, were among the horsemen. When a

'Lidan went down, he was finished. It was then that I noticed there was a man among the women.

"Is that Jesse?" I asked.

"Yes," said Trey.

"He's in danger."

"He's going to be fine," said Silky unexpectedly. "He's strong. We need to take care of *you*, Angel."

"Where's Zinda?" I asked. "Caro?"

"In the thick of it," said Trey.

"I hope you can walk," Silky said. "Because I've been trying to drag you down the mountain, and I don't think I can make it much further, even with Trey."

"What happened?"

"The 'Lidan you killed fell on you and bled all over you, which scared me because I thought it was *your* blood. There was another 'Lidan behind the one you rammed. That's the one Trey took care of. They were hidden by the first ones."

We staggered down the side of the hill in silence. Blood was dripping into my eyes—I had a scalp wound that was weeping red. When we reached the tented area for the wounded, Silky found a clean cloth and pressed it to my forehead.

I don't know how much time passed, but suddenly Renn was there.

"Angel," he said, and he came right up to me.

"She's fine," said Silky. "And don't *touch*; you know better. In getting Angel down the mountain, Trey's done enough touching for both of you."

Silky had a serious want of tact.

Renn looked as if he would take pleasure out of hitting Trey. Trey held up both hands, as if expressing innocence and a desire to placate. "She was unconscious," he said. "She needed to be moved."

"Are you all right, Angel?" asked Renn.

"Yes." I was all right, but the ragged emotions roused by battle were causing all the underlying tensions of our journey to bubble to the surface.

Zinda came into the tent. Jesse was right behind her. Silky made a move toward him, but I held her back, and a moment later he joined us. His face was smeared with dirt and blood, and I thought that in the heat of the moment he was going to touch Silky, but he observed decorum. Perhaps for her sake.

Given a good long period of time, it was possible I might learn to like him.

The wounded women called to Zinda, and she went to one or two cots. She was haggard, and there was blood on her hands and shirt. It was Lark who hurried over to tell us the news.

"Caro's dead," Lark said. "She was killed in front of the pikes, and we haven't been able to recover the body yet. Zinda's been fighting as if she doesn't care about dying anymore. I told her the wounded women needed to see her."

"Maybe she really doesn't care about dying," I said. Caro, I knew, had been like a sister to her.

And I could understand that kind of love. I loved Silky, and I needed no explanation for that love any more than I needed to understand breathing in order to breathe. But I never let anyone else get close. Not even Trey.

Not even Trey.

Then Zinda was with us.

"It's time for you to go," she said.

"What are you talking about?" asked Jesse, wiping his face of blood and sweat.

Zinda looked stern, but her words were gentle.

"You've more than paid your debt to us," she said. "But I realize now we have a debt to you. It's as I said: you have to go."

"But Zinda," said Silky. "We haven't won yet."

"We will, Golden Hair," said Zinda. "But those close to me are having no luck today, and you need to finish your quest. I've spoken with Bard Renn. You didn't tell us the Lady Angel knows The Book of Forbidden Wisdom. That changes everything. Find it; make it yours; change all Arcadia. But forty more 'Lidans will be here within the hour. You have to get out of here now."

The others looked at me curiously, and I knew they were wondering about The Book. But what Zinda said held truth: if I got to the deeds of the free lands, I could shape Arcadia as I wished. I could thank these women properly. If they lived, I could transform their lives.

And Zinda was going to have her way no matter what; there was no gainsaying her in the wake of her terrible loss. We found that the horses had already been tacked up for us. Lark came to us with baskets of food, and I filled my saddlebags, as did the others.

Silky examined the horsemeat as she put it away. "The poor thing didn't even know it was a 'Lidan horse," she said. "It just got unlucky."

"Go on now," said Zinda. "I have 'Lidans to kill." She sounded like a schoolteacher speaking to children.

"Will you please tell the archers to watch their stance and to breathe *out* when they shoot?" said Silky.

"I will, Golden Hair. We'll keep the 'Lidans very busy while you get out," Zinda said. The set of her face was grim.

I didn't want to ask Zinda this, so I turned to Trey and murmured, "What do we do if some of the 'Lidans get through the canyon to us?"

But Zinda heard me.

"None of them will get through," she said.

Once the road wove around a hill, I could no longer hear the noise of battle. The future seemed to open in front of me like a book waiting to be read, but the words were not words I knew, and the letters were not from our world.

When we came out from behind the hill, we could hear the sounds of battle on the wind again, and we could see great carrion crows circling far behind us.

"The 'Lidans will be on us soon," said Trey. "We should move farther north."

"Zinda said the 'Lidans won't make it through," said Silky.

"They're women, Silky," said Renn, "fighting with brooms and rocks against trained soldiers. Before the day ends, all those from the village will be dead."

"Not *Zinda*," said Silky. "Not *Lark*."

At that moment, Renn seemed dark. Not dark and seductive. Just dark.

We were sheltered from the road by some trees, but we pulled even farther back into the brush, because suddenly there were hoofbeats on the road—erratic hoofbeats, as if a horse was scrambling at a gallop in fear.

It burst into the opening.

I never want to see a horse in that condition again. Its saddle had swung down under its belly and was terrifying it into running harder, which made the saddle bang more at its underside, which made it run. Its eyes were wild and red, and sweat and foam streamed down its neck and flanks. I saw the colors of Garth's House on its bridle, and then it was gone, galloping south on the great Arcadia road.

"The battle's over," I said.

No 'Lidans followed the horse. No more horses came.

"They weren't—" Silky spoke softly, but we all stopped what we were doing so that we could hear what she had to say. Silky swallowed and then spoke again.

"Those women," she said. "They weren't very broken at all."

CHAPTER TWENTY-SIX

A SURPRISE ENCOUNTER

The following day, we had stopped for a drink of water and a bit of dried fruit when two riders came out from under the trees behind us. We had passed right by them.

The riders were both women. The one in front was lightly veiled and dressed modestly in sober colors. There was little remarkable about these women other than the fact that they had no chaperone.

And that they had been hiding.

They began coming toward us, but before they could reach us, I had leapt from Jasmine. Silky lowered her bow, and I heard her gasp. I ran to Niamh, and she dismounted into my arms.

"Niamh," I said.

"Angel. I've missed you. And Silky, too, of course. How's my son behaving?"

I glanced at Silky. She blushed.

Jesse laughed as he got off his horse. He came and knelt at Niamh's feet, and she gave him the parental blessing. Then he got up and gave her an informal embrace that lifted her off her feet.

"Well," said Niamh to Jesse after he put her down. "Have you found anything worth seeking?"

Jesse looked at Silky, and then at his mother, and then back at Silky.

I didn't like it.

When Niamh saw Trey, her smile faded. She started to lift a hand as if to touch his face, but he flinched.

"I'm sorry, Trey," she said. She lowered her arm and began speaking with Jesse. It was as if she had given Trey a shield.

Niamh understood pain better than anyone I have ever met.

The second rider was heavily veiled. She sat her small horse awkwardly, as if she wasn't comfortable, and she was holding the reins in such a way that the horse must have wondered what she wanted of it.

Her gauzy crimson veil fell to her stirrup and was embroidered with pearls and small glinting bits of mirror. She had made some concessions to practicality by wearing pants rather than a dress, but the purple silk, just visible when she moved, was not the sort of material that would hold up well to travel.

I was surprised Niamh had agreed to be seen in her company—as a guide for women on the run, Niamh couldn't afford to be stopped or questioned, and this decadent garb was unlikely to pass other travelers without attracting attention.

I tried to imagine this woman as one of Niamh's clients, and I failed.

While Niamh was off to one side, speaking with Jesse, the woman stayed mounted, although she was shifting uneasily. I attempted not to stare at her clothing. Silky and I spoke together in carefully lowered voices.

"Look at her costume," said Silky. "We used to play dress-up in stuff like that."

"I doubt she thinks of it as a costume," I said. "She's standoffish, don't you think? Although it's hard to tell with the veil."

Silky examined the stranger.

"She looks like a giant candy," she said.

Niamh, who momentarily seemed to have forgotten about the woman, now introduced her.

"This is a Lady of one of the Great Houses in Shibbeth," said Niamh. "I'm escorting her to Southern Arcadia." Niamh smiled, almost with affection. But not quite.

The woman didn't speak.

For Niamh's sake, I put on my best manners.

"I'm the Lady Angel Montrose," I said. "And this is my sister, Lady Silky Montrose. And this is Lord Trey, and Renn, who is, who is—"

"A bard," Renn finished. I looked at him with gratitude.

No reply. The veil made it impossible to determine whether or not she was rude or shy or—

Niamh spoke so that only I could hear. "She's difficult. And a stump's got more sense."

We waited politely for the woman to say something.

"They're not going to bow to you," said Niamh, "if that's what you're waiting for. We're all equal now. Why don't you just take off the veil? It must be stifling in there anyway."

The woman delicately lifted the veil. Under the gauzy crimson was another veil, this one in some kind of yellow satin. She really did look like a candy.

Then she removed the yellow veil.

"Oh," said Silky. "My."

For my own part, I could say nothing.

I was looking into the face of Charmian.

"Yes, it's me," she said. "You actually *could* bow. I'm a Great Lady, and I wouldn't be here if you hadn't killed Garth." I realized my mouth was open. She smiled at me. "Yes, I know you killed him," she continued. "Who else? I had to get out of there after. His son and heir is a pig. He's also my half brother, so that makes him an incestuous pig." Charmian gave an unladylike snort.

"The women of The Village of Broken Women let us through," said Niamh. "They're used to my comings and goings. They were just celebrating a victory when we were there."

"They killed the troops Garth's son sent," said Charmian. "Now I'm safe."

So Charmian was the third woman the troops had been looking for.

"Why's Garth's son after *you?*" asked Silky. "If he's your, well, your brother?"

"Half brother. And he wasn't interested in being my brother—he wanted me to be a concubine," she said. "Plus, without Lord Garth, I was *nobody.*"

"I'm so sorry, Charmian," I said.

"That's 'Lady Charmian'—to all except you, Niamh." Charmian was looking at her face in one of the fragments of mirror that decorated her veil.

Niamh sighed. "Get off your horse," she said. "We'll take a rest here and exchange greetings with my son and his friends."

Charmian dismounted, without grace. Her pants caught on the saddle's pommel and almost pulled right off. We were treated to a display of flesh. Renn, Trey and Jesse carefully looked away. Silky was clearly shocked. I wanted to laugh.

Once on the ground, Charmian turned to Silky and to me.

"I still don't understand why you wanted to leave," she said. "Lord Garth was powerful. You could have become Great Ladies of Shibbeth. You, Angel, could have married my-half-brother-the-heir—the money would have made up for a lot. Think of it. Endless baths of roses and milk. Now he wants you dead."

Silky shuddered—not, I knew, at the death sentence, but at the thought of bathing in bruised roses and lukewarm milk.

"Enough, Charmian," said Niamh. She turned to us. "We're picking up the Long Straight Road not far from here. We'll turn south there and then east; we'll seek safe haven in the heart of Arcadia. I know a place."

"Road with us, Niamh," I said. "Even if only to the Long Straight Road."

"Of course," she said. "Of course."

Jesse smiled.

Charmian frowned.

We mounted up and kept riding.

That evening, while Trey and Renn built the fire, Niamh took Silky and me aside.

"We were stopped by two armed men," she said. "They were looking for you two. They thought we *were* you."

"Oh, *no*," said Silky.

"Troops from Garth's heir?" I asked. I wondered if he had, perhaps, sent out more than the eighty soldiers we knew about. And yet nobody from Shibbeth had made it past The Village of Broken Women—of that I was sure.

"They weren't soldiers," said Niamh. "And they didn't recognize Charmian when they made us take off our veils. One of them had a leopard embroidered on his cloak."

"Ugh," said Silky.

"Leth," I said. "The leopard is the sign of his House. He's the man I almost married."

"You have poor taste then," said Niamh.

"I used to," I said.

Niamh smiled at me.

"I bet Kalo was with them," said Silky, and I nodded at her.

"We told them nothing," said Niamh. "I don't think they followed us."

"How did you keep Charmian silent?" I asked.

"A very harsh look."

I was laughing as we joined the others.

Later that evening, Jesse and Silky sat on a nearby log at exactly the right distance apart to please a chaperone—a fact that in itself worried me. They were deep in conversation and seemed oblivious to the rest of us. Occasionally Silky laughed, almost nervously, and I wondered what they were talking about. Silky wouldn't have tolerated anything inappropriate, but that left a lot of topics that I probably wouldn't approve of.

I'm not sure when I realized that Charmian was missing, but when I did, I checked for the little digging stick we kept by a mound of dirt.

Initially Charmian had expected to have her own chamber pot, and it was somehow left to me to explain the facts of camp life to her. For quite a while she had thought I was making a dirty joke, and, until light dawned, she had enjoyed the humor hugely.

Any anxiety I might have had about Charmian's absence evaporated when I saw that the digging stick was indeed gone. I doubted Charmian was far. She wasn't much concerned with modesty.

I sat down to clean one of the saddles, keeping half an eye on Jesse and Silky, when the noise started.

It was breathy little screaming. The sort one might get from a woman who was wearing a corset set a couple of notches too tight.

We all converged at the same place.

Charmian stood in a clearing. She ceased screaming when she saw us.

"A spider." Her bosom heaved. "I saw a spider. A really big one."

"For heaven's sake, Charmian," I said.

"I hate the outdoors," she cried. "I want Garth's son to die. I want to go home."

Niamh bothered to try and comfort her.

The rest of us went back to the fire.

But even as I went to my bedroll, I realized something about Charmian. She was not what I would normally think of as a survivor, but she had managed to increase her chances of success by winkling her way into our group—through her association with Niamh, of course. We didn't want her. We didn't like her. But, until she and Niamh turned south, she was one of us.

CHAPTER TWENTY-SEVEN

THE ROAD DIVERGES

Charmian was excruciating to ride with. In our first hour on the road together, she was far more annoying than she had ever been in the restricted women's quarters of Garth's palace. She rode at a snail's pace and only kept up at all because she was afraid of being picked off by road scum, the lawless who preyed on travelers.

"I'm tired," she said. First day together. First hour. First ten minutes.

"Come on, Charmian," said Niamh. "We have a long way to go."

"Everything jiggles when the horse moves."

I saw Trey raise an eyebrow.

"Don't you dare say anything," I hissed at him.

"I'm innocent," he said.

"Not in front of Silky."

"I didn't say *anything*," he protested.

"She's got a lot to jiggle," remarked Renn.

Renn would never have said anything like that in my hearing had we been at home, and I thought Trey would task him with it.

But they were both smiling like idiots.

Charmian's complaining didn't stop.

"Maybe I should have stayed in Shibbeth," she said.

"Remember when you came to me?" asked Niamh.

"Yes."

"You had no doubts then."

"I'd never ridden a horse then. Not to travel on. Now I have. I don't like it."

"You told me your half brother was going to rape you."

"He was."

"You told me you thought he might poison you."

"That doesn't stop my ass from hurting."

It was my first clue to something new I was to learn about Charmian. Under all her courtly manners and her layers of fine face paint and her elegant clothes, she was a rather coarse little thing. Although *little* wasn't the right word for her. She was short, but she had a beautiful and ample figure.

"It's going to be all right, Charmian," said Niamh.

"I suppose I believe you," said Charmian. "I trust you, Niamh. Nobody else. But you, yes."

"And I won't betray that trust."

Short silence from Charmian. Then—

"You're the only person I've ever trusted, Niamh."

"I understand."

"You'll take care of me?"

"I'll take care of you."

It was like listening to a child clinging to its mother. Over and over and over.

And then, a scarce ten minutes later, the Charmian I knew was back.

"I feel as if my breasts were about to fall off," she said, and in a voice loud enough for all of us to hear. I set my lips in a line. *I can stand this*, I thought. Jesse quickly began speaking about the scenery to Silky. Renn, who had been about to speak with me, turned away. But Trey—Trey started laughing, and he didn't stop until tears came from his eyes.

In the evening, Niamh left Charmian muttering to herself and joined Silky and me.

"You look like you've been through a lot," she said.

"I wouldn't know where to begin, Niamh," I said. "I really wouldn't."

"You could *try*," said Silky.

Niamh looked across the camp. I followed her line of sight and realized that she was examining Trey.

"It's the disease of the flesh," I said.

"I've tried to treat the disease before," said Niamh thoughtfully. "And I've seen worse cases."

"He was a worse case," said Silky. "He was a mouth and a couple of eyes. And some nose."

Niamh looked puzzled. "People don't just get better on their own," she said.

"I finally tried the Aman fungus," I said.

"Tricky," said Niamh. "You need enough to cure, but not enough to poison. Do you think he'd let me examine his face?"

"I don't know." I felt shy. "I can ask."

Trey looked surprised when I went over to him.

"What is it, Angel?"

And I told him.

"If that's what you want, Angel."

"It's not what I want that matters—it's what *you* want."

"It rarely feels that way," said Trey.

Trey sat still while Niamh inspected his face. She was careful not to touch him. Finally she sat back on her heels.

"You were lucky Angel thought of the Aman fungus," she said, "or you could have lost your whole face. How often have you put the Aman fungus on?"

"Once."

She stared at me. "If you poultice it one more time," she said, "some of the effects may be reduced considerably."

"Silky—"

But she was already running for the herb basket.

Trey smiled at me. It was a very small smile, and it was hard to see. But even though Niamh was still there, I knew it was just for me.

When the poultice was ready, I had Niamh and Silky oversee me during the application process. I patted the weak solution on every part of his face and on the inside of his lips and nose and eyelids. Nothing had been left unaffected.

Later, after we all ate, I went and flopped down on my bedding. Niamh's bedroll was next to mine, and she came and sat with her arms around her knees. If she had said something, anything, I would never have spoken the words that followed, but something about applying the poultice had made me unhappy.

"I don't like to feel, Niamh," I said.

Niamh looked at me silently for a long moment. Finally she spoke.

"Feeling is scary, Angel."

"Loving Silky is hard enough," I said. "When she's in danger my whole world is like an eggshell. How could I possibly have room for anybody else?"

But it seemed the conversation was over. Because at that, Niamh laughed.

Silky was slow getting up the next morning. She was still rolling her bedding when all of us but Charmian were standing by our horses.

"Come on, Silky," I said.

"*Coming.*"

"We'll leave without you," said Trey.

"No," said Jesse. "We won't."

"If Charmian's not mounted yet, I have at *least* twenty minutes," said Silky. "Charmian has to mount from a stump and arrange all her scarves and swirling things and put on her veils and make sure her earrings show and *then* use her little mirror to put more stuff on her face. After that we leave. I'll be ready and mounted in less than a minute."

Charmian was too busy trying to apply something blue to her eyelid to listen to Silky. Which was just as well. Charmian was long-winded when she took offense.

We started off.

We had gone maybe twenty yards when we went around a curve, and the road suddenly narrowed. There was a tree lying across it. We came to a halt. All I could think of was that there must be a way to move the tree without allowing Charmian to dismount, or we would be there all day. But I didn't foresee any real problems.

A tree, a road, an unread book.

I was Seeing. The feel of coming events moved in fast and close. I actually reached out with my arm, but it was my mind feeling forward. The future.

We were in danger.

Silky was trying to say something to me, but I had to shed her; I had to shed all of them to concentrate.

The tree was wrong. In a moment, we would be under attack.

Trey's voice penetrated the aura around me.

"Odd," he said. "The tree looks like it's been propped there."

I broke out of the Seeing.

"Crossbows," I yelled. "Charmian and Niamh in back. Silky, flank Trey."

I had to send Silky into danger; there was no help for it—she could handle herself, but even more, she could save us all.

None of them questioned me.

We were almost in formation when they fell on us.

Road scum. Clothes taken from corpses; sores on their faces; ink engravings pressed deep into the flesh to mark how many they'd killed. Matted hair. And the smell.

Their smell overwhelmed my other senses until I could barely think for the stench.

But I cleared my thoughts long enough to see that only one had a crossbow; the others had big Arcadian grooved knives—wicked weapons that left a wound that couldn't properly close, that would be open to infection.

As the one with the crossbow lifted his weapon and aimed at Trey, Silky took him down. As she refitted a bolt, one of the road scum ran to Squab and drew back his grooved knife, ready to drop the pony under Silky.

It was Renn who reached Squab and Silky. He grabbed the knife out of the man's hand and then turned it on him. When he had finished, Squab was splashed with blood.

I thought it was going to be over then, but I heard a scream from behind. One of the road scum was pulling Niamh from her horse. When he had her on the ground, he yanked back her hair and bared her throat and then lifted his knife.

Niamh would be dead in a moment. There was no one close enough to help her.

I was wrong.

Charmian, who took half an hour each morning to put on face paint—who was lazy about mounting and dismounting—flew off her horse and knocked the man down, tearing his weapon out of his hand. She threw the grooved knife down and went for his throat.

With her teeth.

It was Trey who finally got around to pulling her off the road scum. What she was doing was barbaric.

But Niamh was unhurt.

It helped that road scum weren't used to resistance. Three were dead, including Charmian's conquest, and the rest ran away.

And I realized something that I hadn't before: Charmian loved Niamh. Maybe Niamh was the only person in the world Charmian loved, but in my eyes, that love redeemed the coarse, lazy, shallow woman that Charmian had become.

We took turns mopping the blood off Charmian's face. None of it was her own. Silky suggested Charmian might want to use a twig to clean between her teeth. We were all very proud of her, and we listened to her new litany of complaints with something akin to pleasure.

"Who would have thought Charmian had it in her," said Trey.

Niamh, supported by Jesse, came up to us.

"Sorry," she said. "Jelly legs."

"I could have taken his throat out," said Charmian.

"You *did*," said Silky, and she looked at Charmian with new respect.

"We'd better bury them," said Niamh.

"Do I have to help?" asked Charmian. "I'm exhausted from saving Niamh's life." And we all agreed that she didn't have to help.

We moved on until we came to the Long Straight Road. To the left, it ran north to the Spiral City and *The Book of Forbidden Wisdom*. To the right, it went south, until it came to the place where Shibbeth territory bulged into Arcadia, the place where Niamh and Charmian would turn east. And then, after some days of travel, they would finally reach the location where Niamh took the women she rescued. There Niamh's charges stayed in safety until she could integrate them fully into the Arcadian world.

It had been determined that Jesse would escort Niamh and Charmian.

We all stood at the crossroads. The wind was coming from the east, and it was very cold.

Jesse was looking steadily at Silky.

"I'll see you in Arcadia," he said. "I'll see you wherever you go."

"Will you two please stop?" I said.

Trey reached over and grabbed Jasmine's reins. "Come with me," he said, and, as I protested, he led me away from the rest. "Give your sister a chance to say good-bye."

"I need to be there," I said. "I don't want any touching. No. Touching. At. All."

But by the time he let me go back to the rest, it was too late. Jesse had Silky's hand in his. And then he leaned over and kissed it.

Trey bumped me with Bran. "If you say a word," he said, "I'll knock you off your horse."

"But—"

He moved to push me out of the saddle, and I could see in Trey's eyes that he was serious. And perhaps, in this case, for this one time, he was right—perhaps I should let Jesse kiss Silky's hand. Silky was glowing with happiness—and I wasn't sorry that she could feel so deeply.

Now that it was time to say good-bye to Niamh, I found I had no words.

"Don't worry," she said. "I'll be at your wedding."

"What wedding?"

She smiled.

Charmian was more effusive. She kissed Silky. She kissed me. Renn managed to avoid her, but she came perilously close to kissing Trey.

"No wonder you liked roading with Garth," she said to me. "It's a lot more interesting than the restricted women's quarters."

Then Niamh and Charmian and Jesse moved their horses onto the Long Straight Road, but in the direction south. We watched them for a long time.

Only Jesse turned and looked at us again. I couldn't read his expression at that distance, and he didn't wave or gesture. He just turned. And then he turned away.

And that's how we said good-bye to Charmian. And Jesse. And Niamh. I didn't know if we would see them in this world again.

CHAPTER TWENTY-EIGHT

THE SPIRAL CITY

In the northern Arcadian territory, we came to a rolling green land—a land that looked as if it would be a good place to raise horses, cows or sheep, although we saw none. We had moved off the known map of the world into the place of bardsong.

Beyond this land, in the remains of the Spiral City, was *The Book of Forbidden Wisdom*. When my mother gave *The Book* into the care of the Keeper, she could not possibly have imagined that I would one day need it to stay alive. And at first I couldn't think why she would hide a document that would have opened all Arcadia to her children.

And then I understood.

Her children. *All* her children.

Perhaps she had not trusted Kalo.

We began to pass cottages, and, at each dwelling, the inhabitants tumbled out to greet us. They stared at Trey's face, but they showed neither fear nor surprise. The children didn't point or make fun. I realized why when we passed a knot of faceless children. The disease of the flesh had been here too.

When I saw an older woman—maybe in her thirties—hanging out wash, I pulled up Jasmine.

"Is this the road to the Spiral City?" I asked.

"Where be you from?" she asked. Her accent was so strong that I had trouble understanding her.

"Southern Arcadia," I said.

"You be a very long way from home," she said. Or so I thought she said. She said "home" to rhyme with "lamb."

"But are we going the *right way* to the Spiral City?" asked Silky.

"Yes," she said. She showed no curiosity but bobbed her head and went into her dwelling.

So. We were close enough to the Spiral City that people knew of its existence.

As it grew darker, we passed a cottage with warm light coming from its windows. A moment later, three children and a grown woman stood before us. The woman's face was friendly.

"You be strange and strangers both," she said, but she didn't speak with any anxiety.

"We're from the south," I said. "Your land here is beautiful."

She beamed.

"I be Treena," she said. "You're welcome here if you'd like to stop and eat—and I'd be happy for company, should you need a place to shelter for the night." Through the doorway I could see a fire dancing in the grate, and something savory wafted from the dwelling. "It be vegetables tonight," said Treena, "but fresh from the garden. Selt"—she spoke to the tallest girl without waiting for our answer—"go set places."

The meal was a simple stew. Honest potatoes and other vegetables.

She, too, we learned, had heard of the Spiral City.

After dinner, Renn sang. The news seemed irrelevant this far north. Instead Renn sang one of the great epics—the lay of the young lovers who, rather than betray each other, were turned to trees.

We had heard it before, but it was clear our hosts hadn't. Treena and her children wept at the end.

After Treena tucked her two youngest children away in their beds, she and Selt rejoined us.

"It's good to have you here," she said. "It be lonesome sometimes, with my goodman dead these last four years. I have washing water that Selt can heat if you'd be liking that."

Washing. Being clean. It occurred to me that Treena had offered because we *smelled*. And then I didn't care.

Silky and I scrubbed ourselves in the cottage from a bucket of deliciously hot water, provided by Selt. Trey and Renn washed out back. When we had finished, and they returned, we looked at each other—in wonder.

All that shiny, clean hair. Silky's fell around her like silk, and her heart-shaped face was radiant. I noticed again Renn's classically handsome face—I could spend a long time looking at that face—but somehow now my eye lingered mostly on Trey. His face hadn't changed—indeed, I put linseed oil on it earlier, to take away its dry look—but his hair looked shiny and soft, and I wondered what it would be like to put my hands in such hair. I gazed at him, and, for just a second, I looked past his disfigurement and into his eyes, and I saw there again the boy that I had always known to trust.

And Trey gazed back at me steadily. There was so much in his eyes that I had to turn away.

How was I supposed to guide Silky when I couldn't even guard against moments like these?

But it had been a long day.

Silky and I began to bed down—the others would sleep in a lean-to by the side of the cottage. But Treena lingered. I could tell she was curious about us.

"At dinner you said you be going to the Spiral City," she said finally. "They say it's nothing more than a ruin."

"We have business there," I said.

"Ah," she said, in a tone that betokened a complete lack of understanding, "business."

In the morning, Treena and her family saw us off. She pressed food on us, and although I tried to give her money, she refused absolutely, and I saw that to persist would be to offend.

We rode all day. The grass was lush, and there was plenty of food for the horses. The cottages soon spread farther and farther apart until we rode without seeing a single one. All day the wind was brisk; it whipped against my skin. I hoped the linseed oil was protecting Trey's face—I had given the final poultice, so he had little to shield him from the elements. I wondered how much Trey could feel through the disease-mask, and if he were in constant pain.

That afternoon, when the shadows were long, we reached a set of gates that might have been built for giants—but that were now no more than twisted ruins. Flecks of gold leaf suggested that they had been gilded, but now the wood was dark and stained by water and weather. One of the gates had fallen in, and the regular-sized door set in the other was jammed so that it was forever open.

We had reached our destination.

Once upon a time these gates had sealed the Spiral City from the world outside—it had been a forbidden city.

Now we easily rode through them.

On the inside, the buildings around us had crum-

bled, and some had collapsed completely. We picked
our way through streets littered with stone and brick
and timbers. The city curled to the center, where, so
my mother had told me, *The Book of Forbidden Wisdom*
was guarded by the Keeper, her Steward. She had told
me of him when I was a child. Or perhaps now the son
of her Steward was guardian. The Keeper had taken
his family, as well as *The Book,* north.

Squab began limping, and our progress slowed.
Silky dismounted and checked his feet.

"Stone," she called out. "Bruise but no real damage."

"You'll have to walk him for a while," I said.

"We can all walk," she said.

But I did not have the patience.

"I'm riding ahead," I said. "You two stay with Silky."

"Are you sure, Angel?" asked Renn.

"That's a stupid idea," said Trey.

"*No,*" said Silky.

I ignored them. It was as if I were being pulled; delay
would have been almost physically painful. "I'll see
you at the center," I said, and I rode on. Soon enough
the walls of the city curved, and the others were out
of sight. There were advantages to outranking them
all: in the end there had been nothing they could do, in
courtesy, to stop me from going ahead.

And it was a relief to be alone. At home, in Arcadia, I was never alone. There was always an attendant,
a maid, a chaperone, a tutor with me. Here, too, we
were always at close quarters. To be alone, one had
to take the little digging stick and go into the bushes;

then the others would politely pretend one didn't exist.

The air became close as the buildings of the Spiral City drew nearer to one another, as the spiral closed, as the roofs seemed almost to meet overhead. I was in shadow all the time now. I moved slowly, and the others were beginning to catch up to me. I could hear Silky's voice raised above the other two; a moment later, I could see them again.

Then Jasmine seemed to become unsettled, and she pawed at the ground. I thought perhaps she wanted to be with the other horses.

I don't know where the riders came from, except that they must have been somewhere ahead of me, deeper in the spiral. They were dressed in the dark clothes and hoods of freemen, but some of them rode their horses in the style of Great Lords. At first they galloped directly toward me; I screamed a warning to the others and expected to be overwhelmed and taken in a matter of seconds. There was nowhere to go. I braced. But a moment later they galloped past me, all but one. I reined right and left, but he mirrored my movements, and I halted. He came right up to me until our horses were almost nose to nose. The man, I saw, was enormous, and he rode an enormous horse. This was no Lord in disguise but, by the mark I saw on his hand, an indentured servant. There would be no pity in this behemoth of a man.

"You're not the fair-haired one," the man said.

He made me impatient. "Obviously," I said.

"You're the dark one. The Lady Angel Montrose."

"Yes." At my back I could hear outcries and straining horses and the noise of struggle.

"Get off your horse."

There was nowhere to go. I got off my horse. The behemoth dismounted as well.

As the giant approached, I looked beyond him, frantically. I saw that one building in front of me was quite unlike the rest. It had not fallen into disrepair. The façade was covered in what looked like beaten gold, and there were curious devices—serpents, strange land animals, fish—carved on the pillars in front. Its windows were unbroken. If one could get in, it looked like a good place to keep people out.

The door to this building was painted a vivid cobalt blue flecked with gold. It was ajar. Behemoth was close to me now. I measured the distance to the door.

And I ran.

I must have surprised Behemoth, because I got pretty far. My hand was actually on the door when he reached me. He didn't pull me back but pushed me inside, and then, with no regard for the proprieties, he dragged me through a room and then into another. We stopped in front of a window onto the street, and he jerked my arm up behind my back.

I tried hard not to make a sound, but it hurt, and I'm afraid I did.

I stared out the window, pinioned by Behemoth, in

THE BOOK OF FORBIDDEN WISDOM 357

time to see Renn and Trey taken by the men of the dark riders. Silky was on foot, running, and she almost made it to the door of one of the tilted houses, but as I watched, one of the dark riders bore down on her. I was afraid they would shoot her down in the street with their crossbows.

The man still had my arm held high up behind my back until I thought it would break; with his other hand, he covered my mouth tightly. I couldn't scream to the others. All I could do was make small and feeble noises that had no chance of penetrating the glass of the window in front of me.

Silky never had a chance. The dark rider galloped to her so hard and fast that for a moment I thought she would be trampled.

But at the last second the horse spooked and swerved to the side.

As the dark rider's horse swerved, he did not so much fall as swing himself to the ground, and then he was on top of Silky. One of her arms was pinned, but she pushed at him with the other and tried to claw his face. A sharp pain ran from my arm up into my shoulder, and I realized Behemoth had lifted my own arm some more. I must have been trying to struggle. I watched the street, helpless. Up until now all sound had been muffled by glass and stone. But now I heard a voice, high-pitched and desperate.

"*Angel!*" cried Silky.

But there was nothing I could do.

The dark rider hauled her to her feet, and when he

did, Silky reached up and yanked back his tightly fitting cowl.

I recognized the corn-colored hair before I saw the dark rider's face.

It was Leth.

Of course it was.

With one hand Leth held the reins of his horse; with the other he dragged Silky over to where Renn and Trey were being held in check by the freemen and the other dark rider. She suddenly twisted to the side, and I knew, because I knew Silky very well, that she was going to bite him, as she had bitten Garth what seemed like so long ago. But Leth, feeling her struggle, first shook her as if she were a kitten—and then hit her in the face.

I could do nothing.

But at that, the other dark rider left Renn and Trey with the freemen and rode up to Leth. He cuffed Leth on the cheek, and then he pulled back his own cowl.

It was my father.

As I watched Leth drag Silky back to the others, my father at his side, my shoulder and arm were cramping, and I was in agony. But then I felt it. I felt it first as a kind of relief, a very small letup in the pain that was beginning to spread from my shoulder across my chest, and it took me only a second to realize where the relief was coming from—the man holding me was getting tired.

His muscles must be aching, too.

I made a move to get my arm down from behind my back, but he yanked it so far up that I thought he was going to pull it out by the root. I felt sick. But his other arm relaxed just a little bit.

I could bend my arm at the elbow, and I immediately drove that elbow, with all the force I could muster, back into his side.

Reflexively, he released his hold for a moment, but a moment was all I needed. And for that moment, it didn't matter how big he was or how strong or how much someone was paying him for capturing Lady Angel Montrose.

Because I had the image of Silky calling for me.

I elbowed him again, hard; he released the arm he had been holding up my back; my muscles sang in relief.

I turned. He towered over me, and that was a great advantage—for me. I brought the heel of my hand up into the base of his nose.

He didn't fall, but he turned aside. Obviously I couldn't run out into the street—straight into the arms of Leth and my father. It would do Silky, Trey and Renn no good if I were captured again.

But when Behemoth had dragged me into the building, I had noticed an alcove with an overturned chair in it—and behind the chair, a door. I had been looking for doors—for ways out. And the memory of that alcove, that chair, that door, was as sharp in my mind as cut glass. I pushed past Behemoth and started to go back the way we had come.

But when I got to the alcove, the chair was no longer overturned.

Kalo sat there now; a crossbow lay casually across his lap. He held an axe.

"Hello, Angel," he said.

"Hello, Kalo," I whispered.

Kalo smiled at me.

They had us. They had us all.

For a long moment Kalo and I looked at each other, neither one of us moving. Then I glanced at Behemoth. He was doubled over, clutching his face; blood spewed from his nose, and I could hear a steady patter as it fell to the floor.

Kalo didn't say a word to the man. He just let him bleed.

Kalo. My brother.

I wanted to beg for the others, but I didn't. Kalo would not change his mind if I did, and he would have enjoyed it greatly.

"I can't read *The Book of Forbidden Wisdom*," Kalo said conversationally.

"I'm sorry."

In a moment he was on his feet, and the crossbow was leveled at my chest.

"The Keeper says you know how," he said. "The Keeper of *The Book* says Mother would have taught you."

"Mother died young."

"But you seem unsurprised there's a Keeper of *The Book*."

"It's in bardsong."

It wasn't in bardsong. Not so much as a mention of the Keeper had made it into ballad or lay, but then Kalo had never liked bardsong. There was no way he could know.

"You will read *The Book of Forbidden Wisdom* for me," he said. "I'm going to know its secrets, and then I will have the power to own all Arcadia."

"Is it enough to own all Arcadia, do you think? Will you ever have enough?"

"If you don't read, the others die," he said. "They will die without Arbitrators, without witnesses, and in the full knowledge that you could have saved them." He lowered his crossbow. "Is that enough incentive? Shall we go to the Keeper now? Or shall I send this somewhat useless servant"—he gestured toward Behemoth—"to get Leth and Silky? Then you can watch your sister die."

"*Our* sister."

His lips twitched. He was very dangerous now. "All right," he said. "We can watch *our* sister die."

I didn't hesitate. There was no point.

"Let's go to the Keeper," I said.

"And you'll read *The Book*?"

"I will read it if I can."

"I want you to say you'll read it."

"I'll read it."

Kalo smiled and lowered the crossbow. "Thank

you, Angel," he said. He leaned toward me, confidentially. "I'm rather sorry about all the fuss with the wedding. It caused more problems than I'd anticipated."

"You did me a favor," I said.

He smiled. For a moment I thought he was actually going to pat me on the shoulder or take my hand, but of course he didn't. Kalo never touched anyone unless it was to cause pain. Nor could he bear to be touched.

It occurred to me that Kalo had some serious problems.

"You don't know how much I hate you, do you, Angel?"

"I can imagine."

"No," he said, his voice so low I had to strain to hear him. "You have *no* idea."

The dwelling we were in, like the city, was built in a spiral. Kalo prodded me with the crossbow, and I walked down a curving hall and into a room that looked like a study. A man sat on the floor in the center of the room, and a guard stood over him.

"You're back," the seated man said. His hands trembled.

"She can read it," said Kalo. "She's a first daughter of the House of St. Clare. As you stipulated."

So this was the Keeper.

He was a man of tics and twitches. He dressed like an Arcadian freeman, but he wore his long grey hair braided, like a Shibbeth traditionalist. The hair was shiny and clean, and his clothes were spotless.

His wrinkled skin had a reddish glow to it, as if he'd scrubbed it with a stiff brush.

He was a contradiction: a man fastidious amidst ruin, an Arcadian by blood and garb, who wore his hair like a 'Liden.

"Welcome, Lady Angel," he said, as if he weren't sitting on the floor at the feet of a guard.

"We don't need niceties," said Kalo.

"I thought your son might be Keeper by now," I said, ignoring Kalo. It wasn't as if he would kill me—as long as I didn't rouse his temper. For the time being, I actually held some power.

"My family left long ago," said the Keeper. He paused. "You've come a long way to read *The Book of Forbidden Wisdom*."

"Yes," I said. "Very far." I had come so far that I wasn't sure I would have recognized the girl who had set out on the journey.

"I remember when your mother came," he said, as if we were sitting over tea. As if Kalo did not have his crossbow trained on first one and then the other of us. "It was after your birth—she had changed her mind about the keeping of *The Book*. I'm not likely to forget the fuss. Purple and blue tents sprouting up like mushrooms outside the Spiral City. Maids and chaperones and armed men. I went to the edge of the city and saw."

Kalo waved the crossbow at the Keeper, but it had no discernible effect on him.

"I don't understand. Did she take *The Book* back to Southern Arcadia with her?" I was confused.

"No," he said. "I had thought she wanted the power for you, but the Lady St. Clare—I suppose she was the Lady Montrose then—never read beyond the first pages," said the Keeper. "She simply looked at it and then left. *The Book* stayed here."

"Why don't you tell me what's in it?" Kalo asked the Keeper. "You've lived with *The Book of Forbidden Wisdom* for years."

The Keeper looked surprised. "Oh, I can't read it," he said. "I'm the Keeper. Only *she* can read it."

"Why is that?"

The Keeper seemed confused. "Because she's the Lady Angel St. Clare Montrose." As if that were answer enough. "Are you ready, Lady Angel?"

"She's ready," said Kalo.

"Lady Angel?" said the Keeper.

"I'm ready."

There was a stillness in the room. There was a stillness inside of me. I found that now that I was near *The Book*, I didn't care about it at all. Even my terror for the others was, oddly, draining away. I was sure that if I could have dragged my heart out of my bosom, it would have been grey, the color of dead boiled meat.

I couldn't bear to feel.

I just wanted it to be over.

"I'll take you to *The Book* now, Lady Angel," said the Keeper. "It's your right."

We followed him down a hall and into a room like

a small study. Books were everywhere, but I knew *The Book of Forbidden Wisdom* as soon as I entered the room. Backed in silver, bound in dark leather with the St. Clare crest stamped on it, *The Book* rested, closed, on a reading podium.

The air was full of possibility. Despite what was claimed in bardsong, I knew there was no such thing as magic, but I also knew there were vortices in time. How else could one See? I felt that if I were to raise my hand and touch *The Book*, all the various pasts that clamored together would become a single linear story. The past would be revealed, and, as I committed it to my eidetic memory, it would become fixed. There would be no world in which Caro survived the 'Lidan invasion of The Village of Broken Women. No parallel story in which Trey was miraculously healed—or never contracted the disease of the flesh at all. If I read, I might be condemning us to time without possibility—slow and plodding lives plotted out for us.

I didn't know what would happen.

Time flowed around us in eddies and currents, and it all emanated from *The Book*.

"Maybe it shouldn't be read," I said. "Perhaps the wisdom is forbidden."

"Don't be absurd," said Kalo. "It's just a mass of land titles. Enough to make me unimaginably rich."

"It's a book," said the Keeper. "A book is meant to be read. And *you* were born to read it."

I sensed his words were true, but I also sensed that to read would be to reshape the past as I knew it. To read would give birth to the possibility of a new and different and perhaps frightening future.

Land deeds?

I didn't think so. Not land deeds. I thought it might contain something that could overturn our world and drench it thickly in blood.

But I couldn't See anything. I didn't hear my mother. It was my decision alone, and the only thing I knew was that it didn't feel like a decision at all.

I stepped forward, reached up my hand and touched *The Book.*

And with that, everything changed.

I didn't remove my hand. I stroked the exquisite binding. Some long ago St. Clare had lovingly put *The Book of Forbidden Wisdom* together, and she had wielded the power to See. Perhaps she had Seen me, now, standing here, my head bowed. I could See once again, too. I lifted my head and glanced at Kalo, and the thin veneer of his humanity was gone. I saw a grotesque malignity that wanted Silky and me dead—he would thrill to see us die.

I partially lifted the great cover. My mother, I knew, had foregone *The Book*, had, unlike every St. Clare matriarch before her, refused to keep it current. That job might fall to me if I picked up the thread my mother had let fall. If I saw virtue in this wisdom that somehow she had not.

The room was electric with danger.

"Go ahead," said Kalo. "Read."

"Not until I know the others are alive," I said.

"I can make you read," said Kalo.

I searched for fear inside me. I didn't find any. I didn't find anything.

"No," I said. "You can't."

Kalo made a sound of exasperation and waved his crossbow at the guard, as if he were using it as a pointer.

"Tell the Lord Leth I want the Lady Silky Montrose, the Lord Trey and that bard. Here. Now."

That bard. But nothing stirred inside me.

I waited.

And then they were there: two more guards, Leth, my father, Silky, Trey and Renn.

Renn was leaning on Trey as if he could barely stand, and there were dark bruises on his face. But Trey—when he saw me, his whole being seemed to light up, and once again I knew his feelings for me. But I felt only numbness.

Kalo poked me with his crossbow. "Read," he said.

I looked at Silky.

She looked tiny next to the man guarding her. Her gold hair was snarled; there was dirt on her face and the tracks of many tears. She gasped when she saw me.

"*Angel*," she said. "I thought you were dead. Because I called for you, and you didn't come. You've *always* come."

"She was busy," said Kalo.

"She *always* comes," said my little sister.

"Silky," I said, "I'm here now." And I felt a flutter inside, as if my heart had forgotten how to beat and was just now beginning to remember. And for a moment I knew how much I loved them all—Silky, Trey, Renn. For a moment I felt whole.

CHAPTER TWENTY-NINE

THE QUIET COUNTRY

Kalo gave me no time to nurse that flutter of emotion.

"Doesn't it surprise you," said Kalo, "that, except for your own clumsiness in getting captured in Shibbeth, you've roamed almost completely free? You must think us very stupid."

"We certainly *do*," said Silky. "We've known you were following us for *ages*."

Leth spoke up. "What you know doesn't matter," he said. "We've followed you all the way to *The Book of Forbidden Wisdom*. And now Kalo will let me pronounce sentence on you. Because I can't live in peace,

Angel, even with my new wife, Lady Rose, until you, and your lovers, and your foolish sister, are dead."

"Shut up, Leth," said Kalo.

The Keeper spoke.

"Only you can read *The Book*, Lady Angel," he said. "It's not forbidden to you. You have the St. Clare training."

"But I don't," I said.

I removed my hand from *The Book*, and the eddies of time around me stilled. I didn't climb onto the reading stand, because if I read *The Book*, it would be inside me, and Kalo knew that, and, eventually, Kalo would make me tell.

My father was starting to look uneasy.

Kalo came up to me and thrust his face into mine. He couldn't control himself. He had never been able to control his rage; it spread like burning oil across the surface of a millpond. It touched everything, and yet, in some ways, it was ineffectual. He didn't get his way with his temper; he destroyed things.

If he had started with Silky, everything would have turned out differently. I would have defended her; he would have killed me; the journey would have been over.

But something else happened.

He attacked the Keeper.

He beat him and kicked him until he lay senseless on the floor, and I knew we were all very close to death. I had lived with Kalo's temper since the day I was born, and I knew he was now beyond the place where he could help himself. I remembered when, at the age of ten, he had beaten his dog to death for disobedience. And then he had wept and howled when it wouldn't come back to him from the unknown place.

I was numb now as I watched him. He would kill us each in turn, and then he would have a tantrum when he realized *The Book* could no longer be read. I had never felt so utterly helpless, so completely lost.

My father caught my eye for a moment. We both recognized this side of Kalo. To kill him now would be like putting down a mad dog. And had there been a way for us to do it, we would have. Brother or no brother. Son or no son.

The Keeper groaned.

Kalo raised the axe he had been carrying all this time in his left hand and brought it down, severing the Keeper's head from his body. The head rolled to one side, and while the dead man's features were largely hidden by hair, I could see that his lips were still moving. Silky had been nearby, and a fine spray of blood covered her face and pale dress like a macabre bridal veil.

Her lips were pale. She was in shock.

"You need to read," Kalo said to me. "You need to read now."

I doubted, though, that I would be able to read much before his rage engulfed him and he struck me down.

"We can take him," Trey whispered to me, but I shook my head at him.

Instead, I looked at my brother. "Kalo," I said. He stared at me as if he'd never seen me before. "You're going to lose, Kalo. I'm smarter than you are. I always have been." Horror crossed my father's face. I wanted to look at Silky before it happened, but there wasn't time. For a moment, Trey's face was in my mind. I wished there had been a time when I had let him kiss me.

Kalo raised the butt of the axe; he raised it high above my head. I automatically lifted my arm to defend myself.

And he brought the wooden end of the axe down on me.

"**A**ngel," I heard Silky call. "*Angel.*" But the words turned to the sound that starlings make as, startled, they scatter from a tree.

I had only time to take a breath before dark waters closed over my head. At first I struggled, but then the waters took me.

And while I realized that I needed air, or, rather, that I was going to need air soon, there was no sense of hurry in whatever world I was in.

The water cooled and refreshed me. A school of fish swam into my vision; they were small and iridescent blue. Surely this wasn't a dream. I wouldn't dream fish I had never seen before. I wouldn't, in fact, have dreamt fish.

I kicked my legs, and, a second later, I broke the surface of the water and gave a gasp. The air was sweet, like a meadow fully ripe, right before the mowing. And, at the same time, I smelled moonflowers—the sweet and poisonous flowers that opened into deep white blossoms on the nights of the full moon.

Light and dark.

I thought I had been deep underwater, but now I could stand—the water came up to my waist.

And on the shore was my mother. She looked as if she were collecting shells. She stood and gazed out at me, shading her eyes against the bright sun reflecting off the water. Our eyes met, and she smiled. That's when I knew I was still alive in the other world, a world with evil, probably dying on the floor. I hoped it wouldn't upset Silky too much. Here, I didn't seem to mind.

Now, seeing my mother, I was overcome by a feeling of warmth.

This was not my mother as I remembered her when she carried Silky in her womb, when her thick auburn hair streamed down past her waist. Nor was it my mother as I remembered her four years after Silky's birth, with her crinkled smile and a scattering of grey in her hair, supremely happy to be carrying another child, although she was somewhat old to face giving birth. And now the awful, final image I had of her melted away: after her child had been stillborn, and my mother had died, I had glimpsed her chalk-white, still form lying on the bloody sheets of the birthing room.

This woman was not much older than I was, and she bore a deep glow, as if she possessed a joyful secret. And I thought—I will never know that secret. I will never feel that joy. And I thought—I've chosen not to. And I thought, finally—but she will tell me the secret.

I waded onto the shore. She waited, her head tilted, light glowing in her eyes. And then I reached her, and we embraced. I knew I was squeezing her too hard, but this was my mother, the woman Silky had barely known but whose place I had tried so hard to fill for my sister. This was the woman who had burned so bright that her death had sent my father into perpetual mourning.

She held me at arm's length and looked me over.

"You're beautiful," she said finally. "Beautiful and cool as the east wind. Poor Trey. I didn't know what to expect, given all that's happened to you."

"My nose is too long," I said, and she laughed. "But you should see Silky. She's lovely. Can you see Silky?"

"I don't look much," she said quietly. "It's peaceful here. I knew I left Silky in good hands, and that was enough. But come now. You don't have much time."

"And you?"

"I have forever."

And my mother took my hand, and we began walking along the beach. Her hand was warm, but I had to ask.

"Am I dreaming?"

She laughed. "Does it matter?"

I thought about it. "Yes," I said. "It matters."

"No," she said. "You're not dreaming."

I looked around. Sea and sand and, in the distance, dunes.

It was a quiet country.

The odor of meadow and moonflower had grown stronger.

"Can I stay?"

"No," she said.

"Can I stay for a while?"

"No. Time passes more quickly where you come from. Here, time barely passes at all."

"Do you miss me?"

"I do. But there's no place for sorrow here."

Without letting go of her hand, I picked up a shell. The sea had smoothed the outside of it; the inside was pale pink, the color of a baby's ear.

"If I go back," I said, "I'll have to feel." My mother dropped my hand, but I barely noticed. I was looking out at the tranquil bay.

I could walk out into it. I could walk until it was too deep to stand, and then I could just keep going. My mother would watch me to the end, and there would be nothing to fear. Perhaps I would find myself back in the quiet country. Or perhaps I would find oblivion.

And now the scent of moonflowers—poisonous, powerful, alluring— seemed to fill the air completely. I felt as if I were choking on it. The water beckoned even more. The water would wash away everything, even my frightened, confused, agonized and, yes, lonely self. For a moment, my love for Silky, my terror that she would die—these were only burdens to be set down.

And then my mother stroked my arm.

"It's time to go, Angel," she said. The scent of moon-flowers began to fade.

"Don't make me go," I said. "Please."

"I'm not making you do anything. But," she seemed to consider for a moment, "perhaps it's time the book was read. I didn't have the courage for the knowledge. We're all guilty in the book—but maybe it's time for change."

"I don't understand."

She said the words with a sigh, as if they now meant very little to her: "The casteless shall be Great. The Great will be brought down."

I didn't understand her.

"I can't bear it, Mother. Silky—the others—they're probably going to be murdered."

"And what were you thinking about your own fate?"

"That's different," I said. "I'm separate. I'm different—alone already. They're going to be *torn* from the world."

"You love them," she said.

"Love makes it harder." I had said four words too many. Because suddenly I had heard myself, and I realized I was a coward.

"You love many people," she said.

"That's not what I mean."

"Maybe," said my mother, "it isn't love you fear. Maybe you're afraid of being in love."

"I've never been in love."

My mother laughed.

"The St. Clares love deeply," she said.

"But who do I love?" I asked.

"I suspect," said my mother, "that you know the answer very well."

She put a creamy white shell into my hand, and she kissed me softly on the forehead. The scent of roses now was everywhere. She didn't move away, but as I breathed in the scent, the scene began to fade. And then I was under water again, swimming up toward the bright surface, toward loss and sacrifice and pain and betrayal and disease and horror.

Toward love.

CHAPTER THIRTY

THE AWAKENING

I could taste blood. I could smell blood. I opened my eyes, but then the world went away for a little while. When I opened them again, the room was blurry at first, and inclined to spin, but soon my vision cleared. Silky, Renn and my father were standing and looking at me as if waiting for something. I wondered where Trey was, but only for the half second it took me to realize that the warmth and comfort I felt came from the fact that he had me cradled in his arms.

"Angel."

It sounded as if he had been saying my name for

some time. But what I wanted was my mother; I had become, for a little while, a child again.

I was perfectly comfortable in Trey's arms. I reached up to touch his damaged face.

The reaction, somehow, was not what I had expected. He almost dropped me. His expression, so far as I could read it, was one of shyness and chagrin.

"She's *alive*," said Silky.

"I'm sorry, Lord Kestling of Montrose," said Trey to my father. "I didn't mean to take such liberties. I'm sorry, Angel. I thought you were dead."

So apparently it was all right to hold a woman who *might* be dead, but not a live one. There was something seriously wrong with the Arcadian rules of conduct.

"Well, I'm not dead," I said. And then I said "Ow" because my arm ached and my head felt as if it had been hit by the butt of an axe. Which was probably the case, although my arm must have deflected the blow—or I would still be in the quiet country. Trey made a move to put me down.

"Sorry," he said as his arm grazed my breast. Then he grimaced, because, of course, he should have just pretended it hadn't happened. I almost slipped out of his arms.

"Don't drop me," I said irritably, "just because I'm alive. Think of me as wounded. Which I am. Is that my blood?" There was a pool of it on the floor, dark and congealing. I must have been gone for a while, although it seemed I had spent only minutes with my mother.

"You bled like a *pig*," said Silky.

"Thank you for that," I said, and then, because Trey was having a hard time figuring out where to put his hands and arms, I sat up and pulled away from him.

He looked both let down and relieved.

I felt peculiar, but good peculiar, at being held. Illegally held of course. Suddenly the idea that Leth might ever have held me like that—that he might have had every reason to expect to touch me—was horrifying. What on earth had I been thinking to consent to such a marriage?

I hadn't been thinking about Trey.

And I hadn't been thinking about Renn. Strange, dark Renn.

My mother had been right. I hadn't known my heart at all.

Now that I was back from the quiet country, everything looked and felt different—more vibrant. The world dripped with saturated color, and the air pulsated with sound.

Silky came and put her arms around me, and I felt myself coming more and more to my senses. I felt as if I had been traveling a great distance over the vastness of time. In fact, I was fairly sure that was exactly what I had been doing.

"I thought I'd lost you," said my father, which was an odd thing to say, because the last I knew he had been on the side of my sadistic brother and my equally sadistic ex-pre-contract.

"Lord Kestling of Montrose has joined us," said Trey, and I saw a small, ironic smile.

My father came to my side. "I couldn't let Kalo kill you," he said.

"Thank you," I said, although the response seemed a peculiar one even as it came out of my mouth. Thanks-for-not-letting-your-sadistic-son-kill-his-sister. Thanks-for-not-murdering-your-eldest-daughter. Thanks.

I was light-headed.

"Somebody catch me up," I said. Given how hard my head and arm were aching, given how close to death I had obviously come, given that I was quite sure we were still in trouble, I was remarkably cheerful. Crossing the ultimate divide and chatting with one's loving, long-dead mother had that effect.

I considered for a moment whether or not I might have dreamt Leth and Kalo, but there, close by, was the Keeper's body. And there, close by, was the Keeper's head.

"Kalo thinks he killed you," said Silky. "We couldn't hear you breathing. Well, actually, *Trey* thought he heard you, but I thought he was—"

"Let me tell it, Silky," said Trey. "You're already digressing."

"Go ahead," I said.

"When Kalo saw you lying there bleeding," said Trey, "he lifted his axe to hit you again. Your father—Lord Kestling, that is—stopped him. And so did I."

"There was some kind of commotion outside," said

Silky, interrupting. "Shouts and yelling. Kalo and Leth left us with Father as guard and went with some of the soldiers."

I heard voices and a clamor in the distance. Meanwhile, I saw that *The Book of Forbidden Wisdom* was still closed and on the pedestal. Father followed my eyes.

"They think I'm keeping *The Book* from you until they return," he said. "They want to be here when Angel reads it."

"Are you?" asked Silky. "Are you going to keep Angel away?"

"No, daughter," said Father. "I'm tired of Kalo's greed and malice. I had always thought that Angel was my problem child, but I see that I was wrong."

"All this *way*, Angel," said Silky. "And we're finally alone with *The Book*. And you can't read it. If only Mother had told you the secret of the reading."

"If only," I said. "Now will somebody help me over to *The Book* so that I can at least take a look?"

"You *do* know how to read it," said Trey.

"Yes," I said. "I do."

And I felt more in control, stronger, more certain than I had in a long time—maybe ever.

My father moved toward me, but Trey intercepted him and gave me his arm to lean on, which was about as far as etiquette would stretch under the circumstances. He almost slipped on blood as we approached the reading stand. I looked down.

"Move the Keeper's head," I said. "He deserves better."

My father came over, picked up the head, and put it back next to the Keeper's body.

With Trey's help I clambered onto the podium.

The book was a thing of dark and magical beauty. I opened it, and it was as if power were flowing into my fingers. Whatever was there, I knew I wouldn't be left unchanged. The strange markings and notations, the captions under the picture, seemed to rearrange themselves in front of my eyes.

I was reading.

I was reading *The Book of Forbidden Wisdom*.

I turned a page. And then, after a moment, I turned another.

And another.

The world had fallen silent; there was nothing except the markings in *The Book* in front of me.

I read fluently and carefully.

CHAPTER THIRTY-ONE

THE BOOK OF FORBIDDEN WISDOM

I was ready to find the deeds to the lost lands. I was ready to find the power to rule Arcadia under my fingertips. And as I read the first page, I did think it might be an enormous Book of Land, like the ones that were signed at weddings. I found, too, on the second and third pages, that I was looking at dozens of deeds, either pasted into *The Book* (those were easy to read) or scribbled directly into *The Book* in code. An odd thing about the code: I knew it as if it were the first writing I had learned: the squiggles—letters; the dashes and squares—punctuation. My mother must have twined that language into me, and I didn't know when. It was as if I had understood these markings all my life.

After having read only the opening pages, however, I realized that this was no book with the deeds to lost lands. Not in the sense that anyone had ever thought.

This was not a book that would give greater power to the landed.

This was a book with the power to *undo* the Great. To unmake. To unravel the social fabric of Arcadia.

"Well?" asked Trey, and I realized that I had been focused entirely on the book before me. Everything else had fallen away—thoughts about Silky, Trey, Renn, my father. There was only *The Book of Forbidden Wisdom*.

"Give me a little time," I said. "If I read it, it's ours. If I get out of here alive, they can't take it away. Think of my memory. And let me read."

The notations on the first pages had been recent land transfers. Big ones. Some I knew about. A section of prime meadowland had gone to the Nessons, and I remembered when that had happened, but none of the details. I could scarcely make out the hand of the previous owner. The signature was an illegible scrawl.

Now I looked at other deeds, some coded, some not, and the pattern was similar. Large land transfers were being made to Great Houses from people I'd never heard of who could barely write their names.

I heard noise outside the room. "*Hurry,*" said Silky, and she wrung her hands with impatience.

But there was no hurrying. "I need to figure this out," I said. I turned the page.

I was expecting more deeds of sale, but I found myself looking at coded marriage transactions that had resulted in the shifting of land and power. I couldn't read half of the names involved—they were smudged and blotted—but then I saw a name that surprised me.

"Angel?" said Trey.

"Don't let anyone in," I said.

"You read," said Trey. "We'll take care of the rest."

I looked at the familiar name again.

Lady Brynne of the House of Tonnow.

She had married a man named Cor. No title. No other name. But he had brought to the marriage table twenty thousand hectares of timber. And Tonnow, I knew, had been a poor House in the past.

I paused.

Because I knew Lady Brynne of the House of Tonnow. She had been invited to my wedding, although we all knew she wouldn't come. She lived in seclusion in the rambling castle that belonged to the family, and she had not been seen outside that castle for years. It was said that she had vowed never to marry. Being single was allowed if the family approved.

But here was a contract certificate, eight years old. Lady Brynne had been married years before my almost-wedding—she would have been ten at the time of the contract.

Cor. His signature on the documents was like a child's scrawl. His age was given as thirty-two.

I was confused and disgusted by the gross illegality of it—she had been contracted two years before the age of consent for girls.

I raised my head. Noise came from beyond the room.

"I'm going to brace the door," said Trey.

I looked back down at *The Book*—unfolding events were far less real than its contents.

Here was another marriage contract. This time between Wilcomb Surry and one Jane Upton. Wilcomb was the man Kalo had once tried to match with Silky.

I had never heard of Jane Upton, something that was seemingly impossible. I knew all the marriageable men and women of the Great Houses—I knew all of the heirs and the rankings of the children.

Jane Upton? Never heard of her. And she had a low name, like that of a vagabond.

If she were indeed a vagabond, of course, it would explain why I had never heard of her, but it made her marriage to Wilcomb Surry impossible.

Impossible.

I only became aware of the world around me when someone actually began trying to force the door. I looked up from *The Book* in time to see Renn and Silky trying to wedge it closed.

"Read," said Trey.

And it slowly dawned on me what I was reading.

The landless, the vagrants, the casteless in fact owned great swaths of land: they carried the deeds to the lost land—only they didn't know it. Outright stealing might have revealed everything; these thefts had been accomplished through secret marriages. Generations of men and women of no repute had been used and robbed of their inheritances.

Jane Upton and Wilcomb Surry. I saw the details of the land transaction at the marriage: the meadows of Champlain passed from Jane Upton to Wilcomb Surry. But I had been invited to no ceremony.

The land transfer would explain the Surrys' rise in prominence. The meadows of Champlain were famous for grazing and farmland.

I could smell land greed.

In the place for Jane's signature there was an X.

Trey moved to the door. Renn and Silky were already there; Renn was futilely trying to shove Silky behind him.

"Lord Kestling?" said Trey. "We need to block the door." There was a scrambling noise outside, and I thought I heard Kalo's voice and the sounds of fighting in the near distance.

My father joined the others at the door—my father, who had never before acknowledged Trey—except to banish him from my presence. And now, here we were, and Trey and my father were united by a common enemy.

"Hold the door," Renn said. "Hold it."

"Hurry, Angel," said Silky.

I bent my head to the task and kept reading.

Jan Creepow transferred land to Lord Hastings.

Lady Juliet married Egg Morton, who signed with an X.

There was a clamor outside.

"They've left the door," said Trey.

I turned another page. And here I stumbled on something that, had it been known, would have outraged all the Great Houses of Arcadia. It was a signed marriage contract—a full contract—between Pea and Karn of the House of Nesson.

This was all wrong. Pea was pre-contracted to the House of Nesson, yes—to Leth's brother—but she was only six, six years too young to marry, to have a full contract. It was cruelty—barbarism. No wonder the Nessons had kept the contract hidden.

I began to see that Arcadia was rife with secret marriages and alliances; they ran like skeins of wool through the fabric of the country. They held Arcadia together. No wonder this knowledge was forbidden.

But where was the wisdom in *The Book of Forbidden Wisdom*?

I turned another page.

And there was the House of Montrose. Gwen Pan married Lord Kestling Montrose.

Lord Kestling was my father.

But who was Gwen Pan?

In a small hand below the marriage contract, someone had written in code, "Kalo, newly born to Gwen Kestling five months later. Lord Kestling keeps the child." The words were in a black square, as if they were somehow important.

And, indeed, they were.

I looked up at my father. For a moment I felt pity for

Kalo. He was the son of Gwen Pan, whoever she was. Gwen Pan had brought two things to her wedding with my father: a mountain covered in rich timber, and someone else's child inside her.

Kalo existed to torment us all because my father had once shown charity and let a baby live. And I couldn't condemn my father for that.

But what had happened to Gwen Pan? Everyone knew of my father's marriage to my mother. The story was legendary—the Bards still sang of it. The ceremony had lasted three days, and extraordinary amounts of food and drink had been consumed. Whole oxen. Songbirds inside ducks inside turkeys inside great white geese that dripped vast amounts of savory fat into the fire as they rotated on the spit. Skin artists not only decorated the bride and groom but also painted the signs of the House of Montrose and the House of St. Clare onto the hands of the guests. The men and women danced, separately, throughout the night. At midnight, the greatest display of fireworks ever seen in Arcadia exploded in showers of white fire. And finally the wedding couple was put to bed.

No mention of Gwen Pan.

I turned the page.

Fewer documents. More things scribbled directly onto the page. In places there were small sketches next to the writing. I read carefully, and, this time, when I realized what I was reading, I went back to the top of the page and began again.

I didn't want to believe this document, this text that

lay open on the lectern in front of me. I wished I had never opened *The Book*.

But one cannot unread something; I knew that better than anyone. For the first time, I felt the curse of my eidetic memory. My mother had understood the curse when she had turned away from *The Book* before finishing it. And yet—and yet she had made very sure that I would be trained up to read *The Book of Forbidden Wisdom*. She had left it to me to weigh and measure and use the power of *The Book*.

Across time and space, the names called to me.

Cor.

Jane Upton.

Pea.

Jan Creepow.

Egg Morton.

Gwen Pan.

So I did it. I turned the page.

There were sketches on this page. I touched the picture of a coarse-looking woman with lank dark hair. Her face had been drawn carefully, and the eyes looked bleary. There were small earrings in her ears, and I found that detail moving. It was as if, in some small way, she had tried to make herself pretty. I was drawn to that face again and again because I recognized it.

Of course I did.

It was as if Kalo had been staring up at me from the page. It was with no sense of surprise that I saw the name scribbled into *The Book*: Gwen Pan. But this entry concerned no transfer of land, no secret marriage.

Like all the other documents and entries on these pages, this was a certificate of death.

The cause was written in red letters.

Gwen Pan had been born; she had grown; she had married my father in secret and transferred all her land to him. She had given birth to Kalo.

And then she had been murdered.

If it had not been for the baby she had left in my father's care, it would have been as if Gwen Pan had never existed.

The crime committed against Gwen Pan was, in the end, more complete than murder. She and her name had been disappeared.

I looked again at the coarse, large-featured face and the lank hair. Cleaned up, she might not have looked much different from any number of Great House scions. I was beginning to lose my sense of the vast difference between a member of a Great House and a vagabond.

So Gwen Pan had been murdered, and sometime after, my father had married my beautiful, vivacious and charming auburn-haired mother. He had first married Gwen Pan's timber and, then, his House no longer poor, he had managed a match with the richest heiress in Arcadia. My father, even with Gwen Pan's holdings, did not have enough land alone to marry her, but there was, it was whispered, affection on the Lady's side. And so he took in contract my mother, the last of the House of St. Clare. The only woman alive who could read *The Book of Forbidden Wisdom.*

He couldn't have known what was in *The Book.*

I didn't really need to turn another page of *The Book of Forbidden Wisdom,* but I did anyway.

Cor—murdered.

Jane Upton—murdered.

Jan Creepow—murdered.

Egg Morton—murdered.

And other names I recognized from my perusal of the earlier pages—murdered.

I was almost at the end of *The Book.* I read, and as I did, my face must have been transformed. Finally I reached what I thought was the last page. Only a few words were on it. I almost didn't bother turning it over—and had I not, I wouldn't have seen the ragged edge of paper that indicated a subsequent page had been torn from *The Book.*

"They're coming," said Silky.

"Stay behind me," my father said to Silky.

"Trey and I will deal with this," said Renn. I looked up sharply.

"Have you finished reading *The Book,* Angel?" asked Trey.

"I've got it all," I said.

And then, without a hint that he might be doing something untoward, Trey took my hand and pulled me away from the lectern. Renn narrowed his eyes.

"Lord Trey—" began my father, and even Silky's eyebrows were raised by the sight of Trey and me hand in hand, but my father never completed his sentence. Perhaps he thought better of it.

They were at the door again.

"Come on, Renn," said Trey, and the two of them blocked the door with their bodies. A second later, and our father, Lord Kestling, was with them.

"This is it," said Renn.

I wondered if death were upon me, and I wondered if I would be with Silky, Trey and Renn in the quiet country. But I had just awakened, and I didn't want to go back to sleep.

An axe stroke cleaved through the upper part of the door and narrowly missed cleaving Renn's arm.

I wanted to live, and if I lived, I would be heard by all of them—Great Houses, vagabonds, bards. It would be known. The secrets of *The Book* would be known. The Great Houses were built on land greed, on theft, on land transfers from ignominious, secret marriages. The Great Houses were built on the sweat and tears and lives of vagabonds.

The Great Houses were built on blood.

CHAPTER THIRTY-TWO

A REUNION

Trey and Renn weren't going to be able to hold the door much longer. Already they had to stand to either side of it as the great axe blows came through the wood. They could only hope to cut down our enemies— Leth, Kalo, the freemen—as they came through the threshold.

My father watched as the door began to splinter.

"Stop, Kalo," he yelled, "I order you. Lord Leth— the Arbitrator made us allies. The documents will be void, and you'll lose the penalty."

"They're beyond that," I said. "I don't think Leth cares about the penalty anymore."

A piece flew out of the door.

"Leth always had a bad look about him," said my father.

"You loved Leth," I said. "You adored his acres, his meadows, his mines and timber. Leth was just fine by you."

And once, what seemed like so long ago, I had thought Leth was fine enough too.

The door was almost down.

"Trey," said Renn. "Get ready."

And the axe ploughed through the door a last time.

We didn't have a chance. I pushed a protesting Silky behind me as Renn and Trey prepared to take down at least the first man to step through the door.

I heard my father draw his sword.

"Get ready," he said. "Angel, you have *The Book*— you have to get out if you can, if there's a lull in the fighting."

"I won't let them get to her," said Trey.

"We can't be taken," said my father. "Or we die badly. We make our stand here. Silky, we'll probably go down first—you're going to have to fight to the end. I'm sorry."

And that's when I saw that Silky had found a bolt somewhere and was carefully fitting it to her crossbow.

"For heaven's sake, Father," she said. "I'm not a *baby*."

The door was only an empty standing frame now. There was a moment's silence. As if in slow motion, dust and fragments of wood swirled in a single beam of light that came from a high window.

We all waited.

The air cleared; we could just make out two figures, one with the axe.

One spoke to the other.

"If you think I'm just going to walk into the room, you're wrong." The words were measured, but there was a quaver in the voice.

"You're not exactly terrifying the enemy by saying that," said the one with the axe. The voice was light and easy, ironic and very familiar.

I stepped forward; Trey automatically gestured me back, but I pushed ahead of him.

"Zinda." I held out my arms.

"*Zinda?*" Silky leapt forward, tripped, and sent a bolt into the wall. It didn't seem the time to make a point of it.

"Angel?" A head poked in, and then Zinda stepped through. "And Golden Hair?" She embraced me.

"We're all here," I said. "And my father as well."

Zinda and the other figure at the door relaxed visibly. "You might have identified yourselves more clearly," Zinda said. "We couldn't hear you, and getting down that door was seriously hard work. We thought you were the last of the bad lot and were hiding—and we

didn't want you coming up behind us when we left."
Then she gave up the pose of a warrior and put down
the axe, and I embraced her all over again. And then I
hugged Lark, who was staring at all of us in disbelief.

"We didn't know what was behind the door," Lark
said. "I thought perhaps it might be death."

"Seems not," said Zinda. "And it looks like this lot
felt the same way. Last stand?"

"Last stand."

"You all right, Golden Hair?"

Silky lowered her now bolt-less bow and nodded.

"Bard?"

"Here."

"Faceless Trey?"

"Present."

While I didn't like her use of the word *faceless*, she
had called him by his name; she must have grown to
like him a great deal.

"You don't look so faceless anymore, Trey," Zinda
said.

"Perhaps not," said Trey.

Zinda just stared at my father until he began to look
uncomfortable.

"I'm Lord Kestling of Montrose," he said. She
looked blank. "I'm the father of Silky and Angel."

"Ah, I see," said Zinda. "A father."

I laughed. Then I held her at arm's length and
looked her in the face. There were deep lines where
there had been none, and her hair was flecked with
grey. She would not be the same again. Not after Caro.

And I began to have a hint at what I was getting into with all this feeling business.

"Why did you come?" I asked.

"We finished off the 'Lidans," said Zinda. "Then we had some more guests. Two women, one of whom I knew—Niamh of Shibbeth—came through. After that, men came looking for you; they said they were your kindred. We let them pass. But then I began to think we had done the wrong thing."

"And then you had to rescue me *again*," said Silky. She sounded despondent.

Zinda spoke gently. "I think you did well, Silky," she said. "To make it so far. To survive for so long. And you've done your own share of rescuing."

And Silky smiled. For a girl who had been about to fight to her death, she looked remarkably cheerful.

"But where's Leth?" I asked. "And the others?"

"That odious Leth," said Zinda, "is in our custody. As is your odious brother, Kalo. You have a number of unpleasant male associates."

"Hey!" said Trey.

She ignored him. "We had to take down three free-men and one indentured servant. I feel bad about the servant, but he left us no choice."

"Large man?"

"With a bloody face."

"I'm sorry for that."

"Come," said Zinda. "You need cool water and good food. And the others from the village will want to see you."

"You fought the dark riders without knowing we were here?"

"They attacked," said Zinda. "We fought. Although when I think about it, I should have known we'd find you. Trouble follows you around." I was about to protest, but she simply smiled. "And so does luck."

With that, we left behind the blood soaked room of *The Book*. Zinda and Lark led us to an open courtyard behind one of the dilapidated buildings.

"Lark found this place," she said.

I recognized many of the women who were there. I had carted rocks with them, built fortifications and brought down the attacking 'Lidans. I felt I knew them in a way I didn't know the people I had called friends while growing up. These were more like family. Like sisters. Silky moved easily among them, checking to see if the archers remembered the new stance she had taught them right before the attack, asking after women she had known but didn't see there, shedding tears at bad news.

I lacked her touch, but I sat, and Lark brought me water and cucumbers and dried meat (I remembered the 'Lidan horse that had been slaughtered), and we ate our food together, and Lark told me all that had happened after we had left. I didn't know where Trey and Renn were, but I knew that they would be well cared for.

"After you left, Zinda fought to recover Caro's body," said Lark. "It was a foolish chance, but none of us dared stop her. She took that axe she carries now and hacked her way through. When she returned she was all blood, but she had Caro's body in her arms. I tried to speak to her, but she turned away from me. The others were too afraid to approach her."

"Is she—" I paused. "Is she all right?"

"We buried Caro that night," said Lark. "It seemed to help. But no, I don't think she's all right. They were like the closest of sisters."

After Lark said that, I couldn't bear to think about it.

In the afternoon, as I stood with Trey and watched, Zinda released the freemen after first taking their weapons and then confiscating most of their horses.

One of them made as if to complain, but she cut him off short.

"Call it the spoils of war," said Zinda. "You attacked us without provocation, and, in return, we're giving you your lives and freedom. If I were you, I'd call it even." And even the freeman's companions shouted him down, glad to get away with their lives.

That evening we moved out of the Spiral City and made camp in the meadow beyond. Six women guarded Kalo and Leth, and any two of them could have taken the men down. I was not likely to underestimate the women of The Village of Broken Women ever again.

Renn sang as the evening drew in. I could tell nothing of what he was thinking by the songs that he chose. Some of them were comic songs; some were ballads, and he sang the lay of the Great Lady and the Invisible Mountain, perhaps in honor of our hosts. Trey and Silky and I sat toward the back. I was moody, and after Renn made me both laugh and cry, Trey got up stiffly.

"It's time we both faced it," he said to me.

"What are you talking about?"

"You've fallen in love with Renn," he said. "Can we just say it now?"

"Oh *no*," said Silky.

"Please stop, Trey," I said. "You don't know what you're saying."

"Yes, I do."

"Renn is different and dark and interesting," I said. "Is that what you want to hear?"

"No. I don't really want to hear. And I wish I didn't know."

"*Trey*," said Silky, "don't be *obtuse*." She was proud of her vocabulary.

"Sit down," I said, and at first he kept stubbornly on his feet. "Trey—please sit down."

Perhaps he was startled at my "please," or perhaps he was just tired of standing, but Trey sat.

"Renn's a bard," I explained carefully. "He's also—attractive. I'm attracted to him. That's all."

"That's enough. It's pretty obvious what's going on with me, though, isn't it?" said Trey. "I'm assuming the way I feel is no longer some kind of big secret."

"Well," I said, "no."

"But it's not fair to you, is it?" he asked. "If it ever was."

With that, Trey got up and walked off into the twilight.

"Why did you just let him *go*?" asked Silky.

"Trey makes me so unhappy that it's confusing," I said. "And then there's Renn."

"You just like him because he's all *murky*," said Silky.

"I don't know what you mean."

"Yes, you do," said Silky. "But I know how it'll end."

"I wish you'd tell me."

"No," said Silky. "It's going to be a *surprise*."

We sat and listened to Renn for a while longer, and then I stood up and followed Trey into the growing darkness.

CHAPTER THIRTY-THREE

EVERY WISE MAN'S SON DOTH KNOW

I followed him to a dried-up riverbed. The moon wasn't up yet, but I could still make out his pale face and his light shirt.

He didn't turn toward me.

"I was proud of being your rescuer," he said.

"We should take turns doing the rescuing. My turn."

"Better go away, Angel," he said. "You're all right. You can take care of yourself, and I really do know that's a good thing."

"Then what is this about?"

"Nothing."

"Nothing?"

"Nothing."

"Trey."

Silky, I knew, was in anguish over the rift between Trey and me.

So, it turned out, was I.

We walked down from the clearing and onto the dry riverbed. The dusk was moving into night.

"Wait for me, Trey," I said. He stood still. When I had caught up to him, we walked together, and we were silent, although it wasn't like the old days. It wasn't a comfortable silence.

"I always wanted to marry you, you know," he said.

"Maybe you shouldn't say anything," I said.

"No," he said. "I might as well tell it now. All those long years of friendship—each day I knew I wanted you, and each day I knew we could never marry. I had no land to please your father. And I couldn't make you love me—not that way."

"Trey—"

"Not enough to throw away everything and live on a sliver of land," he said. "And then after your wedding was broken, and you came with me, I had hope."

"Trey," I said again, but I could hear the difference in my tone.

We had missed so much.

"I would have married you," he said. "Even if you did it solely to save your honor. Even if you meant it about living together as brother and sister."

"And there was a time," I said, "not long ago, when I would have married you entirely for my honor's sake. I understood nothing. I wouldn't do that to you now."

"I imagine not."

"It has nothing to do with your face, Trey. My whole life I never really loved anyone. Not that way."

"Leth? At the beginning?"

"No," I said. "Even my father saw my indifference. But it seemed the thing I was supposed to do, and I thought it was good that I would become very powerful. I understand more about power now."

"We all do."

We walked on. I thought of all the time I'd spent with chaperones and attendants and those paid to protect my virtue. I took his hand.

"That feels nice," he said.

"To me too."

"I'll never marry now, of course. Even if before I could have brought myself to marry someone other than you, it wouldn't have been fair to her. And no woman would have me now."

"Of course you'll marry." His hand was warm in mine.

"With this face?"

"Have you seen the lumpish, dough-faced man-boys that girls trip over each other to marry?"

"*Landed* lumpish dough-faced man-boys."

I dropped my eyes and looked down at my shoes thoughtfully. They were damp and muddy.

"Do you love Renn?" he asked. "Am I right? If I am, I'll never bother you again. Angel?"

"Yes?"

I forced myself to raise my eyes. Trey stood before me. All Renn's interesting darkness now looked like no more than moodiness. Renn was probably a good man, but I didn't know him at all. Love him? No.

I looked closely at Trey's face. Marred, imperfect, broken. I would have given anything to put him back together again.

I still understood nothing.

As I saw Trey now, standing before me, I also saw all the years we'd spent together. I found I was thinking of his fine-boned hands, and how he could use them to handle a horse, a thousand-pound animal kept quiet, controlled and collected.

I had known nothing about love; I had known nothing about my own desire. I had been stupid from the first moment of Trey's rescue, when I had thrown myself into his arms and let him take me off into the unknown.

For the first time since we had been children, Trey and I were completely alone with each other. And I knew, suddenly, what chaperones were for.

I released his hand and reached up to his face. At first he flinched, and then he caught my hands in his.

It was almost dark. A light breeze ruffled my hair, and from somewhere came the scent of wild roses.

"It's all right," I said.

"What do you want, Angel?" He was hesitant, uneasy. And then he let me touch him.

I touched the shiny new scar tissue with the tips of my fingers. Then I leaned up, and I kissed the edges of the marred space beneath his right eye. What to do next came as naturally as Silky's aim with a crossbow was true. I kissed the left side of his face—here, and there, and there. And then I kissed his mouth.

The voices of my chaperones and tutors and friends and family and Arbitrators were utterly stilled.

At first I could feel him hesitate, and then he pulled me to him, and I grabbed a handful of his thick hair as he kissed me softly, deeply.

I started unbuttoning my shirt, and he put his arms on my shoulders and looked into my eyes.

"Is this what you want, Angel?" His breath was short, and so was mine.

"It's what I've wanted for a long time," I said. "I've just been too stupid to know."

He finished unbuttoning my shirt and then pulled it down, partway down my arms. Then one of his hands was around my waist, and he kissed my throat.

A shock of pleasure ran through me. We were near the bank of the dry riverbed, and he pushed me, gently, against it, and then we were both pulling up my skirt as he kissed my forehead, my eyes, my cheeks.

"I love you, Angel," he whispered hoarsely, and I was about to reply when out of the darkness a form in a flowing white shift materialized.

"Angel?"

It was Silky.

We scrambled. I buttoned my shirt while Trey tried

to pull down my skirt and do up his pants at the same time.

"Just a moment, Silky," I called. I was having a little trouble breathing.

That's when Trey and I started laughing softly. Trey's hands shook with laughter as we both realized that my shirt was misbuttoned.

"Are you all right?" asked Silky. She was fully visible now, which meant that we were visible to her. Trey and I looked at each other, realized that we were too close together and frantically backed away.

"I'm fine," I said to Silky. "And Trey's fine, too."

"Are you two *fighting*? It looked like you were actually fighting."

With that, the laughter bubbled up again.

By the time we got back to the clearing with Silky, Trey and I were both suitably serious and covered in all the right places.

"You've been a while," said Renn, and I thought that maybe he knew. He sounded casual, as if something had happened, but that, whatever it was, it didn't matter much to him. I had never felt farther from his world.

"I needed the air," I said, which was so patently absurd that I almost began laughing again. There was, after all, air all around us.

"Well," said Silky. "This time *I'm* not the one wandering off somewhere."

I felt flustered. I needed something to sew. Something to clean. Something to occupy myself with. I found Jasmine's bridle and started rubbing it with a soft cloth. Trey went to look at the horses.

Silky came up beside me. She was close. So close that Renn and Trey couldn't hear, and I feared, for an instant, that she had understood what had happened between Trey and me. But she was a young fourteen, and, besides, what we had been doing was so impossible and taboo and, well, unlikely, that—

I started to laugh again.

"What's happening, Angel?" she asked.

"I don't know," I said, muffling my laughter. "Maybe it's anxious laughter. I was talking with Trey, you know. He's upset about his face."

I suspected he was less upset now.

"That's what I wanted to talk to you about," said Silky.

"Go ahead," I said.

"I feel bad." She lowered her voice. "Because I think Trey's face is so *horrible*. He frightens me. He looks like a *monster*. He—"

"Come to the point, Silky," I said crisply.

"Well," she said. "I just realized something. Just now. And I wanted to check with you that I'm right. Because it's still *Trey*, isn't it? And his face won't be so scary when I'm *used* to it."

"Oh, honey," I said. "Soon it won't be scary at all."

"At least it's gotten better."

I stopped fussing with Jasmine's bridle and turned and looked closely at Silky.

"What do you mean?"

"It's getting *better*. His face isn't nearly so stiff, and the shiny bits look softer, and—"

"Are you sure?"

"Of *course* I'm sure," said Silky. "Or I wouldn't say it. The Aman fungus must still be working, don't you think?"

"Maybe."

Getting better. For a moment I could visualize such a scenario, and then I stopped—because it didn't matter.

"You two are full of secrets tonight," Renn called out to Silky and me.

"We're sisters," I said. "What do you expect?" And I moved toward the horses then to be with Trey.

"I wish we could race," said Trey. "What do you say, Angel? A race in the dark with unknown obstacles ahead taken at a pace we can't control. What could go wrong?"

"You could break your necks," Renn's disembodied voice called out from the darkness. No privacy. No doubt my father was listening too.

"If there were just a little moon," I said, "I'd take you up on it."

"Bran's faster than Jasmine," said Trey. "I'd win."

I moved until I was as close as I could be to Trey without touching.

"We've both already won," I said.

CHAPTER THIRTY-FOUR

ROAD'S END

Zinda and Lark and a dozen of their sisters guarded Kalo and Leth all the way into Southern Arcadia. We moved quickly and, many times, ate in the saddle.

When we were two days out from home, I finally asked my father.

"Did you kill Gwen Pan?"

"I—no," he said. "She died of the shuddering sickness a month after Kalo was born."

I nodded. He was lying of course.

He wouldn't have done the killing himself; his

Steward probably arranged it. But it didn't matter in the end: Father knew that I knew.

It had been a long journey.

Then we were one day out. We sat around the fire. Renn sang. He was looking forward to seeing Niamh and Jesse in Arcadia—and Silky had already asked me if we could invite Jesse to our House. Even my father deferred to me now.

Silky put her head on my shoulder, as my father took his time ringing the fire with stones. Trey was next to me.

"Will you and Trey get married as soon as we get back?" asked Silky.

"I suppose so," I said.

"Yes," said Trey. He took my hand, and I didn't pull it away.

A wedding.

I had been branded a harlot, and I had brought down both Leth and Kalo. I had seen pain and death and courage and heart. I had been wounded, and the pain from that wound would probably never entirely go away. I could bear all these things.

But a big, arbitrated ceremonial wedding?

I didn't know.

I wound my fingers through Trey's, and, for the moment, that was all that mattered. The flames grew and danced and flickered. My father went to find more stones.

After a while, I stroked Silky's long golden hair. She

would be all right. Much as I had always loved Silky, I had never given her enough credit for her strength and courage.

Father rejoined us.

"So while the door was coming down, you finished reading *The Book of Forbidden Wisdom*," he said.

"Yes," I said.

"So you know it all," he said. "Your forever-memory is still there."

"Yes."

"You read it to the end?" he asked.

"We don't have to talk about it right now," said Trey.

"We certainly *don't*," said Silky. She lifted her head from my shoulder and glared at my father.

"I just want to understand," he said. "What was the wisdom? Why was it forbidden? Did *The Book* ever say? Was there no wisdom at all?" He looked at me with a kind of desperation.

I looked into the flames of the fire.

"There was no wisdom," I said.

My father sighed, but it was a sigh of relief. I had mentioned Gwen Pan, so he must have known that I had garnered knowledge from *The Book*. Wisdom? Wisdom came with time. I had the knowledge to destroy my father's House, and so my own, and also many others', but I didn't yet have an idea of what I should do. Whatever I did, all Arcadia would change.

"We came a long way for nothing," said Silky, but she was looking at me suspiciously.

Trey laughed softly. He knew that I was lying outright, and he knew, too, that I would tell him about *The Book*. I would tell Silky, too. I would tell a lot of people. I would have to reshape our world—because I had read a book.

At the very end, *The Book* had asked a question.

Who owns the land?

We live on it for our time, and then we fade. Other men and women come to live on it for a while. Who owns the land?

Call that question wisdom.

But it wasn't really true that I had read *The Book* to the end. After all, the last page had been missing, torn from the binding a long time ago, if the brown and stained ragged edges were anything to go by.

"Of Love" was the title of the missing section—the title that came before the page that had been ripped away.

I thought I would never know what forbidden wisdom was there. As I watched Silky gazing into the fire, as I raised my eyes and caught Trey looking at me, eyes brimming, as I felt his hand still in mine, I wondered if the kind of wisdom that is truly forbidden could go in books. Perhaps it couldn't be spoken or read; it could only be felt.

Perhaps that was the meaning of the missing last page. Perhaps there had been nothing written on it at all.

The next morning we crossed into my father's estate.

CHAPTER THIRTY-FIVE

WILD ROSES

Silky woke me up.

"How can you sleep so late?" she asked. "It's the most important day of your *life*."

"Again."

"That is *not* funny," said Silky. "Leth does *not* count."

"Not anymore," I said grimly, but Silky didn't catch my ironic tone. One has to be a little mean to use irony, and Silky didn't have a mean bone in her body. Not one.

"I don't even want you thinking about Leth or Kalo," said Silky. "Or worrying about anyone showing up and claiming you." We both knew whom she meant, but Renn and I had become good friends at the end. There would be no challenge from him. Kalo and Leth would be imprisoned for a time and then sent, stripped of Arcadian land, to Shibbeth. I was sure that they would find trouble enough to start there, but first Kalo would have to keep an eye on his lands—his status was now so unsteady that the 'Lidan Lords would be watching his estates like crows waiting for pickings.

Silky threw my wrap to me.

"Time to get ready," she said. "You haven't even had your Ceremonial Bath yet. And wait until you see the *roses*. This time, they're *perfect*."

I had almost come full circle. But no Leth was waiting for me. No soft, spoiled, lazy landowner about whom I cared less than I cared for my horse.

This day was very different.

"Where did the roses come from?" I asked.

"*He* brought them," said Silky.

They would be wild and fragrant cups of scent and color. Blush roses.

"All right," I said, grabbing the wrap. "I'm up. Nervous, but up."

"You weren't nervous *last* time," said Silky critically.

"I had nothing to be nervous about. I didn't care." I saw that Silky had already been to the hand and throat painters. Her loose fair hair set off the dark markings, and I had a glimpse of what she would be like on her own wedding day.

Silky went to the closet. My mother's wedding dress had been ruined during our escape, but this one was a miracle, with portions of the old dress sewn in and the whole softly lit by pearls embedded in silk. Silky gently touched the lace.

I had long ago thought Silky wanted to wear our mother's wedding dress because it was beautiful and because it was our mother's. I had been wrong. She had known I would inherit the dress.

She simply wanted to wear it after I had.

"This dress will be yours," I said. "When the time comes. If you still want it."

"Of *course* I'll want it," she said. "But Father would never let me."

"Ever since the journey, you've tied Father around your little finger. The dress is yours." I paused. "Jesse arrived today, didn't he?"

Silky blushed deeply, but she only said, "Well, *you* invited him." She paused. "You really think someday I'll wear the dress?"

"Yes," I said. "But don't grow up too fast."

Silky smiled. I reached for my robe for the Ceremonial Bath, and the wrapper fell open.

"Your scar."

"It'll never go away, Silky."

"You're still perfect."

"The journey marked us."

And she was unusually quiet for a while.

Violet, again my witness, now a year older and as far from a groom as ever, led me to the Ceremonial

Bath. When I burst out of the water to the surface, there was applause, and, as I made my way to the skin artists, the witnesses began snacking on little lavender tea cakes and lemon drop tarts.

I thought of my trip to the quiet country and of speaking to my mother. This was all very different—bustle and hurry and talk and ceremony. Lots of ceremony.

I wondered how my groom was faring.

Silky talked more about the flowers as the skin artist drew intricate patterns on my hands and up my arms and across my chest and throat. It came to me that Silky was nervous too. The whole ceremony was all too much like the wedding to Leth.

The soft brushes tickled, and I pulled my hand away from the skin artist who was working on my wrist.

"Sensitive skin," said Silky. Then she put something in my hand. It was a little lavender tea cake.

"If you get that down your front," she said, "or if you have sticky hands at the ceremony, I will *not* be pleased."

"It's going to be all right, Silky," I said.

"Look at the blush roses," she said. "I've never seen any so fresh or so plentiful at *any* wedding. Not any."

"He grows them on his land."

"He doesn't have any land."

I laughed. "He has enough," I said.

"I was going to put some wild roses in your bouquet—the way I did when *Leth* was the groom—but he had already done it."

"Show me."

Silky handed me the bouquet, and I touched the wild roses with my fingertips. The skin artist had finished, and she packed up her brushes and pots of ink. She seemed happier than she had been at my last wedding.

"Thank you, Scilla," said Silky.

"A magnificent job," I said.

We both knew the skin artists. They were the most celebrated artists in Arcadia; their work was exquisite. And then, without warning, I was overwhelmed by the past.

So much death.

Someone was tuning an instrument outside the preparation tent. The bard had arrived. Renn wouldn't be singing; he and Niamh and Jesse were guests of honor.

Charmian, Niamh had told me, had reluctantly settled into her new Arcadian home in the west.

The bard was now in tune and had started a quiet ballad. I went to the tent opening, looked out and found myself staring at Bard Fallon.

Silky followed my gaze. "Father found him," she said. "He was singing for pennies. Father's going to pay him *a lot* to do the wedding festivities."

"There isn't enough money in the world to repay him for saving us from Garth," I said.

"He wanted to play for *free*," said Silky.

Bard Fallon looked up from his playing, met my eye and smiled. Technically he was overstepping his station even by looking me squarely in the face, but, given our adventures, we were on even footing. Or, more accurately, I was in his debt. And the rules and ceremonies that so enforced the divisions between high and low were changing. I had already spoken with the heads of some of the more oppressive Houses; I knew their nasty secrets now, and caste lines were beginning to blur. There would be more to come. Much more.

Then Silky was at my side again, pulling me away from the tent opening.

"It's time to do your hair," she said. "Or you're going to leave your groom waiting about an hour with the merger officials and the Arbitrators, and you *know* he'll hate that."

"He will," I agreed. "I wonder what he thinks about all this."

This, apparently, was finally too much for Silky.

She pulled me to a chair, pushed me down into it, and shooed away the honor girls, the hair-wreath maker, the comfit maker waiting for me to taste her samples, the two extra personal maids, the seamstress, my father's legal advisor, my own legal advisor, even Silky's legal advisor—all there to make sure that not an inch of land ended up in the wrong hands. She found two stylists engaged in brief sexual congress behind a screen, and she shooed them out, too. Not much could shock Silky anymore.

She faced me, an arm on each side of the chair.

"Do you want to marry him?"

There it was. Bold and plain and clear.

"There's nothing more I want in the world."

"You're a Great Lady, Angel," she said. "Your dowry is a nice chunk of Arcadia, and if you *wanted*—"

"Don't go there, Silky."

"You're a *Great Lady*," she said. "There. I said it again. You could play the part a little more."

"Let me see your toes."

"What?"

"Your toes."

She had had them painted in three shades—cherry, plum and sunshine—and the designs announced that she was a Lady of a Great House, and single, but of a status that meant that marrying her probably wasn't even worth dreaming about.

"It took *hours*," she said, "and I loved every minute. I wanted to celebrate your wedding, Angel. I hope you don't mind."

"I love your toes, Silky," I said. "And you more than deserve the pleasure they give you. It's not the same for me."

"*Why not?*" she pushed at the chair with each word.

"I'm damaged, Silky," I said. "You're young, and you're bright and fair and wonderful, and you heal fast. I'm one of those stupid little maimed songbirds you used to pull away from the cat and try to nurse to health."

Silky looked deeply unhappy.

"Some of them did all right," she said. "Keet the Robling was all right."

"Keet was a deeply troubled Robling."

"You just have to get through today." She curled up and sat at my feet.

"You know better," I said. I lifted my eyes.

Above Silky's head, through a crack in the tent, I could see towering black storm clouds on the horizon; they were joined to the earth by a dark, sweeping curtain of rain. I watched as bolts of lightning lit up the inside of the clouds. I had never seen anything like it. A storm as tall as Heaven.

"Look, Silky," I said. She stood and peered out of the tent.

"You'll be married before it reaches us." But she looked a little alarmed.

"Maybe."

There was a polite scratching at the tent opening. A servant called in— "The hair artist's here. Havelok." The servant, obviously curious, peeked into the tent. "He's here all the way from the other side of Arcadia."

"Go away," said Silky. "Go away *now*."

The servant left.

Silky, with her fingers, traced the intricate paintings from my hands up to my throat.

"You're beautiful."

"I suppose we should get on with getting ready."

"You want to be rescued again, don't you, Angel?"

"There's no way in the world I can be rescued," I said. "I need to be rescued from myself."

And as I said it, there was a noise at the back of the tent, as if someone were throwing pebbles.

Silky scrambled to her feet. She smiled. And she was sad.

"I think your groom's going to rescue you anyway," she said quietly.

Trey slipped into the tent and into my arms. His face had healed more, but only his eyes, green and deep, would ever give away his thoughts. They did so now.

He smelled of wild air and roses.

"I'll hold them off," said Silky. But just remember—when you're done undamaging each other, or *whatever* you've planned (you notice I *don't ask*), I'll be waiting here. Because I go where you go, Angel."

There were tears in my eyes, but I was giddy with joy. "I'll be back for you," I said.

Trey took a wreath of wild roses and put it on my head. I dressed for the road with the clothes I had originally worn into the tent.

"It looks like we'll be going through a storm," he said.

"We've been through other storms."

"Bran and Jasmine are at the back," he said. "Shamble will be our packhorse—I think the stable boy wonders where you got such a plain beast. I didn't mention you stole him."

"Where are we going?"

"We'll be married on my land. By the old forms. We'll sleep in my bed."

"I'm not listening," said Silky.

"We'll start to heal."

"Trey," I said. "You've given me my life."

"We'll return soon enough," he said. "But a little more on our terms. And, of course, we need to get Silky."

Silky was weeping, but I was too excited now for tears.

The enormous number of wedding preparers waited outside the front gate. We stepped out the back, through the rip that Trey had made into this brittle, artificial world, and soon we were on the outside of all of it.

Renn was holding the horses. Jesse and Niamh were by his side.

Silky stood back against the tent, her golden hair acting as a curtain of protection.

"Stall them, and give us half an hour to get away, Silky," I said.

And Silky ceased weeping.

"Of *course*," she said. And she handed me my bouquet of roses.

I turned to Trey, and I realized I had never seen him look so happy.

Now my mind was on the road in front of me. I mounted, as did Trey, and we turned toward the bridge across the stream that marked the property.

The future, at that moment, curled around me.

Trey. And a child. And Silky and Jesse. And later more children, who had names that marked our journeys. Outside, sometimes, a raging summer storm. But inside, the storm stilled. We would grow older, and the world would change, and we would pass through it together. Suddenly Silky laughed, and I realized we wouldn't be alone. And I understood at last the final word in *The Book of Forbidden Wisdom*. I understood love.

THE END OF
THE BOOK OF FORBIDDEN WISDOM

And they are gone: aye, ages long ago
These lovers fled away into the storm.

ACKNOWLEDGMENTS

Thank you to my indefatigable and wise agent, Richard Curtis.

To David Pomerico, my editor, and his assistant, Rebecca Lucash.

To Judith Gelman, patient copyeditor.

To my creative writing professors at Stanford University, including John L'Heureux, the late Albert J. Guerard and the late Robert Stone. I owe a debt of special thanks to Nancy Huddleston Packer, without whom I probably wouldn't have written either *The Book of Forbidden Wisdom* or *The Garden of Darkness* (Ravenstone, 2014).

To my wonderfully supportive colleagues in the English Department at Smith College.

To Mimi—Irene Dorit—a wonderful mother-in-law.

To my late father-in-law, Murray Dorit.

To the memory of my parents, Paul Murray Kendall and Carol Seeger Kendall, both writers who always just assumed I would be too.

To my sister Callie—Caroline Kendall Orszak—to whom this book is dedicated. Thanks for being a superb critic and reader—at the very beginning, and in the home stretch as well.

To Sasha Dorit-Kendall and Gabriel Dorit-Kendall, for their love and support.

Finally, to Rob. For everything.

ABOUT THE AUTHOR

When GILLIAN MURRAY KENDALL was a child, she spent multiple years in England while her father researched his biography of Richard III, and her mother wrote children's books. She thrived. She had stumbled into a wardrobe, and her enchanted world was England. That sense of belonging-in-the-strange shaped both Gillian's life and her writing. In the 1980s, the months and months she spent in Africa waiting in lines for kerosene and milk and rice or camping while being circled by annoyed lions was a new normal, while Gillian found the once-familiar Harvard, with its well-stocked grocery stores, alien and unknown. She saw things in a way she could not before. Recently Gillian spent two years in Paris, where learning a new culture, a new strangeness, resulted in the writing of her first book, *The Garden of Darkness*, and the beginning of *The Book of Forbidden Wisdom*. Gillian is a Professor at Smith College, where she teaches English literature, primarily Shakespeare. She is married to biologist Robert Dorit and has two sons, Sasha and Gabriel.

You can learn more about Gillian at gilliankendall. org, and follow her on Twitter (@GillianMKendall) and Facebook (www.facebook.com/gillian.kendall1).

Discover great authors, exclusive offers, and more at hc.com.